T0375641

Other Books by Matt Leach

How Can I Believe What Can't Be Believed?
Genesis 1 – 3: Questions for a Logical Mind

You've Got to Know the Territory Before You Pray

PETER, THE PROFESSOR AND THE BLUE ORB TIME MACHINE

A Guide To Prayer Power Set In A Science Fiction Fantasy

MATT LEACH

WestBow Press books may be ordered through booksellers or by contacting:

WestBow Press
A Division of Thomas Nelson & Zondervan
1663 Liberty Drive
Bloomington, IN 47403
www.westbowpress.com
1 (866) 928-1240

ISBN: 978-1-9736-0788-5 (sc)
ISBN: 978-1-9736-0789-2 (e)

Library of Congress Control Number: 2017917636

Print information available on the last page.

WestBow Press rev. date: 11/22/2017

CONTENTS

BOOK 3

Az You Were

PREFACE

Teaching people about prayer, and the power and authority they were given when they got saved has been my passion. The more I learn about these gifts from God the more I am driven to share what I am learning. To this end God told me to write two books. One, *How Can I Believe What Can't Be Believed: Genesis 1-3*, challenges people to momentarily set aside all beliefs and preconceived ideas about the Bible, and follow the Bible's instructions to study it with logic. The second, *You've Got to Know the Territory Before You Pray*, helps the Christians discover who they are in Christ, and to know Jesus as elder brother and Saviour, the Holy Spirit as teacher, and God as a loving Father. Both books are published by Westbow Press.

A few years ago I was surprised by the response I received after giving a talk highlighting many of Glenn Clark's prayer techniques. Many said that I had made some things clear that they hadn't understood before. Out of curiosity I asked if they though it would help if someone wrote a book about applying his teachings. The response was an enthusiastic "Yes". I thought nothing more about it because book writing was not in my repertoire.

I enjoy musing on whimsical ideas to see where they lead. I read the Narnia stories and wanted animals to talk. I read Tolkien's stories about hobbits and elves and dwarves and wanted hobbits and elves and dwarves to be real. Then I read an old legend about nine unknown men and thought, this would make an interesting story if the legend turned out to be true. By this time, I had already written two books, much to my surprise. Again, much to my surprise, I found myself wondering if

I could actually write a science fiction novel with real characters, with a diabolical plot, and use it to teach many things about prayer. Again, to my amazement God said Write!

I started to write, amazed at the ideas that rose up within me. I quickly realized that all those ideas were not coming from my imagination, but were being given to me. The Holy Spirit was helping me write the story. While the story itself is fantasy, the teachings about the Bible and prayer are not fantasy. The fantasy serves as a vehicle for giving examples of how to apply the teachings in real life. I hope you will have as much fun reading and learning as I had fun in writing.

BOOK 1

An Unexpected Journey

Chapter 1

Please Write My Story

I was working in my home office when the front door bell rang. The only people who come to my door without calling first are delivery people, and people collecting for charity. Since I wasn't expecting any packages I thought it must be the latter and grabbed my billfold. Standing at the door was a young man. Well, young to me, as I'm in my eighties. He was neatly dressed and well mannered. I didn't want to appear rude or inhospitable, but I am cautious about admitting strangers into my home.

"Hello, can I help you?" I ask.

"Are you Mr. Leach?" he asked.

I said I was – the sign on the porch gave that away.

"Mr. Leach, my name is Peter. I'm here because I was told to come. I was told that you would listen to my story. May I come in and tell it to you?"

He appeared to be an honest young man. He was obviously alone. I could see no harm in inviting him in. We settled into easy chairs, and he began. His story had me hooked from the first sentence. Time quickly passed. Without realizing it, the afternoon had passed. I invited him to stay for supper and continue his story afterwards. He talked through the night and into the next morning. When he finished I sat still, spellbound by what he'd told me. It was an amazing, fantastic story.

"Why did you tell me your story?" I asked.

"The Professor told me to ask you to write it down for me. He said you've never met. But he seemed to know a lot about you and was convinced you would listen, that you would believe me, and I could trust you to write it all down accurately."

"Peter," I said, "I'm not an author! You need to tell your story to a known author. If I write your story it may never be read or published."

"The Professor wants you to write it."

"I'll do my best if you're sure that's what you want."

"That's all I could ask," Peter answered.

I invited Peter to stay with us a few days while he retold the story and I recorded it. This gave me a chance to ask questions, fill in details, and see if the story changed in any way in the retelling. I hoped it didn't change because it was the kind of story you want to be true. The story didn't change. All Peter did was add more details. Peter's adventure was written indelibly in his mind, even what he thought and felt. He was adamant that the many conversations he had with the Professor about prayer and spiritual truths be included. Those teachings, he said, are integral to the story, as were all the references to Glenn Clark. The Professor liked Glenn Clark because he taught how to connect with God and release his power into our lives and world.

I hope you enjoy the story.

Matt W Leach

CHAPTER 2

The Call

Buzzzzzzz! Startled awake by his annoying clock, Peter crawls out of bed, his eyes barely open. Half stumbling across the room to his desk, he fumbles for the alarm clock and turns it off. Still half asleep, he gropes his way to the shower and steps in, forgetting to warm the water first. The unexpected blast of cold water jolts him fully awake! He dresses, grabs his books, and heads for the dining hall. It's all but deserted. He eats a quick breakfast by himself and heads for class.

From the scowl on Peter's face you wouldn't believe it was a perfect day. But it was. It was warm. The sun was shining. All over the campus the trees and flowers were putting on a show of springtime beauty. But this is lost on Peter as he grumbles his way to class.

"There ought to be a law against Saturday morning classes," he complains to the air. "Juniors shouldn't have to take Saturday morning classes. All the juniors agree. But do the professors listen to us? No! 'It's the only time we could schedule the class,' they laugh."

Arriving at the liberal arts building, he enters, finds the class room, and sits with all the other sleepy students. Only the professor is wide awake. The class finally ends after a herculean struggle on Peter's part to stay awake. He steps outside. The fresh air revives him just enough to make it to the Student Union for a quick cup of coffee, black and strong. He sips his coffee and looks around for any of his friends. They're not there. Probably in class or sleeping in. With nothing else to do, he reluctantly heads back to his room.

"Might as well get started on my homework," he complains sadly to the empty sidewalk. "I'm too wide awake to go back to sleep and there's no one to talk to."

Back in his room he tosses his books on the bed and checks for any new phone messages. The light is blinking: four new messages. "Hey!" he says hopefully. "Maybe Mr. Johnson wants me to come in early. I could sure use the extra money!" He hits the play button and listens while he changes into jeans and his favorite faded blue plaid shirt. George wants to borrow his tennis racket. Jim got the book that Peter wanted. Ed needs help with his physics assignment. Then, the final message: "Urgent! Come quickly. Don't tell anyone. Hurry!" *Click*!

As abruptly as it started, the message ends. Just as abruptly, out of the blue and totally out of place with the message, a strong sense of fear and foreboding grips Peter. The hairs on his neck stand up; his stomach twists into a knot. An overwhelming urge to grab his coat and car keys and rush out to his car pushes him out the door. "What's going on?" he cries out in confusion. "For crying out loud, it was just a phone call from the Professor. He's always asking us to come out. Why this gut-wrenching fear?"

Peter gets into his car. The motor purrs to life. He puts the car in gear and pulls out of the dorm parking lot. Turning right onto College Drive, he heads for Main Street. The Professor lives on a little country road west of town, maybe a 20-minute drive, or 25 if there's a lot of traffic. Students are always welcome. Mrs. McD, his housekeeper, always has a plate of her famous chocolate chip cookies waiting to be devoured. Peter stops at the intersection with Main Street. No one is coming. He pulls out onto Main Street heading west. Suddenly, without warning, Peter becomes totally oblivious to the fact that he is driving a car down main street! His mind flashes back three years. He finds himself setting foot on campus as a new freshman. He relives those first days minute by minute, class by class.

A few moments later the flashback ends. As though waking up from a deep sleep Peter looks around. Startled, he gasps, "What the—! Where am I? I'm stopped at a stop light! What am I doing here? Oh, I'm going to the Professor's. Looking around, he recognizes the gas station on the right, across the intersection. Then it hits him. “Yikes! I’ve driven all the way through town without knowing it! Oh man, this is scary! And why is the Professor’s favorite saying ringing in my head? Why am I thinking of it now? Critical questions reveal truth…”

Peter waits for the light to change. The fear churning in his stomach made worse by the flashback. “Why is ‘Critical questions reveal truth’ running in my head? Has something bad happened to the Professor?” He shakes his head, trying to clear it, trying to shake off the fear. As he tries to make sense of it he goes back over all the things that had led up to the Professor making that statement, starting with the morning he first arrived on campus.

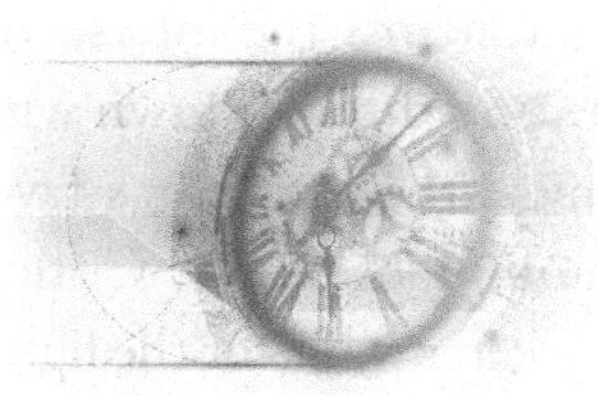

CHAPTER 3

A Tough Week in Physics 101

The day dawns bright and beautiful. Some fall colors are just beginning to show. Peter is so excited he can hardly wait for the long drive to end. At last, the magnificent archway gate that marks the entrance to the campus of this prestigious Christian College comes into view. He opens the door and jumps out before the car is fully stopped. Running up the steps of the college office building, he quickly finds the registration office, checks in and gets his assigned dorm room.

His parents help him move all his stuff into his room. They grab a last meal together, hug him goodbye and leave. He cuts it pretty close to the one o'clock starting time before he finds the classroom for freshman orientation. He quickly slips into a seat, nods to the guys next to him, and settles down for what he is sure are going to be boring lectures. *Here's how you register, here's how you sign up for classes, professor so and so will be your faculty advisor, and here are the rules you're supposed to obey or risk suspension.* The presenters manage to use up the whole afternoon and stuff everybody's hands full of papers to read. Peter and his fellow freshmen are thankful when it ends, and thankful to be heading to the dining room for the evening meal. "I hope the food is better than the lectures," Peter mumbles out loud.

"Amen to that," the fellows next to him agree. As they walk together to the dining hall they introduce themselves. It turns out that all four of them, Peter, Ed, George and Jim are physics majors. It also turns out that all of them, like Peter, are athletes, hoping to get to play on some of the college teams. The next morning they meet together for breakfast, and then head to the book store. The price of their textbooks is a shock! They decide to buy some of them together and share. As a result, they end up hanging out together, playing together and start calling themselves "the gang." Monday comes, bringing the beginning of a very strange first week.

Peter, happy and excited, walks towards the physics building. This is a great day, a dream come true. It's the first day of classes and the beginning of his first year in this small Christian college with its dynamic physics department. More importantly, it's the first day of his first physics class under the Professor. He could have had a baseball or football scholarship in half a dozen other colleges. But they didn't have the Professor. Anyone who studied physics under the Professor was guaranteed to get into any grad school of his choice.

But all is not well. Though happy and excited, Peter is also uneasy. It's something the upper classmen kept saying: "Good luck on surviving your first week of physics." That statement hangs over every freshman's head like a dark cloud. What do the upper classmen mean? What could be so hard about the first week of classes? The upper classmen just look at them with *knowing* smiles when asked what they mean.

Arriving a few minutes early, Peter takes the steps two at a time and enters the physics building. The lecture room is on the first floor, to the right and down the hall. The room is buzzing with chatter. Ed waves him to a seat by him. The Professor, slim but well built, distinguished looking with unruly dark brown hair with streaks of gray, is half seated on the corner of his desk in front of two gas cans. His blue-grey eyes twinkle with joy as he nods his head in greeting and smiles at each student. He appears to be just an ordinary teacher. And yet, as Peter looks at him he senses a hidden power under the Professor's quiet, gentle appearance.

Strange thoughts suddenly and unexpectedly bubble up from deep inside and pour into Peter's mind. *There is more to the Professor than meets the eye. He may appear meek on the outside but he could be a formidable enemy. Our lives are going to be bound together!*

What? exclaims Peter nearly out loud, startled by the unexpected thought. *Where did those ideas come from? I don't think thoughts like those! This is weird!*

Jim and George come in together and find seats nearby just as the bell rings. The room goes quiet. Everyone's eyes are fixed on the Professor. He, in turn, seems in no hurry to begin. He looks each student in the eyes as though taking stock, analyzing each of them. Finally, he smiles and speaks.

"Today you are beginning an amazing adventure. Physics is much more than the facts and figures and formulas you will learn, or the experiments you will do. It is learning how to *use* those facts and figures and formulas. Learn to use them well and you might discover how to travel through time. Or perhaps rebuild a damaged human organ in mere seconds. Or even teleport goods and people across space and continents in a split second of time. Or perhaps stop on the moon for supper on your way home.

What does this statement mean?" the Professor asks as he turns and writes on the blackboard. "'You can take the boy out of the country, but you can't take the country out of the boy.' Anyone?" No one seems willing to answer, probably because the warnings from the upper classmen have everyone psyched out. Is this a trick question? It doesn't sound like a physics question. Eventually, Peter gets up the courage to answer.

"Sir, it means that when the boy leaves the country he takes with him the values, beliefs, traditions, and prejudices with which he was raised."

"Correct," the Professor nods in agreement. "Can anyone give me an example?"

"Business deals," Jim speaks up. "There is a saying in the country that a man's word is his bond, and deals are sealed with a hand shake. City people don't trust anyone. They have to have everything in writing, in triplicate, notarized, and signed in blood!"

"Sounds like you just applied for a student loan!" the Professor chuckles. "The values, beliefs, traditions and prejudices of our country boy were formed in him by his environment, his parents, his neighbors, his school, his community. These form what we call a *country mindset.* All of us have mindsets. Every mindset, whether it be country, city, poverty, or wealth, has both good and bad elements in it that influence how we look at life. Each of you has come to this physics class with your own *physics mindset.* It is made up of ideas, beliefs, and notions that you've picked up from your teachers, your text books, television, movies and science fiction.

"The ideas, beliefs, and notions in your physics mindset that are correct can help you. Those that are wrong can cause you to waste time and money. The question you need to ask yourself is, is there a way to sort the good from the bad? For example, suppose your car runs out of gas. At the spot where you run out of gas you find these two identical gas cans filled with what appears to be gas. You've never seen the gas cans before. You know nothing about them. Unknown to you, the gas in one can is good, while the gas in the other is bad and will damage your engine. You have two choices. You can choose to assume that if the can is labeled 'gas' it must be gas. Assuming, therefore, that both cans are full of gas, you pick one up and pour the contents into your gas tank.

"If you are lucky and choose the correct gas can you'll have no problems. But what if you choose the wrong gas can and put the bad gas into your gas tank? Five miles down the road you will be crying over a ruined engine. If you are like some people I know you might swear never to put gas in your engine again, because gas ruins engines! But being smart physics students, you won't make such a silly decision as that!

"What might have caused you to assume that if it says gas it must be gas? Wasn't it because in your experience people only put gas in red gas cans that are labeled gas? Your experience thus becomes part of your mindset. In this case it turns out that this part of your mindset is faulty. It could lead to an undesired result. You should have made the second choice, the choice not to assume but to examine the gas just in case one or both cans of gas are bad. Having made the choice to examine the gas, how do you determine if the gas is good or bad?"

The Professor waits for an answer, but the only replies forthcoming are the questioning looks on everyone's faces. Everyone seems to share the same assumption that whatever they say will be wrong! No one is willing to take that chance.

"Students! The answer is simple. Become a detective!" the Professor explains, as if it was perfectly obvious.

"Huh?" they all ask instead, completely puzzled.

"The secret of how not to be trapped by a flawed mindset, the secret of how to succeed as a physicist, and the secret of how to pick the good gas," he continues, "means you must learn to be a first-class detective. Who can tell me what separates a first-class detective from all other detectives?"

No one answers, again.

"Isn't it the ability to see clues that others miss? How does he do that? He asks the critical questions no one else is asking. By asking these critical questions he finds clues where no one else saw any clues. He finds them because he is looking for things that are not obvious, things that get easily overlooked. Let's apply that concept to our two cans of gas.

"First, examine the two gas cans. Is there anything that suggests that either gas can had been used for anything besides gas? Any traces of chemical spills, paint spills, rust? Has it always been a gas can, or has it been painted red or repainted? How do the samples of gasoline compare with each other: odor, surface film, color? How do they burn?

"It is the ability to ask critical questions that is the secret of the detective's success, as well as the physicist's success. Unless you can let go of your physics mindset and ask critical questions, your physics car may end up with a ruined motor! The first lesson you must master in physics is this: Critical questions lead to great discoveries.

"I've designed your first assignment to demonstrate the importance of discovering and asking critical questions. To complete this assignment, you must set aside traditional thinking and formulate critical questions that will enable you to discover the answer. This assignment is extremely difficult. It will show you how elusive critical questions can be and why they are important.

"Read the letter to the church in Thyatira in the Book of Revelation, chapter two. Explain what the letter is about. Tell why the Spirit warns them against Jezebel. Like a true detective you must discover the questions no one asks. Do not be fooled. This assignment is far more difficult than any of you can possibly imagine. It is difficult because you will read it with flawed mindsets!"

"Boy," Peter whispers to Ed, "his is one weird assignment for a physics class!"

"Yes, Peter?"

Peter, startled at hearing his name, apologizes, "Sorry, Professor, I didn't mean to say that out loud."

"You didn't, but it was written all over your face. You think the assignment weird. So do the rest of you! It's written on all your faces! I don't do weird, understand? Now, open your books to Chapter One."

After class Peter joins the gang on the way to lunch. George asks, "What does a Bible story have to do with physics? What's the catch? Why would he say it was going to be so hard? What's so hard about reading the Bible?"

"Beats me," Ed joins in. "You got any ideas, Jim?"

Jim shakes his head no. "Guess we'll find out Wednesday, unless Peter knows something we don't. How about it, Peter? You know the Bible better than we do."

"Sorry, guys. I'm as much in the dark as you. I don't think any of us will have it right come Wednesday!"

The rest of the class is just as puzzled. No one has any idea what the Professor's driving at. Or what studying some scripture has to do with physics. One thing's for sure, everybody agrees, they'd better study the passage forwards and backwards. That was Monday. That evening and all day Tuesday the class studies the Letter. They look at commentaries and compare notes. By bedtime on Tuesday everyone can recite the passage backwards and forwards.

Wednesday morning begins all too early for Peter. That is when he discovers that there are some things for which you can never prepare! Hearing the alarm go off at five-thirty is one of them. The day is dawning bright and clear, but not Peter. He struggles out of bed mumbling and groaning. A quick shower and a brisk walk brings him to the local grocery and his appointment with Mr. Johnson, the owner.

He hires Peter on the spot. Peter rushes back to the campus, happy as a lark. Without that job he couldn't stay in school. He eats a quick breakfast, grabs his books and heads for the science building. Peter arrives at the class room with just enough time to compare notes with some of the others.

Everyone seems to have come up with the same conclusions. The Professor sits at his desk, watching and listening. From the look on his face, he does not seem impressed or pleased with what he's hearing. The bell rings. He stands and walks around to the front of his desk. He folds his arms, his piercing blue-grey eyes examining each face. Finally, he speaks.

"You've all read the letter to Thyatira. Apparently all of you have come to a common consensus on the answer. So I assume you all agree as to what the critical questions are. Would someone please volunteer to give your combined answer?"

The Professor's tone of voice does not sound good. No one's willing to speak up and take a chance on being wrong. Finally, George volunteers. "We thought the passage sounded like Jezebel was trying to convince the Christians that there's no harm in a little compromising with the world. Otherwise they were just cutting themselves off from society."

"Do you all agree? Does anyone want to add to this?"

The stern look on the Professor's face makes everyone afraid to speak. The room is silent.

"In that case the whole class gets an 'F' on your homework! This is the sorriest excuse for homework I've ever heard. You are all wrong! Dead wrong! None of you has the foggiest clue about what was going on in Thyatira. You've no idea why Jezebel was such a threat. I told you to think like a detective, to ask critical questions. You didn't. Now, do the assignment again and this time ask the critical questions. Understand?"

The Professor's voice is harsh, almost angry sounding. This is a side to the Professor no one had expected. After all, it's only the second day of physics classes. Why should he be so upset? The room is still silent. Everyone looks stunned.

"Sir," Ed breaks the silence, "what do you mean by critical questions? We thought we did ask them."

"Use your common sense," the Professor answers, his voice stern. "You've let yourselves be trapped by how people traditionally interpret that passage. Ask questions that get you inside the story. What was happening behind the scenes? You're a detective, remember. You are trying to get at the truth. Now open your text books to where we left off Monday."

Boy! Everyone is glad when the class is over. The Professor is great. Everyone really likes the way he teaches. But this thing about critical questions hangs over their heads like a black cloud. Outside, the whole class stands around bewildered. George takes the lead and makes a suggestion.

"Let's research this letter between tonight and tomorrow night, and then after supper tomorrow let's gather in the Union and compare notes."

Everybody agrees, relieved to have a plan of action. By the time Peter gets to the library he finds all the reference books on Revelation are already checked out! Fortunately, the passage is short and everyone is eager to share the books and compare notes. The Thursday night get-together doesn't produce any new insights, or ideas, or any clue as to what the Professor is driving at. Everyone wracks their brains trying to come up with "critical questions" but still come to the same conclusion everyone had reached on Wednesday.

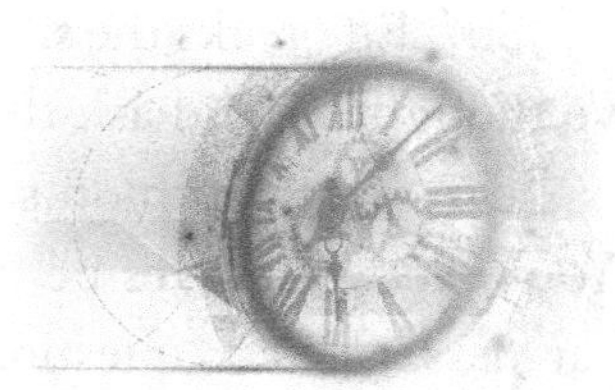

CHAPTER 4

What Do You Mean – Flunked?

Friday morning Peter is rudely awakened by his alarm clock. "It's four-thirty in the morning! It's still dark out, for crying out loud!" he sputters as he forces himself to get out of bed. "Why did I tell Mr. Johnson I'd be there at five? It sounded good yesterday. But not now. Every cell in my body wants to crawl back into bed!" Somehow he manages to get up and dress and arrive at work on time! It is with no small pleasure Peter discovers that Mr. Johnson has brewed a pot of coffee and set out a tray of big, gooey, delicious donuts! Those donuts make restocking the shelves a lot easier and the work go faster.

His work done, Peter rushes back to the campus. He barely has time to get through the class room door before the bell rings. Jim has saved him a seat. Everyone has a pile of books and notes on their desks, prepared with every bit of information on Thyatira they could find. The Professor is seated behind his desk. His face looks stern, emotionless. All is quiet. Finally, he stands and comes around to the front. He half sits on the edge of his desk, his arms folded. Once again his eyes search every face. The look of sternness does not leave. Whatever he was looking for he didn't find.

"I understand the whole class has worked together on this report," he finally speaks. "Since you all have the same answer I've decided to ask George to speak for you again. George, please stand up. Give the report in your own words. When you are finished tell me the critical questions you asked."

"We dug up every fact we could find," George begins. "Thyatira was located on an important trade route. It was a prosperous city. It had an extraordinary number of trade unions, guilds and associations. You couldn't do business or practice a trade if you didn't belong to a trade union or association. It would be certain business and professional suicide if you refused to join one.

"The trade unions all held common meals. These meals were usually held in a pagan temple and always began and ended with a formal sacrifice to the gods. This put Christians between a rock and a hard place. Christians do not eat in pagan temples. They don't eat meat sacrificed to a pagan god. That would be worshiping the pagan gods. Christians worship only Jehovah God, and Him alone.

"To make matters worse for them, these meals usually turned into drunken orgies; all in the name of fun! Christians couldn't join in. They believed their bodies were the temple of the Holy Spirit. These Christians were caught in an impossible situation. They were cut off from just about all social contact with non-Christians. They couldn't belong to trade unions or guilds or associations. There was no way they could earn a living or practice a craft."

"Good, George. That's a good description of how things were in Thyatira," the Professor nods in agreement. "Now, what about the woman Jezebel? What did the Spirit have against her, and why?"

"We figured Jezebel was just trying to help the Christians survive. If they would only compromise just a little, they could stay in business."

The Professor turns to the rest of the class and asks, "Do you all agree with this report as George gave it?"

Everyone nods YES.

"Does anyone want to add anything to it?"

Everyone shakes their head NO.

The Professor stands up. He looks at the class, shaking his head as if to say "it's hopeless." He walks around to the back of his desk, pulls out his chair, and sits down. Without looking up he speaks. "All of you might as well leave now!" His voice is sharp and biting. "Not one of you has any idea what the letter to Thyatira is about. You didn't ask a single critical question. You don't have what it takes to study physics. You have all flunked! I'm giving all of you an 'F' for the semester. There's no sense my wasting any more time on you. You are dismissed." He begins writing.

The class sits - stunned. No one moves. No one speaks. How can you flunk after just one week? Whatever they've missed must be pretty big for the Professor to act like that. The room is wrapped in silence, the only sound being that of the Professor's pen as he writes. After what seems like an eternity, Peter breaks the silence.

"Please, Sir, tell us where we missed it."

The Professor looks up and in that same biting tone responds, "I said, you didn't ask any critical questions."

"But, Sir, we were sure we had."

The look of shock and disbelief on everyone's face is replaced by a look of bewilderment. The Professor continues writing. Peter speaks up again, "Professor we don't know what you mean by critical questions. Please explain it to us."

The Professor looks up with the same unyielding expression. His eyes search each student's face. Suddenly the sternness leaves and he smiles, asking, "Are you finally ready to learn?"

"Yes!" everyone answers in unison, relieved.

"Good!" the Professor exclaims as he stands again. "You all missed something extremely important in the letter. Remember, I told you that being a scientist is like being a detective. That means you must break free of traditions and preconceived ideas. Come as though you are the first one on the scene. Take note of every little thing. The key to discovery may be something simple that everyone else overlooks. A detective doesn't overlook anything. An important clue might be what others think is unimportant and totally unrelated to the case.

"The reason you all missed what this passage is about is because you were focused on the last part of the letter. When your focus is wrong you overlook the obvious or pass over some simple little thing which turns out to be the key that unlocks the mystery. Critical questions are never obvious. They come from pondering the data, from examining the minutest things that may seem irrelevant, from reading between the lines and filling in logically what isn't said.

"All of you overlooked the second verse of the letter: 'I know your deeds, your love and faith, your service and perseverance, and that you are now doing more than you did at first.' (Revelation 2:19 NIV)

"Based on that verse, what was the critical question you didn't ask?"

Still, no one has any idea what he is talking about.

"Students, look at the last line of that verse. It says that those Christians are 'now doing more than' they did at first. Your first critical question is to ask how. Logic tells us that the only way they could be doing more is if they weren't poor! It is telling us that they were both prosperous and gaining in converts. Critical questions are never the obvious questions. But when asked, they reveal a depth of information that brings clarity, insight, understanding.

"Now, let's look at the critical question of how. Imagine that you are one of the non-Christians living happily in Thyatira. You belong to a trade union. You are successful and fairly wealthy. Your life style is pleasurable and you enjoy the occasional orgy. Imagine that one day someone comes along preaching Christ. It sounds good until you are told followers of Jesus can't belong to trade unions because they meet in temples and eat meat sacrificed to idols.

"Everyone knows if you don't belong to a trade union you can't buy or sell in Thyatira. You are also told that followers of Jesus can't party either and you love your parties! Becoming a Christian is beginning to sound pretty dumb. It sounds like becoming a follower of Christ is a fast trip to unemployment and the poor house!

"Go back to the key verse. It tells us that the Christians were prospering, and that the people of Thyatira were becoming converts. How do you explain it? What accounts for this strange turn of events? That brings us to the next critical question you failed to ask. That question is: What would have to be happening with these Christians to cause you, a Thyatiran, to take them seriously, to listen to their witnessing, and receive Christ as your Savior? What would make you give up your membership in a trade union?"

The class is silent. Eventually, Ed breaks the silence. "The only thing that would get me to take them seriously is that the Christians would have to be more successful, have more money, and be far happier than me."

"And that," the Professor adds emphatically, "is exactly what that verse is telling us. From the world's point of view, they were committing financial, social, and economic suicide. From a human point of view these Christians should have been starving, homeless beggars. Is that how you attract non-Christians and get them converted? 'Become a Christian like me and you too can be homeless, dressed in rags, starving and begging!' No! Absolutely not! This verse tells us that against all odds the impossible was happening.

"The Christians in Thyatira had a winsomeness about them. There was joy, and generosity of spirit. There were miracles and signs and wonders. Instead of being in the receiving line, they were in the giving line. Instead of being on the public dole, they were doling out to the public. Instead of living like the child of a beggar, they were living like children of the King. This against all odds! Now we can answer the question, what was the real danger of Jezebel? Peter, you look like you've got the answer. What about Jezebel?"

"To follow her would have destroyed the miracle life they enjoyed."

"Yes! Do you see that, class? It's not until you look at the verse others overlook, and then ask the critical question of 'How could this be so?' that you begin to see the whole story. Critical questions reveal truth. Many times in physics it is the scientist who examines the overlooked verse who makes the great discoveries. Christians, like scientists, often miss the truth because they look at it through their prejudices, preconceived beliefs, and traditions. If we want to learn and discover we must break free of those mindsets and adopt the mindset of a great detective.

"Rene Alleau, a French scientist, gives a perfect illustration of this. He was studying certain chemical processes as practiced by the Ancients. He was surprised that he was not able to repeat some of their metallurgical experiments. He used the same raw materials they had used, and followed their descriptions. But the experiments didn't work. *Why*, he asked? He had been very careful to duplicate each step. Like a good detective, he began to ask questions. Were the raw materials identical? Any difference there would account for his failures. But they were identical.

"Then he examined the flux, the purifying agent they used. He had assumed that the ancients had been correct in identifying the flux as the cause of the reaction. With that in mind, he had used a pure flux, and the reaction failed. Then he asked the critical question. Was it possible that it wasn't the flux but an impurity in the flux the ancients had used caused the reaction? When he used the impure flux, the experiment worked. Asking critical questions enabled Alleau to advance his metallurgical studies rather than spend fruitless hours chasing a wrong belief.

"Now to answer your unasked question. Yes, I designed this lesson to help you discover the importance of asking critical questions. Yes, I knew you would fail! And no, you are not getting an 'F' for Wednesday or the semester. Asking critical questions will make your study of physics much easier. You will need to use it in almost every lesson. It is also a good life lesson. How often have you jumped to a conclusion about someone or something that someone did, only to find out, often to your embarrassment, that you were wrong? Now, open your books to where we left off Wednesday. Don't forget, critical questions reveal truth."

As his thoughts return to the present, Peter remembers how shocked everyone had been. "Wow!" Ed had spoken for everyone. "When he drives a point home he really drives it. None of us will ever forget it."

That's true, Peter muses to himself. No one ever forgot it. *But why am I being reminded of it in this crazy way? Is something going on I don't know about? Maybe there is. Maybe I'm being warned to keep my eyes open, to ask questions. But why? Why such a dramatic way to warn me?*

Impatient, driven by the knot in his stomach and the weird flashback, Peter shouts to the traffic light, "Come on, change!" It turns green and he heads down the road mumbling, "Can this morning get any weirder? I wonder if Mrs. McD's made any cookies? Speaking of Mrs. McD," Peter reasons, "if something is wrong she would have called. She's very fond of the Professor. Dotes over him like a mother hen. She's a bit of a character but a great housekeeper and cook. She'd let us know immediately if something was wrong. So why the fear? Why is my stomach tied in a knot?"

Seemingly as soon as Peter asks the question a scream bursts from his lips, his heart in his throat. In a blink of an eye he has gone from pulling away from a traffic light to racing down the highway, passing another car. He doesn't know where he is. Fear propels him to slam on the breaks, pull over to his right, and turn off onto a farm driveway. Fear surges through his body. He sits, breathing hard, his knuckles white as he grasps the steering wheel.

"What's going on?" he cries out. The fear and knot in his stomach twist further. As he tries to get control of himself, he discovers that now *two* phrases are bouncing around in his head: *Critical Questions Reveal Truth*, and *Nine Unknown Men*. "Nine Unknown Men? Oh come on! Why is that nonsense filling my head? It doesn't mean anything. It was just an old legend that wasn't true.

I've got to figure this out. I'm not going back on the highway until I've got an answer or I may end up dead! God, please help me. Why Nine Unknown Men? It wasn't as big a deal with the Professor like *Critical Questions Reveal Truth*. It was just an old legend, like a fairytale. The Professor agreed with us. If that's true, why is *Nine Unknown Men* bothering me now? What's that got to do with the Professor?

Maybe if I go back over more of the strange events of that week something will come to me. We were in the quantum physics classroom, waiting for the class to start. We were puzzled because the Professor was missing...

"Where is the Professor? He's never late without telling us," everyone was asking. The Professor was always there to greet everyone with a cheery hello. While the class waited, Peter's thoughts wandered back to the last class session. Just as it was ending, the Professor had given the class another of his strange assignments.

"Your next assignment is to explore the truth, if any can be found, behind a strange science fiction movie. This assignment has two parts.

First, watch the movie *My Science Project.*[1] Second, submit a written report covering the following: On what scientific theories is the movie based? Of the many things that happen in the movie, which do you think might be possible and which do you think impossible? Explain why, referring to what you've been learning in quantum physics."

With those words the Professor picked up his notes and walked out just as the bell rang. He was gone before anyone could ask any questions. Still, it sounded like this assignment would be a piece of cake. *Boy! How many times have I said that and regretted it?* thought Peter. On the way out Peter was hailed by the gang. It was quickly agreed that he would pick up a copy of the video at work, and they would meet at the Union that night to watch the movie.

[1] "My Science Project", Directed by Jonathan R. Betuel, Distributed by Buena Vista Distribution, 1985, Film.

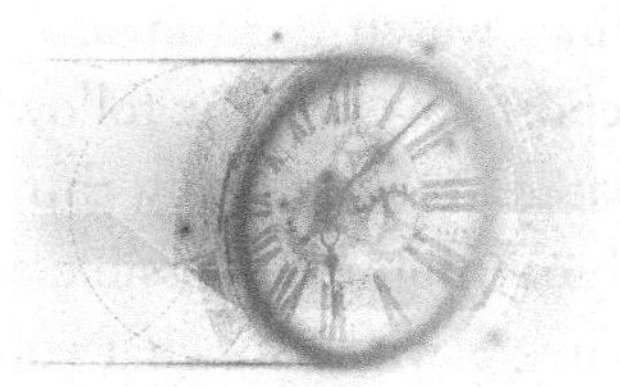

CHAPTER 5

Weird Science

Peter was very tired by the time eight o'clock came around. Restocking shelves is hard work when you're the only one doing it, and the shelves were nearly empty. But he got it done. He checked out the movie and headed back to the campus. Stepping into the Union, Peter was hit full in the face with the smell of fresh popcorn. It set his mouth watering. He grabbed a big bag, buttered, and headed for the video room. The guys were already there.

"Hi guys! Boy, am I glad to sit down! Here's the video, George."

"When you think about it," Ed said thoughtfully, "it's a weird assignment for a quantum physics class! The stuff in science fiction movies isn't real. It's pretend science."

"Still," Jim added, "we better be on our toes. The Professor has a reason why he wants us to watch the movie. If we don't get it right, he'll nail us to the wall like he's done before! He may be a great guy, but he's one tough teacher!"

Peter's reverie is broken by the bell, signaling the start of class. That's strange. The Professor still hasn't arrived! Suddenly everyone's attention is drawn to the doorway-like frame that has been standing by the Professor's desk for several days. No one's paid much attention to it. It looked ordinary enough. You could see through it and all around it. No one had asked what it was for because it looked like something maintenance was working on. The door frame was sitting in front of the door way to the Professor's supply closet. The supply closet door had started to stick and had been taken away for repair. A dark curtain covered the opening.

Suddenly, tiny lights hidden in the doorway-like frame start blinking! Beeping sounds and a faint whooshing noise start coming from the frame. The whoosh begins to increase in volume, like something coming from a great distance away. Then suddenly: *poof*! There is a burst of smoke, a brilliant flash of light; and the Professor steps out of the frame! Everyone gasps in surprise.

"Wow!" Peter exclaims. "That's some entrance!"

The Professor gives Peter a scowl that says "Don't say another word." Then, gazing intently at each student, he asks, "Why do you look so surprised? Is there some reason why I shouldn't use a transporter beam? It's a very efficient way to get from one place to another. This is a class on quantum physics, isn't it?"

"Professor," George speaks up, "that was just an old magician's trick! And a pretty good one the way you did it."

"Was it a trick?" the Professor asks, looking directly at George, a dead serious look on his face.

"Professor," Jim protests, "according to the laws of quantum physics, neither atoms nor sub particles of atoms can be physically sent between two points. A transporter beam is an impossibility."

"Are you sure?" the Professor asks, looking at Jim with the same dead serious expression. "Then how do you explain what happened to Philip who suddenly found himself transported to a distant town in the eighth chapter of Acts? How do you explain what happened to the apostles who suddenly found themselves transported to the outside of a locked and secured prison, as told in Acts chapter 5?"

"So it's gonna be one of those days," Peter observes to those around him. "All kinds of questions, and not one straight answer."

The Professor is silent for a couple minutes. "From your unimaginative comments, I highly suspect that not one of you has done a good job on your homework assignment. Remember what Glenn Clark wrote about expanding your thinking to God size? It sounds more like you've let your thinking shrink to amoeba size! Expand your thinking. Rewrite your assignment and bring it next time. For the rest of our class time we will continue our study of the Standard model of Particle Physics."

Peter takes notes fast and furiously. The Professor has a gift for making things easy to understand. Even so, sometimes it sounds like a foreign language! The bell rings just as Peter's hand cramps up for the tenth time!

The physics building is built like an old mansion with elegant front doors. Its wide, marble steps are a favorite place for sitting with one's back against the stone railing warmed by the morning sun. That's where Peter finds George. Ed and Jim have already gone off to their next class.

"Have a seat," George greets him. "That was some entrance the Professor made! What do you think he was getting at? Was he serious, or was he pulling our legs? Are we missing something?"

"I'm with you on his dramatic entrance," Peter replies. "It was an old magician's trick. He jazzed it up a bit. But, knowing the Professor, he had a reason."

"That was my conclusion," agrees George, "but I can't quite put my finger on the reason."

"It was the same reason why he had us watch that movie. He's still teaching us to ask critical questions, to think on God's level of possibilities. That's why he referred to those two stories in Acts. We know God works by the laws He built into His creation. If He were to break just one of His laws, everything would disintegrate into chaos."

"That's obvious," George agrees, "but what does that have to do with those two incidents from Acts where Philip, and then the disciples, were instantly transported from one place to another?"

"It's simple," Peter laughs, slapping George on the knee. "Even if the present level of scientific research says it's impossible, the Professor is saying that if God did it, then it must be possible! Start thinking on God's level!"

"So that's it! I better rewrite my paper like the Professor said."

While they'd been talking, a stranger dressed in a black business suit ascended the steps near them. Overhearing their conversation, he stops and listens with interest. When they finished, the man speaks.

"Pardon me," he says politely, "but your talk about those two events in Acts caught my attention. This professor you're talking about sounds like a fascinating teacher. It almost makes me wish I were back in college!"

From the moment the stranger speaks, Peter's sense of danger goes on high alert. Something isn't right. He can't quite put his finger on it. He senses danger and evil, but he hasn't a clue why. Unless, this man is spying on the Professor for some unknown reason. *Why would I imagine that?* Peter wonders.

"He's an excellent teacher," George answers. "Maybe not orthodox. He gives us strange homework sometimes. But he has a way of making things easy to understand. This is no small task when it comes to teaching quantum physics!"

"In my experience, scientists who make the best professors are also the ones who are involved in the most cutting-edge research. If your professor is as good as you say he is, he must be doing some pretty exciting cutting-edge research, too. Do you know what projects he is working on?" the stranger asks.

"This is a small Christian college. It doesn't have money for any research facilities," George replies. "The only research he's doing is with his hobby, mushrooms. He grows the most delicious mushrooms you can find anywhere."

"Are you sure he's not working on any of these things you were talking about? I've heard reports that he is. He's reputed to have a very brilliant mind. Rumors say he has been making a great deal of progress. Are you sure he doesn't have a research facility near here?"

"Sir," Peter speaks up, "we don't know what you have heard, but it wasn't about this professor. Somebody has given you a lot of wrong information. There is no place around here where he could do research even if he wanted to."

The stranger studies Peter. Peter's skin crawls with goose bumps, and again the warning flashes through his mind.

Finally, the stranger says, "Perhaps you are right," then turns and walks away.

Peter turns to George, "Did you get a funny feeling when he was talking?"

"No. I thought he was a little strange, but that was all."

Peter shakes his head. The feeling of danger soon passes and is forgotten.

"Let's get a cup of coffee. I'll buy" George offers. They head for the Union.

When the gang files into the class room Wednesday morning, a few of their fellow students gather around George. They want to know if George still thinks the Professor's dramatic entrance was a magician's trick. The Professor seemed to insist that teleportation was possible. Peter says nothing. As they talk, they notice the Professor listening to their conversation, as he often did. The bell rings just as they find their seats. The Professor turns and, without speaking, writes the name Glenn Clark on the blackboard. Turning back to the class, he speaks.

"From your conversations this morning, I think we need to stop and talk about mind stretching once again. A few weeks ago, I asked you to read chapter 18 of Glenn Clark's autobiography, *A Man's Reach*.[1] You were to write a brief summary of the course of study he had set for himself. What was his motivation for this course of study?"

"Dr. Clark was troubled," Susan, another classmate, speaks up. "What the religious experts of his day were saying didn't fit with what he read in the Bible. It was as though the theologians had put God in a box. What didn't fit, they explained away. Dr. Clark decided he needed to break free from the theological teachings of his day. Only so could he find out what God actually said."

"That is an excellent answer, Susan. One more question: What brought him to that point?"

"Only one thing brought him to that point. Having become a new creature in Christ, he set out to be 'transformed by the renewing of his mind,' so that he could 'prove what is that good, and acceptable, and perfect, will of God' according to Romans 12:2. Only the person who is born again can understand the things God reveals in Scripture."

"Susan has summarized it very well, class. Now let's see what that

---

[1] Clark, Glenn, *A Man's Reach*, ©1977. Minneapolis, MN, Macalester Park Publishing Company, pp158-172.

meant to Glenn Clark. He was born into a world where scientific and religious thought was stagnant. In 1875, a director of the US Patent Office resigned because, he said, there was nothing left to invent. In 1887, the well-known chemist Marcellin Berthelot wrote: 'From now on there is no mystery about the Universe'[1].

"Theologians chose to listen to the world's ignorance rather than listen to God's wisdom. They reverted back to being what the Bible calls 'the natural man.' I Corinthians 2:14 makes it plain, 'The natural man receiveth not the things of the Spirit of God: for they are foolishness unto him: neither can he know them, because they are spiritually discerned.'

"Their minds were closed to the things God had revealed in Scripture. Everything inside Dr. Clark said 'This is wrong.' The only way out of that stifling swamp, that paralyzing mindset, Clark reasoned, was to force his mind to break free. What was the course of study he chose to help him break free?"

The Professor looks around, waiting, and then chides the class in a stage whisper, "They say short term memory is the first to go!"

"Professor," Ed volunteers, "Dr. Clark said that he mapped out a three-way course of study. First he would forget about what the churches and theologians were saying. He would let the Bible speak for itself. He would study the teachings of Jesus – and everything in the New Testament – as his anchor and guide. Second, he would study the writings of the Christian mystics whose goal was 'union with reality.' Third, he would study the writings of the unconventional scientific thinkers, the dreamers who dreamed of doing the impossible."

The Professor nodded, "That is correct. All of you would do well to follow Clark's example. Your minds are caught in that same kind of closed science trap. That is why you had trouble believing that I could teleport to the classroom. What is important is that you be open to such possibilities without being gullible. Developing that openness means that sometimes you must take drastic measures to break your mind free from the trap of old ways of thinking. Clark was forcing his mind

---

[1] Louis Pauwels & Jacques Bergier, *The Morning of the Magicians*, ©1963, New York, NY, Avon Books, p34.

open, breaking free of the debilitating, crippling bondage of a mindset that knew only a sterile and powerless form of religion and scientific thinking.

"Science had lost its vision. Scientists had declared that going to the moon was impossible. Television was an unbelievable flight of fancy. And the very idea that you could actually expect God to hear and answer your prayers all the time wasn't even to be considered. If you've made up your mind that those things are impossible, you won't study and experiment until you learn how to do them.

"Clark challenges us to set our minds and spirits free. Expand your concept of the universe to God's concept. Be open to all possibilities. Even the possibility that the Bible's description of creation is what actually happened, and that it is our understanding that is flawed! The problem with people in every age is that they tend to explain away what they do not understand and are unwilling to accept as true.

"Clark set for us the task of embracing truth and questioning theories that could not be proven. Think on the level of the stars. If you had been thinking on the level of the stars, you wouldn't have been at all surprised to see me use a teleportation beam. For you, science would be full of wondrous possibilities. There would be no such words in your vocabulary as 'that's impossible; it can't be done'".

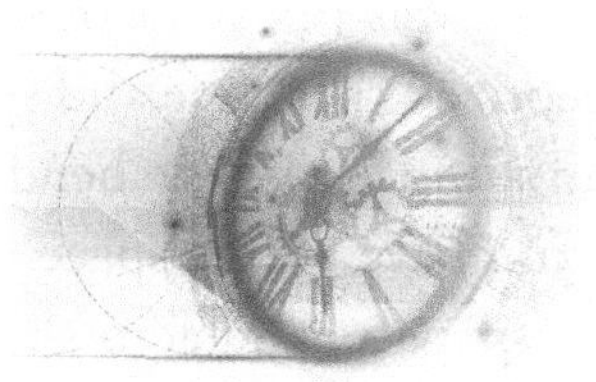

CHAPTER 6

Legends or Strange Facts?

Perched on his favorite spot at the front edge of his desk, the Professor asks, "Ed, you're a *Star Trek* fan. How did they explain the workings of teleportation?"

"It's based on the theory of quantum entanglement. An object, or person, is broken down into atomic particles, sent across a distance and then reassembled at the other end. But of course it can't really be done."

"And why is that?" the Professor asks.

"In quantum entanglement only information is sent between two points. The actual matter is destroyed at the sending end, and is constructed new on the receiving end. It's great for spies who need to instantly send information. But living matter would be utterly destroyed."

"That is true, as far as it goes," cautions the Professor, "but you have fallen into the 'can't-be-done' trap. You failed to ask the simple question, 'Why not?' There are physicists working on it today who believe they can send matter across space instantly. Or, perhaps that has already been done, as you saw last time . . . or didn't see! The question is, what is impossible and what is only a matter of time?

"Are your minds closed, or are you open to what may seem to be impossible possibilities? What about the movie you watched, *My Science Project?* Is your mind open to the possibilities it suggests? Or do you see them as impossibilities? Who can tell me the scientific theory behind the movie?"

"It was like a lot of science fiction stories," Jim answers. "Einstein theorized that time and space bend. That gave rise to the idea that you can jump across the bend, or warp, from one place in time to another. If you have a time/space machine you can warp, or jump, across time, across space, and across universes."

"Correct! Now, who can tell me the plot of *My Science Project*?"

"It starts with the crash of an alien spaceship," George volunteers. "The Air Force finds a strange looking gizmo in it that they hide in a bomb shelter in an Air Force junk yard. A few years later a guy looking for something he can use as a science project sneaks in and finds the gizmo. When he hooks it up to a battery, it starts ripping holes in both time and space. Everything from dinosaurs to the Viet Cong start showing up in his school."

"The wonderful thing about science fiction," the Professor smiles as he holds up a book by Jules Verne, "is that it can take you on exciting adventures. The best writers can take a scientific theory, such as quantum entanglement, and make a convincing argument why teleportation is possible. You end up with wonderful stories like *Star Trek*.

"Jules Verne's stories were like that, too. His science fiction stories were so on target that they became today's truth. Some of today's science fiction will become tomorrow's truth. And speaking of truth," he pauses, and looks at everyone in the class, "keep this fact in mind: truth can be stranger even than science fiction! Ask yourself, is your mind open to turning impossibilities into possibilities? What if I were to tell you that there were learned men who hundreds of years ago made scientific discoveries that we are only now rediscovering? Is such a thing possible?

"You're going to get a chance to think about that. Your next assignment is designed to stretch your minds and imaginations further than you've ever stretched them. It's going to stretch your ability to think scientifically. Are you ready to consider that the unbelievable is believable? For your next assignment, I'm going to tell you a series of stories. Some will be true. Some will be legend. Some will sound like fairy tales. I'm not going to tell you what is true and what isn't. That will be for you to figure out.

"Remember, this assignment is about mind stretching, mind stretching without being deceived. To make it easy for you, I am taking all these stories from a book titled, *The Morning of the Magicians*[1] by Louis Pauwels and Jacques Bergier. Louis Pauwels is an author and writer. Jacques Bergier is a nuclear physicist and chemical engineer. All the names and events I describe come from their book. The book has a bibliography of sources. You will need to do much research on the internet, as well as search the library, to complete this assignment.

"Your assignment is to be an investigative science historian. You will search through old records and writings. Some records date back hundreds of years. Some are written in foreign languages and you will need to find translations. Seek the truth behind each story. If the story appears to be fiction, try to discover what events gave rise to the story. Give facts, not opinions. Always give a reason for your conclusions.

"These stories date from the Third Century B.C. to the Seventeenth Century A.D. A problem you will encounter is that science and witchcraft were often considered to be one and the same. That's why scientific experiments were carried out in secret. When things are done in secret, strange tales have a way of cropping up. It was said that one goal of the scientist or alchemist was to turn lead into gold by means of a legendary substance called the philosopher's stone.

"A story is told that in 1666 a man by the name of Johann-Friedrich Schweitzer was visited by a stranger. The stranger asked him if he believed in the philosopher's stone. Schweitzer answered 'No.' The stranger then opened a little ivory box in which were three pieces of a substance resembling glass or opal. The stranger said that these three pieces were all that was needed to produce twenty tons of gold.

"Schweitzer asked to hold one of the pieces. He asked if he could have just a tiny fragment. The stranger declined. Then he asked the stranger to prove his claim. In answer, the stranger said that he would come back in three weeks and do the transmutation. He did come back in three weeks but he refused to do the transmutation. He said he was

[1] Pauwels, Louis & Bergier, Jacques, *The Morning of the Magicians*, 1963, New York, Avon Books.

forbidden to do so. But he did give Schweitzer a grain of this mineral the size of a mustard seed. When Schweitzer said that wasn't enough, the stranger took back the tiny mustard seed sized bit and broke it in half. That little bit, he said, was all that was needed.

"The story goes that Dr. Schweitzer then confessed that he had removed a few small particles of the mineral when the stranger came the first time. He said that he had tried to transmute some lead into gold but all he got was glass. The stranger replied that Schweitzer should have covered his fragment with yellow wax. According to the records, it is said that Schweitzer followed the stranger's instructions and succeeded in transmuting lead into gold. The gold was examined and found to be the purest, finest gold the assayer had ever seen."

"Boy! That's quite a story. I could sure use a bit of that philosopher's stone right now!" Peter remarks wishfully.

"So could I!" chimes in everyone else in the room.

"I don't suppose there's any way to find out if this story is true, or where we can get some of that philosopher's stone?" he asks hopefully.

"Sorry to dash all your hopes," the Professor smiles. "No gold for you today! But you do have a golden opportunity! See if you can find any evidence to prove or disprove the story. Bear in mind that transmutation of one element into another is the basis of atomic energy.

"Did a man by the name of Schwenter investigate the principle of the electric telegraph in 1636? Did the German poem *Salman und Morolf*, written in 1190, have in it a drawing of an underwater vessel made of leather and navigable in stormy weather? Was the diving bell described in a 1320 manuscript of Alexander's Romance? Did Tiphaigne de le Roche publish a work in 1729 telling how to make both color and black and white photography through the use of a chemically prepared surface? What is truth and what is fiction?"

The Professor stands quietly for a few moments, letting his words sink in. Peter asks the question that is troubling everyone, "If there is any truth to these stories, why was their knowledge lost?"

"That is a question for you to answer. Legend has it," the Professor continues, "that alchemists were men of conscience as well as men of science. They were afraid to let common men know their secrets for fear common men might use them for war and bring untold destruction. So they kept their discoveries and identities secret. That of course leads to more rumors and more tall-tales.

"For example, it is reported that one morning in Paris in 1622, the people of Paris awoke to find a strange poster plastered on the walls of their city. It read:

> We, the deputies of the principal College of the Brethren of the Rosy Cross are amongst you in this town, visibly and invisibly, through the grace of the Most High to whom the hearts of all free men are turned, in order to save our fellowmen from the error of death.[1]

"These Rosicrucian Brethren, it is said, possessed the secret of changing one metal into another, and of living for hundreds and hundreds of years. They worked in secret. The trouble with doing things in secret is that rumors fly. The truth gets stretched. The doers of good are charged with being doers of evil. That is not a good position to be in. It could get you killed! Absolute secrecy was the only protection these people had."

"Being a scientist in those days wasn't a good profession to be in, was it?" George asks. "Man! And we thought your tests were killers!" The class bursts out laughing – even the Professor laughs.

"That brings me to my final example, and possibly one of the most intriguing. Is it legend or is it fact? You tell me, and give scientific reasons for your answer. This story begins in India after 273 B.C. during the reign of Emperor Asoka. He had just ordered a great massacre. When he saw the carnage for which he was responsible, Asoka was so overcome with remorse that he renounced war as the way to win men's hearts.

"Since he had used the inventions of science to massacre the people, he vowed all natural science to secrecy. All people involved in experiments, advances in knowledge, and scientific studies were to be hidden behind a mask of mysticism. To this end he founded the most secret society on earth, the Nine Unknown Men. It is said that Pope

[1] Ibid. p56.

Sylvester II had contact with the Nine Unknown Men and received some sort of computer from them which he used until his death in 1003. It has been reported, that in times of great need, when sickness threatened all human life, some unknown gentleman would step forth and show how to make an antidote.

"It was also said that they had discovered a liquid, an elixir of life, that gave them immortality. The liquid was a byproduct of the process they used to make the philosopher's stone. Modern science knows that the human body is designed to never grow old. Why it does is a problem modern scientists are trying to solve. People spend millions of dollars trying to defeat the ageing process. The Nine Unknown Men, so the story goes, found the secret hundreds of years ago."

The Professor pauses, looks around, and asks, "If the legend is true, do you realize what it means?"

"Professor," Ed answers hesitantly, "this is really farfetched. But I think it means, that if the story of the Nine Unknown Men was actually true, and if they really had discovered this elixir of life that gave them immortality, then there is every reason to believe that the Nine Unknown Men are alive today and could be living secretly among us!"

"Precisely. That's exactly what it means. A fascinating possibility, isn't it? Did the Nine Unknown Men ever exist? That's unknown. Are they alive today? That's unknown! Did they learn how to live for hundreds of years? That's unknown. Have they recruited others to take their places and did they pass their knowledge on to them? That's unknown because it is unknown if the men themselves actually exist or existed.

"Play around a bit on the internet. Type in any words you think might turn something up. You will discover some very weird web sites. Some people, who are convinced science is not telling them the truth, are willing to believe anything without proof. They will tell you the Nine Unknown Men are alive today. But that is only wishful thinking. If their existence is known they can't be unknown, can they? And yet, maybe they are alive and among us! That is a possibility, isn't it?"

"Professor," asks Jim with an incredulous look on his face, "are you serious? You sound like you believe this Nine Unknown Men story.

Do you? It's too farfetched. Look how old they'd be! Be very skeptical of anything you can't prove, you tell us. So, how can you suggest this story might be true, when there is no evidence that it is anything but a legend? If we can't prove it, how can it be true?"

"Are you sure it isn't true? Are you sure we can't prove it? Have you thought it through? Be a detective and ask critical questions, such as, what would be telltale evidence of their presence among us? After all, doesn't the Bible tell us that Methuselah lived to be 969 years old?"

Just then the bell rings and Peter slaps Jim on the back, laughing, and says, "You know you'll never get a straight answer out of him!"

Peter doesn't mention it to Jim, but something about the Nine Unknown Men legend bothers him. The Professor knows something he is not telling. It's like deep reservoirs of knowledge the Professor keeps hidden: knowledge greater even than what scientists know today. Peter has sensed it before. Ever since that first day of classes something keeps dropping these bits of knowledge into his mind. He's found himself asking many times, "Who is this man?"

Outside, Peter notices a stranger entering the physics building. He is dressed and acts similar to the man he saw a couple days before. The feeling of uneasiness he had then returns. He shakes his head, thinking "My imagination's playing tricks on me again."

With those thoughts, Peter's reverie ends. His grip on the steering wheel lessens as, thankfully, he begins to see a pattern, a possible reason for the phrase *Nine Unknown Men*. "It has to have something to do with those strangers. The first stranger kept insisting that the Professor was doing some kind of cutting edge research. Maybe he was one of those fanatics who believe the Nine Unknown Men are real and has decided the Professor is one of them. All the time the man was speaking I kept getting the feeling that he was evil and up to no good.

"If that's what the Nine Unknown Men is about, maybe the Professor is in danger. Maybe he needs me to help convince them he isn't who they think he is. That would explain his urgent phone call and the flashbacks. I'm being forewarned to be on the alert. When we looked up Nine Unknown Men on the internet we found some really weird stuff. Like all those people who think science is hiding the truth. Some of them sounded dangerous."

Just to be sure he hadn't miss anything, Peter quickly reviews the events from that strange week. Satisfied, he begins to relax and breathe a little easier. "I don't think the Professor is in danger or he would have said so. Why can't I shake this fear? Why doesn't this knot in my stomach let up? Is it possible I've got it all wrong?"

Suddenly, from out of nowhere, the last thing Peter would ever have thought, shouts in his mind. Danger! The Professor's brilliant mind is starting to snap. He is starting to believe he's one of the legendary *Nine Unknown Men*. He is becoming delusional. There's no telling what dangerous things he might try.

"Delusional! Oh c'mon. That's nonsense. That's a ridiculous idea. I'm not going to sit here and let that fill my mind." Peter takes a deep breath and pulls back onto the highway. About 10 miles down the road Peter comes to the turnoff to the Professor's. He turns right onto the familiar country road. As he turns, the fear that has gripped him starts to grow stronger. In spite of his efforts to be logical, his imagination works overtime. He starts imagining all kinds of bad things.

Then suddenly, startled awake, Peter finds himself jamming on the breaks. His arms fly up to shield his face. Adrenalin races through his body. His heart beats rapidly. He keeps his eyes closed, afraid to look. The car stops. There is no crash. He doesn't know where he is. At the same time a third phrase joins the other two. *There Is an Enemy*. No! No! No! Peter shouts.

His eyes slowly begin to focus on the road. There are no other cars, nothing he was going to hit. Why did he stop so suddenly? Then he sees it. He stopped for a duck! A mother duck, ambling along without a care, unaware of the turmoil in Peter's mind and the sense of dread that is driving him. Trailing her ducklings behind her, she had expected him to stop and wait for her!

Peter's nerves are frazzled. He can't think. His heart is racing. The fear knot in his stomach feels bigger. Weird and unwelcome thoughts flood his mind. *Danger!... The strange men have taken the Professor prisoner... No! It's not the strangers who are dangerous, it's the Professor...*

He has become delusional!... He thinks he is one of the Nine Unknown Men... I'm in danger... There is an enemy... Don't go on... But I've got to go... The Professor needs me. No! The Professor is the enemy! Like water spewing from a burst dam the thoughts come.

Just then Mother Nature gets his attention. In the midst of his fears, the unnerving driving, the unwelcome thoughts, Mother Nature has set before him a scene of peace and beauty. He forgets the turmoil in his mind for a moment. His latest flashback has evidently lasted about five miles and he is stopped at one of his favorite places on the road.

Flowers carpet the fields in a rainbow burst of color. A sweet fragrance fills the air. As he looks, the peace and beauty calm his nerves. If only he'd brought his camera. What a picture it would make! The country road winds along the east edge of the wooded hills until, in a grand sweeping curve, it turns to the right, races down to a distant stream, crosses an old bridge, and disappears into the distance. That picture would be sure to win a prize. The moment of peace is forgotten, and the unwelcome thoughts again flood his mind.

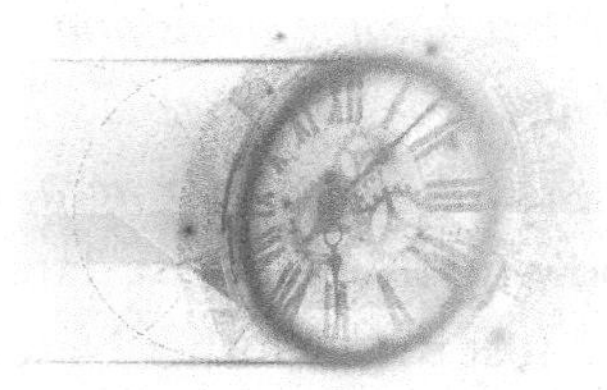

CHAPTER 7

The Duck and the Tesseract

Desperate for answers Peter prays, "Father, please help me understand. I know you are trying to tell me something. But it has gotten all mixed up in my head. I know this fear isn't of you because you did not give us 'the spirit of fear but of power, and of love, and a sound mind.' (2 Timothy 1:17). I let fear grab hold of me and now it won't let go. I'm sorry, Father. Help me see what it is you are trying to tell me. Thank you."

Feeling a little better, Peter tackles the meaning of this third flashback. It came at the end of an ordinary trip that turned into a strange adventure. It started just before the spring break when the Professor called him into his office…

"Peter, how would you like to do a research paper for extra credit?"

"I'd love to Professor. In fact, I already know the subject. The fifth dimension. I just read a book by Madeleine L'Engle called *A Wrinkle in Time.*[1] In her story she describes a fifth-dimensional phenomenon in which the fabric of time and space folds. She calls it the tesseract and has the characters in her story tesseract across the folds of time and space. Some scientists suggest that might be possible. I'd like to find out what is known about it."

"Hmm. That would be a good research project. Some who have studied Einstein's Theory of Relativity think the tesseract might be

[1] L'Engle Madelyn, ©2007, *A Wrinkle in Time,* New York: Square Fish.

possible. In fact, I've a friend who is researching the fifth dimension. I'll give him a call. Maybe he can help you. In the meantime, see what you can find out on your own."

In the days leading up to spring break Peter spends all his free time researching the fifth dimension. Discouraged by what he doesn't find, he shows his notes to the Professor.

"This study has been confusing, Professor. Most authors seem only interested in their own drawings and formulas about dimensions. I was hoping to learn the characteristics of the fifth dimension and what new possibilities the fifth dimension holds for us. Is anyone really researching it?"

"One man in particular did. But he wasn't a scientist. He was Glenn Clark, a football coach and professor of English. His understanding came because he let the Holy Spirit transform and renew his mind according to Romans 12:2. If we take a moment to look at what he said, we will be amazed where we end up! Can you quote the opening words of Genesis?"

"In the beginning God created the heavens and the earth."

"There is more, Peter. Go on."

And the earth was without form, and void; and darkness was upon the face of the deep. And the Spirit of God moved upon the face of the waters. And God said, Let there be light: and there was light. And God saw the light, that it was good: and God divided the light from the darkness. And God called the light Day, and the darkness he called Night. And the evening and the morning were the first day. (Genesis 1:1-5)

"Just think Peter, what it must have been like at the moment of creation. Imagine the power that was released when God spoke, 'Light Be.' This was not the light we call day. That came later. The power that was released when God called the universe into being and flung the stars into the heavens and filled the emptiness with galaxies was a power beyond our imagining.

"Scientists want to learn all they can about God's creation, how it works, and its secrets. The concept of dimensions is part of that quest. A straight line is the first dimension, length. A second line, perpendicular to the first, is called the second dimension, breadth. To this add a third line to form a cube and call it the third dimension, depth. Einstein added the fourth dimension, time. Are there more dimensions?

"Glenn Clark in his book, *God's Reach*,[1] describes dimensions from God's point of view. Think of dimensions as a cone or funnel, with each new dimension greater than the last. The smallest end of the cone, the bottom, is the first dimension. The largest end of the cone, the top, is God's dimension of unimaginable power. Glenn says man was designed to live at the top, in God's dimension of unimaginable power!

"Glenn used dimensions to help us understand spiritual truth. The fifth dimension Glenn calls the Secret Place of the Most High, or the dimension of prayer. Prayer releases the power of the fifth dimension. Atomic energy of the fourth dimension can disintegrate a mountain, but Jesus said prayer, the power of the fifth dimension, can make a mountain get up and move without disintegrating it. This kind of power is greater than atomic energy. Joshua demonstrated it when he commanded the sun to stand still (Joshua 18:31).

"Glenn calls the sixth dimension Love. What kind of power was released when God spoke 'Light Be,' and 'Earth Be?' Perhaps the creative force was love. Glenn calls love the strongest force in the world. Science is just learning how to measure the power released by prayer. What will they find when they begin to measure the power released by love? It might be that from which all creation is formed.

"Glenn proposed a seventh dimension. In the Bible seven is a perfect number. Glenn's seventh dimension is the Kingdom of Heaven. It is the dimension of abiding so completely in the Father that you and the Father are one. Each higher dimension has a power that far exceeds the power of the lower dimensions. A fourth dimensional atomic bomb that you can carry in a small briefcase has a destructive power that exceeds enormous tons of the dynamite of the third dimension.

---

[1] Clark, Glenn, ©1951, *God's Reach*, St. Paul, MN, Macalester Park Publishing Company, pp13-53.

"The same is true of God's dimensions. Even though our feet are planted on the earth, God is calling us to come up and live on His level. He invites us to live a life where miracles and the miraculous is the very air we breathe. It's also interesting to note that the higher the dimension the smaller it is on the outside and the bigger it is on the inside. For example, prayer comes from the inside, and cannot be seen, weighed, tasted, heard or smelled. But prayer, the size of a grain of mustard seed, Jesus said in Matthew 17:20, is all it would take to move a mountain."

"I had always thought that was just an expression Jesus used," Peter marvels. "But He really meant it, didn't He? He was trying to help us connect with God's dimension."

The Professor smiles in agreement. "When you asked Jesus to be Lord of your life, you connected on the inside with all the power of God, the power that created the universe with one spoken word, as Paul wrote in Colossians 1:16-17; 2:9-10. The greater your level of union on the inside, the greater the power that is released on the outside. What are some examples of Jesus releasing power?"

"Jesus walked on water," Peter answered, "took authority over the weather, called up a fish for money, raised the dead, healed the sick, cast out demons, passed through crowds and walls unseen and told us that if we did not doubt, the wind and storms would obey us and mountains would get up and go where we sent them."

"All that was possible, Peter, because Jesus, living among us as a man, was also living on God's dimension. That was the basis of his comment in John 14:12, that we will do even greater works than he did. Follow Jesus' pattern, Glenn writes, because He is the Way. Are there events in Jesus life, as well as in other places in the Bible, that give us clues about the fifth dimension, and perhaps even about other dimensions?"

"That's a fascinating idea, Professor. There are many unexplainable events. But I don't have the foggiest notion how one would even begin to develop a scientific treatise using those stories from the Bible. Do you?"

The Professor, with a pleased look on his face, answers, "I'm glad you asked! Remember the friend I told you about? He is researching the fifth dimension from the Biblical point of view that Glenn Clark described. My friend begins with the premise that if it is in the Bible then it's doable. He asks: 'What possibilities are suggested by these Biblical events?' Since these events are not normal, he theorizes they could represent a higher dimension. He then asks himself: 'What might this infer about the characteristics of that dimension?' He has come up with many intriguing ideas and some fascinating experiments. How would you like to meet him?"

"I would like that very much, Professor. Does he live near here?"

"Actually, he lives in another country."

"Then I guess meeting him is out of the question. I don't have any extra money. I can't afford to take a trip," Peter answers, disappointment in his voice. "I could sure use a rich uncle right now!"

"Better than that," the Professor smiles, "you've got me! I want you to meet my friend and visit his lab. But it will cost you! It will cost you a well written paper with a lot of original ideas. Are you up to the challenge?"

"Boy am I! That's too good an offer to pass up! I'll even rewrite the paper as many times as I need to get it right."

"We'll skip the rewriting. I don't think my head is up to rereading one of your papers a dozen times! Get your things packed, and I'll take you to his laboratory next week during spring break!"

True to his promise, when spring break arrives Peter finds himself sitting beside the Professor on an airplane, headed for the Netherlands to meet the Professor's friend. When the plane lands, they disembark and make their way into the terminal. Peter does not know the language and would have been lost if the Professor wasn't leading the way. They find the signs pointing to the baggage area and make their way there. While they wait for their suitcases to come on the conveyor, Peter looks around. He sees a man coming towards them looking as though he has recognized someone. He looks strangely like the Professor and yet unlike him in many ways.

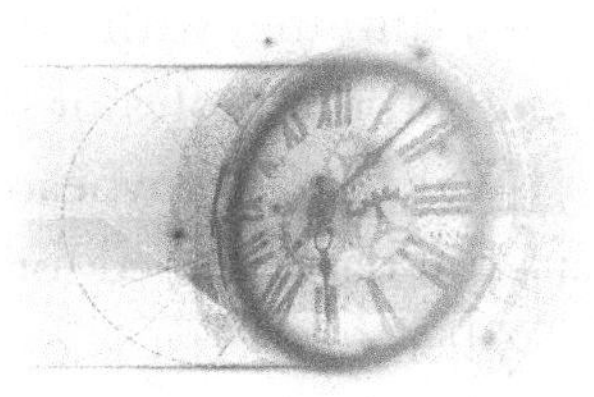

CHAPTER 8

Nightmares and Secrets

Professor! It's great to see you again." The stranger grasps the Professor's hand warmly, and then Peter's. "And you must be Peter! The Professor has told me much about you. Very proud of you, he is. You can call me TPF, short for The Professor's Friend! I keep my real name secret and this seemed as good a substitute as any. It helps avoid some unpleasant encounters."

They start to chat when Peter's stomach growls. "Forgive my manners," TPF smiles. "You must be famished after that long flight. My car is waiting just outside. I've got a cook, Peter, who's just as good as Mrs. McD, better I say. She has a tasty dinner waiting for us."

After many turns and twists the car pulls up in front of a modest home on a hillside overlooking the city. Peter grabs his luggage and follows the Professor and TPF. Even before the door is opened, he catches the delicious smells of a roast beef dinner with all the trimmings. After dinner, when Peter's stomach is so full he can't possibly eat another bite, he follows the rest into the living room and sits in an overstuffed chair by the fireplace. He dozes off only to be awakened by TPF, who leads him to a guest room. Soon as he sinks into the soft warmth of the bed he's sound asleep.

Peter's sleep is disturbed by a strange dream. In the dream he is running. An unseen enemy pursues him. The enemy wants something Peter's got. He knows he mustn't be caught. The Enemy must not get it. Peter dashes down streets and around buildings. Suddenly he is in a tunnel, running, with no way out. Just when it looks like he is about to be caught, the Professor shakes his shoulder and wakes him up.

"Wake up, sleepyhead! Breakfast is calling us. After breakfast TPF has a full day planned for us. Hurry!"

When breakfast is over, they hop into TPF's car and head for the city. "You two will have to bear with me as we go to work. I'm taking you to our research facility. Visitors are welcome and we often have school children come for a tour. In the lab they see us working on microchips, robots, and the very latest innovations in home entertainment. Most of it is contract work for other companies, although we do come up with some original technology of our own that we lease to other companies.

"However, we won't be visiting that facility. We're going to a secret lab hidden underneath. We take great pains to protect our secrecy. It would be dangerous if any of our research fell into the wrong hands. Unfortunately, there is always the possibility something will attract attention. We try to be very discrete. But you know how easily rumors can start. You can't always explain away some things just by saying they are projects we are working on at Microtechnologies."

These words set Peter's imagination racing. What could they be working on, he wonders, that would attract public attention? Usually the public is only attracted because you tell them. Or you are doing something that draws attention to itself, like launching a rocket or experimenting with aircraft. TPF's company isn't working on projects like that. So what could be attracting public attention? Does it have something to do with his research into the fifth dimension? And if so, what kinds of experiments?

"We thought it best to use a little diversion to throw people off their guard just in case someone tries to spy on us and tie us to the strange anomalies that are being rumored about," TPF explains. "We needed to be able to park our cars and enter the secret lab without being noticed. The best way to hide things is out in the open, don't you agree? Ah, here we are. I'm going to ask you to be quiet for a few minutes in case there are any listening devices on the ramp."

TPF pulls into a multistoried public parking ramp. He drives up several levels and parks his car. Motioning to Peter and the Professor to follow, he leads the way to the stairs. They descend down several levels. Much to their surprise TPF opens the door to one of the lower levels and walks towards a car. He unlocks the doors and motions for Peter and the Professor to enter. He backs out of the stall, drives down to the street level and exits the ramp. Finally, he speaks. "Just in case someone is watching we park on one level and drive off in another car we've parked on a different level. It's a simple ploy, but it's the simple things that get over looked."

He drives to the outskirts of the city. The road ascends up through a residential area before coming to open country. "The city was originally built in a valley between two hills," TPF explains. "But as it grew, it began to crawl up the sides. We'll be pulling into a parking lot near the top of the hill where you see that big sign. This is one of two parking lots. This is for employees and visitors who want to get a little exercise by climbing the steps to Parking Lot B above. The hill levels off up there with room for a visitor parking lot and for our Microtechnologies facility. We're not going up there. Our destination is the shelter recess you see at the bottom of the steps. Brief storms sweep through the valley unannounced. They last only a few minutes. The lucky ones who use this lower lot, and who spot the rain in time get to keep dry in the shelter."

The shelter is dug into the hill. One side is open to the parking lot and benches line the other three sides. TPF takes a seat on the bench in the rear and beckons Peter and the Professor to join him. From there they can see any cars coming up the road as well as any people who are in the parking lot or on the stairs. Seeing no one, TPF stands, turns, and faces the back wall. He speaks, "This is TPF. Please open. Being polite, Peter, is part of our security code."

A small door suddenly appears in the wall, opens, and a retina scanner projects out. TPF leans forward and lets his eye be scanned. A metallic voice speaks: "Retina scan passed, voice recognized. Welcome TPF. How may I help you?"

"May we please enter, Carlos?" TPF asks.

"Yes," the computer answers. The back wall of the shelter quietly swings backwards to reveal a dark tunnel. They quickly enter and the door closes, leaving no trace.

"Wow!" exclaims Peter. "This must be what it felt like to the Hobbits when the door to Moria[1] closed behind them and they stepped into total darkness."

"If you were a spy, or agent of our enemy, and you were able to figure out how to get past the eye scan, and get the door to open, you would be as trapped as a Hobbit in the mines of Moria. You would find this tunnel just as treacherous with sudden holes in the path. But we don't have to walk in the dark or look for sudden holes. Once the door closes, our friend, Carlos, will give us light, and close all the holes. Good morning Carlos, this is TPF speaking. Would you please turn on the lights?"

"Yes TPF. I'll be glad to," the metallic voice answers.

"Thank you."

The tunnel fills with a dim light. They walk for what seems like a mile to Peter. The tunnel, which actually was only the length of a football field, ends abruptly as though the diggers had suddenly stopped. There is no door and no sign of a door. TPF places his hand on the wall. An orange colored hand print appears under his hand. A small opening suddenly appears and a retina scanner projects out. A metallic voice announces, "Hand print recognized. Retina scan recognized. Did you have a nice walk, TPF? When you're ready to enter just ask."

"Would you please let us enter?"

Silence. Then the metallic voice speaks again, "I recognize your voice, TPF. You may enter." Where there had been no sign of a door, a massive stone door quietly opens to reveal a magnificent laboratory, the likes of which Peter had never dreamed existed.

"Welcome to Tesseract Dimensional Research. Everything you see here we have developed to help us research the fifth dimension. Here you will find all the material you'll need for your research paper."

"But first," the Professor interrupts, "before we look around, why don't you tell TPF what you told me?"

---

[1] Tolkien, J.R.R., ©1965, *The Fellowship of the Ring*, New York, Ballantine Books.

It is hard for Peter to takes his eyes off the amazing lab, and collect it his thoughts. With difficulty he brings his mind back to his study and tells TPF, "This study has been confusing. I couldn't find a single theory about what the fifth dimension is like or about practical applications."

"That's how research into the unknown begins," TPF observes. "Our first task is to ask critical questions like a detective. To help us do this, Tesseract Dimensional Research is using a guidebook few scientists use: the Bible! It has led to amazing discoveries. The Biblical record contains a number of events for which we have no natural explanations. These form the basis of our research.

"We begin with the premise that the universe is a law and order universe. If God were to break one single law the whole universe would disintegrate into chaos and vanish. Therefore, we conclude that all the supernatural events recorded in the Bible follow law and order and therefore must be repeatable." With a sweep of his arms, taking in the whole array of electronics and devices and work in progress, TPF turns to Peter and asks, "As you look at all this, do you have any idea what we are working on right now?"

Peter studies the array of equipment, the instruments, the massive power generator. "From our conversation and the name you have given this research facility my guess is that you're working on the tesseract, or wrinkles in time"

"We aren't just working on it; we are actually perfecting the tesseract."

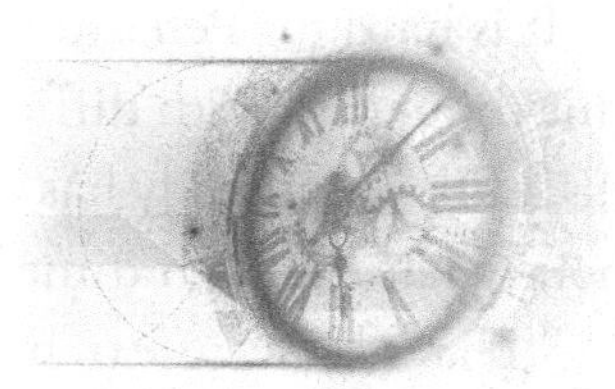

CHAPTER 9

Worm Holes in the Bible

Star Trek used warp drive for speed. Do you remember the other form of travel they used, Peter?"

"They used a theoretical concept from physics, called an Einstein-Rosen Bridge, or wormhole. It is a shortcut through space and time," Peter answered.

"Man has long dreamed of traveling to the stars and beyond. But his dreams have always been hampered by the hundreds and thousands of years it would take to travel that far," TPF muses, a twinkle in his eye as though he had a secret. "Wondering what is possible is where science begins, Peter. Some struggle with theories and how to turn them into reality. Some ask 'Suppose there are stories in the Bible that give us clues to what is possible?' In 2 Kings 6:12, we find the comment that the prophet Elisha, even though he was in Israel, was able to hear the plans the king of Syria made in his own bedchamber. In 2 Kings 2:11 Elisha sees Elijah ascend in some kind of chariot of fire and a whirlwind. In Ezekiel chapter 1, Ezekiel describes a strange vehicle that is not of this earth. In Acts 8:39 Phillip is instantly transported from one spot to another.

"John 20:19 says Jesus suddenly appeared in a room whose doors were locked. Eight days later He did it again. Luke reports in chapter 24 that when Jesus suddenly appeared in their midst the disciples thought they were seeing a ghost. Not only did Jesus show them that He was flesh and bone, but He ate a boiled fish in front of them. Just as quickly as He had appeared, He disappeared.

"All of these strange events described in the Bible happened in accordance with existing laws. How could Jesus pass through walls with a physical body that could be touched and that ate food? The only logical explanation is that He was functioning from a higher dimension that allowed Him to tesseract, as it were, between places in our world, and between our world and heaven, or wherever He chose to go. Based on these stories we believe we can discover the scientific laws of those dimensions and build the equipment that will enable us to tesseract like Jesus did."

"Wow!" Peter exclaims. "That would be some feat! Have you been able to do it?"

"Well, yes and no. First we had to find a way to step outside of the time-space continuum to create a time-space free zone. As you can see, it has required very elaborate equipment – far too big and elaborate to be practical. Experimentation comes first. Miniaturization comes later. But on the positive side, we've been able to create an opening in the time-space continuum and to direct this opening to specific locations. So far all these openings have been directed to locations nearby. We needed to be sure of our accuracy. Once we were sure of our accuracy, we started sending things through.

"At first we tossed toys through the opening. We always had a driver waiting to pick up the toys and bring them back. We tried to be secretive but the drivers wore anti-radiation suits and put the toys in radiation proof containers. So that raised a few eyebrows whenever someone chanced to see us. We found no evidence of radiation, though. Next we used live animals. It was a little trickier catching the animals on the other side. But our accuracy is so precise we can drop an animal into its cage. If we used a dog, I'd toss a bone through the opening. The dog would chase it right into its cage. Anyone who saw it would assume that the dog had been let out to run and had suddenly come back.

"After months of testing and making sure the animals were not harmed or changed in any way by passing through the opening, I went myself. I was sure I'd picked an isolated place where no one would see me. Instead I popped out in the middle of a group of star gazers! I don't know who was the most surprised."

"You always were a bit of a show off, Friend," the Professor laughs. "Serves you right. How'd you talk your way out of that one?"

"Just in case something like that might happen, I wore black clothing. I apologized for startling them, and said they must not have seen me coming because of my dark clothing. We can't look into the opening from the other side. So there was nothing for them to see except me!

"That brings us to the next part of the project that we're working on. You can't see the opening from the other side. If it were visible, there is no telling who or what might see it and decide to come through. As I said, we've learned how to put it exactly where we want it. Now all we need is a way of locating the opening from the other side. It wouldn't make sense to step through onto Mars soil if you can't find the opening to get back!"

Awestruck by what he just heard, Peter turns to the Professor. "Most of my classmates think you talk about the Bible just because you love it. Now I'm beginning to understand. You really meant it when you kept telling us that to the recreated human spirit God gives clues to many scientific mysteries in His word! The clues are there if we will take time to search them out."

"That's right, Peter," TPF speaks up. "That's the upside. There is a downside. It is the ever present menace of evil. For each good or benefit God has for us, evil is always present to corrupt it and use it for evil purposes. One whom we loved as a brother and worked with side-by-side, turned traitor and became our enemy. He is looking for this lab because he wants to steal the tesseract machine.

"We've kept this facility secret, but we've not been able to keep our testing secret. The average man on the street thinks nothing of the anomalies, but to our enemy these aren't anomalies. He's sent Watchers to our city to try to find the location of our secret lab. There was at least one Watcher in that group of star gazers. It's because the enemy is closing in on us that our window of time for conducting experiments is fast closing. So I must warn you both to be prepared for anything when we go through tomorrow."

"What! Are we going to go through the tesseract opening?" Peter asks hopefully.

"That's the plan, Peter," the Professor laughs. "A little adventure we've planned for you! To go through and come back. Are you ready?"

"You bet I am!"

They follow TPF into the Cone of Silence. It is a round room of shatterproof glass set in the middle of the lab. The door closes and immediately the room is enveloped in silence. In the center is a large round table with a dozen chairs. In front of each chair is a computer terminal and a Bible.

"Grab yourselves a cup of coffee or a soft drink. There's some gooey rolls if you'd like one. We do a lot of praying here, a lot of thinking and a lot of dreaming."

"It looks like you do a lot of eating, too!" accuses the Professor as he reaches for an especially gooey roll.

"Who is this enemy you were talking about?" Peter asks.

"He once was one our Order, Peter," TPF answers. "A very brilliant man, but misguided. He got it in his mind that if he could rule this world he could eliminate all war, all poverty, and all of society's ills. He wants a time machine, but there isn't one. So instead he's after the tesseract machine. That's why we have to be very careful."

Opening a locked briefcase, TPF removes a cell phone and hands it to Peter. "Look carefully at this cell phone. You might call it a key to a magic doorway. It can be used as a cell phone. But when you dial the correct combination of numbers, it activates the tesseract doorway. Wherever you are, when you activate the doorway, an arrow will appear on the screen pointing in the direction of the doorway. If you walk in the direction the arrow points you should instantly be inside the doorway, stepping out into this lab.

"I've sent one of these to each of the members of our Order. When it's okay to test them, we'll see if the tesseract machine will latch on to their signals. Then we'll try sending things back and forth. We were able to coax that dog to chase a bone back into the lab using this one, so we know it works.

"Peter, you and the Professor are going to help me test it tomorrow! Today we'll pick out sites for our test. Take this cell phone and carry it safely secured in a pocket when not in use. You can make any calls you want to anyone you want. When it's time to tesseract, I will give you the code. When you punch it in, it will lead us back through the opening.

"Now, about your research, Peter. In this folder you will find tesseract theories and references, along with some suggestions for experiments and practical applications. Feel free to use any of it in your research paper."

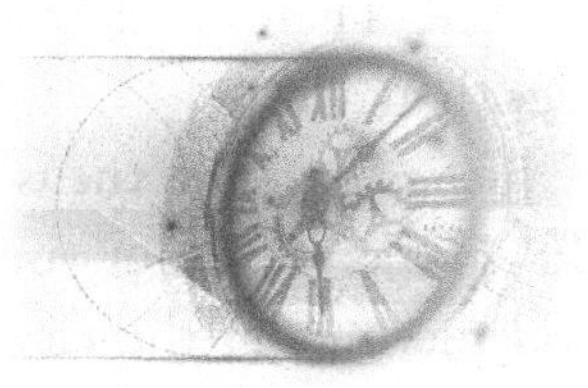

CHAPTER 10

Run, Run for Your Life!

The next morning Peter, TPF, and the Professor go back to TPF's secret lab. Gingerly, Peter steps into the opening of the tesseract doorway, half whispering, "This is how the astronauts must have felt as they disembarked from the Lunar Lander onto the surface of the moon." The cell phone/transmitter is safely secured in his pocket. For a moment he feels the sensation that he has stepped outside of time into a timeless nowness: a place of just being. The next moment he steps out of the opening into dark shadows. The Professor and TPF follow.

Yesterday the three of them had carefully picked out this dark secluded corner in a room opening onto a turret in an old castle. They could step out of the tesseract doorway into deep shadow. No one would notice them. Then they could easily blend in with all the tourists. But that's not what Peter finds! Without a word he holds his arms out to keep TPF and the Professor from stepping out of the shadows.

There is no crowd of tourists in the turret. Instead there are two men, dressed in black suits, wearing dark sunglasses, bending over some kind of electronic device. Peter's stomach tightens and he senses danger. TPF stiffens and then motions everyone to silently back up over to the steps and begin to descend backwards, silently. They barely breathe as they move. TPF is hoping to make it look like they are just coming up the stairs.

"See! There it is!" exclaims one of the men. "It's just behind us. Over there."

Just as the man turns to point to where the three had materialized, TPF speaks up. "Got your cameras ready? We should get some really good pictures of the city from up here. It's one of the most popular spots for tourists."

"Hey! What are you doing here?" snaps the man holding the electronic instrument. "Didn't you see this is closed?"

"We thought it was a mistake," TPF answers. "They told us at the desk that this is a favorite place to take pictures. No one told us it was closed."

"Well it is," the man snaps back.

"Since we're already here, would it be okay if we take a couple of pictures? Then we'll get out of your way."

"Make it quick and then go," the man answers grudgingly.

TPF and the Professor step up and quickly snap pictures as fast as they can.

"Thanks," says TPF turning and heading down the stairs.

"Hey, just a minute," the man holding the instrument demands in a sharp voice. "Did you see anyone on the stairs when you came up?"

"There was someone acting rather strange, now that you mention it," answers the Professor. "He kept looking back this way like he was looking to see if anyone was following him. I guess he thought the stairs were closed by mistake, too, and got scared when he saw you two."

"Quick," cries the other man, pushing Peter aside. "Maybe we can catch him before he gets away."

Once the men are gone, TPF asks in a low voice, "Did you see their instrument? It was designed to pick up traces of a tesseract. Only our enemy has that kind of technology. Well, I guess that ends our experiment. We don't dare try to tesseract back to the laboratory. They'll pick up the signal and know where the lab is."

"I think," the Professor advises, "it is time to disappear. It won't take them long to realize that we're the ones they're looking for."

"Head for the basement of the castle," whispers TPF. "There's an exit into a wooded area. Not far beyond that is an entrance into an old tunnel system. We want to make for the tunnel. Peter, don't let anyone get their hands on the transmitter."

They race down the stairs, sticking to the shadows, watching for the two men. So far so good. No trace of them. They make it safely to the basement exit. TPF opens the door slowly, looking cautiously outside. He motions for the others to quickly follow as he races out and into the woods. Just then they hear the two men shouting: "There they are! They're headed for the old tunnel. Cut them off."

"Well, so much for the quick escape," pants the Professor. "What next?"

"We'll have to make them think we aren't heading for the tunnel after all," pants TPF. "Follow me."

Suddenly Peter's strange dream of a couple nights ago comes back. They run down alleys and sneak around corners, until TPF finally starts back towards the tunnel entrance. They barely make it when they hear the men shout: "They're going into the tunnel. We've got them now. There's no way they can escape."

They run down the tunnel, turning several corners until the only light is TPF's flashlight. Finally, they reach a place where TPF whispers to Peter to press back into a deep recess in the wall. He and the Professor press back into a deep recess on the other side. Peter's heart races a mile a minute. He struggles to keep his breathing slow and quiet. They hear the sound of voices and running feet coming towards them.

"Are you sure they came this way?"

"Yes, there's no other way out. The tunnel ends up ahead, around the bend. The cover at the top of the ladder is bolted shut. Set your phaser on stun. We want all three of them alive for questioning. We'll grab them when they try to climb the ladder"

"The boss will be really mad if they get away."

"Don't sweat it. We've got 'em."

Two dimly lit figures run past, their flashlights probing the darkness ahead of them. As their steps echo around the bend in the tunnel, the Professor and TPF step forward.

"This way," whispers TPF. He leads them back the way they came, stopping in front of what looks like a bracket to hold a torch. Reaching up, TPF tries to turn the bracket clockwise. It doesn't move. The Professor grabs the other side of the bracket and pushes. It still doesn't move.

"Peter, you help the Professor," whispers TPF.

Slowly the bracket turns. Just then, they hear a shout from the far end of the tunnel, "They're not here! We lost them."

"Nonsense," shouts the other voice. "We must have run past them in the tunnel. Quick, shine your light in every corner and crack. They're here somewhere. There's no escape. We locked the entrance."

"Push!" whispers TPF. "The door slides noiselessly, but it'll still take all our strength to open it."

The three of them push hard against the stone wall. Slowly it begins to move, revealing another tunnel behind it. The sound of running feet gets closer and closer. With one more hard shove the opening is wide enough to slip through. Once through, they all push as hard as they can to close the door. The running foot steps are right outside. Everyone holds their breath, listening, hoping the armed men running past do not notice that the torch bracket has been turned. When it seems safe they force the bracket back upright. Steel rods attached to the bracket slide back into their slots, barring the door.

Again TPF cautions them not to whisper and to move quietly away from the door. They walk quietly down the passage, ears alert, listening for any telltale sounds coming from the tunnel behind them, or in front. Finally, in the distance ahead, they see a faint glimmer of light. TPF raises his hand to stop. He whispers, "We'll sit here quietly until dark. We don't want to alert anyone to the existence of this tunnel. And we need to allow enough time for any search party to satisfy themselves that we are not to be found." In the silence, the danger over for the time being, Peter falls asleep.

"Peter." The Professor's voice, barely more than a whisper, rouses him. "It's time to go. The day has past and it is dark. The entrance to this cave is hidden behind trees and brush on a steep rocky bank. Grab the tree roots and let yourself down as far as you can, then drop. It's about twenty-five feet down to a thick bed of moss and fern. Drop and roll when you get to the end of the tree roots. At the foot is a hiking trail. We'll follow it to the Park. If it's safe, a ride will be waiting for us. If there is no ride, we'll lose ourselves in the thickets and go to another spot in the Park where TPF has a secret shelter."

First the Professor, then Peter, and then TPF drop onto the moss. Surprisingly, the moss deadens the sound to no more than a pebble falling off the cliff. On the edge of the moss bed they can just make out a hiking trail. Quietly, they walk along the trail, listening intently for any sign that they're being followed. At last they come to the Park. Peter freezes in his tracks. An elderly man is bent over, tending a camp fire. A pot of coffee is nestled in the coals, sending up its tantalizing fragrance. He scoops up some live coals in his frying pan and uses them to clean his pan. The Professor pulls on Peter's sleeve and points. The man's van is parked in deep shadows with the rear door open. TPF leads the way. Keeping to the darkness, they circle around to the back of the van and one by one crawl into it.

As if some secret signal had been given the elderly man packs up his camping gear, douses the fire with the coffee, and puts his things in the back of the van, closing the door. He gets in and drives off, seemingly unaware that he has passengers. Back in town, he drives around, going down one street and then another. Finally, he speaks. "Well boss, it looks like you've given them the slip! They'll be more convinced than ever that you know how to use a tesseract. They will believe that that is the only way you could have escaped."

With a great sigh of relief, Peter turns to the Professor and asks, "Professor, how did I end up running for my life when all I wanted to do was write a research paper on dimensions?"

The Professor only chuckles and says, "It is rather amazing when you think about it! Friend," he turns towards TPF and asks, "do you always entertain your guests this way? You really didn't have to go to all of this trouble to convince us that the traitor wants your tesseract machine!

"This wasn't exactly what I had in mind, Peter, when I said TPF would help you. Think of it as an extra lesson, a freebie. There is a real enemy, and you've met some of his Watchers. To safeguard his work TPF, will disappear. The Watchers will give up watching and leave.

You and me? We're nobodies. They don't know we exist. Is supper ready, TPF?"

As he sits in his car, remembering his tesseract adventure, Peter muses, *I'd never thought about scientists having enemies, not until I met TPF. If I understand it right, this flashback its telling me that there is a major, big time Enemy. It was his Watchers we met in the castle turret. That explains why the Professor forbade me from mentioning anything I saw and heard in my term paper. In fact, he told me to make the paper boring. "If you make it boring enough I'll give you an 'A'!" He didn't want anything in writing that might fall into the wrong hands.*

But why go to all the trouble to tell me that in a flashback? Were those weird strangers hanging around campus some of the Enemy's Watchers? Are they spying on the Professor? Maybe they think the Professor is experimenting with something the Enemy wants. Anyone with half a brain knows that's impossible. There is no place around here big enough for a laboratory. And no money to run one. Is there a possibility they've started watching the Professor? That can't be; Mrs. McD would have told us.

That leaves another possibility: delusional. Ever since the word delusional popped into my head I haven't been able to get it out of my head. Is it possible that the strangers coming to see him at odd hours and the phone calls from people who can barely speak English have started to affect his mind? No! Stop! The Professor is not becoming delusional. Why does that word send my fear soaring? Can this morning get any worse?"

Afraid to start. Afraid not to. Hoping against hope he won't have another flashback, yet knowing he will, Peter starts his car and cautiously begins to move down the road. The Professor's home is just a couple minutes away. The picturesque road runs along under the overarching branches of the trees. The quietness and beauty and blanket of flowers makes a stark contrast to the churning in his stomach.

Well, so far so good. Move slowly. Breathe deeply. Try to relax. Enjoy the scenery…

Without warning it happens again.

"What the! Not again! Where am I? I don't recognize this road at all." Peter exclaims aloud as he pulls off the road and stops. Bewildered at first, he finally recognizes where he is. "I must have blacked out for three or four miles." At the same time, he becomes aware of a very strange fourth phrase now bouncing in his head: *A Time Machine.* "A time machine? Why a time machine? I could make some sense of the other three phrases, but this is way off the wall. Not even TPF talked about it.

"Wait a minute! Just a couple days ago, some tough looking strangers accused the Professor of working on a time machine. Maybe that's the answer..."

It had been mid-terms. Peter, like everyone else, dreaded mid-terms. He was savoring a last cup of breakfast coffee and was bracing for a grueling morning. All his classmates agreed that college would be enjoyable if the professors weren't so hung up on giving tests. "They say it's for our own good," Peter had complained to George. "Then say it shows if we're learning anything. Sometimes I wonder if it isn't just revenge."

Breakfast finished, Peter reluctantly walks towards the science building. Arriving at the classroom, he walks in and takes his seat. There's not much talk as everyone gathers and sits. The Professor smiles but no one smiles back. The bell rings. He hands out the test papers. Everyone begins.

"Finally, the last answer," Peter half whispers as he breathes a sigh of relief. This has been one tough test! He puts his pencils in his shirt pocket, gathers up his test papers, and heads for the Professor's desk, just as the bell rings. He looks around. The test is over but there's not much talking. More like everyone is suffering from shell shock! The Professor's tests can do that to you. He sighs as he hands his test to the Professor.

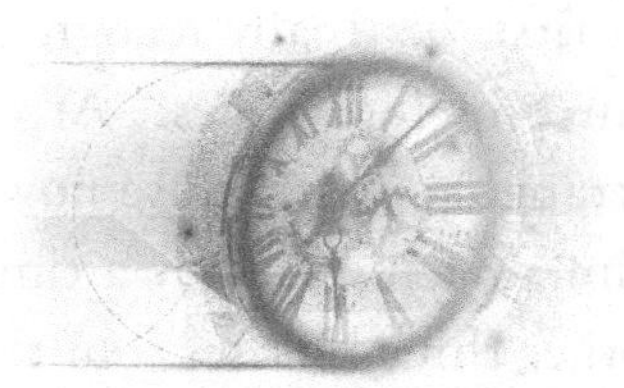

CHAPTER 11

Unexpected Visitors

Thankful to be rid of the test papers, Peter turns and heads for the door. Before he can take a couple steps the Professor calls: "Peter!" Peter cringes thinking, *Oh, oh! I did something wrong.* Slowly he turns to face the Professor, who is smiling as he asks, "Peter, how about joining me for a cup of coffee? I'd like to get away from all these tests and relax a bit."

"Sure. We can grab a table outside the Union," Peter answers with much relief in his voice.

The Professor smiles, "Did I have you worried about the test, Peter? If there is anyone who doesn't have anything to worry about, it's you. Let's walk." So saying, he stuffs the tests into his briefcase, and they walk outside together. He stops and looks around, like he's looking for someone. They quickly cover the distance to the Union, grab their coffee, and settle down at one of the tables on the sundeck.

Once again the Professor scans the campus, and then turns to Peter, saying, "I love springtime. There's a feeling of freshness mingled with the delightful fragrances of the flowers. You should drive out my way, Peter, and look at the glorious sight I get to see every day. The meadows are lush with flowers this spring."

"Professor, you weren't just looking at flowers. You were looking for someone; someone you want to avoid. And you still are. May I ask what's going on?"

"I'm tired of strangers asking questions. I don't want to see any today."

"That's not like you, Professor, to want to avoid people. What brought this on?"

"Well, Peter, it's a long story. We scientists have a scientific journal in which we share our ideas. The idea of time travel holds a great fascination for many of us. But few have any idea of how to go about researching such a project. A couple of my fellow scientists and I decided to have some fun with it. We share our ideas on how we'd build a time machine. And then we point out the flaws in each other's ideas.

"When it came my turn to share my ideas, I wrote a sort of tongue-in-cheek article. Einstein theorized that time is curved, so the machine would need to be able to jump from one spot on the curve to the next. Navigation would be a major problem because no one knows how to navigate once you get outside of time. We don't even know where outside of time is.

"I drew attention to the wheel-within-a-wheel that Ezekiel describes. I called it a working time machine. I suggested the two wheels, or spheres, rotating in opposite directions, one inside the other, could theoretically generate a neutralizing electromagnetic field around the time machine that would set it free from time. I gave some mathematical formulas I'd worked out, and some ideas on setting up experiments. This was only a fun article. But I guess it was a little too convincing.

"I started getting calls from people who wanted to know if they could come and see the time machine. Some wanted to be taken backward or forward in time and left there. I finally put a message on my phone saying there is no time machine. The article was a tongue-in-cheek article written for my fellow scientists. No one would believe me! Well, a few days ago, things began to take on a disturbing note. It started when two strange, foreign looking men cornered me outside my office. They started asking strange questions."

"What kind of questions?" Peter asks, his curiosity aroused.

"They insist I'm doing research on a time machine! Isn't it strange, the ideas some people get? You're not likely to find a college anywhere that has the money to fund that kind of research, especially this college.

That's what I told them, but they wouldn't believe me. Ah, Peter," the Professor sighs, "I'm afraid the world is full of men of power, unscrupulous men of wealth, and governments bent on ruling through controlling ultimate power. So they look for clues of some scientific research that can help them. They want more power. They want bigger and better weapons. Nothing would suit them better than a time machine . . ."

The Professor's voice trails off, as if he's lost in thought. Peter looks down at his coffee mug, clasped between his hands, wondering if time travel might be possible, like the tesseract.

"Hello, Professor!" the voice, almost a snarl, startles them. Two men, wearing wrinkled black suits, with the hint of concealed weapons, have slipped up to their table, unnoticed. "You are the Professor, aren't you?" asks the shorter one. "We have an offer for you. Our employer knows what you've been working on. He is prepared to pay a very high price for your services. He will give you all the funds and research facilities you need. He wants your answer now."

"Gentlemen, gentlemen," smiles the Professor. "I'm sorry to disappoint you. Unlimited money and the best research facilities are all a scientist could ask for. But I think you've been misled. My research is breeding better mushrooms! I hardly need more than the mushroom cellar I already have."

"Don't mess with us, Professor. Our employer read your article on time travel. He knows you're working on it."

"Oh that," the Professor laughs. "This college can't afford a research laboratory so I review papers written by fellow scientists, and comment on them. We decided to pool our ideas on time travel for fun. But none of us are trying to build one."

"Professor, our employer does not take NO for an answer. We have ways of getting what we want," answers the taller man in a low menacing voice, patting the side of his jacket. "We'll be back for your answer." They leave. The Professor shakes his head from side to side, with a look that says, "They just don't get it, do they?" Maybe they don't get it, but Peter sure gets it! He gets cold shivers like something evil was just here.

"Well, Peter, time is growing short! You're soon going to have an opportunity to apply all I've taught you these last three and a half years."

Whatever the Professor meant by those last remarks he obviously isn't going to say any more. Peter's imagination begins filling in the gaps. *It has nothing to do with my application to grad school. No, the Professor is expecting some kind of trouble. My gut tells me that that trouble is going to involve me – without my asking to be involved! Could it possibly have anything to do with this idea of a time machine? No! The Professor said he knew of no one who was experimenting with a time machine.*

"But is it possible that he is secretly working on one? There is no place for a lab here, but his friend has plenty of room in his secret lab. Whoa! What am I thinking?

As the Professor starts to get up to leave, Peter hurriedly asks, "What about these men who came to see you, Professor? Won't they be back? Aren't you worried?"

"There's no need to worry, Peter. I've dealt with people like them before. All they're doing is putting out feelers, and letting me know that they will be watching for any signs that suggest I'm doing research in time travel. They will report back to their employers what I said. They've seen no evidence of research facilities either on campus or off. Unless I start building a research facility they will leave me alone. It's just a pain having to deal with them."

"That's a relief! By the way, how is the time machine coming along?"

"Peter! Any more questions like that and I may decide to flunk you!" the Professor laughs. "Well, it's time to start correcting your tests. Yours alone will probably take me the rest of the day and half of the night! So I'd best get started. See you in class Monday." With those words the Professor gets up and leaves.

Frustrated that recalling the time machine incident gives him no clues, Peter groans, "It still doesn't make sense." Hitting the steering wheel doesn't help either. "There is no time machine. TPF's enemy can't be after something he knows doesn't exist. Maybe there are crackpots like those two men at the Union. But they weren't TPF's enemy because they wanted to pay the Professor to build one, not steal it. This flashback doesn't make sense at all."

Frustrated, Peter feels the knot in his stomach tightening. "I want to believe the Professor is in danger and needs my help. Maybe the Enemy believes the Professor is one of the Nine Unknown Men. If he does, and if he's read some of the Professor's essays on the time machine, that would make sense of all the memories.

"But the idea he is becoming delusional won't leave me alone. Maybe his mind has started to crack under all the pressure. Maybe he's becoming maniacal. Maybe I'm the one in danger, not him." Peter's heart sinks. Pictures begin to flash back and forth in his mind. Unbidden and uncalled for they invade his head. Visions of a mad scientist ranting and raving, intent on evil, flash before his eyes. *Warning! Warning! You're in danger. Be on your guard. Go back! Run while you can*. Peter's confidence, his careful analysis of the flashbacks, lay in a wild heap at his feet.

"Is this some trick of my mind? Is some outside force trying to stop me? If it is it is only making me more determined than ever to find out what is going on. My only choice is to do the thing that must be done. I must go to the Professor's." His mind made up, Peter grits his teeth and resumes driving.

At the curve where the road turns away from the woods, a driveway branches off to the left. Peter turns onto the familiar driveway, pulls up onto the gravel parking area, and comes to a stop in front of the Professor's house, relieved to finally be there in one piece. Cautiously he opens the door and steps out.

The Professor's old stone house is nestled under the edge of the woods. It's an attractive home with thatched roof and grey fieldstone walls flecked with faint streaks of bluish grey and rusty red. A flagstone path bordered by yellow daffodils leads from the driveway to the porch. The overhanging porch roof gives shelter from the sun and protection from the rain. Wooden chairs made for sitting and talking and soaking up the beauty of the fields and hills rest on each side of the porch in front of two large picture windows that flank a large rustic cottage door.

Peter shivers involuntarily. What danger does this tranquil scene hide? The knot in his stomach tightens. Slowly he walks up the stone steps and onto the porch, looking for any signs, any clues of danger. He looks through the windows. Everything appears normal, although he sees no sign of the Professor. His mind floods with pictures of the Professor injured and swathed in bandages, or held at gun point by strangers. Or waiting with a maniacal look on his face. He takes a deep breath, rings the doorbell and waits in trepidation. Waits to see what is on the other side of the door.

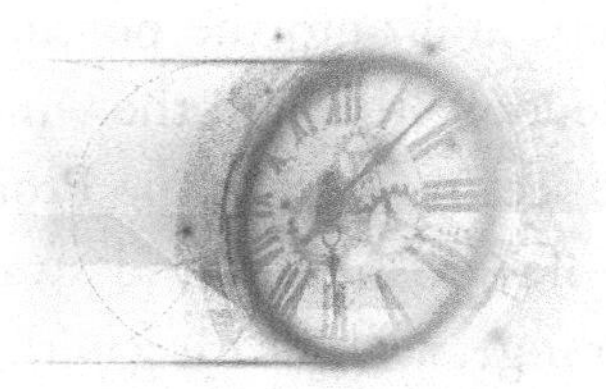

CHAPTER 12

Ancient Secrets

The doorbell, unaware of Peter's fear, chimes a cheerful welcome tune and then is silent. After waiting a few seconds, which seems like an eternity, he hears the Professor's familiar footsteps coming down the hall. The door opens. What he sees flies in the face of all the feelings of dread, the wild imaginings of his mind, the unsettling drive. In fact, he sees quite the opposite, which puts him in a state of greater confusion, but extremely alert for any signs of danger.

Standing there in his white lab coat, face wreathed in smiles, eyes twinkling with laughter as though he had not a care in the world, stands the Professor! His smile and cheery greeting seem wrong to Peter. The haunting sense of dread does not diminish. Something isn't right.

"Well, Hello Peter! Come in! Come in! I'm so glad to see you. I was hoping for some company. Mrs. McD baked a fresh batch of her famous chocolate chip cookies before she left for town. I've just started a fresh pot of coffee. Nothing goes so good with hot cookies straight from the oven and fresh brewed coffee as good friends to share them with. Come in! Come in!"

Peter starts to speak, but the Professor interrupts, beckoning him again, "Come in! Come in!" Peter follows, questions tumbling over each other in his mind and almost choking him as they struggle with each other to get asked. *What is going on*, Peter wonders? *He did tell me to come. Yet he acts surprised and pleased that I showed up unexpectedly. He doesn't give the slightest hint of danger, yet he won't let me speak or ask questions. It was his voice on the phone. I sense dread and warning all around. But he's acting like things couldn't be better. What's going on?*

Glass paneled double doors on the left open into the Professor's library and living room. The room is spacious and comfortable. Encircling the large front picture window and lining the walls from floor to ceiling are bookcases, filled to the full. Still more books lie on top of books. The ceiling, and what can be seen of the walls, is white with just a hint of the rusty red color from the stone walls. The picture window, shaded by the porch, looks out on the magnificent view of colorful meadows and rolling hills. In front of the window is a small reading table. On it is a laptop computer, a digital projector, a pair of white gloves, and what appears to be an ancient manuscript.

Built into the wall opposite the picture window is an old fashioned fireplace. It's tall enough that a young child could stand upright inside. A few embers still glow from an early morning fire. In front of the fireplace are two oversized stuffed chairs that invite you to sit and enjoy the fire and each other's company. Between them is a round table cut from a tree trunk, smooth as glass. Sunlight, where it can find room between an open book and a folded newspaper, dances off the polished surface.

The professor's library is a fascinating collection. There are the usual science books, plus a collection of very old science manuscripts. There are the classics and all the usual books one might expect in a college professor's library. There are other books too, books that reveal the Professor's childlike joy of life and his deep faith in God. There's a collection of Walt Disney Comics. Next to these is a complete set of books by C.S. Lewis and J.R.R. Tolkien. These are followed by a large collection of books on faith.

The Professor has often said, "You cannot be a true man of science and be an atheist. The more science discovers, the more it proves the claims of the Bible. It is ignorance, people assuming they know it all and that there is nothing more to know, that has caused confusion."

Peter takes all of this in at a glance as he looks for some clue as to what's going on. *Ask the critical questions,* his mind is shouting. *Look behind the scenes and between the lines.* But everything looks normal.

Only the Professor's behavior seems out of place. That is, it's out of place only if something is wrong.

"Make yourself at home." The Professor's cheery voice interrupts Peter's thoughts. "I've just come into possession of an old manuscript. It arrived last week. The language is one of the 'forgotten languages.' You might find it interesting. Why don't you look at it while I get the cookies and coffee?"

Peter walks over to the library table to look at the Professor's new old book. When he touches it, he feels a strange sensation as though it were a magical book. Clearly this book has something to do with the answer he is seeking. A pair of white gloves and the Professor's translation notes are lying on the table. He puts on the white gloves and begins carefully turning the pages. The binding appears to be several hundred years old. The parchment is faded but still legible. He recognizes the ancient language, but cannot translate it.

He gently turns the brittle pages. On many of the pages are detailed illustrations of what appear to be scientific discoveries and inventions or experiments. Many, Peter realizes with a shock, are of recent discoveries and inventions! Yet the text describing them is the same 2500-year-old dead language the Professor has been teaching him. A chill of excitement goes up and down his spine. At the same time the sense of dread that has his stomach in a knot increases. The mystery deepens. What is this all about?

"Coffee time!" The Professor's cheery voice breaks into Peter's thoughts. "Come. Sit with me in front of the fire. We'll have some cookies, some coffee, and talk a bit. You must have a lot of questions about the book."

It's the Professor who does most of the talking. He seems determined not to let Peter ask any questions. This aggravates the sense of dread Peter is feeling. Draining the last bit of coffee from his cup, the Professor sits quietly looking at Peter.

Now's my chance, Peter thinks. He starts to ask, "Professor . . ."

Again the Professor interrupts, "There's an old saying that if something sounds too good to be true, it probably is. Take that ancient manuscript, for instance. What did you think of it?"

"It appears to be written in that ancient language you've started to teach me. But that went dead over 2,500 years ago," Peter answers. "It's the drawings and formulas that have me puzzled. They are in the style that would be appropriate for 2,500 years ago, but they are totally out of place in such an ancient manuscript. The technology they illustrate is too modern, like some of the fake documents we studied. They don't belong in a manuscript that old. Some of the things it shows may not have been discovered yet! It can't be for real, can it?"

"Is it for real?" asks the Professor. "That's the question I was asked to answer. Like the saying goes, if something sounds too good to be true it probably is. Remember your assignment when you learned how old manuscripts can be faked? It's always the same. The victim is so eager to buy what he thinks is a great bargain or a great discovery he just *happened* to stumble across, that he is willing to accept the most superficial of tests."

"But an ancient manuscript with drawings and illustrations of today's modern technology is illogical," Peter protests. "The two don't go together. It's like trying to mix oil and water. There were some rare examples in what we studied, but nothing of modern technology. If this is real, it would be the greatest scientific discovery of the century. But logically, this has to be a fake. Why would anyone fall for it?"

"It could be a forgery," the Professor agrees. "Why would anyone fall for it? That's where stories and legends come in. This particular manuscript has a legend attached to it passed down for many centuries. According to the legend, an ancient manuscript once existed that was filled with scientific wonders beyond our wildest dreams. It had in it, according to the legend, drawings and formulas of a highly advanced science. One of those wonders was detailed plans for a vehicle that could carry you anywhere in time and space.

"The experiments, research, and discoveries described in it are said to have been carried out in the strictest secrecy. The authors did not want their knowledge to be lost. But, mankind was not mature enough for such knowledge. To keep their research and discoveries from being used for evil, they devised a unique plan. They recorded all their knowledge in a manuscript using a language long forgotten.

They reasoned, the legend says, that when man had advanced enough to translate the forgotten language and interpret the scientific language, mankind would be ready to make beneficial use of the knowledge in the manuscript. But the manuscript was lost."

"I'd love it if such a manuscript actually existed! It would be fun to translate and repeat their experiments," Peter replies wistfully.

The Professor looks at Peter thoughtfully for a moment, and then says the last thing Peter expected to hear. "There is always the possibility that the manuscript does exist!"

"Huh!?"

"What if I told you the manuscript does exist, and that its existence was supposed to be a secret? Scientists are overheard talking. A misplaced confidence is betrayed. Stories and rumors start to grow and spread with the speed of gossip. Rumors like that make a great hunting ground for scam artists. All he needs is an ancient manuscript, written in some forgotten language. It would be a great temptation to doctor up the manuscript and try to pass it off as the lost manuscript."

"Are you suggesting this manuscript is for real?" Peter asks.

"There are only a few people who can translate these ancient texts. I am one of them. Every once in a while I get asked to examine some ancient manuscript. Each time it has been a cleverly designed forgery. This manuscript, however, seems exceptional. It's written, as you noted, in a language that went extinct about 500 years B.C. The author, however, had quite an imagination."

The Professor moves to the edge of his chair, a look on his face like he was about to reveal a great secret. He learns forward, and whispers, "In the introduction the author tells us that this book was written for future generations yet unborn."

"Wow! That's some claim!" Peter whispers back in awe, almost forgetting the fear that clung to him. "It's hard to imagine that they could possibly have had all that knowledge over a thousand years ago!"

"Whoa! You're jumping to conclusions," the Professor sits back and laughs. "Haven't I taught you not to jump to conclusions? That is how a fake needs to begin in order to trap a buyer. The real test is going to be whether or not the text matches the illustrations."

"Sorry, Professor. My hope that it was real got the better of me. Do they match?"

"It's not that simple," the Professor answers. "You have to put the text into the context of the time and culture in which it was written. How do you describe a space ship and its propulsion system to someone whose experience is limited to walking and riding a donkey? For example, some suggest that in chapter nine of Revelation, John's locusts that spit fire could be a description of helicopter gunships firing rockets."

"Professor, that doesn't make sense. You're talking about two different things. The Bible is not the same as this manuscript. The Book of Revelation was written for and meant to be read and understood by John's contemporaries. It's not a book of secrets. It's a book of revelations. Whereas you said the writers of this manuscript wanted to hide their secrets. They wanted to write so that their contemporaries could not understand their writings, nor make use of their discoveries. So the real objective was not how to explain a space ship to their contemporaries, but how to hide it from their contemporaries, while explaining it so that a future, matured generation, and only that generation, could understand it."

"That is an excellent rebuttal, Peter! Insofar as this manuscript is concerned, it means that we must look for any attempt to simplify or explain. In other words, is it a straightforward presentation of the material? Or is it doctored?"

"Which is it?"

"Which is it? Yes, that is the question. That applies to the Bible, too! The Bible was written by ordinary men and was meant to be understood by the contemporaries of the writers. Trying to force it to be something different, or reading into it things that are not there, gets us into trouble and leads to much misunderstanding."

"Professor, you're not answering my question."

"Ah, yes. Which is it? You know, Peter, the ability to know which critical questions to ask can make the difference between good science and bad science, between the right interpretation and the wrong interpretation. I'm glad to see you're learning to ask the right critical questions. That will be especially important today."

Argh! thinks Peter, as the fear and knot in his stomach come back full force. *He's not answering my question. And I don't like the way he said, "especially important today." The Professor is holding back on something that's going to involve me, and I don't want to be involved. Maybe I'm the one in danger, and not the Professor!*

"Professor, I asked if the manuscript was real. We've talked about forgeries, communication problems, and asking critical questions. But you still haven't answered my question!"

"Have another cookie!" smiles the Professor.

"This is turning into one frustrating and confusing morning," Peter purposely mumbles loud enough for the Professor to hear him. Another cookie doesn't help. His stomach is uptight. The cookie doesn't set well. The Professor sits, watching him, making him nervous. When the cookie is about finished the Professor speaks again.

"Well, enough about old books and legends. There's lots of exciting new things being discovered every day. NASA's space probes are sending back some amazing pictures. I've downloaded some of the latest ones. Would you like to see them before you leave?"

"Yes!" Peter answers enthusiastically, relieved that this strange and confusing morning with all its unanswered questions, fear and dread, will soon end. "That would be awesome."

"I'll project them onto the big screen and then you'll see how awesome they really are! Turn on the computer and projector and I'll lower the window shades and the big screen."

Instead of using the switch he had always used before to lower the big screen, the Professor pulls a brick out of the side of the fireplace, opens a concealed panel, and flips a switch. The sound of motors lowering the curtains fills the room. Peter turns on the computer and projector and makes sure everything is hooked up and working. As he finishes, the sound of the motors stops.

"That's strange!" Peter exclaims when he looks up. "The curtains are down but the room isn't any darker!" He stares at the curtains. "These aren't window darkening shades! What are they?" he asks. He looks around and discovers that they encircle the whole room! "What kind of material is this? It appears to be both visible and invisible!" He touches the strange looking fabric. It feels cold like metal! When he moves it, it reflects light like golden crystal.

"DON'T TOUCH!"

Peter jerks his hands away, startled by the urgency in the Professor's voice. The sense of dread rises up within him shouting *Danger, beware the Professor.* He hears the click of another switch. A faint humming sound surrounds the room.

"There are a million volts of static electricity surging through that curtain," the Professor explains. "The fabric is a crystalline metal that can be woven like cloth. When a high voltage static charge is applied to it, it becomes a secrecy curtain. It blocks anyone from seeing into this room, or listening to what is said. Meanwhile, we can look out and see clearly what is happening outside."

This sudden, and unexpected, action by the Professor causes Peter's fear to grow alarmingly. Not only is he stunned by the Professor's strange behavior and the strange curtains, the warning that flashed in his mind makes him anxious about his own safety! *What is going on? The Professor is always doing strange things, but this is way off the wall, even for him. What's going on? What's with the Professor? It's like he's switched personalities. Almost like he has become delusional…*

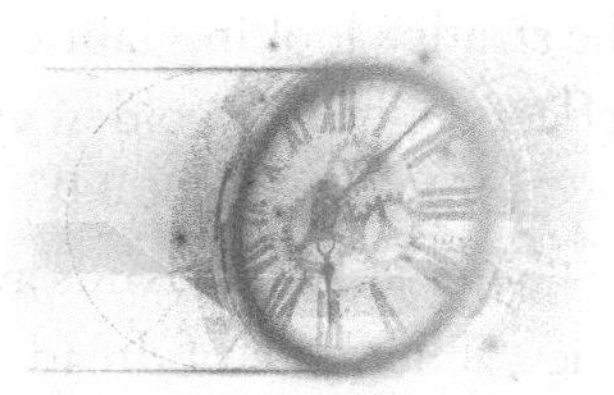

CHAPTER 13

Through the Fireplace

Peter can't wait any longer. He's got to have answers. The phrases in his head and the feelings in his gut are warning about something. Is the Professor safe or is he becoming paranoid, delusionary? Desperate for answers Peter blurts out, "Professor, I've got to ask you some questions. I need some answers."

The Professor, smiling, replies, "Sometimes the simplest explanation seems the most absurd, and yet is the correct one."

This comment doesn't make sense to Peter. But before he can get a question out the Professor speaks again.

"In a moment all your questions will be answered. But first, did you tell anyone you were coming?"

"No, no one."

"Good. Were you followed?"

"No, I was the only one on the road."

"Good! But even so, we cannot take chances. You can never be too cautious where the 'Men in Black' are concerned. That's why I acted as though you had just stopped by for a visit."

Peter is stunned by the Professor's words, Men in Black. *Men in Black are characters from UFO stories, not real life! Could it be the Professor's mind has snapped? Were the flashbacks telling me the Professor has become unstable, delusional? That I am in danger?* Peter tries to dismiss these thoughts. Still, when he adds the secrecy curtain to the fear in his gut… Peter struggles to apply the four phrases to what he is hearing. "The only thing that makes sense is that they were warning me that I'm in danger".

"Up until today, no one has ever used the secrecy shield," the Professor continues. "You see, the plans for making it were lost because the plans were in the lost manuscript. When I turned on the secrecy shield that told the enemy that the lost manuscript has been found. But that's not all. Instructions for building the time machine the enemy wants are also in the lost manuscript. Our enemy knew I had a manuscript, but he didn't know if it was *the* manuscript. Now he does. He also knows that anyone who has the technology to build the secrecy shield will also have the technology to build the time machine. He wants the time machine. That, Peter, is why the Men in Black are coming. They are coming to get the manuscript. I'm in great danger for that reason."

Peter's head is swimming in confusion. *Either the Professor is spinning one tall tale, or he really believes what he is saying. If he really believes it, then he must be becoming delusional. I've got to find out. Maybe he'll respond to reasoning.* With that thought in mind Peter asks,

"I understand that you are in danger. But what does that have to do with me? I'm just a college student."

The Professor is silent for a moment. He then says the last thing Peter wanted to hear. "What you don't know is that you are in danger too."

"Whoa! Professor," Peter interrupts as his fear rises up stronger than before. "Back up! You're not making sense. If I'm in danger, too, you haven't told me why. What's going on that I don't know about?"

"The Men in Black have been interested in you ever since you were with me and TPF. When we escaped from them in the tunnel, we went on their most wanted list. By now they know all there is to know about you. Before that, you were just one of many students, another name in their surveillance records. That event, plus your being here when I turned on the secrecy shield, is part, but only part, of the reason you are in danger."

"Professor, why are these Men in Black interested in either of us, especially me? Why are we in danger? There's got to be more to this story than you're telling me." *Boy*! Peter thinks to himself, *he makes it really tough not to believe he is becoming delusional, living in some fantasy world.*

"Before I answer all your questions, let me first put the manuscript away. It is the legendary lost manuscript!"

A drawer, hidden by a false front, slowly ejects from the wall to the left of the fireplace. It is made of stainless steel and hermetically sealed. The Professor places the manuscript gently into the container, closes and seals the lid. The drawer recedes back into the wall. It leaves no trace of an opening. Peter did not know that such a drawer existed. Seeing it now deepens even more the question he has asked so many times, *Who is this man*?

"Peter," the Professor continues, "the manuscript was not why I asked you to come. I had you look at it because it's part of my own story. Now, for your questions. First, about my phone call. I asked you to come because I was told to do so. You have been chosen to go with me on a voyage in time. I have not been told why you were chosen, or where we are going. I only know that the order has been given and our task is to obey. We are about to take an impossible journey and see unimaginable things!"

The Professor may have meant for this message to excite Peter. It does! But not the way the Professor intended! As the words sink in, the sense of foreboding he hasn't been able to shake shouts *You are in danger. Get out of here!* Peter's survival instincts kick in! He reacts in alarm! *It's me, and not the Professor, who is in danger! So that's what the four phrases were all about.* The knot in his stomach tightens. In the grip of this momentary fear, any attempt at reasoning deserts him.

Peter's mind races to plan his escape. And yet, as he looks at the Professor, Peter's bewilderment deepens. The Professor's eyes are not those of a wild man. His actions and words suggest a calm spirit, not the frenzy one would expect from one suddenly gone mad. What he sees flies in the face of his feeling of danger, flies in the face of the words the Professor just spoke.

The Professor's expression is like a little boy's with a great surprise he's been wanting to share, and now he finally can. But Peter, gripped by fear, sees it as the maniacal expression of a mad scientist. No longer able to hide his fear, it shows on his face. His thoughts race to plan his escape and get help for the Professor.

The Professor, seeing the fear, suddenly asks, "Has something happened since yesterday that you haven't told me about?"

"Yes," Peter answers. "It started with your phone call. All of a sudden I felt an overwhelming fear, a sense of foreboding, almost terror. My stomach went into a knot and I was compelled to grab my coat and car keys and rush out here."

"I'm sorry Peter. I never meant to alarm you. I only wanted to arouse your curiosity and excitement, nothing more. There was no reason for fear. As you remember Paul said that 'God has not given us the spirit of fear; but of power, and of love and of a sound mind' (2 Timothy 1:7). For some reason Satan must have taken advantage of you. When your guard was down, he must have sent a spirit of fear on you. Fear distorts the facts. It causes us to worry and fret. It renders us powerless because we are consumed by the problems. God intends us to be victors in life, not victims (Revelation 5:10). Take your authority and bind the fear dumb and powerless."

This Peter does, saying, "You spirit of fear that is tormenting me I bind you dumb and powerless in the Name of Jesus." As quickly as the fear had come upon him it leaves. It was gone but it left behind all the doubts and questions still racing through Peter's mind. Peter pushes ahead, wanting answers.

"There is more," Peter continues. "The trip out here was alarming." He briefly describes his unsettling drive, and the four flashbacks. He does not mention the four phrases. The Professor's response doesn't help. He agrees with Peter that they were from the Holy Spirit.

"It might be Satan doesn't want you to interfere with his plans. As you remember, TPF said our enemy wants a time machine. Satan wants our enemy to get it. Satan wants to use our enemy for evil. Our enemy doesn't know he is Satan's slave because he doesn't believe Romans 6:16.

"Satan never had a reason to stop you before. But that has changed. It has to do with the manuscript. Our enemy has been watching all of us who are experts in the language in which the lost manuscript was written. Fake manuscripts turn up periodically. But lately a rumor has spread that the genuine lost manuscript may have been found. Word was passed around to each of us experts warning us that we were being watched. Finally, the lost manuscript was brought to me because I am the most proficient in this particular forgotten language."

"Professor, I can't translate the manuscript, to say nothing of doing any of the science. I'm no threat to anybody."

"You weren't. But the enemy thinks you are! Our enemy has designed highly sophisticated surveillance technology. That is how he knew about the tesseract machine, and how he knew this manuscript had come to me. No one has ever been able to devise a shield that the enemy's surveillance technology could not penetrate. That is, with one exception, the secrecy shield. It was developed hundreds of years ago. The plans for it are in the manuscript.

"As you already know from your visit with TPF, men of great learning and wisdom continue to study and learn the secrets of the universe. You also saw that powerful men, wanting to rule the world, unscrupulous men of wealth, governments bent on ruling through controlling ultimate power, are searching for these men of great learning. They want their secrets. They want more power. They want bigger and better weapons.

"The Men in Black are employed by our enemy. I don't know why he has them dress in black. You've already escaped from two of them. TPF calls them the Watchers. They are the 'they' who are watching us. They will be here any moment."

"But why?" Peter asks, hoping to make sense of what the Professor is saying. "I'm just a college student. You're just a physics professor. Why would anybody be interested in us? These Men in Black you're talking about, surely they've got better things to do than spy on a physics teacher and his student? Aren't you being a little paranoid if you think they're interested in us?"

"That might be true except for two facts."

"What facts?" Peter is troubled by the Professor's words. *What if the Professor says he really does have a secret laboratory? Where is it? Certainly not here. What if there really is a time machine? He's always denied it. In my heart of hearts, I wish both were true. Part of me wants all this to be true, and part of me is afraid he's become delusional.*

Peter decides there is only one course of action he can take. He'll listen carefully to what the Professor says. If he says he has a secret lab, he'll ask him to show him the lab. If he can't, that will prove he's become delusional! Then Peter will escape and go for help!

"Peter, there are many secrets about me and this house you do not know. Now it is time for you to know the whole truth. We'll begin with this house. As you know, beneath this house is a cavern. You've seen it, and helped me harvest mushrooms. What you don't know is that behind that cavern, on a lower level, there is another larger cavern. In that cavern, I really do have a secret laboratory! That is fact number one."

Even though he was hoping it was true Peter is stunned to hear it. This is what he wanted the Professor to say, and at the same time he didn't believe the Professor would actually say it. Now, when he says it, it shocks Peter because it seems so unbelievable.

"The Men in Black keep constant surveillance over the earth looking for signs of unusual energy emissions, anything that would suggest research being done on a time machine, as well as research being done on a tesseract. They have detected energy emissions of a power unknown to them coming from my laboratory. I am not speaking about my experiments with mushrooms. I'm talking about the energy emissions that come from a time machine! That is fact number two."

The Professor speaks softly. "Because you are here, they have reason to believe I've chosen you to go with me on a trip in the time machine. Their master, our enemy, does not want the trip to happen because he thinks we might do something he will regret. He is determined to stop us at all costs. He wants to divert the time machine to his own evil purposes. If he knew the real purpose of our trip, he would be even more determined to stop it."

Peter's mouth drops wide open, stunned at hearing what he didn't want to hear, and yet hoped he would hear. Shivers run up and down Peter's spine. The cloak and dagger tone things have taken is more than alarming. *It's time to know the truth, once and for all. If the Professor needs help, now is the time to break away and get it. I'll ask to see the laboratory.* He starts to ask: "Professor . . ."

The Professor smiles and says, "Come. It is time to go."

He reaches inside the fire place on the right hand side and removes a brick that is hidden from view. He pushes a switch and replaces the brick. The back of the fireplace slowly swings open to reveal a long passageway. The passageway slopes down for about a hundred feet and then levels off. A soft, dim glow lights the passageway. It appears to be made exactly like the tunnel that led to TPF's secret laboratory, except this one is illuminated.

Peter, wide-eyed in amazement and with a great sense of relief, exclaims, "There really is a secret laboratory!"

"Yes, there really is," the Professor laughs. "I've longed for the day I could share this with you, Peter. I was waiting until I was sure you were ready. But last night, that was taken out of my hands."

The full meaning of the four flashbacks is suddenly clear. They weren't about the four phrases. They were about the Professor! From the first day of classes, Peter had sensed that there was something different about the Professor. There was a hidden power in him. He had depths of knowledge, and secrets, he did not share. He dropped little hints from time to time that only Peter picked up on. Hints that said he was far more than just a teacher. Now the pieces of the puzzle were fitting together.

The traitor/enemy is also the Professor's enemy. The future of the world is at stake. The Nine Unknown Men were real, or maybe even are real. The Professor has their manuscript. Maybe the Professor is one of them! No, that's too absurd. He'd be almost 2,000 years old! There is a time machine, and the Professor built it! Peter looks at the Professor with wonder and admiration as he finally understands. Well, almost understands.

Those last words of the Professor, 'last night that was taken out of my hands,' have set Peter a new mystery! What happened last night? Peter quickly follows the Professor into the passageway. They walk along the long tunnel as it delves deep into the hill behind the Professor's home. Peter senses an atmosphere of reverence as though he was entering a great cathedral where anxiety and fear cannot exist. The Professor smiles and speaks in a hushed voice.

"In all your physics courses, I have challenged you to think that the impossible is just something we haven't learned how to do. It was God's plan in the beginning that whatever we can imagine, we can do. In Genesis 1:28, God commands the man to develop and utilize all the earth's vast resources. What we see today in scientific and technological achievements is only a drop in the bucket of possibilities. In Genesis 11:6, God states that nothing man has imagined he can do will be impossible for him.

"Sin changed everything. First, man lost the glory in which he had been created and clothed, as well as his home and kingship. Second, he became the slave of evil, as Paul writes in Romans 6:19. Satan may have planned to use man's godlike abilities and intelligence in his war on God. Man's situation had become very dangerous. Not to God, but for man himself. That is why God, to protect man from his own self destruction, sent confusion.

"The Bible is a love story. It is the story of his love for man and his plan to restore man to the glory he lost in the Fall. God loves us so much, Ephesians tells us, that long before he laid the foundations of the Earth, God had a secret plan to redeem us and restore us. When a man puts his faith in Jesus Christ, he is immediately adopted into God's family as a son, and the restoration of his original godlikeness begins."

The tunnel ends at a blank wall, no markings or anything to suggest a door. The Professor places his hand against the wall. There is a slight glow where his hand touches. A small door becomes visible and opens to reveal a retina scanner. A voice speaks, "Hand print accepted. What is your name?"

"I am the Professor. May we please enter?"

A pause.

"Retina scan accepted. Voice recognized."

The little door closes and slowly a massive door takes shape in the stone and then opens. Peter steps into the Professor's lab and instantly gasps in wonder! Wonder, amazement, excitement, awe! He has stepped into a futuristic physics lab! Scientific equipment, the likes of which he has never seen, line the walls. But these Peter barely notice.

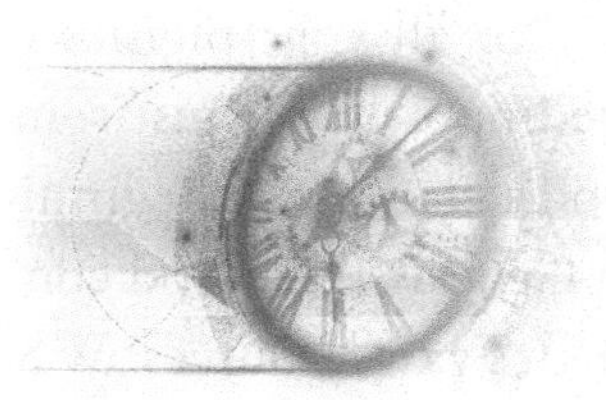

CHAPTER 14

Back to the Beginning

In the center of the room is a brilliant blue orb, about seventeen feet in diameter. It pulsates with energy. It appears to fade in and out. One moment it is fully here, the next it almost disappears. One moment it is a brilliant transparent blue, a wheel spinning within a wheel. The next it sparkles like a blue crystal diamond with circles of light. The blue seems to change with each pulsation of the orb.

"What is it?" Peter whispers in amazement.

"You might call it a time machine, or a space machine or a trans-dimensional machine." The Professor's face glows with joy. "It is of this world, but it isn't. It exists here and everywhere. It is present in the here and now and the then and there."

"A time machine! Is time travel really possible?

"Yes, and no!"

"What do you mean, 'yes and no'?"

"Keep in mind that Daniel wrote that in the last days knowledge shall increase. Today, knowledge is increasing exponentially. The Biblical prophets, the alchemists, the Nine Unknown Men were the first to experience this increase in knowledge. They dreamed of doing the impossible. From dreamers like them have come great scientific achievements. This isn't one of them!"

"Now you've got me really confused," Peter complains.

"Look at Glenn Clark. He was a dreamer of impossible dreams. He believed God had given the prophets keys to releasing God's power into our world. He believed when Jesus taught about the Kingdom of God, He was instructing people on how to step up into God's dimension of life."

"Professor, I know how much you like Glenn Clark, but what does that have to do with time travel?"

"Everything!"

"Everything? I don't understand."

"It was what Glenn taught. Glenn taught us to seek guidance and answers to our questions in the Bible. Glenn understood that when you let the Bible speak for itself, it reveals many secrets men have overlooked. One of those secrets has to do with what the Bible says about time. Paul writes that in the fullness of time, God sent Jesus (Galatians 4:4), and that in the fullness of time He will bring all things together in Christ (Ephesians 1:10). Daniel prophesies about the time of the end and the last days (Daniel 8:19; 12:9). Isaiah and Micah speak of what is to happen in the last days. The Bible understands that time is God's design. God controls it."

"Professor, what does that have to do with time travel?"

"It has to do with what is possible. Some want to go back and change the past. But that cannot be. What is done is done. Only the future is in flux. But that future can only be changed by the people living in it. One cannot travel into the past or into the future to change it. One can only observe as an unseen observer."

"Then that means a time machine can only be an observation booth?"

"That's right," the Professor agrees. "We can watch what is happening but we can't get out and take part in it or change it. God does not allow it. Only God, who created time, and for whom all time is NOW, can participate in all the dimensions of time and timelessness because He dwells both outside of time and inside of time. In Him 'is no variableness neither shadow of turning' (James 1:17). He is the great I Am. He is unchanging.

"A time machine enters God's dimension where all is now, and then moves out of His dimension into time at the point we want to observe. The Orb appears to fade and then come back because it exists in both dimensions at the same time. There are some," the Professor continues, "who reject any thought of God. They deny any possibility of a Creator. For that reason, they do not understand the true nature of time. They want to manipulate time and change events. If they cannot manipulate time they want to see into the future so that they can manipulate the present to their future advantage. They are propelled by greed and the lust for power."

The Professor's voice fades into the silence. A soft musical humming emanates from the Blue Orb. Suddenly the quietness is broken by an alarm. Red warning lights flash. A voice warns, "Danger! Danger! The perimeter has been breached. Transformation to complete in 20 seconds! 20. 19. 18. 17 . . ."

"Quickly! We must be gone before they come."

The Professor turns and dashes towards the Orb. An opening appears and he steps inside. Peter follows on his heels. The opening closes as though it never existed while the Orb becomes almost transparent. The grating noise of massive rocks moving and rearranging themselves echoes in their ears. The countdown continues: 16. 15. 14. 13. 12. 11. 10 . . .

Inside the Orb there is a simple and elegant instrument console. It is formed of the most beautiful gems Peter has ever seen. The dials and instrument lights emit an inner glow as though they are alive. Opposite the instrument panel are cushioned seats, upholstered in a rich blue fabric unknown to Peter. The Professor, already seated in the pilot's position, quickly adjusts the jeweled levers and dials. Peter sits down beside him. The Professor pushes a ruby red lever. The musical humming is suddenly drowned out by a gentle *woosh* sound as of a cylindrical object being sucked through a tube. The warning flashing lights of the laboratory vanish. The counting and sounds of massive rock scraping on rock cease.

Suddenly the Orb is immersed in a wild dance of brilliant colors in constantly changing patterns. It looks like everything around it is rushing past while the Blue Orb sits still. Just as suddenly it all stops. Everywhere Peter looks through the crystal clear walls of the Orb there are millions of glistening stars and planets. Coming from the stars and planets themselves are the most beautiful sounds and melodies he has ever heard, blending into a vast symphony. For several moments Peter drinks in the beauty and the music.

The Professor speaks in a hushed voice, "It is the music of the spheres (Job 38:7)."

The beauty, sweetness and holiness of the melody are overwhelming. Neither speaks.

"Where are we?" Peter asks reverently.

"The Orb has transported us into another dimension. We are no longer present in the lab. And we are not present anywhere else. You might say we are in between. For us, it is a resting place for asking questions."

"Tell me, what just happened?"

"The warning you heard was the house warning us that our enemies were closing in. When the perimeter was breached the house began to transform to protect us. The secrecy curtain raised and made itself undetectable. The fireplace entrance to the lab sealed itself and was replaced by a simple cellar door off the kitchen leading to the underground mushroom garden. The laboratory itself has been hidden. When they search they will find mushrooms in various stages of experimentation, and a laboratory equipped with an electron microscope and a radiation gun. They will see my instruments for cutting and splicing the mushroom genes for altering the genetic code of the mushrooms. They will find that the radiation gun has developed a defect and emits erratic radiation signals. That is all they will find."

"Won't they try digging it up?"

"No. Men like that think only of big. They think of Europe's 5.3-mile-long underground particle accelerator and all the equipment it takes to make it work. They cannot envision something that is small on the outside being bigger on the inside. There are no records, no evidence that anything exists as big as they think the facility must be."

"How did you build the Orb? It must take an immense amount of power to work."

"I didn't build the Orb. It is not of our world, even though it exists in our world."

Peter didn't expect this answer. The Professor looks out reverently at the wondrous beauty of stars and galaxies and planets surrounding the Orb. The music coming from the stars proclaims the glory of God.

"I was at prayer in my lab." The Professor's voice is a reverent whisper. "With my hand in Jesus' hand, I had approached the Throne to ask for knowledge on a project that had me stumped. I heard an unusual sound. When I looked up, this Orb was resting where you saw it. Out of it stepped a man in gleaming white.

"He said 'Come, I will show you how it works.' He showed me the controls and showed me how to set them. Then he said, 'Call your student. It is time. But hurry. Danger awaits.' With that he disappeared."

"Wow!" Peter marvels. If he hadn't seen the Orb and if he wasn't in it, he would have found the Professor's story unbelievable. He had passed it off when the Professor said he was chosen. But the Professor really meant it! The full force of the idea of being chosen by God for a special mission makes Peter feel totally inadequate.

For a moment an irreverent thought crosses his mind. "Does God know what He is doing?" Peter asks. "Well, if He can use me, I'm willing. I hope that's okay."

The Professor turns towards Peter and smiles. "He knows your heart and you have given Him all He asked for. Your 'Yes.' Continue to acknowledge Him in all your ways, and He will continue to direct your paths. Delight in Him and He will give you the desires of your heart." (Proverbs 3:6; Psalms 37:4)

Peter is quiet for a few moments, soaking in the wonder of what he is experiencing. Suddenly he hears a gentle bump on the side of the Orb, like someone knocking. A strange looking object acts like it is trying to get inside the Orb. Suddenly, with a *thunk*, it plunges into the Orb. It looks like a small version of the wheel within a wheel Ezekiel described (Ezekiel 1:16).

The Professor reaches out, picks it up reverently and places it gently on the seat beside him. "So this is where you ended up!" he exclaims, obvious joy in his voice. "Thank you, Father. I'll tell you about it sometime, Peter. But for now let's enjoy the beauty and music." Then he is silent.

The beauty and music around them fills the Orb with an indescribable peace and joy. Peter thinks about what the Professor has been saying. It is clear that if scientists leave God out of their consideration, they will be forever frustrated in their research. Only when they seek God first will they come face to face with the power that creates: the Word from the mouth of God.

"Professor, there's something I've always wished I could do. I've always wished I could have been there and watched God create the universe, and create man. Do you think there is any possibility that we could go back to before the beginning of time and watch God create?"

"That, Peter, is the task for which you were chosen! I do not know why. My visitor in white said that you had been chosen to join me on a trip back to before time began. There is evidently something God wants us to see, or perhaps do. I suspect there will come a time when you are to report what you see and hear. Until then, keep what you see and hear in your heart."

The ruby lever begins to flash. The Professor reaches out and pushes it. Suddenly, the whooshing sound surrounds them again, and then all is quiet. Everything becomes a total, utter black nothingness. Never had Peter seen, or not seen, such dark nothingness. Even the Orb is totally dark. In some other place and time, he might have been afraid. But here it is impossible to be afraid. This is no ordinary nothingness. It is a nothingness uncorrupted by sin.

All around the nothingness is filled with the awesomeness of Love. It is a nothingness filled with Joy and anticipation. It has in it all the sweetness of a bright sunshiny day filled with the delicate fresh fragrance of flowers in air just washed by rain. That sweetness and freshness and fragrance are in the nothingness. A nothingness filled with jumping-for-joy Joy! A nothingness electric with excitement, with expectancy! A nothingness so full of Love that it caresses and bathes and electrifies and exhilarates! A nothingness Alive with Life!

How can nothingness be alive with life? As Peter wonders, it comes to him that in the Beginning, when all was New, that is how the nothingness was. It was a nothingness whose name was Love. From that

Love would come all that is. This is how it is when it all begins; in the time when as yet there is no time.

As Peter watches, suddenly, in the midst of the darkness of nothingness, there is Light! It is the most beautiful, breathtaking Light of shimmering, iridescent colors. It has the brightness of the green translucent jasper and the fiery deep-red sardis. Surrounding it is a halo, like a rainbow of emerald colors. All the beauty one knows, multiplied by a thousand times in intensity, would look dim and colorless by comparison. From the Light come flashes of lightning and rumblings and peals of thunder. The lightning is a Glory of the most beautiful, brilliant fireworks, and the rumblings and thunder are music indescribably beautiful.

In the Light he sees, as it were, two Men and a Flame of Fire. They are in the Light, and They are the Light. The shapes of Light dance and laugh and sing with the utmost joy. The Darkness shimmers around Them as They dance, and Their Laughter and Joy and Song are as sparks of Light bursting in Glory in the Darkness, like millions of diamonds catching and reflecting the rainbow of colors of light.

Suddenly, all becomes silent. The deep silence of waiting in great expectation. Then, one of the Man shapes of Light stands apart. He begins to sing. The song is beautiful, intense, full of joy and life and love, and power. Each note of the song, each high, each low, each soft and each loud, has a purpose. The song ends.

"LIGHT BE!" sounds forth from the Man shape, and Light IS. The song has set the limits of the light. Each note has shaped some part of it. Light becomes what the song had sung. And there is joy and laughter and shouting and dancing as Father God and the Son and the Flame look upon their handiwork, and proclaim, "IT IS GOOD!" The light that has come into being has a music of its own, as though the light is alive.

The Son begins to sing again. He sings of hills and rivers and cities of indescribable beauty. He sings of walls of green jasper, cities of pure gold, clear and transparent like crystal, gates made of a single pearl. As the song draws to an end the Son shouts out, "HEAVEN BE!" and

Heaven is. And the Father and the Son and the Flame make their home on the beautiful planet, singing and dancing and laughing for joy.

And then the Son begins to sing again. And as He sings a heavenly host begins to form, and the heavenly host takes up the song and sings with the Son. For with a burst of joy from the Son, the heavenly host comes into being - angels and archangels and cherubim and seraphim.

Still the song goes on. With each new creation, comes more joy and more dancing and more laughter. Each part of the creation has its own order and its own life within itself. The Son sings: "UNIVERSE BE! STARS BE! WORLDS BE! SUNS BE! MOONS BE!" When each song has determined all things, the Light that creates speaks the Word, and it is so.

Peter becomes so absorbed in what is happening, that as each thing is created he finds himself shouting "YES!" He is aware, too, that the Orb has been protecting him from being utterly destroyed by indescribable power coming from the Father and Son and Flame. Every hair on his body is standing straight up and his muscles tense, as though he had grabbed hold of a million-volt high voltage wire. Then comes a moment when all that had been created watches. The Son sings a very Special Song. The morning stars sing together and all the sons of God shout for joy as it begins to take shape and form. Peter knows what it is going to be and a great thrill races through him as he watches the creation of a great jewel in the midst of the heavens. The Earth.

The Father calls out, "Lucifer!"

"Here I am, Sir," speaks a voice beautiful and melodious beyond anything Peter could imagine.

"Lucifer, I have made you perfect in every way and endowed you with great wisdom. To you I give the highest position and honor in my presence." At those words great singing and joy and worship burst forth across all of heaven.

"Lucifer," the Father continues, "I entrust to your care this planet to govern wisely. I have endowed you with every grace so that you can lead all creation in singing and worship. Of all my creation, none is wiser than you, none more gifted, none more privileged." With those words, the most beautiful man shaped Being Peter has ever seen leaves the Father's presence and takes its abode on the planet earth.

"Professor," Peter whispers. "What we've seen, what we've experienced, I can't put into words. It is so breathtaking. I can hardly take it all in. But something isn't right. I know that that's the earth, but it doesn't look like our earth. The polar ice caps are missing. The geography is all different. It has a brilliance I've not seen on our earth."

"Watch!" the Professor whispers.

As they watch, Peter has the impression that a long period of time is passing. Suddenly, he is aware of great discord and the presence of evil. A force opposed to the Joy and Laughter and Love, to God Himself, begins to grow on the earth and suddenly bursts into the very heavens. Just as suddenly, a great upheaval of lightning and thunder flash and crash through the heavens. When it ends, a burning and smoke blacker than the blackness of space envelopes the earth, covers the earth, plunges the earth into a blackness deep and dark and ugly. Where there was once a beautiful jewel there is now only a swirling black and evil darkness.

Gone, too, is the joy and wonder. The darkness that was once so vibrant with life is now plunged into a darkness where evil hides. The very atmosphere reeks of judgment on evil. All is silent. Once again, Peter has the sense of time passing. Slowly, Peter becomes aware of singing once again. Once again stars sing the glory of God. Once again Love and Joy and Laughter and Wonder fill the darkness and the darkness does not overcome it. As Peter watches, once again in the darkness appears the brilliant shimmering lights of the Father and Son and Flame. The Father Light looks upon the earth that now is only chaos and darkness, without form and an empty waste. And the Father says, "Let us make it more beautiful and more glorious than it was before. Go," the Father Light commands the Flame.

The Flame goes and hovers over the darkness of the face of the earth, burning it away. Where the darkness had been there emerges a crumpled chaotic mass that once was the earth. The Father lovingly begins to recreate the earth. He speaks "LIGHT BE" and Light once again surrounds the earth. And God says, "THAT'S GOOD!" The morning stars sing together and all the sons of God shout for joy.

As Peter continues to watch, it is as though a voice speaks, telling him that what he is about to see is far greater than all he had seen before. The Father Light lovingly refashions the earth. After each thing He does, God pauses and says, "THAT'S GOOD!" And a new burst of song comes from the morning stars and all the sons of God.

God divides the waters and dry land appears. He sets the sun to rule the day, and the moon to rule the night. He surrounds the earth with what appears to be a crystal clear shield to protect it from harmful rays from the sun. He commands the earth to bring forth vegetation and trees to bear fruit. He makes what appear to be blobs of various undefined sizes and shapes that must be animals. When all is done God says, "THAT'S VERY GOOD!"

Suddenly a great hush comes over all the creation. Peter discovers he can actually hear the words being spoken. The silence is broken as Father God speaks, "THERE IS ONE MORE SONG TO BE SUNG. HE WHO I HAD LOVED SO MUCH HAS BROUGHT A GREAT EVIL TO MY CREATION. BUT IT IS MY WILL TO TURN HIS EVIL INTO A GREATER GOOD. THIS SHALL BE THE GREATEST SONG OF ALL . . .

"SON, LET US MAKE MAN IN OUR IMAGE, AFTER OUR LIKENESS. AND LET HIM HAVE DOMINION OVER ALL THAT HAS BEEN MADE. LET HIM BE WHAT WE ARE, CREATE WITH US, RULE WITH US, BE GODS WITH US."

The Light that is the Son begins to sing, and the song is the most beautiful song, the most joyous song, the most love filled song of all the songs of creation. The Light that is the Father appears to kneel on the Earth. With his hands, he shapes an image of himself. It strikes Peter that this is the first time he has actually seen a man shape. For the Father and Son and Holy Spirit are all hidden in Light. But there, on the ground, is the most perfect and beautiful sculpture of a man he has ever seen.

"I am ready," Father God speaks to the son.

"MAN BE!" shouts the son.

The Light that is the Father bends over the head of the man shape, and breathes into it the breath of life. As Peter watches, the statue of the man begins to glow, and suddenly bursts into the same brilliant Light that is the Father and the Son. The Man Light rises and joins with the Father Light and the Son Light and the Holy Spirit Flame and they dance for joy.

The Father Light speaks and says, "Man has become a living soul."

So great and joyous and love filled is that moment that the joy and laughter and music of the heavens cannot be contained. God has created a Being like unto Himself. Man has come into being, born of Love and Joy and Laughter and Power and Wonder. In him is the Mind of God, the Heart of God, and the Wisdom of God. For an instant, it appears as if the Father Light and the Son Light and the Flame all stand back and look at the Man Light. And Peter hears God speak, "IT IS VERY GOOD!" And then silence.

The ruby light blinks, and the Professor pushes the lever.

They are back in the resting place. Neither Peter or the Professor speak. Both are overcome by the emotion and wonder of what they have just witnessed. They sit in silence, listening again to the music of the spheres.

The ruby red lever blinks. The Professor reaches out and touches it. With a gentle bump, the Blue Orb lands back in the Professor's lab. Still too overcome to speak they step out in silence. The Orb disappears. They make their way back to the mushroom cellar, to the door of the kitchen, and to the Professor's living room. Peter sits down, and is instantly sound asleep.

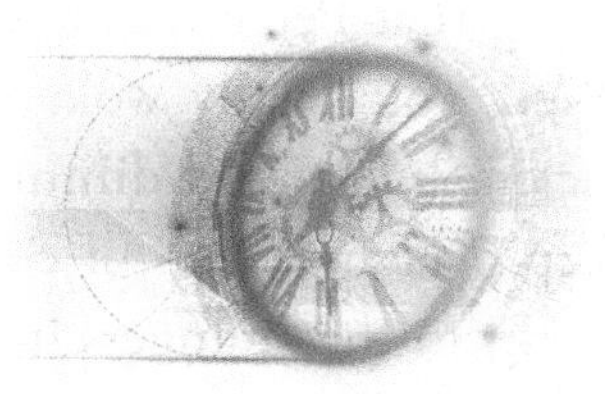

CHAPTER 15

A Whale of a Weird Dream

A gentle hum brings Peter's mind back to the present and a most startling awakening. "Where -- where am I!?" he exclaims, surprised and confused. "I… I thought I was in the Blue Orb. But instead I'm sitting in a stuffed chair in front of the fireplace in the Professor's living room!" He looks around and sees a tray of cookies, five coffee cups and a pot of coffee freshly brewed. Just then, he hears voices. It is the Professor, outside the picture window, talking to three men dressed in black suits and wearing dark sun glasses.

"I wish I could help you gentlemen. As you saw, all there is here is my garden and my mushroom cave. Some are pretty delicious mushrooms, too, if I do say so myself. Like I told you, I'm trying to improve their flavor and nutritional value by altering their genes."

A cell phone rings. One of the Men in Black answers. "Hello! You say you've double checked the origin of the emissions you detected about a half hour ago? Are you sure you got the coordinates right? Are you sure it was the right kind of emissions? Are you sure it came from here? The Professor claims he knows nothing about it. We've searched and searched and all we can find is a mushroom cellar and a leaky radiation gun. We've been unable to detect anything. We pick up no emission residue here at all. If something happened only a half hour ago we should have been able to find a residual energy trace. If he's causing it, we don't know how. Yes, sir, we'll continue our search."

The Professor and the three men enter the room. The Professor, seeing that Peter is awake, smiles and with a twinkle in his eye says, "Well, you finally woke up! I'm afraid my rambling on about those ancient books and dimming the lights to look at pictures put you to sleep! Maybe a cup of coffee will help you perk up. Gentlemen," he speaks to the strangers in black, "won't you join us for a cup of coffee and a fresh cookie? My housekeeper makes the best chocolate chip cookies you'll ever sink your teeth into."

"No!" The strangers appear agitated. "We've got work to do. There's something strange going on here. My superiors believe you're hiding something. If you are, what you're doing is against the law and we're going to stop you and confiscate your equipment."

Just then Peter notices, and hears, Mrs. McD's old '59 Ford coming careening and banging into the driveway. She slams to a stop, jumps out of the car, grabs an old shot gun out of the back and comes running to the house. Standing in the doorway with all the fire of a mother lion she bellows, "Get out of here!" Waving the shot gun menacingly at the strangers she adds, "Land O' Goshen, ain't anybody safe in their own home anymore? No good ever come from men dressed up like you messin' around. Now get out of here fast before I fill you full of buck shot!"

The Professor laughs. "It's okay Mrs. McD. I'm afraid these gentlemen are all mixed up and don't have the slightest idea what they are doing. They seemed to think that in the midst of all my mushrooms they would find a space ship to a distant galaxy. I told the gentlemen they could search the house, tap on the walls for secret doors and trap doors. But now that you're here with your shotgun I should advise them to go through you before they touch anything!"

The Men in Black are obviously angry. From what they say, Peter gathers they have seen nothing to contain equipment big enough to generate the emissions they've been monitoring. Yet they are convinced, beyond the shadow of a doubt, the emissions came from this house.

The Professor offers a suggestion. "Perhaps, gentlemen, your instruments are picking up an atmospheric anomaly. Given the correct angles and atmospheric conditions, signals that originate in one place have been known to bounce back and appear to originate from another place." This suggestion does not please the Men in Black. They stalk out angrily.

The Professor watches them leave, and remarks, "I've no idea what they thought they were looking for. But come. You've had quite a long nap. Mrs. McD, let's all have a cup of coffee and another of your cookies. I know it's close to lunch time, but I don't think it will dull our appetites too much. Besides, this sleepyhead needs to wake up before he heads back to town. If I remember right," he turns and speaks to Peter, "you work this afternoon, don't you?"

To say Peter's head is swirling is an understatement. *Could I have fallen asleep and dreamed it all? The Men in Black seemed real enough. But, the Blue Orb? The trip to see God create? Was that real or just a dream? I woke up in an easy chair instead of stepping out of the Blue Orb. Maybe it was just a dream; a wild quirky dream that seemed real, like dreams can do sometimes.*

Peter decides not to say anything to the Professor. Some other time, maybe. He thanks him for the coffee and cookies and leaves. By the time Peter arrives back at his room he's convinced he'd just had one wild dream. He chuckles about the absurdity of it. The weird drive to the Professor's. Time travel! Other dimensions! The manuscript the Nine Unknown Men wrote! Absurd!

As is his habit, Peter checks his phone messages. George wants to borrow his tennis racket. Jim got the book he wanted. Ed needs help with his physics assignment. Then, the final message: "*Urgent!* Come quickly. Don't tell anyone. Hurry!" *Click!*

BOOK 2

Escape To Danger

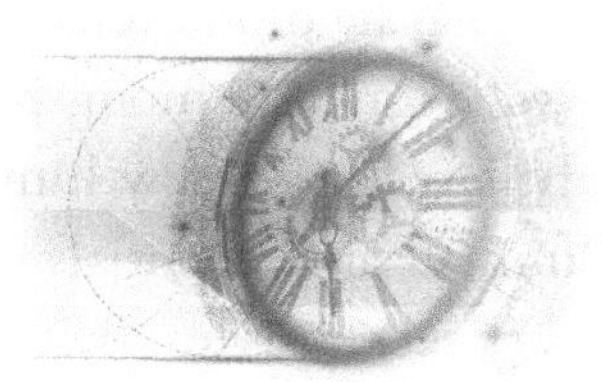

CHAPTER 16

The Man in The Chair

In a distant city, a man sits in his chair, alone in his office, in front of his computer. He is lost in deep contemplation. On the screen is the message he has waited long months and years to see. *An energy emission occurred at 2:00 a.m. this morning, and again at 10:00 a.m. We analyzed the emission footprint and it's the one we've been looking for. Our men are checking out the location now. Our initial survey of the area has not revealed the presence of a lab large enough to support such research. But all our data points to the home of a physics professor. We are certain he is now in possession of your ancient manuscript and has begun to translate it.*

The man in the chair smiles. Now, at long last, all the pieces of his great plan are falling into place. It is just a matter of time. Yes, time and a time machine! He chuckles at his little play on words. It is time; time for breakfast, time for his morning walk, time to put the finishing touches on his plans, time to sweep down on the builder of the time machine. At his command, the computer retracts into the desk top. He pushes back his chair, rises, and prepares to leave his office.

Who is this man? By his design, no one knows. It amuses him to listen to his employees speculate. He neither denies nor encourages their ideas and questions. The more the rumors and their imaginations grow, the greater the cloud of mystery that surrounds him. This pleases him. Once, in a talkative mood, he had told his most trusted employees that he had spent some time among the high priests in their monasteries high in the Himalayas.

What he didn't tell them was that the priests had taught him how to walk unseen among people. He had learned how to cause people to believe they knew him when they didn't, and to believe they had examined his credentials when they hadn't, and then permit him access to very secret places. By so doing, he had learned many secrets that had proven to be very useful to him. Lastly, he had learned how to erase men's memories so that not even hypnosis could bring the memories back.

He uses this power of forgetfulness when he mingles with the public. Those with whom he has just done business cannot describe him. "He appeared to be of average height and weight, neither young nor old," they would answer with a puzzled look on their faces. How was he dressed? "Well, like everyone else." His facial features? They couldn't recall or remember, not even the color of his hair. A few moments after meeting him, or talking with him, or doing business with him, most seemed to forget all about him.

It cannot be said that in the public eye mystery surrounds him because no one seems to be aware of him. Only to an inner circle of trusted men has he ever revealed more of himself. And that was only when he found it necessary. They knew him as Mr. Az. Az was not his birth name. It was a name he had chosen for himself. No one knew why. Some speculated that it was the English version of the Greek "Alpha and Omega," the first and the last. Others thought it may have been the abbreviation of the name of Azazel. According to the book of Enoch, Azazel was the leader of the Nephilim who educated humankind and revealed heavenly secrets.

His facial features were those of a scholar. His steel grey eyes reflected depths of wisdom. But it was a cold, calculating, and malevolent wisdom. If someone crossed him or displeased him, those same eyes would reveal a depth of malice and hatred just before their memories of him were erased. But they were not the eyes of a despot who ruled by violence.

"Despots, dictators, kings, emperors: all fools," he said. "They think they are powerful because they have the power of life and death. But it is only make believe power that feeds their egos. They want to be worshipped, admired, and feared. But those that fear them also seek to destroy them, so they themselves live in fear. The fearful are not powerful. Fear is a task master that will betray you, whereas an enemy who has no memory of you, is an enemy no longer. Probe his mind to gain any useful information, and then wipe his memories."

Mr. Az, believing himself to be both intellectually superior and benevolent, has developed his own plan to make himself the absolute ruler/dictator of the world. He will be the absolute ruler of the world without the administrative headaches dictators have faced. He assures himself that he will be the most benevolent dictator the world has ever known. Of course, there will be some freedoms men will have to give up. But in exchange they will live in a world without wars.

Mr. Az has developed a secret plan to achieve his goal. His most trusted men know only parts of his plan, the parts they need to know. They serve him gladly, out of loyalty, not fear. He treats them well. If they desire to leave his employ, or are no longer needed, he erases their memories of their employment. Violence was not his way. He has rejected violence and war as a means of conquest because it is too costly in both goods and lives. Violence and cruelty are not efficient ways to deal with opposition or punish failure. It makes enemies. A conquered people might rebel at any moment, causing additional problems and cost. Chemicals and mind control drugs reduce people's efficiency and productivity. No, the way of the monks was a better way.

As Mr. Az studied history, it became quite clear that real power belongs to the ones who control the world's wealth. Kings and dictators cannot wage wars without money. Science cannot discover and industry cannot progress without money. Governments cannot function without money. All political systems would crumble without money. Without money, civilization comes to a standstill.

Working secretly, quietly, testing his plans bit by bit, Mr. Az has developed a master plan. He theorizes that by going back in time and making very minute changes at strategic points this plan could be achieved. He has pinpointed the exact points in history where he would intervene – a slight alteration in events that would not change history per se, but which, when they all came together, would deliver all the world's wealth into his hands. Once he has the wealth, ruling the world would be automatic.

All politicians, all scientists, all would-be kings and rulers would have to come to him for money. They would do the governing and ruling according to his plans. If they didn't, he would cut off their money and wipe their memories, thus insuring he would never have enemies, and install others to take their places. His plans were ready. It was now time for the time machine.

His search for a time machine was not a flight of fancy. He had knowledge that in the ancient past, working plans for a time machine had been put forth. A model had been built and he had seen it vanish into the future. All that was lacking was the technology to produce the energy to power it. He was certain that the day had come when science was advanced enough that the time machine could be built.

He employed many scientists to do research and development in the areas of surveillance and detection. Some of his inventions, when he no longer needed them, he sold to governments for spying. His most secret he used in a constant surveillance, looking for any evidence of the kind of energy emissions that would suggest research and testing of a time machine. Whenever the intelligence looked promising, Mr. Az sent his scientific investigators. He had them dress in black suits with black overcoats and hats, and wearing dark sunglasses. He said that since the idea of "Men in Black" had been popularized it might intimidate people and make it easier to get information. Lately, it was beginning to pay off. The right kind of energy emissions had been detected. At long last all the pieces of his plan were coming together.

"Ah, yes," he smiles. "It was only a matter of time before all the parts of my plan would come together."

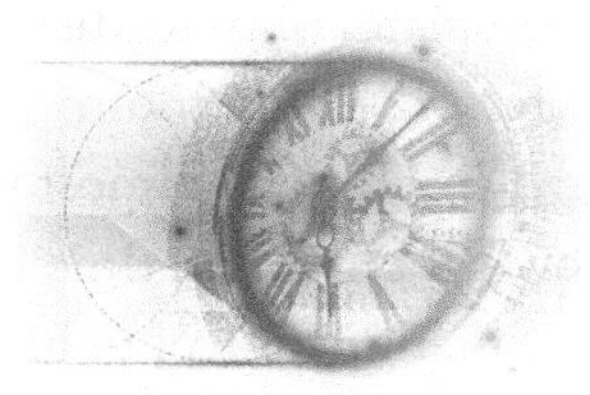

CHAPTER 17

Nightmares Become Daymares

"B*zzzzzz - ACKKKKK - ACKKKKK – ACKKKKK - ACKKKKK - CRASH! - TINKEL - tinkle. It's 5:30 a.m. Time to get up*," announces the jarring voice of Peter's annoying alarm clock – a Christmas present from his mom. "Yeesch! What an alarm!" Peter grumbles as he hits the off button. "At least it gets me up!" Sleepily he plants his feet on the cold floor only to jerk them back quickly. "Brrr!" he shouts. "Well, I'm awake now!"

He finds his slippers, crawls out of bed, grabs a towel, and heads for the shower. The hot water feels good but the cold draft from the frosted windows sets his teeth chattering. "Winter is not my favorite time of year," he complains to the empty shower room, donning his bathrobe, grabbing his towel, and heading back to his warm room as quickly as he can to dry off and dress. "Early morning physics lectures aren't my favorite thing either," he sputters. "If anyone but the Professor was lecturing, I'd crawl back into bed. The Professor . . ."

His thoughts instantly flash back to last spring and the strange dream he had had at the Professor's home. "Why does that dream keep taking over my head? I dream it at night and now I've started dreaming it in the daytime. I've got to talk to the Professor about it today. It's driving me bananas!" Suddenly the dream takes over his mind again. It always begins with the part he didn't dream; the Professor's strange phone call and the nerve wracking drive. Then comes the part he dreamed at the Professor's, about a secret laboratory and a trip to see

God create, only to discover it was a dream when he woke up in the Professor's living room.

"Argh!" Peter almost yells several minutes later. "It happened again! Now I'll only have time for a cup of coffee for breakfast!"

Sticking his feet in his overshoes, grabbing his jacket and his physics notebook, Peter rushes out into the snow and heads for the dining hall. At a table near the door, George and Jim are enjoying a last cup of coffee. Peter grabs toast, jelly and coffee, and sits down with the guys. They want to talk. "Sorry guys, can't stay and talk. Gotta eat and run!" Peter exclaims, gulping down his toast and coffee. He asks them to take care of his dishes, then darts out the dining hall to the physics building. "Whew!" he gasps in relief as he slips into his seat just as the bell rings, "I made it."

The Professor begins to speak.

"Peter. Peter."

Peter looks up, startled and dazed. He looks around, exclaiming, "Where am I? I thought I was in the Blue Orb! No, I'm sitting in the Professor's living room! No, I'm in the physics class room!"

"Peter! The class is over. Sorry it was so boring. Did you have a good nap?"

Confused, Peter questioningly looks up into the Professor's merry face and asks, "The class is over? No!" Then he desperately pleads, "The dream, that nagging dream has just made me miss the most important class of the semester! Professor, you've got to help me!"

"We do need to talk, Peter."

Peter forces his mind to focus on the Professor, who is looking at him with an amused look on his face.

"People usually don't dream with their eyes wide open. Yours were open but no one was home! I apologize if my lecture put you in a trance. You weren't snoring, so that rules out sleeping! You aren't dating, so that rules out reliving a hot date! So, something else must be going on, right?"

Peter, nods, relieved to finally get to talk about the dream.

"We'll grab a cup of coffee at the Student Union. It'll help you wake up. Then we'll talk. But, we need to hurry. Time is running short!"

Those last words startle Peter. He's fully alert now, including a sudden knot his stomach just like last spring! They step outside. The campus is deserted, except for a couple students running past, late for class. The fresh brisk air clears Peter's mind. He looks around and realizes it's turned out to be a beautiful day. The sky is bright blue with billowy white clouds. A thick coating of hoarfrost coats the trees, the bushes, everything. The campus has been transformed into a white winter wonderland.

"Hasn't God painted a beautiful picture?"

There is pleasure and deep appreciation in the Professor's voice, who is also enjoying the beauty of the frost. But Peter is distracted by the memory of the dream and the tension in his stomach. Questions burn in his mind. Needing answers, he turns to the Professor and asks, "Professor, why did you call me last spring and tell me to come quickly?"

"Remembering lets us build on the past, not repeat it," he answers, bending over and making a snowball. "Think of all the things a simple snowball teaches us. What do you think this snowball might be saying to us right now?"

"DUCK!" answers Peter, ducking down as the Professor lobs the snowball at him. As he ducks Peter grabs more snow and fires a snowball back. A brief snowball fight follows, ending in a draw.

"See, Peter. You remembered the past and learned from it! You knew I would throw my snowball at you."

The Student Union is filled with the clamor of people talking, cups clinking, and a jukebox playing. The Professor and Peter are both well liked. No sooner do they step inside and invitations to have a seat come from all over. The Professor smiles and waves a "No." Peter gives his coffee order to the girl at the counter, who, he notices, is one of his fellow physics classmates. She brings his order, cappuccino for himself, and regular with cream for the Professor.

Peter follows the Professor as he winds his way through the crowded room, saying, "Let's sit in back, by that door, where we can talk in private."

From this out-of-the-way table they have a clear view of the whole room. The Professor moves his chair to the back side of the table, facing the front. Peter senses that this is important, and the knot in his stomach tightens. He wants to know what is going on. He wants the answers to his questions. He waits impatiently, sipping his coffee. It's hard not to speak. But the Professor looks thoughtful, as though something very important is bothering him, and he wants to talk about it. Peter decides it is best to wait with his own questions until after the Professor speaks.

"Peter, am I correct that this morning in class you were reliving what you thought was only an old dream?"

"Yes."

"Remembering is important. Often understanding what is before us depends on remembering what is behind us. We've learned how to combine atoms in different combinations to make all kinds of things. A piece of chocolate cake is a whole gob of atoms linked deliciously together. It would be a tremendous waste of time and energy if we had to learn all over again how to combine the atoms every time we wanted chocolate cake!

"Some scientists fall into the error of forgetting. They want to learn the atom's secrets. But they forget that God made the atom, and that if they would turn to the Bible and seek his guidance they would find what they are looking for. But man is arrogant, unwilling to listen to what the Bible teaches, so he wastes his time relearning what is already explained. Do you remember Elisha?"

"Sure. Elisha was Elijah's servant. When Elijah caught a chariot ride into heaven, Elisha saw it. Because he saw it, a double portion of the anointing that had been on Elijah fell on Elisha."

"There is much more to Elisha than meets the eye. The secret to Elisha's success is that he remembered what others forgot. That's why he had more prayers answered and did more miracles than any other person in the Old Testament. At the same time, he was the laziest of all, a true scientist!" the Professor adds, laughing.

"You're a scientist, and you're not lazy. Why did you say that?"

"You've heard the old adage, 'Work smarter, not harder'?"

"Yes," Peter answers, puzzled.

"Do you remember what Archimedes said about the lever?"

"He said 'Give me a lever long enough and a fulcrum to rest it on and I can move the world.'"

"Right! Think of all the wasted effort that would be spent if people forgot the lever. Using a lever to move an object makes a lot more sense than trying to move an object by brute force. Using a lever is working smarter, not harder. Elisha applied this law on the spiritual level and miracles happened. Elisha was remembering what others forgot. He remembered that he had been created in the image of God, designed to live in God's dimension. He was, first of all, a spirit who had a soul and lived in a body, just as Paul wrote in 1 Thessalonians 5:23."

"Professor, what does that have to do with my questions?"

"The natural man has forgotten that he is a spirit," the Professor continues, ignoring Peter's question. "Having forgotten who he is and where he came from, he looks at the animal kingdom and thinks he must have evolved from an ape. Elisha knew he was a spirit designed to walk and talk with God. As his spiritual eyes were opened, he saw things the way God saw them. He discovered that if he found the right lever and the right fulcrum, and used them to apply spiritual laws to problems in the soul and body realm, miracles happened."

"Professor, you've lost me! What does all this have to do with my dream?'

The Professor looks at Peter with an amused smile. Peter hates that. It makes him think of a cat playing with a mouse!

"Some scientists get hung up in their thinking and forget that when you move up to a higher level, or a higher dimension, things that were impossible on the lower dimensions now become possible. Once Einstein discovered the dimension of time, it opened the way to amazing discoveries that had been impossible prior to that. It is the same in the spiritual realm. What is impossible in the natural realm, the realm of the natural man that Paul describes in 1 Corinthians 2:14, becomes possible in the spirit realm, or spirit dimension."

Peter puzzles over this. "It's hard wrapping my mind around the thought of putting Elisha and Einstein together on the same level. Elisha was not a physicist. He was a prophet. What do you mean?"

"I know just the Elisha story that will make it all clear. It's one of Glenn Clark's favorite examples. Clark was an educator, a college professor and football coach. Elisha was also an educator, the headmaster of a school of prophets. Elisha had a student who forgot who he was. When a need arose, he panicked. Elisha had to show him what he'd forgotten.

"It happened like this. One day Elisha's students came to him and said, 'This place where we are living is much too small for us. We want to go down to the Jordan and build a bigger house with plenty of room for everybody. We can do it if everyone pitches in and works together.'

"'That's fine,' said lazy Elisha. 'Go and build. I'll just stay here and finish my nap!' 'But sir,' one spoke up, 'Please be willing to go with your servants.' 'Okay, I'll go,' he said. And so they all went down to the Jordan and started felling and trimming trees for the house. That is, everyone except Elisha. Elisha was sitting back, watching them, enjoying the show.

"Suddenly one of the young men yelled 'help!' His aim was bad. He over reached the tree trunk and hit it with the axe handle instead of the axe head. The handle busted clean in two, sending the axe head sailing off towards the river. There it landed, in the middle of the Jordan. 'Alas, my master,' he cried, 'for it was borrowed.'

"The young man was frantic. If he didn't get that axe back to its owner, he was going to be in really big trouble. But lazy Elisha just said, 'No sweat!' The student had forgotten all about living on God's level. Instead, he was living on the scared level of his soul and body; the level of 'Oh dear, what am I going to do?'

"Elisha knew that all of creation was designed to live on God's level, and see things as God sees them: in harmony and wholeness. When the axe head came off, the harmony of the axe was broken. It was hurting and wanted to be healed. Harmony and wholeness are spiritual laws, as well as physical laws. Everything seeks to be in a harmonious relationship with everything else. Everything that is broken seeks to be healed. We claim it for ourselves when we quote Psalm 37: 4-5 and Proverbs 3:6.

Delight thyself also in the LORD; and he shall give thee the desires of thine heart. Commit thy way unto the LORD; trust also in him;

and he shall bring it to pass... In all thy ways acknowledge him, and he shall direct thy paths.

"Elisha knew that the laws of God's dimension apply universally and work on both living and nonliving objects. How to apply the law is a principal Archimedes taught us. We start by asking four questions. The first question is 'What got lost that caused the disharmony?' The second question is 'Where was it lost?' The third question is 'What can we use as a fulcrum.' The fourth question is 'What can we use as a lever?'"

"Professor, now that you've thrown Archimedes into the mix you're confusing me! All I wanted to do was ask you about my dream."

"Shut up and drink your coffee!"

"Professor! That's not very polite!"

"No, but it was fun to say it! I'm not forgetting your dream. I'm giving you tools to help you. Archimedes' lever is a very important tool of prayer. Let me give you an example. We'll pretend that what Archimedes lost was the earth. Considering its size that was very clumsy of him! But it was lost, missing from its orbit, and the whole galaxy was out of kilter. Next, Archimedes had to find out where he lost it. He must have been an absentminded professor, because it turns out he was standing on it all the time! Now that he knows where the earth is, Archimedes has to figure out how to get the earth back into orbit and restore harmony to the galaxy.

"Let's switch our attention back to Elisha. The first step, identifying what is lost, was easy. It was the axe head. The second step, identifying where it was lost, was easy too. His student could point to the exact spot where the axe head entered the water. He couldn't point to where the axe head lay on the bottom because the water was deep and muddy and they couldn't see anything. He needed a way to find his axe head and get it back.

"Getting back to Archimedes, he needs a way to pop the earth back into orbit and restore harmony to the galaxy. What he needs is a fulcrum and a very long lever. The fulcrum is what makes the lever work. When we apply this to prayer, the fulcrum of prayer is the Word of God. His promises give us the authority and power to get results.

"The lever is what we use to apply the authority of the Bible to the problem or need. Some call the lever a point of contact. It is the thing that enables us to turn our faith loose. To the woman with the issue of blood, her of point of contact was the hem of Jesus' garment. The Centurion's point of contact was Jesus speaking the word. In each case the lever released faith and enabled harmony to flow into the need. With harmony came wholeness. The lever enables us to turn our faith loose and believe."

"What does a lever have to do with my dream?"

"Our Elisha story brings all this together. The fulcrum is our Biblical authority for restoring harmony. Our lever rests on the spiritual law of harmony. To apply the law of harmony to the axe head, Elisha needed a lever, something he could get his hands on. Just a little effort on our part, when it rests on the fulcrum of God's Word, exerts mighty power. What better lever than a new handle to replace the one that broke? So he made a new handle for the axe. He threw it out over the spot where the axe head lay. The axe head, seeking harmony and wholeness, seeking its handle in order to be whole, floated up to its new handle. You see, Peter, how important it is for people to remember that man is a spirit being, designed to live on God's level. Elisha remembering that is what made the miracle possible."

Peter thinks about the Professor's words as he drinks the last of his cappuccino. "I understand the importance of remembering, of building on what's gone before, and using the authority of the Bible. What I still don't understand is what that has to do with my dream. How does my dream fit into what you've been telling me?"

"I was just getting to that." The Professor pats Peter's arm reassuringly, when suddenly his grip tightens.

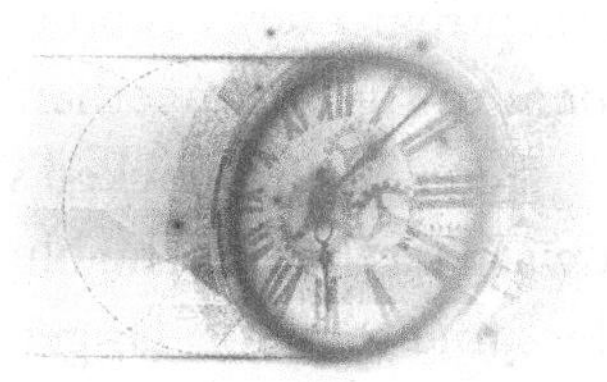

CHAPTER 18

Escape to A Loaf of Bread

The Professor is looking towards the front. Three strangers, dressed in black with the collars of their heavy overcoats drawn up against the cold, black hats drawn down over their eyes and wearing dark sun glasses, have just walked in. They look around, and begin talking to the girl at the cash register. They do not seem pleased with the answers she is giving them.

"Quick," whispers the Professor. "Let's slip out before they see us." He grabs Peter's arm and drags him out of his chair and rushes through the back door, closing it quickly behind them. Without talking, they run behind the buildings to the faculty parking lot by the science building. They stop to catch their breath. The Professor looks quickly at all the cars in the lot.

"There are no strange cars here. So it is safe. Hop in my car and we'll go visit an old friend."

Peter hops in, his heart racing as though he were running for his life, although he doesn't know why. The car quickly roars to life. The Professor drives it like a race car. Peter hangs on for dear life, trying to keep in his seat as the Professor turns first one way and then another!

"Thank goodness the roads have been sanded!" Peter blurts out.

"I know who they are," the Professor explains. "I do not want us to meet them. They are the same ones who invaded my house last spring. They are looking for us. My guess is they've detected another high energy burst from a time machine, like the one they were searching for last spring. They've come back again looking for the source. I don't want them to find us together."

Peter sits in shocked silence. "Energy burst!? Time machine!? Then it wasn't a dream!" he blurts out. The Professor's words have awakened the same sense of danger Peter felt last spring. "Something's up. It has to do with my dream, doesn't it?"

The Professor remains silent. Finally, after so many turns Peter loses count, the Professor turns into the driveway of an old farm house on the southeast edge of town. The garage door opens as he drives up to it. He drives straight in and stops next to Mrs. McD's car! Peter would know her old clunker anywhere. Immediately the garage door closes.

"Well Peter, I think we gave them the slip. They won't find us now. And, by the delicious smell, I'd say Mrs. McD has been baking. Let's see what she's got."

The side doorway of the garage opens onto an old fashioned mud room for slipping out of mud or snow covered boots and slipping on slippers or shoes. It was covered with a multicolored carpet like stepping into a flower garden. On the left, a large formal door leads directly outdoors. To the left of the door, an upholstered corner bench fills the space between the front door and the garage door. On the right, carpeted steps lead down to the basement. This basement was built for parties, and the wide basement stairs are elegant, with a graceful curve and finely turned balusters. In front of them, another set of carpeted steps turns to the right and leads up to the kitchen. The house was built with all the charm of an old fashioned farmhouse, although it had never been used as one.

As Peter and the Professor ascend the steps to Mrs. McD's homey kitchen, the wonderful fragrance of fresh baked bread sets their mouths watering, especially Peter's, who remembers his scanty breakfast.

"Hello Professor! Hi Peter! Now Professor, don't tell me you came racing down the street that fast just to get a slice of my fresh baked bread!"

"No, Mrs. McD. As much as I'd be willing to race a hundred miles an hour for your bread, that wasn't why we were in a hurry. They've come back. They came into the Union. I don't think they saw us and I'm sure we weren't followed. But first, Mrs. McD – about your bread . . ."

With a happy smile on her face, Mrs. McD quickly sets three places at the table, cuts the fresh hot bread into generously thick slices, sets out a big dish of butter and opens a jar of her homemade strawberry preserves. No one talks, except to ask for more, as they savor each delicious mouthful.

Bright sunshine streams through the spacious windows of Mrs. McD's kitchen. A soft shade of yellow on the walls, white cabinets with glass paneled doors and bright bits of color from decorations and flowers made it a place that invites you to sit for a cup of coffee, a piece of pie, or a cookie, and a bit of chat. Neighbors and friends often stop in to visit, and many times to ask for prayer.

The loaf of bread quickly disappears. Nobody speaks until the last crumb is devoured. Then Mrs. McD rises and starts to clear away the dishes. "You go into the living room while I clean up. I'll join you shortly. I've got some questions I've been meaning to ask."

The living room is full of old country charm. On one wall is an old fashioned brick fireplace with an opening large enough for old St. Nick to come down the chimney. The white ceiling is crisscrossed with dark wood beams. The tall windows stretch from the floor to the ceiling, each with leafy potted plants, seeming to invite the outside to come in and be a part of the living room. The shelves on the walls are filled with books and dishes and pieces of art. Every chair invites one to come and enjoy its comfort.

The Professor walks over to the fireplace, carefully lays a log on the fire, and sits in one of the chairs. The look on his face is of a man without a care in the world, enjoying the comfort of a warm fire. Perhaps now, Peter thinks, maybe he can ask his questions. But as usual, just as he is about to ask, the Professor speaks! What he says startles Peter.

"Peter, remember what happened when you came to see me last spring?"

"Yes! Professor, what did happen last spring? You said 'time machine' just as we left the Union. Does that mean it was real and not a dream?"

The Professor begins to speak in the most serious tone of voice Peter has ever heard. "It is time for you to learn secrets known only to a few. They are secrets you must never tell. You must never breathe a word of them to even your closest and most trusted friends. The future of the world may depend on your silence!"

This comment startles Peter even more. His stomach responds by trying to make knots on top of the bread and jam. He shivers as if in dreadful danger. He stares at the Professor, his mouth opening to speak, but no words come out.

"Everything you remember about that morning actually happened. After the Blue Orb landed and we got back to the living room, you sat down. Then suddenly, as though someone had flipped a switch, you dropped off into a deep sleep. I thought how wise that was of the Holy Spirit, for it gave me all the explanation I needed when the Men in Black arrived. The house had warned us that they were coming. I didn't want them to know that we had just returned from a journey in a time machine. I thought it best to let them see you sleeping through the window.

"Afterwards, for your safety, I let you go on thinking it was a dream. I knew that it wasn't the kind of dream you'd go around talking about. The Holy Spirit kept bringing it back to you so that you wouldn't forget. Today I had to tell you that your dream was real, that it had actually happened. You see, the Blue Orb has returned to take us on a second journey back in time."

"I'm glad it was real! But if we're taking another trip, why aren't we at your home? Or in your lab?"

"The Orb is here. The Men in Black have also returned. They believe we're getting ready to use it again. The men who came into the Student Union were looking for you, not me."

"Looking for me? Why? I don't have a time machine."

"They know you were at my house."

"Why not go directly to you?"

"They're looking for me as well. But they believe they can make you lead them to the time machine. They suspect I'm a very uncooperative and bright scientist who won't tell them anything. They think it will be easier to get the information they want from you. They had no idea where to find you. They were just asking questions. They weren't expecting to find either of us in the Student Union. That's why it was easy for us to get away. I don't want you to fall into their hands, Peter."

Mrs. McD, having finished her work in the kitchen, interrupts their conversation. She refills their cups with fresh coffee, saying, "If you two are going to do a lot of talking you'll need some coffee to sip on. Let me refill your cups. Now Professor, before you get started again, I could use your advice. Mary Belle Hines is coming for prayer this afternoon. She has a list of troubles a mile long! Gall stones, a growth on her neck, and severe headaches. And I'm thinking, 'How do I pray for all this?' Any suggestions?"

"Funny you should ask, Mrs. McD! Peter and I were just talking about Elisha and about Archimedes' lever. Do you remember how Glenn Clark loved the idea of levers?[1] In one of his talks, he told about a lady who came to him with more problems than your lady's got. This lady was scheduled for surgery, but talked her doctor into putting it off until she'd had a chance to go to one of Glenn Clark's camps.

"Glenn was not a doctor. He had no idea what could be causing her problems. So Glenn did what he always did when he didn't have a clue how to pray. He asked for guidance. As Glenn prayed for guidance a memory from his childhood flashed into his mind. When he was a boy, homes didn't have vacuum cleaners. Instead, every spring, housewives would hire a vacuum cleaner truck to come and vacuum out their homes. You remember those, Mrs. McD? The truck would park out in the street and a crew of men would come with their hoses and give your house a complete cleaning in just a few hours.

"Glenn realized that, like Elisha's axe handle, the idea of a vacuum cleaner was a lever this lady could grab hold of. He had her invite Jesus to come in with his crew of angels to vacuum out all the toxins and poisons that had gotten into her body. That meant cleaning out her memory rooms too, because resentments and anger and self-pity can cause physical problems. The lady was able to picture Jesus and the

[1] These and other stories and teachings by Glenn Clark are available for listening at: www.cfoclassicslibrary.org

angels doing a thorough cleaning and airing out. In less than a week, she called and said the doctors could find nothing wrong with her.

"It is God's will for us to be whole and healed. That's how Glenn prayed. Once he knew the lever to use, his prayers were always short and to the point. Nothing long, nothing fancy. It is important that the people for whom we pray be enabled to release their own faith. All he did when he prayed for this lady was ask Jesus to bring his vacuum cleaner angels, and then instructed the angels what to do as they went about cleaning. Why don't you try something like that with this lady?"

"Thanks, Professor. That's exactly what I'll do. I should have thought of that myself! These latest events must have driven it from my mind."

"These events are why we showed up to eat your bread. Why don't you tell Peter about what's happening, Mrs. McD?"

"I was working on some projects yesterday, Peter. Suddenly the Blue Orb showed up. I called the Professor right away and gave him the message I seemed to be hearing. The Orb has been here ever since. Well, as here as it ever gets, seeing as how it keeps appearing and disappearing. I don't think the enemy has detected it, else I'd have had some visitors. Not that they could have found anything in this house!

"The message was for you too, Peter," Mrs. McD explains. "Both of you are to take the trip. Professor, I'm worried about what our enemy will do to you if he catches you. He won't believe you didn't build it. He saw your designs. He saw the model disappear. He knows the time is right for building one and that you had started experimenting once again. He needs it now to complete his plans. Does Peter know how serious this is and what will happen if either of you, or the plans, fall into his hands?"

Peter's heart jumps to his throat once again. A sense of impending danger has his adrenalin pumping. "What's going on?" he asks. "Is the traitor/enemy here, in town?"

"Peter, Mrs. McD is right. It's time we disappeared. Finish your coffee and then come and I'll show you a secret about this house." The Professor leads the way back to the garage.

"Many years ago," the Professor began, "when this was still a secluded place in the country, a very rich and eccentric gentleman built this house. He was a collector of valuable things. He loved to show them off, but he was deathly afraid of being robbed. One day he noticed the hydraulic lift used to raise cars up so the mechanic could get underneath the car to service it. And he thought, *why not use a hydraulic lift to help protect my possessions?* He built an underground showroom and covered it over with several feet of dirt and planted a garden. He had a custom-made hydraulic lift installed under the garage floor. When the floor was up and locked in place it looked like any other garage floor. But when he pushed a hidden switch, the floor would sink down until it was level with his underground showroom.

"The only other entrance to his showroom was a narrow, barred, doorway opening off the basement. The hydraulic lift was hidden behind a wall panel so that visitors to his collection couldn't see it. Everyone assumed he must have had the showroom built up around his collection as the doorway was too small to move most of his collection in and out. He could show off his treasures without fear of robbery.

"When the city began to crowd in and his home was no longer isolated, the gentleman moved out, taking his treasures with him. Everyone assumed he dug up his showroom and filled in the hole. But the truth is that the showroom, and the hydraulic lift, are still here. When Mrs. McD and I moved to town, we bought this house for her. I converted the old showroom into a second secret laboratory where both Mrs. McD and I do some work. Mrs. McD is quite a gifted scientist in her own right. I hid the basement doorway so that no one but Mrs. McD and I can find it. We come and go at leisure and a monitor lets Mrs. McD know who is at the door.

"We are going to disappear into that room. Since we need to hide my car we'll use the lift. So hop in and down we go."

The Professor pushes a button on his key ring, and the floor begins to descend. It comes to rest about 20 feet below the garage floor. He eases the car forward onto the parking ramp, pushes another button on his key ring and the floor slowly rises back up. The Professor places his hand on the wall in front. Instantly it glows under his hand as it recognizes his hand print. "Open the door, please." He was always polite, and *please* was part of his command code to a machine. A thick concrete door slides effortlessly open. They step through into the lab. Peter stares in wonder.

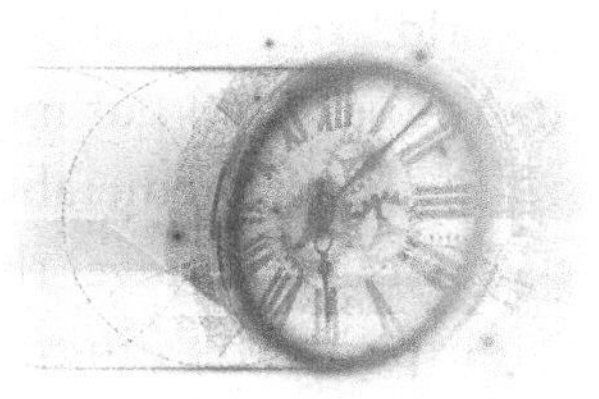

CHAPTER 19

An Unbelievable Story

Futuristic-looking electronic instruments line the walls. Light from the instrument panels and computer screens bathe the room in a soft glow. In the far corner, behind a thick transparent wall, is a power generator. There's a particle accelerator, a fusion reactor, an electron microscope, and banks of computers and screens monitoring and analyzing the sophisticated equipment, much of which Peter has never seen before. On the other side of the room, across from the power generator, is a kitchenette, a table, and two plush recliners. The Professor, an amused smile on his face, watches Peter as he gazes in wide-eyed wonder at this physicist's dream laboratory.

"Wow!" Peter exclaims. "You can do here what others need enormous facilities to do. It reminds me of what TPF said. 'Experimentation comes first. Miniaturization comes later.' This would be a fun place to work. What kind of experiments are you conducting here? May I see them?"

"There's not time now, Peter. We have more pressing concerns that require our immediate attention. I've much to explain. Mrs. McD packed us a huge lunch basket for later."

Peter settles down in a recliner beside the Professor. The events of these last few moments had so fascinated him that he'd forgotten the foreboding he'd felt moments before. The Professor's words bring the fear flooding back and Peter's not sure he wants to hear what caused it.

"Professor. What's going on? Why will keeping my mouth shut save the world? You talk about some sinister plot, saying I'm in the middle of it. You say God put me here. Why?"

"Life is not predictable," the Professor answers. "Things we did not expect, things we never thought could happen, suddenly happen. Some are unexpected blessings. Some are unexpected troubles. Having an old friend become a deadly enemy and want to kill me and steal my time machine was not in my plans.

"But in the midst of the unexpected, there is one thing we can always expect. We can always trust and expect that God is with us guiding, helping, and making us more than conquerors in Christ Jesus. That is the sure thing and the source of our confidence. That also makes our lives exciting. When we give our lives to God we give him permission to use us in any way He needs. Sometimes He uses us in ways we never dreamed. When He does, we discover in the doing that He gives us the strength and resources to accomplish his will. Do you remember the story of Corrie Ten Boom?"[1]

"I think I see your point, Professor. Corrie would never have dreamed that when she was fifty-six she would be hiding Jews in a secret room in her bedroom. Neither would she have dreamed that she and her sister Betsie would be imprisoned by the Nazi's in Ravensbrook. Nowhere in her biography did she declare, concerning what might happen, 'I can handle that!' When the time came, God gave her the strength to handle it in His strength.

"She never dreamed of writing a book, or that her book would become a movie or that she would become a world renowned speaker. Yet her story is full of how God gave her the strength and inner resources to endure, including the miracle of her release due to a clerical mistake. If Corrie could do what she did, I don't have a thing to worry about, do I?"

"The trouble with us, Peter, is that when we look at ourselves, we tend to see only our limitations. When God looks at us, He sees our possibilities. Remember what God said to Jeremiah? 'Before I formed you in the womb I knew you, before you were born I set you apart'

---

[1] Ten Boom, Corrie, *The Hiding Place*, 1971, Bloomington MN, Chosen Books.

(Jeremiah 1:5 NIV). We have this confidence that when God is for us, no one can successfully stand against us, as Paul said in Romans 8:31. Besides, 'Greater is he that is in you than he that is in the world' (1 John 4:4).

"Each of us chooses to either become all that God has planned for us to be, or else find a box and crawl into it and hide. Glenn Clark stepped outside the box theologians and scientists had built and sought to ignite people's minds to join him in the adventure of discovering what is possible with prayer. People flocked to his Camps Farthest Out to venture farther out with God.

"Venturing farther out is what you are doing. You gave God permission to use you any way He needed. You spend time in prayer and in His word, seeking His daily guidance. As a result, He brought you here to me, and together we've been chosen to go on these marvelous journeys in His Time Machine."

Wow! thinks Peter. *When I asked God to take me and use me in any way He wanted I never dreamed it would be anything like this. It wasn't because I was worthy, which I'm not, but simply because I was willing.*

"Now it's time to tell you my story," the Professor breaks the silence. "It is an old story that began many hundreds of years ago. It is a story most people will not believe. Even you may have trouble believing it, Peter. Last spring, one of your assignments was to investigate an ancient story about the Nine Unknown Men. The class concluded that the story was a legend! It was not a legend, Peter, although many legends grew up around it. What I am about to tell you is the true story.

"When the secret Order of the Nine Unknown Men came into being, their knowledge was already immense. Each of the Nine had an area of knowledge for which he was responsible. At the wish of the Emperor Asoka, their identities were known only to each other. Only Asoka knew who they were. At his request their identities died with him.

"However, Asoka made one more request. He did not want their knowledge lost. He believed that in some future day, mankind would mature and would use this knowledge for good and not for evil as he had done. He instructed them to search for gifted young men to take their places so that there would always be nine. This they did. And that was the pattern that was followed for the first few hundred years.

"It all changed one day when one of the Nine discovered an elixir with amazing properties. It was a byproduct of one of his experiments. In theory, it should have only been pure water. Being thirsty, and believing it safe, he drank it. The next morning, he received the shock of his life. He came running into the dining room. Running, in itself, was most unusual for an old man with rheumatism in his joints. But that was not all. His white hair was gone, replaced by a thick unruly mop of red. His skin was smooth and ruddy like a young man in his prime.

"He explained what had happened. The water in his experiment had been changed into an elixir of life. He had made meticulous notes so that he could repeat every part of his experiment. Each of the other Nine then duplicated the experiment. Each ended up with what should have been pure water. And when they drank it, they too were rejuvenated! Those same Nine Unknown Men are still alive today, Peter, even though this is many hundreds of years later."

"Professor, that can't be possible. Nobody can live that long."

"It's not such an impossibility as you might think, Peter. Man was originally created to live forever, remember? Methuselah lived 969 years (Genesis 5:27). Theoretically man's body has been designed to keep on renewing itself. But for some unknown reason, it stops. Millions have been spent studying the aging process. While no solution has been found, science has been learning how to help people to live healthier. Others, hoping science will learn the secret, have their bodies frozen in anticipation of the day they can be brought back to life.

"The fruit of the Tree of Life in the Garden of Eden prevented ageing. That suggests that there is an elixir that renews life. The Elixir of Life discovered by the Nine Unknown Men does what the Tree of Life would have done. It reverses the aging process and allows the body to return to its youth and vigor.

"With our youth renewed, the accumulated knowledge of the Nine became vast indeed. So vast in fact that not even the minds of the Nine could remember it all. The Nine decided that now that our youth had been restored and our memories were sharp, we needed to write all our knowledge in a book. Having the book handy would save the time we would have spent going back over old memories, and sorting them out to find the bit of information we needed at the moment. We could refer to the manuscript as needed, and never again be concerned about forgetting anything.

"For many years this book was the center of our library. In the course of time we added to it, made notes in the margins, and added pages. As civilization expanded around the world, establishing centers of learning on every continent, the Nine spread out. Today, each continues his research in secret. When a crisis arises that mankind seems unable to handle, such as an epidemic, one of the Nine will step in and anonymously show them the cure.

"Our immediate concern is the manuscript and the time machine described in it. Our enemy has his heart set on getting the time machine. You've seen the manuscript, Peter. It is real. Our enemy is also real, as you already know from the close encounter we had with his Watchers. He is after the part of the manuscript that has the detailed plans for building a time machine. But what he really wants is me with a working time machine."

"Whoa, Professor! You've got to admit your story has all the earmarks of science fiction. I saw enough of the old manuscript to know that a remarkable old scientific text exists. I've been in the Blue Orb so I know that is real. But two things in your story bother me. First, the idea that there are men living now who are almost two thousand years old is a little hard to swallow. Second is the matter of a time machine and the amount of power it takes. Asking me to believe that two thousand years ago ancient scientists figured out how to build and power a time machine is going beyond believable. We've only recently developed the technology to create microchips."

"Peter, let me show you something." The Professor reaches up and removes a large beautifully finished wooden box from one of the cabinets and sets it on the table. He tips the top back and lowers the front revealing a plush blue lining. Sitting inside is the strange looking object that had penetrated the side of the Blue Orb.

"Peter, you do recognize this, don't you? You knew I knew what it was when it came into the Blue Orb and set it carefully on the seat beside me. Now let me tell you what it is. This is the working model, a prototype, of a time machine. It looks like a wheel within a wheel, almost. The full scale version is what is described in the manuscript. It is driven by its own internal power source. You see the small round yellow can with the wires attached to it? We didn't have a nuclear power source because we felt it was too risky. Instead we learned how to harness the power in lightning and store it for our needs. That box is a high capacity battery into which we were able to concentrate millions of volts of energy. It was charged from power garnered from the lightning. I measured it and it still retains a significant portion of its power.

"At the time I built it I did not understand the true nature of time travel. I programmed it to go into the future. We knew it couldn't return to us because there was no one on board to reverse the settings. We did not know it would come to rest in the in-between place. Our assumption was that sometime in the future the time machine would reappear in the same spot from which it had disappeared. The Nine of us watched it fade and vanish! That's how our enemy knows it works."

Again Peter is stunned by what he hears. He stares at the Professor for several moments. Finally, he exclaims in disbelief, "You keep saying 'I' and 'we' as you talk, just as though you had been there, maybe even built it yourself. There is no way you could be that old!"

"But I am that old, Peter. The story I've told you is true. I designed the time machine and built this model. By being unknown and staying unknown, we Nine Unknown Men have been able to do many wonderful things. We plant ideas and give suggestions to help scientists and inventors. When needed, we redirect their research if they start to invent things or discover things mankind isn't quite ready for. We were fearful when atomic energy was discovered, but its time had come. We felt like fathers watching their children drive away on their own for the first time.

"Life has been good and we've enjoyed it to the full. Jesus is our Lord. Our greatest joy is knowing him and serving him. That is, all of us except one. One chose to follow the path of hate, the path Satan chose. The light that was in him has grown darker and darker."

Peter has been watching the Professor's face very carefully for any hint he might be telling a very tall tale. The Professor's expression continues to be both serious and sad. There is not the slightest suggestion of a smile or a mischievous twinkle in his eye. His words were spoken with the greatest earnestness. Peter finally realizes that the Professor's amazing story is true.

"Peter, the reason God sent us back in time to watch Him create was to make you a witness. You have witnessed what man was really like when God first created him. God wants you to proclaim to the world that we were created in glory, but lost it. He wants you to proclaim that, in the fullness of time, because Jesus bore all our sins on the cross and died in our place and shed His blood to cleanse us of all sin, because of all that, God has raised us up together in Christ and made us to sit down together at the right hand of God. Evil has been defeated, and God is undoing all the evil that evil has done. He is restoring us to the glory that once was ours.

"The natural man does not want to believe this. He wants nothing to do with God. The natural man wants to believe he evolved from some primordial soup. He does not want to believe that he was created after the image and likeness of God, or that once he possessed immense knowledge and wisdom. Or that he lost it all in an event called the Fall. To help get this message out, God is beginning to call on others besides the theologians, such as scientists, businessmen, people of all description, to be His spokesmen. God has chosen this time to show you creation as it happened. Many Christians have forgotten who they are. They have listened to the world and the hype of politicians. They've started looking to the government as their source, instead of looking to God Who is our real source. It is God who supplies all our need 'according to His riches in glory by Christ Jesus' (Philippians 4:19)."

Peter thinks about the Professor's words. Then, with a note of sadness in his voice, he speaks softly. "I've tried so many times to share that message, only to have people argue with me and reject it. It feels like they are saying, 'It's too much effort to believe God and trust Him to meet my needs for everything, when the government will give it to me for free!'"

"Peter, do you recall Ezekiel's prophecy against the King of Tyre? 'This is what the Sovereign LORD says: In the pride of your heart you say, "I am a god; I sit on the throne of a god in the heart of the seas." But you are a man and not a god, though you think you are as wise as a god.' (Ezekiel 28:2 NIV)

"One of my Order fell into that same sin of pride. A long, long time ago he tried to talk all of us into becoming rulers of the world with him. He had given up on God and believed we could rule more wisely, benevolently and fairly than God. We refused. But his words alarmed us. In secret, without his knowledge, we hid the manuscript to keep him from using its secrets. Then we disappeared, hiding our identity, our whereabouts and our knowledge from him. We kept in contact with each other, alerting each other to what the traitor was doing.

"What we had done he would not forgive. He blamed me for turning the others against him. Plans of revenge have been festering in his heart for hundreds of years. So too have plans for achieving his goal of ruling the world without us. The key to achieving his plans is the time machine I designed, although the tesseract machine would also be extremely useful to him.

"He had the elixir of life. He could live as long as he desired. Civilization wasn't ready yet for him to execute his plans. It needed to become much more advanced. He was willing to wait for the time machine until civilization was ripe for the plucking.

"He surrounded himself with brilliant engineers and set them to work designing highly sophisticated surveillance devices. With these he spies on every inch of the world. Do you remember in the *Star Trek* series they talked about their warp engines emitting an ion trail that they could follow? The time machine emits a unique energy trace. By searching for this energy trace he can tell exactly where the time machine is once it's activated. He plans to swoop down on it and steal it. He is so angry with me that his plans have become as much about revenge as about becoming the world's ruler. He wants to find me and force me to witness his triumph, and then kill me.

"We Eight felt responsible for creating this monster who threatened the world. We dared not die while he still lived. We had to be sure we kept the world safe from him. So Peter, welcome to our cloak and dagger stuff, as you call it."

The Professor sits back in his chair. He sighs, and smiles. Peter continues to digest all he has just heard. Finally, he speaks, "From the first day of my first physics class I've had the sense that there were great mysteries about you that you kept hidden. I wasn't prepared for them to be what you've just said!"

"I now have the equipment I need to build the full size time machine. I had begun experimenting again. I'd worked out a way to program an onboard computer to land the time machine, take pictures, and return to me. I started to build it and test it. Our enemy was expecting it and was watching for me to start experimenting again. He deployed his surveillance devices so that he could detect and watch what I was doing. I instantly stopped. The other members of my order sent up similar emissions from their labs. This confused him, but he kept watching. That's how he learned the manuscript had been found and brought to me to translate. I was warned the enemy was ready to grab the manuscript.

"He has developed a diabolical plan whereby he plans to go back in time, and, by changing a little thing here and a little thing there, we would suddenly discover that he controlled all the world's wealth, and had made himself the supreme ruler of the world. This was the very thing we were trying to prevent.

"Some of my fellow scientists and I were having fun theorizing about time travel in our research magazine. Rumors started to spread. Foreign powers, evil and greedy men began looking for me, probably led on by rumors our enemy planted. I thought we had put them off. Then, the Blue Orb arrived! I was told to get you and take you on that journey. The presence of the Blue Orb and the energy trace it emitted alerted our enemy that a time machine was here and working. My call to you last spring was urgent. We had to get away before they came.

"Well, that's the story, all too quickly told. Hundreds of questions unanswered. I don't know about you, but all this talk has made me hungry. Mrs. McD has a splendid meal waiting for us over there. And the Blue Orb will materialize any moment to take us on our second voyage."

With those words, the Professor hops up and walks over to one of the tables on which is a gigantic basket filled with sandwiches and salad and apple pie and a thermos of hot chocolate. Peter suddenly realizes how hungry he is and quickly joins the Professor. One of Mrs. McD's picnic dinners requires the utmost attention. Succulent Potato salad! Chicken salad sandwiches made with almonds and grapes. Apple pie made with the best kind of pie apples, rich with cinnamon and sugar and spices, and candy-like goodness oozing from the holes in the crust. This was not a time to talk but a time to enjoy and loosen your belt.

As soon as Peter and the Professor eat the last bit of pie and swallow the last bit of hot chocolate the Blue Orb suddenly appears. "Quickly," the Professor grabs Peter's arm and rushes into the Orb. Once again they are seated inside this marvelous machine.

"Those Men in Black will know the Orb is here. We must be long gone before they come to bother Mrs. McD."

The Professor's hands gently adjust the jeweled levers and dials. Peter sits on the cushioned seat. The Professor pushes the ruby red lever. The musical humming of the Orb is drowned out by a *WOOSH* as of a cylinder being sucked through a tube.

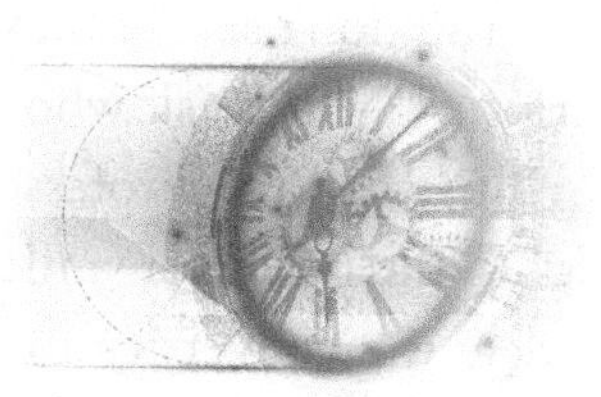

CHAPTER 20

The Unflappable Mrs. McD

The Professor had no sooner closed the door than Mrs. McD got busy. Once the Blue Orb arrived, the Men in Black, and who knows who else, would be pounding on her door. "I'll have to work fast," she said to herself. She gathered all the dishes and washed them and straightened everything up like no one had been there. Fortunately, the Professor and Peter had taken their coats and boots with them. In the garage she cleaned up the tracks and melted snow left by the Professor's car. And lastly she swept the driveway clean.

"That should do it," she said to herself. "Never a dull moment with the Professor around. I just wish those people would leave him alone."

It seemed like only yesterday when she first met the Professor. Dr. McD had talked about him many times. Scientists were so close-minded in those days. It used to drive Dr. McD up the wall! Until the day he met the Professor. It was a chance meeting in a book store. Jules Verne had just released his new book *From the Earth to the Moon*, and Dr. McD wanted to buy a copy. When Dr. McD saw the Professor pick up a copy too he said, "My colleagues laugh at the idea of traveling to the moon. They say it will never happen. What do you think?"

"According to Genesis 11:6, man was once capable of doing whatever he could imagine. He was stopped when his ability to understand other people was confounded. And according to Daniel 12:4 in the last days knowledge shall increase. So, according to the Bible, a time is coming when fantasies like Jules Verne's will be everyday realities."

"You don't say!" Dr. McD almost gasped. "Now you've aroused my curiosity! May I ask who you are, and are you a scientist?"

"Just call me Professor. And yes, physical science is my field, Dr. McD," the Professor smiled. "Yes, I know your name. I've followed your work at the University and heard you present a couple papers. Your work is most impressive."

"Thank you," said Dr. McD appreciatively. He was liking the Professor very much. He was obviously extremely intelligent, gentle spoken, and one with whom one could have fascinating discussions.

Dr. McD came home excited over finding a fellow dreamer of impossibilities. Soon the Professor was a regular guest in their home. Mrs. McD was something of a scientist, too. She had been a student of Dr. McD's and often worked alongside him in his research lab. She was interested in the things the Professor and Dr. McD talked about and often joined in their conversations. The McD's were never blessed with children. But their big hearts took in all the children of the town and there were quite a few families who were able to struggle by because of the McD's generosity. The Professor enjoyed helping this giving couple.

Time flew by fast. By the end of the century Dr. McD's great heart grew weak and he had only a few days to live. On his last visit the Professor asked to be alone with Dr. McD. When he left, Mrs. McD went into the bedroom. Dr. McD's eyes were glistening and a look of wonder was on his face. "Mrs. McD," he laughed, "I die a happy man. I've just learned that our dreams and visions of the future are already here! Now, go take care of the Professor. He's a bit older than he looks, and needs looking after. I'll see you up there." He pointed to heaven, and was gone.

The days that followed were hectic. There was a never-ending stream of people coming to visit. Both the McD's were popular and beloved in the community and on the University campus. Many felt they had lost a best friend. Finally, the visits began to taper off and Mrs. McD could get back to a normal life, as normal as it could be without Dr. McD. It was on one of these normal days that her life changed completely. It was a beautiful morning in May. Her yard was a feast of color and fragrance. There were yellow daffodils, white narcissus, and purple hyacinths standing tall.

As she stood admiring them, a cup of coffee in her hand, the Professor drove up, tied his horses to the rail, and walked up to the porch. She poured the Professor a cup of coffee, and they sat down together admiring the beauty of the flowers. Finally, the Professor broke the silence.

"Have you given any thought about what you are going to do now?"

"I kinda thought all along I'd stay here as long as I could take care of it. Maybe take in a student or two. I've no family."

"Mrs. McD, I have a proposition for you. I talked it over with Dr. McD before he died and he seemed to think you might be interested. I need a housekeeper. Would you consider being my housekeeper? Think about it and pray about it and let me know your answer."

As she thought about it and prayed about it, Mrs. McD came to believe that being the Professor's housekeeper was the right thing to do. She sent him a letter tentatively accepting his offer. Little did she dream of what being his housekeeper would mean!

In reply to her note the Professor wrote back: *Before we finalize this I must ask you some additional questions. Please meet me for dinner at the old Country Inn at 5:00 p.m. Monday.*

Mrs. McD had always been handy with horses. In no time she had them hitched to the buggy and drove out to the old Country Inn on the edge of town. The Professor was already there, having a good chat with some students. As she came in the door they looked up and waved hello, then excused themselves, and left the Professor alone to talk with her.

"Before we make this final, Mrs. McD, you need to know that I move around a lot. Would you be willing to move and live in a variety of locations?"

"Of course! True, I'd miss my friends, but it's easy for me to make new friends. But there's something I need to know about you."

Mrs. McD told the Professor about researching the legend of the Nine Unknown Men with a view of writing a mystery story. She explained how she analyzed the story and began to look for the evidence suggested by the story. And how her search turned serious when her detective instincts began to kick in as she began to uncover things that were more than coincidence, not the least of which was the Professor himself.

"All this sounds like a wild flight of my imagination, I know. But you've made it worse. Things you've said over the years, the fact that you haven't aged a day since we first met years ago. And those final words Dr. McD said to me, 'Mrs. McD,' he laughed, 'I die a happy man. I've just learned that our dreams and visions of the future are already here! Now, go take care of the Professor. He's a bit older than he looks, and needs looking after.' So tell me Professor, are you who I think you are?"

The Professor sits silently, studying Mrs. McD's face. Dr. McD was right. Detective instincts like hers would be desirable to have around.

"Professor," Mrs. McD takes a deep breath and plunges in. "I understand the gravity of the situation. The traitor needs the time machine to complete his plans. He searches for it. The eight have vowed to remain alive as long as the traitor lives. Your identity and your whereabouts must never be known. Being a doughty old housekeeper is a task I can easily handle. I can also help you remain invisible and shield you from prying eyes and ears. I can stall for time when you need to escape. I understand what's at stake and I want to help."

The Professor is silent, apparently lost in thought. Then he speaks.

"Dr. McD was right! You do have a detective's mind," the Professor chuckles. "Well, I hate to be the one to burst your bubble but the job I'm offering isn't as exciting as all that! In fact, it's rather dull. At least, I think housekeeping is dull. Occasionally I move if another location is more suitable for my research. Having a housekeeper who can move with me, and who knows my whims and needs would be a great boon. Do you want the job?"

Mrs. McD notes with satisfaction that the Professor did not deny her conclusions. He side-stepped them. "I'll take the job, Professor. You can count on me."

"Thank you, Mrs. McD. That's a load off my mind. Oh, and there is one more thing. Since we'll be working closely together I want you to drink this. It'll keep you healthy for a good long time."

Taking out a small marble bottle, the Professor removes the stopper and gives it to Mrs. McD. She drinks what appears to be and tastes like ordinary water. The Professor puts the empty bottle away. They work out the final details, eat their dinner, and leave. The next morning when Mrs. McD awakes she feels and looks twenty years younger, and life and energy flow through her body. And she knows the Professor has given her to drink of the elixir of life.

That was how it all began. And it seemed like only yesterday, not one hundred years ago. A knock on the door brings Mrs. McD's mind back to the present. Marybelle Hines has come for prayer. Glenn Clark's vacuum cleaner prayer soon has most of Marybelle's symptoms disappearing.

"Why, I feel like a new person," she says as she leaves. "Thank you ever so much. I never dreamed I was carrying around so much junk that needed to be vacuumed out! That is a terrific way to pray. I'm going to tell the other ladies about it."

Mrs. McD watches as Marybelle's car backs out of the driveway and heads down the street. As she watches, a black car drives up; the same car she had seen last spring at the Professor's. Quickly she phones her friend, the chief of police. "Hank those same men I told you about last spring have just pulled into my driveway. I'd really appreciate it if you'd come by just in case. There's a loaf of my fresh baked bread in it for you!"

"Now Mrs. McD, you know you don't have to bribe me! I'd like to get a look at these men myself. I'll be there in a couple minutes."

Mrs. McD has barely time to hang up the phone when there is a very loud banging on her door and a demand: "Open this door!"

"Goodness gracious! What's so important you nearly broke my door down?"

"Out of our way," says the leader of the three Men in Black, pushing his way past her. "We want the Professor. Where is he?" The other two men burst into the house behind him. One runs into the living room. Another runs down into the basement. She hears doors being opened and slammed shut. The first man stands there glaring at her, doing his best to try to dominate her with the force of his look.

"What on earth are you talking about? What gives you the right to come bursting into my home and go through all my rooms?" Mrs. McD demands, stamping her foot in obvious displeasure.

"Don't mess with us lady. We know he's here. We know he's got a time machine and we want to see him now!" The other two men come back, saying they can't find anyone. The three men, acting as one, do their very best to look very menacing and scary. They had come up against Mrs. McD once before. Then she had a shotgun in her hands. They made the mistake of thinking that without her shotgun she wouldn't be so brave. They were mistaken. She was not someone you tried to scare or dominate or bully around. That was just asking for trouble and she could dish it out!

"Gentlemen, gentlemen," she scolds, walking over to the stove to get the coffee pot. "I'll make a pot of coffee and we can sit down at the table like civilized people. Then you start from the beginning. What is this nonsense you're talking about? A time machine?"

Just then Hank arrives and knocks at the door.

"Well hi Hank! Come on in. What brings you out here? As if I needed to ask! You just can't pass up a loaf of my fresh baked bread, can you?"

"You got me, Mrs. McD! The boys knew this was baking day and they begged me to stop. Oh, I see you've got company."

"Well, I don't know if they're company or not, Hank. They just burst in here like mad men. They've run all over the house. They demanded to see the Professor, thought he was here. But the strangest thing is they think the Professor has a time machine!"

"A what?"

"A time machine. And they think it's here!"

"Gentlemen," says the police chief, unable to contain his laughter, "I don't know what you've been drinking. But you are way out of your reckoning if you think the Professor has a time machine! And keeps it here? In this house? That's the most ridiculous thing I've ever heard. The boys will get a great laugh over this one!"

The leader of the Men in Black is not accustomed to having people laugh at him. This outburst from the police chief is making him furious. He begins to seethe, and finally explodes saying, "You don't know who you're dealing with. We've got power you've never dreamed of. You may be the police chief of this podunk town, but you're no match for us. We don't take this kind of messing around from nobody. Our satellite intelligence has shown us that there is a time machine here. We can turn that same electronic surveillance on you and burn you to a crisp in a second. We have all the proof we need. The Professor is here and he has built a time machine. We know he is using it. We know it was here just a few minutes ago. And we are not going to leave until we get both the Professor and the time machine. So back off!" he almost shouts.

While the man was raving, Hank had pushed the call button on his shoulder radio and asked for back-up. These men were not going to leave just because he asked them politely. That was easy to see. He didn't know who they were, but they had over stayed their welcome.

"Tempers, tempers," scolded Mrs. McD. "Just like men. All swagger and talk and no one explaining what it's all about. You definitely need to sit down and start from the beginning. If we can make some sense out of all this, maybe we can help you."

The Men in Black are puzzled. The overpowering intimidation of their mere presence had always worked before. It had always gotten them any information they wanted. Local authorities always backed off when they started threatening. This police chief and Mrs. McD were not about to move. Maybe, they began to reason, Mrs. McD didn't know anything after all. Perhaps the time machine had stopped here for a short time and she didn't know it. She did appear naive enough not to know what was going on. It would make sense for the Professor to have a naive housekeeper.

Just then they hear sirens as two patrol cars pull up. This was not a time for any entanglement with law enforcement. The Men in Black quickly exit without a word, followed by Hank, who can't pass up the opportunity to have the last word, and he does. Just as they start to get in their car he shouts, "I'm warning you men to get out of town now and don't come back. We'll be watching for you. If you show up again I'm slapping you in jail!" With that, he slams their doors shut.

"Thanks, Hank," calls Mrs. McD from the doorway. "No telling what damage those men would have done to my house. I'm glad the

Professor wasn't here. They looked mean. I just don't know where people come up with their weird ideas nowadays. Well, they've gone and I think this was worth more than one loaf of bread. Call the men to come on in and we'll heat up the bread and coffee. I'll get out the jam and butter and we'll have a little feast"

Well, muses Mrs. McD to herself, *we got rid of them for now. And I'm pretty sure they think I'm just an old naïve housekeeper who has no idea what's going on. But they will be back. Things are starting to heat up. And one of these days the Deserter will come out into the open.*

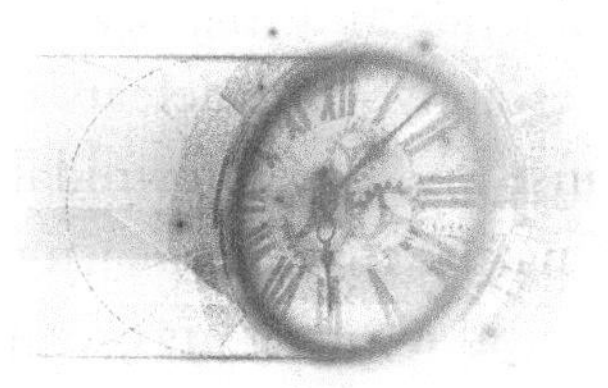

CHAPTER 21

The Would-Be God

Surrounding the Blue Orb are millions of glistening stars and planets. Coming from the stars and planets themselves are the most beautiful sounds and melodies blending into a vast symphony. Peter and the Professor drink in the beauty and the music.

"We're in the in-between place, aren't we?" Peter asks.

"Yes. I believe I'm to review some things with you. As you know, God called and anointed prophets to bring messages to His people. Sometimes it was a message of hope and deliverance. Sometimes it was a call to repentance. Sometimes it was to teach us about Satan, Satan's fall, and God's plan of redemption laid down before the foundation of the world. Do you remember when I pointed out that there is no room for the God of the Bible in most science fiction?"

"Yes. You said that science fiction stories are usually built around the idea of different races evolving from some primordial soup. Some races evolve in like manner as the human race. Others often develop in forms that are hostile to all human life, and often in forms we would consider grotesque. The stories are centered around the clashes of these races in battles of good versus evil. Almost always there are supernatural forces of good and evil that they tap into with the good always winning. There is no deity and no creator. The closest they come to it is to suggest a guiding force or destiny that is inherent in nature itself."

"Isn't it strange, Peter, that the writers of science fiction, in spinning their tales about the battle of good versus evil, always celebrate the resilience and majesty of the natural man? It is the natural man who rises above and defeats evil. In order to have their heroes rise to the cause and battle formidable odds he has them discover hidden powers in nature that they learn to master. Using these powers to help him, the natural man, in his own power, defeats the evil.

"That is the tragedy of science fiction. It is the mistaken belief that man, in and of himself, can and will rise above evil and conquer it. But man, according to Romans 6:16, by virtue of the Fall, has become the slave of evil. Evil cannot conquer evil. Ever since the Fall there have been men in every generation who embrace the science fiction idea that the God of the Bible does not exist. But even more tragic are those who know that the Creator God exists and yet hate Him because His nature is love. Like Satan, they believe He is a weakling. They believe they are more powerful than Him and can outsmart Him."

"Is that what happened to the traitorous member of your Order that you call 'the enemy'?"

"Yes. Last spring, when I lowered the secrecy curtain, he immediately suspected that you were traveling with me in the time machine. He was afraid we would alter history in a way contrary to his plans, and he didn't want that to happen. He does not suspect that it is God who is sending us on this journey."

"Man!" Peter groans. "It's like I'm being drawn into some sinister plot. Are the Men in Black looking for me around every corner?"

"Peter," the Professor chuckles, "slow down! Your task is to help people open their eyes, to see beyond traditional ways of thinking. People are missing out on so much God has for them because they have listened to too many lies about the natural man that have been taught as truth. Just as your mind is being stretched, you are to go and stretch their minds, that the eyes of their understanding will be opened."

"That I can handle!" Peter exclaims with relief. "It's this cloak and dagger stuff that was starting to get to me."

"Unfortunately, my wayward friend is gumming up the works! He has been making plans of his own that depend on getting control of the time machine. Our traveling in the time machine is very upsetting to him. He doesn't know where we are going, nor what we are doing. That makes him afraid."

The Professor pauses as though he is listening. "Yes, Lord, I'll do that." The Professor smiles at Peter. "Peter, do you remember when we watched the creation, the earth we saw then was totally unlike the earth we see today? Do you remember how that earth was suddenly immersed in darkness and the atmosphere changed from goodness to evil? It wasn't until the darkness of evil was removed and the earth was remade that Adam was created. Did you notice that the remade earth, Adam's earth, did not look like ours either?

"The earth God remade for Adam was an amazing piece of engineering. The earth itself was fashioned like an atomic engine. There was a thin crystalline firmament made of crystal clear metallic hydrogen suspended above the planet. It filtered out short-wave radiation, and acted as a radio receiver serenading the earth with the morning melodies of the stars and planets. This caused a mist to rise up from the ground to water the earth. The whole system was a self-sustaining system. It's all there in Genesis, in the literal definition of the words.

"That earth is not the earth we know today. That was the earth before sin spoiled it. That was the earth before the cataclysmic flooding when the metallic hydrogen firmament fell to earth as water, and before the internal upheavals that formed our present-day continents."

"Did you say that is all in Genesis? Are you sure you aren't indulging in science fiction, too?" Peter asks the Professor. "You taught us to question everything and demand proof. Boy, this needs proof if anything ever did!"

"The word firmament means to be beaten down into a thin layer. Some scholars believe the word actually means a crystalline metallic hydrogen. Scientists have been able to produce a crystalline metallic hydrogen that can exist in the metallic state above our atmosphere. Research has also discovered that at one-time oxygen levels were much higher than they are now. The breakdown of this canopy, combining with oxygen in the air, answers the question of where the water came from in the flood, how it could have covered the earth, and what happened to the oxygen level."

Peter is silent. These are new ideas. They will take some thinking about. The enchanting music of the stars fills the Orb. No words are spoken and yet he hears them singing the praises of God, rejoicing in His handiwork. Love and joy and delight seem to be everywhere.

"Peter." The Professor's voice breaks in on Peter's thoughts. "Peter, we need to review Lucifer's story. As you remember, God created him perfect. He was vested with every grace. He was full of beauty. He may have been the guardian of God's Glory. Paul suggests in Colossians 1:16 that he may have been created by Jesus. Lucifer was endowed with a beautiful voice. The sound of it was of liquid beauty that reached out and embraced the listeners. No one who heard it was left unmoved. Those qualities were given to him to equip him to lead worship in heaven. Lucifer was also given a kingdom and a throne befitting his status. It was located in a place called Eden on a planet we call earth."

"I know Lucifer's story, Professor. But what is hard for me to wrap my mind around is why he gave it all up to become Satan. He had everything. He was God's right-hand man. I think anything he wanted God would have given to him. So why rebel?"

"That's the thing, Peter. We can only guess from the little bits of information the Bible gives us. We think he fell in love with himself, and became dissatisfied with God. His power and authority went to his head. The more he watched God, the more he interpreted love in action as a sign of weakness. He began to sow seeds of dissent among the angels. About a third of the angels came over to his side. Lucifer, self-deceived and self-deluded by his position of importance, began to want to be God. Perhaps he even thought he could use words like God used words."

"Wasn't he acting like a little kid who thinks he can do the things his dad does? I remember getting in trouble because I thought I could drive my dad's tractor just as well as he could. I got the hay wagon hung up, and knocked out a door post. After dad got it unstuck and put in a new door post, he grounded me for a month!"

"It went a bit farther than that, Peter. You didn't try to get rid of your dad and take over the farm. Satan did. He thought that with the angels on his side, all he needed to do was speak the words of power and he would immediately put himself above God. We cannot say for sure, but we do know that it came to pass that Lucifer made that fateful decision and spoke what he thought would be undefeatable words of power: 'I will exalt my throne above the stars of God. I will ascend into heaven. I will sit also upon the mount of the congregation, in the side of the north. I will ascend above the clouds. I will be like the Most High' (Ezekiel 14:13-14).

"Satan may have been an archangel, the greatest of all the angels, but he was still only an angel. Lucifer was undaunted. In his pride, he still believed his might was greater than God's. Marshalling all the great forces at his command, Lucifer assaulted God's throne, only to discover that God was not weak. Lucifer did not have the power to do what he thought he could do. Instead he lost everything—his position, his kingdom, and the angels who rebelled with him who were put in prison (Jude 6). He became the accuser of the brethren. He did not admit defeat. A battle was lost but the war wasn't over. He still believes he can defeat God. Evil and hatred have become his nature. He is, as Peter wrote, lurking around like a roaring lion seeking whom he may devour (1 Peter 5:8)."

The ruby lever begins to flash. It is time to continue their journey to the beginning of time. The Professor gives the lever a gentle push. They hear the familiar *WOOSH* and suddenly they are there.

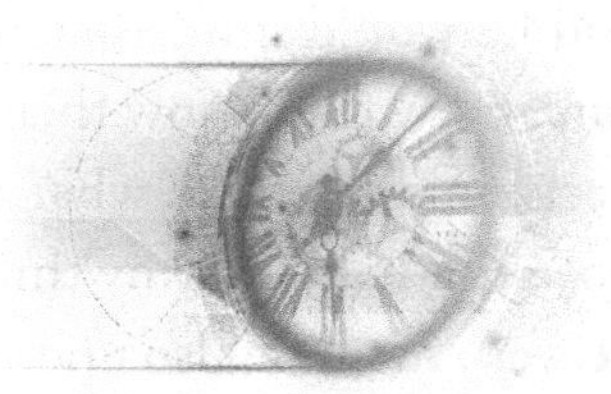

CHAPTER 22

The Calm Before the Storm

The memory of what Peter saw the first time comes flooding back to him. They seem to have come back to the moment when God breathed life into the man. Again Peter is caught up in the wonder of what has just happened. So great and joyous and love-filled is that moment that the joy and laughter and music of the heavens cannot be contained. God has created a being like unto Himself. A being that is a little less than God and greater than the angels, whom he is destined one day to judge (1 Corinthians 6:3). Man came into being born of Love and Joy and Laughter and Power and Wonder. In him was the Mind of God, the Heart of God and the Wisdom of God. For he was the image and likeness of God.

The Father Light and the Son Light and the Flame all stand back and look at the man light. God speaks, "IT IS VERY GOOD!" Then God looks on the man he has made and names him Adam. God blesses Adam, and says to him, "I have made you to be just like me. When I look at you I see Myself. You have My personality, My intelligence, My mind. I have put into you the creative power of words that I used to create all things. But remember, you are not Me. I am the Creator. You are the Creature.

"Look about you. This is the Garden of Delight. I made it all for you! This Garden is for your pleasure, a place to enjoy. It is yours. I have crowned you with glory and honor. You are its King. Rule wisely. Utilize it to its fullest. Develop all its resources to their fullest potential. Come now, and let us together create animals to fill the earth."

As Peter watches, he is amazed at what he sees. Something he had learned from his Bible study flashes into his mind. In Hebrew, the name of a person or thing defines its nature. Jacob meant 'cheat', and he turned out to be quite a cheater. But later his name was changed to Israel because his nature got changed when he wrestled with God.

The Father Light takes one of the formless lumps of clay that had come into being as the Son sang. He gently molds it as Adam speaks. "I want an animal that is regal and proud, a leader, who can be both fierce and gentle as need requires. His voice will shake the trees when he roars. Around his head he will wear a crown of golden hair. I name him LION."

As Adam speaks, the clay in God's hands becomes a mighty lion. No sooner does his body take its final shape and a golden mane surround his head, then he lets out a mighty roar that shakes even the Blue Orb. The lion turns to Adam and, in his lion voice asks, "Ah, that felt good! How may I serve you Sir?" The Man Light and the Father Light laugh, and Adam speaks, "Lion, that was a mighty roar! I have made you King of all the beasts. You shall help me rule and govern all the animals. Sit here, beside me."

As Peter watches, the Father Light forms a lump of clay into the shape Adam describes and it becomes what Adam names it. Laughing, the Father Light brings a great big lump of clay to the Man Light. "What shall this big lump become, Adam?"

"I know! It shall be a big HIPPOPOTAMUS!"

The hippopotamus begins to move - *ga-lumph, galumph.* In a very deep voice he speaks: "Sir, do you think it might be alright, if I ahh, if I ahh, step into the river? It looks ever so nice."

"Yes, you may go, hippopotamus, and play in the water to your heart's content."

"Oh, thank you sir." Turning towards the river he lumbers off – *ga-lumph, ga-lumph, ker-splash.*

The Father Light, chuckling to Himself, brings Adam another lump of clay. This time it seems to have a very, very long neck. "Why, all the better to eat the leaves of the trees," exclaims Adam. "This I name GIRAFFE, leaf eater."

The giraffe shakes itself, looks around and immediately says, "Excuse me, but those leaves look very delicious."

Turning to the Father Light, the man light says, "Sir, let me describe one first, and then You form the lump of clay. I would like an animal that would take delight in jumping and playing with me. I would like a DOG!"

"A dog it shall be," answers the Father Light as the lump of clay in His hands suddenly comes to life and jumps down. That formless lump of clay becomes all that a dog is, jumping and barking and laughing and licking Adam's face. Suddenly the dog notices its tail. "There's someone behind me," he barks. "I'm gonna catch him!" Barking for all it is worth, the dog chases its tail. The Father Light and the man Light laugh and laugh, until finally the man Light says, "Dog. There's nobody behind you. You're chasing your own tail!"

"Grrrr, ruff. I knew that," says the dog, panting, and trying to hide its embarrassment.

God and Adam together create all the animals as Peter watches. It soon becomes a gigantic menagerie of animals talking and animals laughing in their animal voices and God and the Son and the Flame and man joining in the laughter. With the help of the lion and the dog, they shoo the animals off to play elsewhere in the Garden.

"Adam, you're going to need a little more help taking care of the animals. I'm going to create another animal to help you. He will be wiser than the rest. Because of his importance I will adorn him with a coat of colors adorned with living jewels."

So saying, God creates the serpent. It is a beautiful creature. Its attractive face, almost human in shape, as one might imagine a merman's face, seemed to glow with great wisdom. Using its tail to balance itself on its short legs, it stood a little shorter than the man. Its arms and hands, while shorter than a man's, seemed almost human.

The work of creating done, the God Light and Son Light and Spirit Flame and man Light are left alone. The God Light reaches out and in His hand is a scroll. The man Light takes the scroll and unrolls it. It is a legal document, a lease. This startles Peter. But then he remembers that in the writings of Isaiah and Paul and John, and in Jesus' own words, there are references that suggest the existence of such a legal document. Peter senses that this is an extremely important moment. Suddenly he catches a movement out of the corner of his eye. He turns and looks. What appears to be a man shape, but without the glow, is creeping up to where it can hear what God is about to tell the man. Peter senses that this is Satan himself. Whatever he is up to, Peter senses at once, it will not be good.

"Adam!" God's voice is very serious. "This document is a lease. A lease is a legal document that transfers a piece of property or an object to another person for that person's use for a stated period of time. The lease spells out in detail what can and cannot be done to, or with, the property. It explains the rights, privileges, liabilities and responsibilities of the lessee and lessor. Lastly, it states the duration of the lease, at which time the property is returned to its owner.

"With this document, I give the earth totally and absolutely to you. I give to you, and all your vast family that shall come from you, complete and absolute control and ruler-ship of the earth. You are to develop the earth and utilize all its vast resources to their fullest potential. Do all you do in love. The earth is yours to love. The plants and animals are yours to care for lovingly. (Genesis 1:28-31)

"Adam, while this lease is in effect, I will not and cannot interfere with or violate the ownership and rulership right I have given to you. I will act only when and if you ask Me. The duration of this lease is six thousand years. (Psalm 90:4; 2 Peter 3:8) Remember, too, even though you have the lease, I own the earth." (Exodus 9:29; Psalm 24:1; 1 Corinthians 10:26-28)

Peter keeps his eyes focused on the God Light as he asks, "Professor, remember how John said we are to test the spirits to see if they are of God? (1 John 4:1) I want to believe what I am seeing and hearing. How can we be sure this is of God?"

"When we get back we'll dig into the scriptures," the Professor whispers back. "Many times the truths we are seeking are scattered throughout the scriptures. When we search them out and put them side by side, we begin to see the whole story. But even then, not everyone will believe. But listen," he whispers as they turn their eyes back to the scene and hear God say,

"Adam, there is one thing more about which I must caution you. In the midst of this Garden of Delight are two very special trees. One is the Tree of Life; the other is the Tree of the Knowledge of Good and Evil. All the fruit of the trees in the Garden are for you to enjoy. But don't eat the fruit of the Tree of the Knowledge of Good and Evil. If you eat it, that very day, you will die. In time I will talk to you about the tree and why it is here.

"And now, Adam, you need a helper who is just right for you. The lion will help you look after the animals. The serpent will be a good advisor. But you still need someone like yourself, to stand by your side, and help you rule and govern my creation. Did you see any animal that would be suitable?"

"None, Sir. There was none suitable."

Peter can't see into the light, but he suspects God has a twinkle in his eye as He says, "Adam, you need a helper who is just like you, bone of your bone and flesh of your flesh. So I'm going to put you to sleep. When you wake up I will have a surprise for you!"

As Peter watches, God causes a deep sleep to come over Adam. From Adam's side He removes what looks almost like a duplicate of Adam. He molds it into the shape of a woman. Then He breathes into her nostrils and the woman shape begins to glow with the same brilliant light as Adam.

"Adam! Adam!" God calls. Adam awakes. He looks at the help God has made for him. While Peter can't see, it is easy to imagine Adam's mouth dropping open in surprise, for he hears an exclamation that sounds like, "Wow! She is so beautiful. Yes, God, this is a perfect helpmeet for me. Together it will be a pleasure to look after the earth and plants and animals."

"Be fruitful, multiply, and fill the earth," says the Lord God, who looks upon all He has created and pronounces it Good.

There is a great love between the man and the woman. There is a great love between the man and the woman and God. There is a great love between the man and woman and the animals romp and play around them in great joy. Soon Adam and the lion walk off together, sorting the animals out, and helping them pick their homes in the Garden. The leopard brushes up against Eve and she strokes his soft fur. The sounds of their talking and laughing drift into the Orb as they take pleasure in each other.

While Peter and the Professor are watching there is a sudden gentle lurch of the Blue Orb. It's as though some great period of time has suddenly passed. The scene changes dramatically. The Garden is now different. Stones of different colors have been beautifully shaped and sculptured into walls, garden paths, and fountains. Flowers of outstanding beauty line the paths. Orchards of every kind of fruit imaginable stretch as far as the eye can see. The fragrance of their delicious fruit seeps into the Blue Orb. A house of brilliant white marble, accented with colored pillars and window arches trimmed in gold, with open windows and doors and a spacious patio festooned with beautiful plants is set in a prominent corner of the Garden. It is a breathtakingly beautiful scene. The land has indeed flourished under Adam and Eve's care.

Movement catches Peter's eye. A lion and a lamb are playing together on the grass. He can't help but laugh as the lion tosses the lamb up into the air and then gently catches it in its paws. Other animals come into view. They do not act at all like wild animals or tame animals. They seem to treat each other as equals. He's sure they are talking to each other.

The man Light and woman Light come into view. The animals gather around them, and the littlest ones jump up and down for joy. At least that is how it looks. The lion gives a gentle roar and the animals part. The man Light turns left and walks towards a large building Peter had not noticed. The words "highly advanced scientific laboratory" pop into his mind.

The woman Light turns to the right and walks over to the house. She sits on a wicker chair, and beckons the animals to come to her. An animal Peter hadn't noticed before joins her, standing on her right. It stands upright on its hind legs, its skin beautifully colored as though covered in jewels. It is the serpent.

"It's time to go home, Peter." The Professor's voice interrupts Peter's thoughts. "The ruby lever is flashing." He reaches out and gently pushes it.

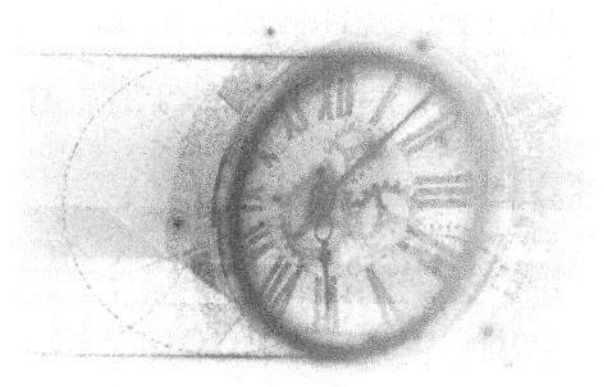

Chapter 23

Tricking the Trickster

Once again they are back in the in-between place. There is so much to think about. So many new ideas to digest. Peter promises himself he will write a detailed account of the whole experience as soon as he gets back. He wonders when and where that will be. The first time it seemed like no time at all had passed, even though he was sure they had been away for many hours.

"Peter," the Professor again interrupts Peter's thoughts. "We can't return to Mrs. McD's or to my house. Our enemy is watching both houses, ready to pounce on us. We need to draw him away from both houses so that it will be safe for us to return. We'll need to materialize somewhere far away."

Peter's nerves begin to tense with fear of the unknown dangers they are about to face. He anxiously observes, "Professor, we didn't bring any clothes or provisions with us. If we land in another country, we will have to buy them. Do you have enough money? And what about passports? How will we get back home?"

"The other members of my Order will help us do that. My main concern right now is our enemy's mind control technology. He will try to use it on you if he gets a chance. He mistakenly considers you to be weak-minded, an easy mark. He does not believe in physical violence. Instead, he uses a helmet that emits highly intensified thought waves that can pierce your mind. He can ask questions, 'hear' your answers, and tell you to do things. It is impossible to resist him, unless you know how. He believes he can force you to tell him where the time machine is, and how to operate it. That's why the Men in Black were looking for you."

"Professor, there's one thing you've taught me. God doesn't put us in hopeless situations. He makes a way where there seems to be no way." (Psalm 37:23; Proverbs 1:33; Proverbs 3:6) If the enemy uses his mind probe on me, God will provide a way for me to shield my mind."

"God does provide, Peter. That's why we need to get quiet now, and ask him to guide us." The Professor sits back quietly, closing his eyes. A few moments later, a smile crosses his face. He studies the instrument panel. He reaches out, gently moves several controls, and looks up chuckling.

"Our enemy thinks he knows how I think. We can't materialize in public. We'll have to materialize in the secret lab of one of my Order. He expects me to create a diversion, to draw his men away from that location, so that we can land safely, and then sneak back home. While the Eight of us keep our identities secret, he has used his surveillance technology and his spies to pinpoint where each of us lives. He will have Watchers at each of those locations, all equipped with instruments to identify the presence of a time machine.

"Only one location is ideal for disappearing. That's the mountain lodge of my friend in New Zealand. My friend has a beautiful hunting and vacation lodge hidden from view at the opening to a valley with steep hills and thick woods. It's an ideal place to get lost in the woods and not be found. Our enemy will send his best men to the lodge to wait for us. That is where we will land. But we're not going to do it the way he expects! We are going to create a diversion that will force him to keep his men searching in all of the locations! I've set the time machine to land in each of the other locations, too - all at exactly the same time!"

"How can you do that, Professor? It takes time to appear and disappear."

"How? This is a time machine! A time machine can do that. Plus, I've added a new location he doesn't expect - a château in southern Italy. He's never suspected the chateau so no one will be watching it! That's exactly what he would do; pick an unknown place and have everything he needs there. He'll immediately dispatch his top men to the chateau and that will leave fewer men to search for us. What he doesn't know is that a member of my Order owns the chateau. All the Men in Black will find is vacationers! And a staff that is very unfriendly to Men in Black!"

"You enjoy being sneaky, don't you, Professor? I'd sure hate to have you for an enemy."

"I do enjoy taunting our traitorous enemy because he has such an exalted opinion of himself. There's more yet. Mrs. McD and I, with TPF's help, have cooked up a little something else. After the Blue Orb showed up, the traitor stopped watching TPF and concentrated on watching us. So TPF began testing again. When the other members of our Order dialed the code on the cell phones he'd sent them, the tesseract machine successfully latched onto the signals. When we land, they are going to start activating the cell phones to make it look like we are tesseracting back and forth from one location to another! That, and the new location in Italy, will cause our enemy to spread his men out even more. We can't actually tesseract because it hasn't been tested for safety. But our enemy doesn't know that.

"My mountain friend's lodge, where we are going to land, is much more than a vacation spot. There are secrets about that place that our enemy knows nothing about. Even though he expects us to land there, and even though he will be there himself to supervise the hunt, we will easily escape from him."

Peter is not sure he likes the idea. When the Professor says something is easy that usually means it is anything but easy!

"Good!" the Professor grins as he finishes setting the controls. "Now that that is settled, we shouldn't have any trouble getting back home safely. All we'll have to do then is create an airtight alibi for why we were gone. No one will be left to bother Mrs. McD or watch my house. My friend, where we land, will be well looked after by the local police. The Blue Orb will leave as soon as we step out of it. We'll have plenty of time to get away before the Men in Black know what's happened! Pretty sneaky, eh! Don't worry about clothes or mountain climbing gear. My friend will have everything prepared thanks to Mrs. McD. She'd already set this up before we got there this morning!"

Mountain climbing gear? What's the Professor talking about, Peter wonders as once again there is the *whoosh*ing sound as of a cylinder being sucked through a tube. The sides of the Orb turn an opaque blue. There is a slight jar as the Orb lands. An opening appears in the side of the Orb. The Professor steps out and motions for Peter to follow. As soon as they step out, the Orb begins to fade in and out as it did when it first arrived at Mrs. McD's. Then, suddenly, it vanishes completely.

Peter, looking around to see where they are, gazes in wonder. They are in an underground laboratory just as amazing as the Professor's and TPF's, except this one is equipped for chemistry. There are the usual test tubes and beakers and flasks of a chemist, and instruments and banks of computers and a whole lot more Peter doesn't recognize. A man, who appears to be both very old and yet very young, with a crop of red curly hair, is sitting in an easy chair, a book in his lap, a pipe in his hand. He seems not at all surprised to see them.

"Hello, old friend," he smiles with a wave of his pipe, his voice deep and rich. "I've been expecting you. Mrs. McD passed the word that you might stop here to throw our enemy off your trail. He's so overconfident and so obsessed to get his hands on your time machine that he doesn't try to act in secret anymore. He's getting careless," he adds with a chuckle.

Turning to look at Peter with a big smile of approval, the Mountain Friend continues. "Hello Peter! So you are the chosen one. Welcome to my lab, and to my home. You've got to come and be my guest sometime. You'll love it here. But quickly, we must get you off into the woods and secure the lab before anyone comes. No time to sit and chat, I fear.

"Word has come to me from town that he's moved in a small force of specialists. The first ones to come have been acting like a bunch of bullies. Not a smart move on their part! The sheriff stuck them in jail for a couple days! Nothing he could keep them locked up for, though, or they'd all be sitting jail right now."

Peter is surprised to see mountaineering gear laid out on a table. Following instructions, he changes into the camouflage clothing and hiking boots. There is a backpack on the table for each of them. Peter swings his pack over his shoulders and the Professor adjusts the straps for him. A multifunction tool, rope, and several SL-CDs—spring-loaded-camming-devices—are strung on a utility belt. The Professor explains these are to help them scale the rock cliffs. Peter, whose only contact with mountains has been via pictures, is becoming a little alarmed at this new twist this day has taken. Mountain climbing?

"All your special gear is packed, Professor," the mountain friend explains as crosses to the table and picks each one up. "I checked everything out and all is working fine. Don't worry about your clothes. I'll send them up to the cabin in a few days after our enemy leaves the area. You'll not want to leave before he does, anyway. There is no question but that our enemy himself will be here. It will be easier to escape and disappear from here, than from the homes of any of the other Eight. He is going to be so frustrated when he can't find a trace of you, and you'll be right out in the open under his nose all the time!" he chuckles.

"Our enemy thinks he is so smart but he is so easily fooled. He suspects I'm either a member of our Order or good friends with one, since I absolutely refused to let him come here once. I've been able to keep him confused, even though he's had a man watching the lodge for some time. This little event may remove all his doubts. But I don't think that matters anymore. I've a feeling everything is drawing to an end now, don't you? Are you ready? Let's go."

He hurries them out the door and down a long passage. Behind them, they hear the sounds of heavy stone sliding on stone. As they move forward, the strange glow lighting the tunnel dims and goes out behind them. After what seems like many twists and turns, the tunnel begins to rise. They come to a massive stone wall. To the right is a control panel with a security monitor. The Professor's friend directs the security cameras to inspect the inside of the lodge and to sweep the grounds. Seeing no one, he places his hand on the stone wall. The wall glows under his hand, and a retina scanner suddenly appears. A voice speaks, "Eye scan recognized. Please speak." Their host answers, "Please open." The voice responds, "Voice recognized, please enter."

A massive stone wall turns, revealing the back of a large fireplace. Stepping through, they find themselves inside the magnificent great hall of a mountain lodge. It is built entirely of logs. The logs are shaved smooth and fit tightly together. The furniture is carved from logs and cross sections of large trees, polished smooth. There is no time to see more. The mountain friend leads the way to the back door and ushers them out onto a worn path.

"Quickly," he half whispers, his voice urgent. "You need to get to the stream and the cover of the trees before they get here. Keep low and hidden. I've put a GPS marker in your bags. Do not use it unless you are in trouble. About a half mile to the west, just inside the woods on your left, is a small stream. Hike up the stream for a couple miles and no dogs will be able to pick up a scent to follow.

"The path from here to the stream is smooth and full of the scents of many people. My staff goes back and forth all the time to a vegetable cellar we built in the middle of the stream. The water keeps the cellar at a constant temperature all year long. Step into the stream right at the entrance to the cellar. The dogs won't be able to pick out your scent from all the others. Beware of echoes. Keep your voices very low. Notice how we can hear cars going around the hairpin turns on the climb up to the lodge? They are still about twenty minutes away. The echoes make it easier for the dogs to pick up any sounds you make if they are near you.

"Now, quickly. There's no time to delay. The enemy will bring a chopper. Their high tech scanners can pick up the slightest movement, body heat, shapes, even heart beats. Fortunately, the stream has stone outcroppings for the first couple miles along the way, with a lot of natural lead in them. It pollutes the water so don't drink any water until you get past the outcroppings. Meanwhile, the lead will shield you from their scanners overhead. Stay under them as much as you can. If their choppers are in stealth mode, you won't be able to hear them until they are on top of you. Wear your ponchos once you get under cover where you can put them on. Don't put them on now. They will slow you down. You need to run while you are on the path. Good luck and God Bless. Go!"

As though the mountain friend's voice had been a starting pistol they race towards the stream. The first quarter mile is easy. But before the end of the second quarter Peter begins to feel a pain in his side. By the time they reach the mountain stream he can't run another step.

"Whoa, Professor!" he pants. "Running with a loaded back pack . . . is not like running the half mile . . . in track and field . . . I've got to catch my breath . . . I feel like I've been running . . . for hours!"

Just as he finishes talking they hear the sound of the Men in Black's cars and brakes reverberating off the walls of the canyon. Peter suddenly discovers he has more energy than he thought! They quickly step into the water and head upstream. The going is slower because they have to be careful where they step. Fortunately, the mountain shoes keep their feet dry and give good traction.

Even so, Peter almost falls several times. Meanwhile, the Professor steps along as though he had been doing this all his life. About a half mile upstream they come to the beginning of the overhanging rocks. They pause for a minute to listen. There is no sound of any movement on the path from the lodge. The Professor assures Peter that his friend will be alright.

"He's a good friend of the local police. They like to stay at his lodge and go hunting. So whenever it looks like there may be trouble my friend sends a signal and the police come roaring up. The police have been watching the Men in Black closely. They won't get to start looking for us immediately. Our friend will see to that.

"About a half mile east of the lodge, just off one of the hairpin turns on the main road, there is a little hiking trail that breaks off from the road. The Men in Black won't be allowed to take their dogs through the lodge. Dogs aren't allowed in the valley. They will have to hike up that trail with their dogs before they can use them to follow us. That will give us more needed time. It's their use of choppers that has me more concerned. We need to get under cover of those outcroppings quickly.

"Our enemy expects us to do what he would do. He knows about the lead in the rocks. He would hide the time machine in an underground cave. Then he'd hike along the valley floor, hiding among the trees and boulders, and climb out of the valley at the far end. But that's not what we're going to do. We know a secret he doesn't know. We're going to leave the valley floor shortly and climb way up there, on the left, to the top of the rock cliff."

Peter glances up at the sheer rock wall that ascends up several hundred feet above the shale and tree line. He can't believe the Professor actually expects to climb up that rock face. As hard as he looks he cannot see any ladder or any steps up the face of the cliff. Only a spider could climb that! There's no time to stop and ask the Professor if he has plans to turn them into spiders!

"Sending the Blue Orb to the chateau in Italy was an unexpected twist and will sow a lot of doubt in his mind," the Professor adds. "He'll send some of his best men to check it out. But still he will favor this spot and will oversee the search."

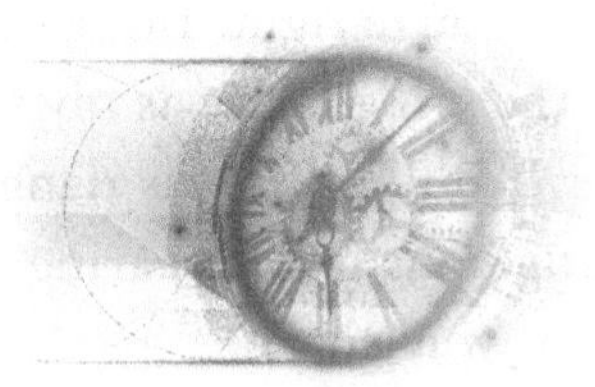

CHAPTER 24

Hiding in the Open

The Professor sets a fast pace as he leads the way upstream, stepping carefully from stone to stone. About a mile upstream they come to an outcropping. Over the years the water has undercut the bank, creating what looks like a veranda. It is high enough to stand upright underneath. Along the back is a ledge just the right height for sitting down. It's almost like Mother Nature wanted to provide all the comforts of home to the weary hiker. And they are weary; at least Peter is. They stop to rest a few moments, slipping off their backpacks, thankful for the protection the lead-laced stone gives them. For Peter, the athlete, it is more a collapse than a rest! He stares at the Professor who looks and acts as though he's just getting ready to start, instead of resting after a grueling run and hike.

The Professor puts his pack on the ledge. He removes a close-woven net-like camouflage colored poncho from his pack. He slips his backpack back on, adjusts his utility belt, and then slips the net-like poncho over his head. He looks up, smiles, and whispers softly, "You've got a poncho just like this in your pack. Put it on."

Peter opens his backpack and removes his poncho. He puts his backpack back on and adjusts his utility belt. The poncho feels like it is made of the same fabric as the secrecy curtain back at the Professor's home. He slips it on and then asks, "If their surveillance is as good as you say it is, there is no way these flimsy ponchos can help us hide"

"You're right. But these are not ordinary ponchos. These are made of the same fabric as my secrecy curtain."

"You said it was dangerous to touch the fabric. Isn't it even more dangerous to be wearing it when the power is turned on?" Peter asks, a bit worried.

"The threads of this fabric are insulated. That's why it's safe to touch them. They're woven together, positive to one side and negative to the other. In that little slit on the side where you can insert your hand is a plug receptacle. There is a battery pack on your utility belt with a short cable attached. Plug that end into the plug receptacle in your poncho. Turn the switch on. Surveillance systems are designed to pick up body heat. They are so sensitive that they give an exact outline of the animal or person. These ponchos disguise our body heat so that the sensors do not see us.

"The ponchos won't fool the dogs. We'll use skunk odor to do that. It's not a nice smell, but dogs won't chase a skunk. The strong odor will dull their sense of smell for a few minutes. And it will cover up any scent we leave behind. Keep the wind to your back, and the scent won't bother you as much.

"The biggest problem will be concealing our movements. Even though our body heat is hidden, their hand held scanners are also designed to pick up movement. Fortunately for us they have to be nearby first. We're not going to let them get nearby. We have plenty of time to hide and we want to stay hidden as much as we can. We'll have to stay perfectly still if a chopper comes along, or a foot patrol comes along using a scanner. I've got a few tricks that may fool them, so hopefully we're pretty safe. We've still got a long way to go before night. A couple miles farther and we will leave the stream bed and start climbing. All set? Off we go."

They step out from the safety of the outcropping back into the stream. The Professor douses the area with skunk odor. Then he turns to Peter who is getting a good look at the valley for the first time.

"About fifteen miles ahead of us to the north, the sides of the rock cliffs come together and enclose the valley like a box canyon. The only way out of the valley at that end is to climb a primitive stairway that has been chiseled into the rock. This stream originates up in the hills at the far end. It cascades down the steep wall of rock in small cataracts. It follows a natural groove in the rock that funnels the stream down to the west side. On its way to where we are it stops to make a pool here and a mini lake there. We're at the point where the stream bed begins its slow climb to the north. It's also the point at which the lead in the rock ends. So we will no longer have that protection."

The frequent outcroppings over the stream give good overhead cover as they hike. In places it's like walking in a tunnel whose side had collapsed when some gigantic flood ripped through the valley, washing away the earth. They hurry in silence, listening for any telltale signs that they are being followed. Several times they hear a faint humming, and the Professor pulls Peter under the outcroppings to wait. In the distance they hear the echo of dogs barking. Peter's heart races.

"The dogs are a long way back," the Professor speaks softly. "From the sound of their barking, they have not been able to find our trail. Good! That gives us more time. Dogs need a scent to follow. Even though they may have found something back at my home to give them a scent, it does no good if they can't pick up that scent anywhere. We left none. They are running in circles."

The stream bed becomes increasingly hard to follow. Several times Peter slips on the unstable stones and almost falls. The bank on each side of the stream begins to rise higher. The sun starts to go down. When they've gone as far as they can, they climb the bank and leave the stream. For good measure the Professor empties the can of skunk odor to cover their tracks. Finding shelter under some brush, they sit and rest.

"The sun will set soon," the Professor speaks in a low voice. "We need to climb up there, and take shelter in the shrubs," he adds, pointing to some thick growing brush, a thousand or more feet up on the slope. "Be careful of the shale. A little falling will erase our tracks. A lot might draw attention to us. We'll eat when we get up there. Our enemy will have someone stationed up at the end of the valley, watching for us. That's where he'll look, but that's not where we're going! We're going up there," he adds, pointing to the high cliff face above the shale.

Peter can see no possible way to scale the steep cliff. But scale it is what the Professor said they were going to do! "Sure, you're going to turn us into spiders," Peter whispers. The Professor does not answer. The climb up to the brush is difficult and takes far longer than Peter had anticipated. If it weren't for the gnarly bushes digging their roots into every crack and clinging stubbornly to the hill, they never would have made it. His hands would be bruised and bloody if it weren't for the gloves he wore to protect his hands and leave no human sent.

The bushes are a strange variety Peter had never seen before. Some of them have thorn branches that arch out over the ground, forming a canopy like a tent where one could crawl under and not be seen if he could avoid the sharp thorns. Little animals would find it a great protection from bigger predators.

They slowly inch their way upward. The sun goes down behind the hills, and still they climb. There is no moonlight. The darkness makes the climb difficult. Each step is followed by listening for any sign of dogs, or men. A step meant finding a foothold that didn't send a lot of shale cascading down, and then, pulling on the brush, hoisting yourself up a couple more feet, finding a new foot hold and hoisting yourself up another couple feet.

CHAPTER 25

Saved by The Animals

After what seems like hours the steep slope levels off a little. There, close to half a mile up from the creek bed, the Professor halts. In front of them is an especially dense thorn bush that rises up like a tree, with its thorny branches arching out like an umbrella. They crawl underneath, carefully avoiding the thorns. Even though there is no moonlight, the Professor is extremely cautious.

"We can't count on the darkness hiding us. Their search lights are very strong and their scanners can penetrate the darkness. The slightest little thing will give us away. Body heat, movement, sounds. Sounds especially. That's good because we'll hear them coming. It's bad because they can also hear us! We'll anchor ourselves next to the trunk of this bush so that we don't move or send any shale sliding down. The bush is fairly dense above us. That will help shield us from above. Nevertheless, we are exposed to heat sensors, and their extremely powerful search lights can penetrate this bush. We'll make a tent of our ponchos to shield us."

Peter removes his poncho, unplugging it from the battery pack. The poncho has a non-metallic zipper running diagonally from the hood to the hem. The Professor unzips each poncho and then zips the two ponchos together. They make a small two-man tent. Speaking softly, the Professor explains, "When we fasten them together and turn the power on they become a secrecy tent. It will hide our body heat and shield us from all prying eyes, radar, search lights, and whatever else they use. We'll be invisible so long as we don't move or make a sound. But we won't be invisible to the dogs if they come sniffing around. That is our biggest danger. So to fool the dogs if they bring them, we'll pull the poncho tight to the ground all the way around us. The ponchos emit a chlorine-like odor of static electricity. As long as that is all the dogs smell, they will ignore us, provided we breathe softly and don't make noise.

"Most people would have put their dogs back in the kennel by now. But sometimes our enemy gets hung up on an idea and won't let it go. He's done that with dogs before. It never did any good, but he doesn't always trust people. He knows he can trust the dogs. We are too far above the trail for them to catch our scent even without the secrecy shield. Nevertheless, these dogs are trained to spread out and hunt down anything within a mile of their trainer. If they bring the dogs, hopefully, the steep hill and loose shale will keep the dogs from coming up to sniff us out.

"Our enemy will not give up easily. Tonight will be very dangerous. He'll estimate how far he thinks we can go on foot. Then he'll send his men out to search the sides of the valley and the valley floor. He knows we won't travel at night when we can't see and don't dare use a light. He thinks that is to his advantage. He thinks we will be sitting ducks if we came this way.

"Now, let's eat. There is food in your knapsack. Eat only as much as you need. We don't know how many days it will have to last. It won't be like one of Mrs. McD's meals. This food will be almost odorless and tasteless so that dogs can't pick up its scent. But once you start to eat it, it tastes pretty good. It will give you all the strength you need. In fact, the longer we eat only this food, you'll find that very little of it will keep you going strong for a full day."

Peter eats in silence, thinking back over this strange day. His nerves are tense. His ears strain for the slightest sound: a twig breaking, a stone sliding. *How could this possibly be happening to me?* he wonders. *I woke up this morning to go to a physics class, and now I'm in a strange country, holed up under thorn bushes on the side of a steep slope in the dark, hiding from who knows what danger!*

"We'll take turns keeping watch," the Professor whispers. "I'll keep the first watch while you sleep. Don't talk out loud. Don't break a twig. Don't move any more than you must. Sounds carry a long way in this valley."

Sleep? How could he possibly sleep? He lays his head on his backpack. The next thing he knows, the Professor is gently shaking him to wake up and take his turn. He sits up, takes a last sip of cold black coffee, and waits. The sounds of the night fill the air. Out of curiosity he tries to identify as many as he can. There are crickets chirping. In the distance he hears a night owl. All around is the scampering of the little creatures that come out at night.

One little animal, out for a stroll, stops behind their bush. Peter can barely see it through the secrecy mesh of the poncho. *I bet I know what you're thinking*, he almost speaks. *What is this strange thing? There is something in there. It feels harmless. I wonder what it is?*

Suddenly the night birds are quiet! The little creatures stop scampering. The little animal behind their bush freezes in its tracks. Peter's heart skips a beat, and then lodges in his throat. In the distance he hears faint voices.

"Sarge, if they came this way I don't know how they escaped us. We've not seen hide nor hair of them, nor any sign that they are in this valley. Nothing along here looks disturbed like it would if someone had walked this way."

"I agree Corporal, but we have to keep looking until we've gone as far as he said to go. Keep scanning the sides as far as the beam will reach. This is a long range scanner and they just might be hiding within its reach."

Peter nudges the Professor, with his finger over the Professor's lips to keep him from speaking. He checks the edge of the poncho to be sure it is snug to the ground. The faint crunching sounds of someone coming in the distance booms in their ears. They barely breathe. Looking through the fine mesh of the poncho Peter can make out the faint red glow of the scanning beam as it sweeps along the hill side. It reaches their clump of brush and stops.

"Sarge, I think I've got something. See, there's something hidden in that clump of brush way up there."

"Hold the light on it Corporal," the Sergeant calls out as he starts to scale the steep slope. "I'll have a look."

Fear, panic, adrenalin floods through Peter. He sits absolutely quiet, hardly breathing. Will they be discovered? What will the soldiers do to them? Just then the little animal behind their bush bolts and runs off into the night.

The Sergeant stops. "Corporal, do you think a wild animal would get up close to humans?"

"I don't think so, Sarge. The townsfolk do a lot of hunting in these wilds. Wild animals are very wary of people. It takes all of a hunter's skills to spot the game, to say nothing of bagging it."

"That's what I thought. I didn't think wild animals would get that close to humans. Let's move on."

Peter and the Professor remain every quiet. They don't dare make the slightest sound until the patrol is out of ear shot. Finally, the Professor speaks in the softest whisper, "Praise You Lord for sending us that little animal. It saved our lives. But I don't think the danger is over yet. They'll either have to come back this way or get picked up. Rest if you can and I'll keep watch."

Rest? Who could rest after that! Peter lays his head down on his pack. He barely closes his eyes when the Professor nudges him. A helicopter! The familiar sound of blades beating on air drifts up the valley towards them, getting louder as it approaches.

"This is a new threat. It will be hard to fool them. We must act fast. Put on this face mask to protect your nose and eyes. The chopper blades will stir up a great deal of dust. Then empty out your backpack."

Peter puts on the face mask and empties his pack. It is very cramped, and they have to be careful not to jostle each other as they rearrange everything. But they get it done.

"Once the chopper picks up the patrol it will come back this way. When it does it will shine high intensity spot lights on every inch of this area. If they see our ponchos flap in the wind stirred up by the propellers that will give us away. If our ponchos do not look like a boulder, that will give us away.

"We'll scrunch down behind and under the bushes and stick our back packs under the poncho to hide our shape and make it look like the shape of a boulder. There's an old magician's trick called the Stiff Rope. Short pieces of wood are hinged together and stuffed into the shell of a cotton rope. Held one way the rope hangs limp. Rotate the rope a quarter turn, and it becomes stiff. A miniaturized version of the stiff rope goes all the way around the hem of your poncho. Rotate it now, and it will help us hold the ponchos tight to the ground and reduce some of the flapping."

They work quickly, keeping hidden under the ponchos. When the Professor seems satisfied, they lay motionless, without a sound, waiting.

"Father, we'd much appreciate it if you'd send some of those little animals to come and stay behind our bush. I think three or four would be enough. Thank You, Sir."

It strikes Peter that when the Professor prays, he speaks as though God is right there with him, as a companion would be. Immediately he hears the scrambling and scampering of little animals. Because of his position he can't see them. But now they're sitting behind the bush, looking curiously at the strange bolder.

Soon the beating of the helicopter's propeller is heard as it comes slowly back down the valley. Peter can make out the floodlights scanning the ground as it comes towards them, dust billowing up. Soon the dreaded moment comes. The chopper pauses right above them. The ponchos try to break free and flap. One edge gives way. Peter catches it with his foot.

"You! In the bushes! We know you're there. We've got you covered. Come out with your hands up." The voice they dreaded to hear bellows out from the chopper. The Professor remains dead still. So does Peter, even though everything in him wants to get up and run.

"We're warning you. Come out now!"

Someone on the chopper fires a warning shot that ricochets off the stones and sends splinters flying everywhere. Peter feels a sudden sharp stinging pain in his left shoulder. "Ow," he starts to cry, but bites his tongue just in time to keep from crying out. The little animals, fearing for their lives, run off in all directions.

Over the noise of the chopper they just make out the voice of the Sergeant, "That's what happened before. They must have a den behind the brush." The chopper continues its journey on down the valley.

When the chopper can no longer be heard the Professor lifts his voice in gratitude, "Thank you, Father, for sending the animals. I didn't mean for them to get scared. Please thank them and apologize for us." Turning to Peter, whose face is grimaced in pain, he speaks softly. "Now Peter, let's look at your wound. Hmm. The blood is coming from your shoulder. I'll have to remove your jacket to see how bad you're hurt. I'll be as gentle as I can but I'll have to move your arm a little. Try not to cry out."

The Professor carefully pulls the jacket off Peter's shoulder. "This is lightweight protective clothing. It's not designed to be bulletproof, but it will stop a bullet fired from a distance. This was fired up close, and ricocheted. Ah, here's where it hit. It isn't deeply embedded. Good."

"Good! What's good about it?" Peter winces. "It hurts like the dickens."

The Professor opens one of the pockets on his backpack and removes a small kit with a red cross on it. He opens it and takes out a small vial. He puts just a drop on the wound. Almost instantly the pain disappears and the bleeding stops. Using a surgical forceps, he removes the bullet. He puts a drop of liquid from another vial directly on the wound, and covers the wound with a bandage. He puts the first aid kit away and takes out a canteen and offers it to Peter.

"A scare like that takes a lot out of you, and a wound even more. Drink some of this. It's the mountain man's drink. We need a bite to eat too."

The food quickly satisfies, and they soon feel their energy renewed. Peter suddenly realizes he has been using his arm and shoulder as though nothing had happened.

"What kind of medicine did you put on my shoulder? There's no pain and it feels like nothing had happened."

"The Nine have made many discoveries in medicine, too. Man is not ready for them. Man does not value human life enough to seek to protect all men everywhere. They seek to destroy, maim, and hurt. We will not help them prolong their lives until they have learned to use well the lives they have. We'll leave some of this food for the little animals if they come back. Our enemy will keep searching the forest and watching the sides until he is sure we are nowhere to be found. Now, let's sleep."

The morning breaks bright and clear making the bullet hole in the poncho look ten times bigger than it was. Dismayed Peter asks, "That bullet ruined the Poncho, Professor. What do we do now?"

"We fix it and then we eat," smiled the Professor. "We have patches that will reconnect all the wires and make the poncho good as new." They repair the hole, eat breakfast. Before reloading their backpacks the Professor places a generous amount of food on the rocks, a thank you to the animals. Finally, they reload their backpacks. To Peter's surprise the Professor rolls up their ponchos and straps them to the backpacks.

"Are we out of danger now?" Peter asks. "If we don't wear those ponchos anyone can see us."

"No, we aren't out of danger. We're going to fool the enemy by doing what the enemy doesn't expect. Remember what TPF said about hiding when we visited him?"

"He said the best place to hide is out in the open."

"That's exactly what we are going to do! In our enemy's mind only a fool would try to escape out in the open where he can be seen. What he would do is use his woodland skills to take advantage of the boulders and dense foliage. He would keep hidden under cover of the forest. They checked the sides of the valley last night and couldn't find any trace of us. So today his men will focus all their attention on the valley floor. Meanwhile, this part of our climb will be much easier if we aren't wearing the ponchos."

They begin to climb. Peter is disappointed to find his backpack is still as heavy as it was when they started. He knows he shouldn't be groaning, but he used muscles yesterday he hadn't used in a long time, and they're not happy. Pausing to give his poor muscles a break, Peter looks back. "Professor!" he calls in a loud whisper. "The animals have come to eat." As they watch the animals pause in their eating, turn and look up at them as though to say "thank you", and go back to eating.

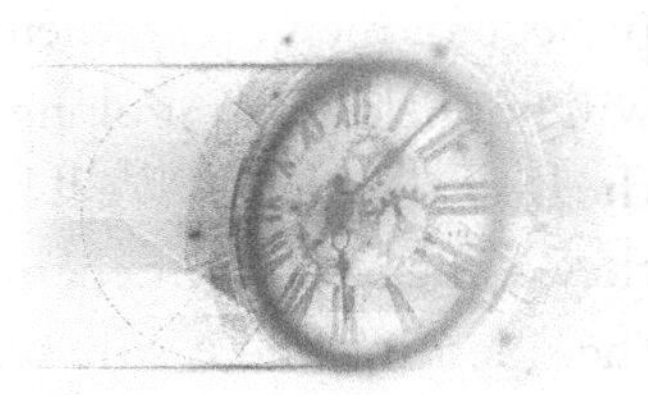

CHAPTER 26

Rock Climbing 101

The hill is so steep they have to zigzag back and forth, balancing against the hill with one hand, trying not to disturb the loose shale. Time and again Peter's foot slips. He slides back a little and digs in again. Two hours pass as they slowly inch their way upward, pulling themselves up from bush to bush. Half way through their third hour of climbing, they hear the dreaded sound of a chopper coming. Peter's fingers ache as they dig into the shale, grabbing the roots of a bush. The chopper flies on by a couple hundred feet below them. The Professor was right, the pilots were too busy concentrating on the trees and boulders to look up and see them.

Finally, they come to a place where the steep hill is interrupted by a narrow shelf running horizontally across it. It is just wide enough to barely sit on. They take their backpacks off and sit gingerly on the shelf. Facing the valley from this lofty perch they see the chopper in the distance following a search pattern over the valley floor.

"When they come back this way I doubt if they'll see us," the Professor reassures Peter. "We're too high up. They expect fugitives to keep to the cover of the trees and boulders down there below us. Up here we look like a couple rock climbers. Tonight it will be different. They will be making another thorough scan along the sides of the valley looking for any cracks or crevices in which we could hide. I don't know about you, but I'm ready for lunch."

Pulling a package out of his backpack, he serves their meal. "It'd be nice if we had a table and chairs and a bit of coffee, but this will have to do. We'll finish off with another swallow or two of the mountain man's energy drink. We should make it to the ridge up there by early afternoon. Then we can stop and have a well-deserved rest. It'll be easier to hide up there."

Peter had woken up this morning tired and aching. The climbing, along with the fright when the chopper flew by, have left him drained. He can hardly move; his muscles are so sore. For that last hour he'd been climbing in a daze. Mechanically he eats the "mountain man's" food. As he eats, strength returns, causing him to whisper, "Wow! Professor! What's in this food? I was so tired I couldn't move. Now I'm feeling like I could go on forever!"

"It does wonders for you, doesn't it? You can hike in the mountains many days on just a little of my friend's food. But we aren't hiking many days, if all goes well. There is a hidden ledge that goes along the side of the cliff way up there. We're heading for it. If we'd headed for it straight out from the lodge, we would have been exposed to the enemy's men right from the start. This way we've set them quite a puzzle. We've left no trace of our having been here, just as there is no trace of us in any of the other eight places the Blue Orb landed. They will have to conclude that we are tesseracting all over the place!

"Well, it's time to move on," the Professor adds, examining the hill above them, and removing a coil of rope from his pack. "We're going to need some help to get up to that next bush. Tie the rope around your waist. I'll see if I can toss this grappling hook to catch on that boulder behind the bush."

The Professor gives the hook a vigorous swing and sends it hurtling over the boulder. That had to be a throw of over 100 feet! Peter marvels at this man who seems to be as much at home scaling cliffs as he is teaching in the classroom. He follows the Professor up the rope. Just as he puts it away, they hear the chopper coming back.

"They didn't see us the first time. If they do see us out in the open now, carefully scaling the steep rock face above us, they won't give it a second thought. Like I said, they don't expect fugitives to be out in the open. We'll look like ordinary rock climbers to them, and that is what we will be. Have you ever done rock climbing before?"

"No! And I don't want to now!"

"You'll soon catch on," the Professors smiles. "We're going to go straight up. The ledge is about five hundred feet above us. Up there we can sit and rest and eat and plan the rest of our climb. Ready to go? There are plenty of good places to put our feet and grab hold with our hands, like climbing a ladder. Just be sure there is no shale or broken rock where you step and grab. Put your hands and feet where I put mine and you will be fine."

They begin to climb. It is slow going and hard. After about two hours Peter's hands ache.

"Professor, I've got to stop and rest. I don't think my fingers can hold on any longer."

"Just a couple more feet and there is a good place to rest."

Peter has his doubts about any place being good. Surely not the place the Professor is talking about. "A fissure in the rock? It's a bit too small to crawl into, Professor! How are we supposed to rest in that crack?"

"Welcome to rock climbing 101! On your utility belt are several spring-loaded camming devices, or 'cams' for short. Leave the carabiner snapped to your harness. Do exactly what I do. Hold your cam by the handle, flat side parallel to the rock face. Push the cam straight into the fissure like I do. Now, pull the handle down and give it a jerk. See how the lever pushes the cams against the sides of the fissure? The harder you pull, the tighter the cam jams into the sides of the fissure. That cam will support several times your weight. Now just relax and let the cam support all your weight and rest."

At first Peter is cautious and not sure about trusting the cam to hold. As he watches it, it digs in harder the more weight he puts on it. Finally, Peter relaxes and looks around to survey the valley from this new height. The view is so breathtaking he wishes he had his camera. He also notices how easily things echo at this height. Spring has already come to the valley. The trees are leaved out, looking like a green carpet covering the valley floor, punctuated by large boulders sticking up through the foliage. Wild flowers cover the open spaces and banks of the stream with reds and purples and yellow mixed in with moss and fern. To the south, the spurs of the two sides of the valley come together with the mountain lodge barely visible between. To the north a fine line of white can just be seen where the stream begins its descent in cataracts and falls to the valley floor.

Cautiously Peter whispers, "I still don't like rock climbing but now I realize that there are views you only get to see if you are a rock climber. I'm reminded of that old hymn that goes 'I want to scale the utmost heights and catch a gleam of glory bright.' It's true, isn't it? The things most valuable and rewarding in life are the things that come only as we scale the utmost heights? To be one whose prayers are always answered, you must scale the heights of prayer. To be a scientist, I must first scale the heights of study and research. To be a renowned pianist, I must first scale the heights of practice. To be a fully functioning child of God, I must first scale the heights of obedience."

"Rock climbing is turning you into a philosopher, Peter! But you are right. There is no easy path to achievement in any endeavor except by scaling the heights to the top. And speaking of tops, we'd best go on. We don't want to stay visible too long. It's best to arrive at the top with plenty of daylight left."

Releasing the cams, they continue their climb. They reach the ledge in the middle of the afternoon. Peter is surprised to discover that the ledge, sometimes narrow and sometimes wide, stretches both south and north as far as he can see. In the cliff in front of them is a man-made alcove. It had been dug into the rock, slanting gently down towards the back. It was fairly high and wide, but not quite high enough to stand upright. It was meant to be a place for climbers to rest, to sleep, and store supplies. At the back of the alcove, heavy steel anchor pins had been driven deep into the rock. Climbers could use it to hoist supplies up and not have to carry heavy back packs.

"It's time to disappear again," the Professor speaks in a low voice to avoid echoes. "If we were seen today, we do not want to be seen again. We want them to think we finished our climb and went back to the lodge. We don't want the enemy to suspect there is anyone up here. They'll be out searching again tonight, especially if they saw us climbing the rock face. We'll put our poncho secrecy screen in front of us to shield us. We'll anchor the hem to those wind break hooks you see stuck in the wall. The secrecy shield will block their search lights and keep them from sensing our body heat."

While they eat an early supper of the mountain man's food, the Professor tells the story of how the ledge and alcove came to be. A few hundred years before, the Professor's mountain friend had hired a crew of men to help him cut the ledge into the side of the cliff. Starting near the lodge they cut the ledge into the rock to support one side of a very long foot path. First, they drove anchor pins into the back side of the ledge. About six feet above the ledge they chiseled slots into the rock about every four feet for cams. Using the anchors and cams they built an ingenious wooden walkway along the side of the cliff.

"My friend disguised his real purpose for the walkway by making this a public attraction. It was a favorite place for painters. When he no longer needed it, he tore it down, and it was forgotten by the towns people. It happened so long ago no one remembers. He and his staff use it now and then for sport when they want to get away from the noise of the lodge."

Peter is suddenly overcome with sleep. The strain of hard climbing and then the relief of being in a safe place catches up with him. He falls sound asleep with his back resting against the back of the alcove.

Peter is suddenly awakened from his sound sleep. "What was that?" Peter whispers. The Professor sits quietly, leaning against the back of the alcove. After a few minutes the sound comes again. Peter recognizes the swishing of a helicopter running in stealth mode. This time it is closer. It passes and fades. After a few minutes it comes back again. This time he can see the reflection of a searchlight. Again the sound fades. The chopper is going back and forth, making a sweeping search of the tree line and rock face, double checking each crevice, searching under every bush and scrubby tree.

A few minutes pass and the swishing sound returns, getting louder. Suddenly, the full force of the search light is aimed at the alcove. Peter holds his breath. The chopper halts. The search light sweeps back and forth across the alcove, finally halting with the beam focused directly on the opening of the alcove. After what seems like hours the light passes by, continuing its search along the narrow ledge. The swishing sound disappears into the dark. Peter is so unnerved he can't go back to sleep. His only comfort is the Professor's words: "If they had detected anything suspicious they would have kept the light on us and lowered rock climbers to come and find us."

"Professor, while the search light was focused on us I was praying, asking God to blind their eyes. He must have, because the light was getting past the edges of the ponchos. It had to look like something was blocking the middle of the alcove."

"You're right, Peter. I was praying too. Do you remember hearing Brother Andrew[1] tell how God blinded the eyes of the border guards, when he was smuggling Bibles into Russia during the Cold War? His car would be loaded with Bibles, all out in the open, but the border guards never saw them. We can call on God to help us in every difficult situation, provided we've done all we can. Last night, after we had done all we could, He sent the animals to help us."

Peter is quiet for a moment, and then speaks. "The words of an old hymn keep running through my mind: 'He hideth my soul in the cleft of the rock . . . and covers me there with His hand.' I've been thinking about God's promises and how each one has a man side and a God side. If we had had no choice but to sit fully exposed, and had done all we could to hide, we could have prayed in faith believing, and God would have covered us. But if I don't study for a test, I can pray until I am blue in the face and God will not give me the answers. We do the man side first and then God does the God side."

"That is a good bit of wisdom, Peter. It's too bad so many Christians miss it. But enough talk! Good night!"

They get as comfortable as possible, and soon are fast asleep.

---

[1] Andrew, Brother w/Sherrill, John and Elizabeth, *God's Smuggler*, 1967, 2001, 2015, Bloomington MN, Chosen Books.

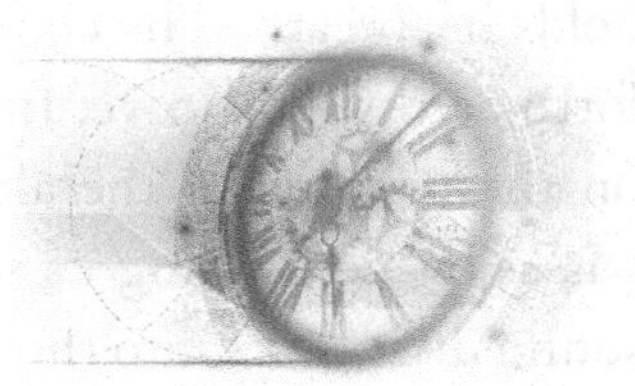

CHAPTER 27

Spiders on the Wall

At first light they eat breakfast. Next, the Professor shows Peter how to convert the ponchos into capes that hide their backs. The two bottom corners of their capes they fasten to the back of their shoes. They pull the tops of the cape up over their shoulders and heads. The top two corners of the capes have straps that fasten to their wrists, and project out over their hands. Lastly, they plug their ponchos into their battery packs.

"The side of the ponchos that's showing now is designed to blend in with the color of the stone cliff. From a distance we cannot be seen as long as we keep the ponchos plugged in. If a chopper comes up close, we need to immediately stretch our legs and arms out forming an X. As long as we don't move they won't be able to see us. Only if we give ourselves away will they come in close to look at us. If the sun is directly behind us, and we move away from the cliff, we will cast a shadow and that can be seen. So we need to hug the cliff face to minimize the shadow. Anyone watching us inch our way along will only see what looks like a ripple moving along the ledge. That could be dangerous if someone is watching."

The Professor decides that instead of moving steadily across the rock face they will go in spurts, stop, wait, and then go again. But each pause will be different in length. He will also vary how far they go between stops. "That will help fool the watchers and make them think they are just seeing a mirage caused by the heat," he explains.

This time they attach two cams to their harnesses, one for each hand. The Professor leads the way, telling Peter to do as he does. Holding on to the edge of the alcove he reaches out and slides a cam into the first crevice. Hanging on to it with his right hand he gingerly steps out, changes hands, and slides his right hand along the rock to the next crevice and slides the second cam into it. Steadying himself with the second cam he slides his feet along the ledge, and unhooks the first cam. Following this pattern, he moves slowly along the ledge.

Peter cautiously follows the Professor's example. He puts the first cam in place, moves his feet, reaches to put the second cam in place when his foot slips. He falls about a foot when he is caught up tight by the first cam. "Whoa!" he blurts out.

The Professor looks at him, shakes his head, smiles, and says, "That was not what I meant when I said you'd soon get the hang of it! With those cams in place you are perfectly safe. You could even hang around all day like that. Unfortunately, we've got a lot of distance to cover. So, if you're through playing we'd better get moving."

"I was not playing! That slip gave me an awful scare. My heart's in my throat and its beating a million times a second. Boy, from now on I'm gonna make double sure those cams are stuck tight!"

In that moment Peter gained much respect for the cam and his harness. The cam easily held. He only had to step up about a foot to regain his footing on the ledge. Knowing he is safe with the cams wedged in the crevices, he follows the Professor along the ledge. But his heart still races like crazy each time he slips. He notices the Professor never slips. Slowly a suspicion rises in Peter. "Why didn't you give me shoes like yours that don't slip?"

"It's not the shoes," the Professor answers. "It's who's wearing them! You have to pay more attention to how you place your feet on the ledge. The more you practice, the surer footed you will get. Many professional rock climbers don't use cams except to rest, or in extremely difficult places. They'd think scaling this wall was easy, not worth bothering with cams."

Peter is not impressed. In fact, he is getting very tired. By mid-morning he can go no further. They stop and rest, letting the cams support them. They nibble on some of the mountain food and take a couple swallows of the energy drink. They are just about ready to start again when they hear the sound they hoped they wouldn't hear: a chopper in the distance.

"Quick," the Professor warns. "Back up on the ledge. Spread your legs as far apart as you can and stretch your arms up to cover the cams with your hands. That will help you hold the poncho taunt. If the chopper comes in close, the wind from the props could make the ponchos flap in its breeze. It's not safe for a chopper to get that close to the rock wall, but these are our enemy's choppers, and they do what he tells them to do. If they keep a proper distance, they will only see a faint shimmer where we are.

Again Peter's heart is in his throat as he waits. It seems to him that lately his heart has been spending most of its time in his throat. The chopper takes it time. He's sure it's looking for them. Suddenly he gets the oddest feeling like someone is trying to get into his mind. **Tell me your name. Tell me your name.** The words thunder in his mind. They are so loud and commanding they drive every other thought out. His ability to resist rapidly diminishes. He knows he must not think his name. He must not say it. But the pressure is too great. Just as he is about to yield, he cries out, "Father help me."

Tell me your name. Come out and show yourself, the voice in his head commands. Just when he can hold out no longer, words begin to well up inside him. *Greater is he who is in you than he who is in the world. (*1 John 4:4) "Yes," Peter cries out in relief. "I have the mind of Christ. (Philippians 2:5) Greater is he that is in me than he that is in the world. I can do all things through Christ who strengthens me." (Philippians 4:13) As he speaks those words, he feels the voice in his head stop abruptly as though in great pain. The chopper, which seemed to have paused there forever, continues on its way. When it has gone, the Professor speaks.

"That was the most dangerous moment of our whole journey. The enemy himself was in the chopper. I could not warn you. I had to shield my mind from him; else he would have detected my presence, too, and all would have been lost. When you quoted the scripture, you blocked his mind probe. No one has ever done that to him before.

Up to now, he has believed he was invincible. And yet you blocked it in the only way it could be blocked. It was very painful to him. We can be sure another patrol will be out looking for us tonight. So we better get going."

The urgency to get to a safe shelter and get out of sight gives Peter a new burst of energy. He follows the Professor along the ridge with renewed vigor. "I don't want to encounter that mind probe again. Won't he come back just to double check what happened?"

"No, not until tonight. He is in too much pain. He will want to think about what happened. He didn't know until just now that quoting the scripture can stop him. If he thinks the scripture came from you or me he will probably want to come back to check it out. Hopefully we'll be in our next stop before he comes. It'll give us good cover, and the minerals in the rock should provide a good shield against his mind probe. So you can put that worry to rest."

Finally, after what seems like hours that run into days, the ridge they are following begins to rise to a higher level where it suddenly widens. The rock face changes to rust-colored stone. To Peter's great relief he discovers their cams are no longer needed. The ridge widens to form a path with a natural curb on the valley side.

"One could walk this path in the dark without fear of falling several hundred feet!" the Professor whispers.

"A mountain goat might feel at home up here, but I'm no mountain goat," Peter complains, while admiring the agility of the Professor. "Are you half mountain goat? I wish we could take time to enjoy the view instead of having to hurry all the time."

"We've got about an hour before it gets too dark," the Professor whispers as he pauses to rest. "That should be just long enough to reach our next safe niche. The ridge we're following gets very narrow for a while. Keep your eyes on me, and do as I do. The cliff slants in quite a bit so we can lean against it as we go. There are lots of little hand holds to steady yourself. This should be a piece of cake!"

"A piece of cake!? What kind of cake do you eat?"

Following the Professor's example, Peter faces the cliff and side steps his way along the narrow path. When the path widens enough, he half faces forward, ready to turn back to the cliff if he hears any noise. That's when he sees how far down it is on the right! Ugh! He's sure thankful for the Professor's guidance and assurance as they inch their way along.

Suddenly, tiredness overwhelms Peter. Time is forgotten as he drearily struggles along, one uncertain step at a time, until they come to a place where the ridge on the right rises up about five feet. On the left, the wall is undercut with a deep alcove about four feet wide and five feet high. It seems almost homely. There are signs that it has been used many times. They shed their ponchos and their backpacks. The Professor leans his back against the far wall of the alcove, closes his eyes and relaxes. Peter joins him.

"The only way anyone can see us here," the Professor speaks softly after a few minutes, "is to be on the ledge standing directly in front of us. Since the enemy does not know about this place, we're safe. He'll be thinking about what he would do if he were us. If it were him he'd start moving at night, heading for the stairway at the upper end. There are lots of good hiding places along the path. He'll use stealth mode tonight, hoping to catch us on the path with his mind probe. When that fails he'll scan the rock face again. Now, let's eat and relax."

They are both famished and make short work of the meal. But try as hard as he can, Peter can't relax. Finally, he asks the Professor the questions that are bugging him.

"Professor, how did you know our enemy was in the chopper? Tell me more about his mind probe."

"I sensed our enemy's mind probe when the chopper came near. He has developed a way to strengthen the force of his mind so strongly that no one can resist it. Then, like Satan, he plants thoughts and commands in your mind, except that his are electronically intensified and cannot be resisted by sheer will power. When I warned you about it, your answer to me was, 'God makes a way where there seems to be no way.' It seems God had already taught you how to resist. Just as you do with the thoughts Satan plants in your mind, you reject them by filling your mind with the Word of God which is more powerful than a two-edged sword." (Hebrews 4:12)

"Until today, no one has ever used God's Word to resist his mind probe. Any resistance makes him angry. He is vengeful and he does not forget. When you meet, if he knows it was you who resisted him in the valley, he will attack you with the full force of his mind probe and try to destroy your mind just because you resisted him. We'll delay that meeting as long as we can."

"Thanks," Peter sighs as the old feelings of danger rush back! Even the hairs on his neck stand up. Again his stomach starts to knot with fear and foreboding. His mind tells him it's just nerves and a wild imagination, but his body isn't listening. The Professor gives him another sip of the mountain man's cordial and his nerves calm down.

"Our Order was designed to protect and help mankind grow and develop and mature. We looked forward to the day when men would be able to take our knowledge and use it for the benefit of all mankind. As I told you before, at first Mr. Az was in harmony with this. We worked together like brothers. But as mankind continued to war with each other, he became disillusioned. He suggested that we end the wars by becoming the rulers. We reminded him that that was not what our Creator wanted us to do. As time went by, he became obsessed with his idea.

"Our immense amount of knowledge we had written in a book using an extinct language known only to us. One day Mr. Az asked us to give him the book. He would keep it safe, he said. But all our instincts said 'Danger'. The eight of us hid the book and disappeared without his knowledge. At first he was furious. Then he designed a plan to become the ruler of the world. He will go back in history and make minute changes in events. These will be accumulative so that the world's wealth will fall peacefully into his hands. All the world leaders will have to come and bow before him.

"His search for a way to control men took him to the monks in their monasteries high in the Himalayas. Normally the monks would not share their secrets. But just as Lucifer had been specially equipped with a voice to lead the worship in heaven, Mr. Az also has a voice that is hypnotic, irresistible. Just as Eve and a third of the angels fell under Lucifer's spell, the monks fell under Mr. Az's spell and shared their secrets with him.

"The monks possessed great stores of gold and jewels and silver. Rumors of their wealth passed into legend and story told around camp fires. Bandits and fortune hunters, lured by these stories of enormous riches, searched for the monasteries, hoping to find the treasures. When they got too close, the monks took them prisoner. Caring for prisoners became a great burden.

"One day they discovered one of the prisoners was so scared, his hair had turned white. He cowered in a corner. They did not know what caused his fear, but it was obvious he was now harmless. They carried him down the mountain and deposited him on the outskirts of a village. The people found him and cared for him but he would never again set foot outside the village.

"The monks reasoned that if they could induce extreme fear in every prisoner it would make the prisoner harmless. They found a simple technique. They plant the suggestion in the prisoner's mind that he will forget everything he has seen and heard and that the thought of going back up the mountain will fill him with terror. Mr. Az overheard them using this treatment on a prisoner. This was what Mr. Az was looking for. Using this, he could control men and render enemies harmless by erasing their memories.

"He also learned how the monks were able to walk unseen among the villagers when they needed information. Mr. Az began to use the techniques he had learned. People who worked for him were discharged with no memory of ever having been in his employ. In this way, when he no longer has use for someone, he simply erases their memories.

"Mr. Az, however, let some of his thoughts slip and the monks quickly caught on. They were fearful of what he would do with the knowledge they had given him. They sent out messengers to search for us. They explained what had happened. And then they taught us something they had not taught Mr. Az. They taught us how to protect our memories, and how to restore lost memories.

"Mr. Az has been perfecting his skills for several hundred years.

Likewise, we in my Order have been perfecting our skills. Our skills are in prayer, listening to the Holy Spirit, and obeying the guidance we are given. When the chopper came, I sensed the mind probe. I could not take time to teach you how to resist. I had to close my mind to him because he would have detected my presence, and all would be lost. Since God had called us to make this trip I trusted Him, that He knew you better than I did, and that you would do the right thing. And do the right thing, you did!

"When you started speaking the Word in your mind it cut Mr. Az off. It didn't just cut him off, it hit him like a slap in the face. It brought back memories he's suppressed all these hundreds of years. When he was young, sitting at his mother's knee, he gave his heart and soul to the Lord Jesus Christ. He came to us as a very devout young man. But then tragedy struck. In bitterness, Mr. Az denied the faith he once knew. He made the same mistake as Lucifer; he mistook love for weakness. He rejected the way of love. He rejected God.

"You stirred up those memories. It made him angry. Tonight when he comes, he will use the full force of his mind probe to force you out. Finding nothing, he will stew over it. Was it a fluke, or has someone dared challenge him? That's the question that has him worried. He knows someone has been chosen by God to bring a message of love to the world. He cannot allow that to happen. When people lose their spiritual grounding they reverse their values. Immorality becomes the norm. When God's Name is removed from the door posts of our universities, when we remove all reference to God from our schools, we promote wickedness. That is just the milieu evil people like Mr. Az need. Evil has nothing to fear when evil is in power."

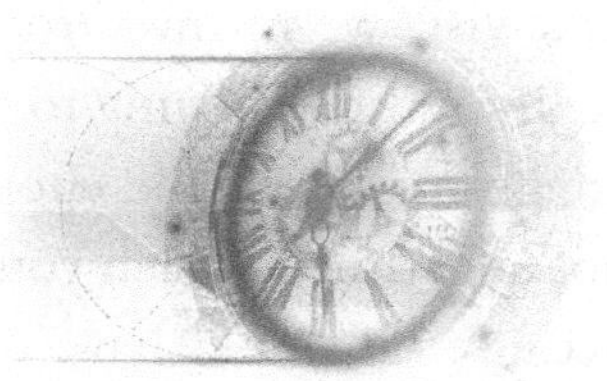

CHAPTER 28

The Hidden Cave

Peter. Peter. It's time to be up and on our way. It's already five in the morning and we've some hard climbing ahead of us. We've come about ten miles so far in three days, and we've got another four or five miles to go. Have some breakfast and another sip of the mountain man's elixir. Pack up as quickly as you can. Believe me, it will be well worth it when we get there. You are in for quite a surprise."

Where is there? Peter wonders. *It's hard to get anything out of the Professor. And when he does open up he tells you far more than you want to hear! After last night, I'm not sure I want to know where 'there' is. What's the surprise? Another ten mile climb down the other side?*

"Have some breakfast. It's not ham and eggs, but it will stick to your ribs a lot better. Eat all you want. Things have gone well. We've made good progress. This should be our last breakfast on the trail. We'll leave our leftovers here for any animals that come along."

They eat in silence. Peter wonders what kind of animals would climb up here. As he eats he notices that the Professor seems to deliberately avoid letting his head get above the ridge.

"Professor, why are you staying below the edge of the ridge? Is somebody out there? Are the choppers back?"

"We need to be very cautious today, more cautious than we have been. There are secrets on this mountain we want to keep secret. If someone is up at the upper end by the falls scanning for us, we don't want him to see our heads bobbing up and down."

"How are we going to get out of here? Crawl on our hands and knees?"

"No! No! When we're ready to go we'll put on our ponchos and be on our way.

"As usual, no explanation," Peter mumbles, sorting out the extra food. "Only save enough for a snack on the way," the Professor said. "That will leave a nice pile of food for the animals. I hope they like it. Now, to put on my backpack and my poncho."

"Plug your poncho into the battery pack on your belt," the Professor instructs. "Now, open the pocket next to the battery pack. See the red switch? Turn it on and behold: another sneaky thing about your poncho."

The Professor has a look of pure enjoyment on his face. "I love outsmarting Mr. Az. He is so sure his surveillance technology cannot be defeated. Yet we are going to step boldly out into the sunlight and we won't be seen! The sunlight will bend around us. Anyone looking at us will only see the wall. The ponchos will scramble their detection signals, making them think their equipment is malfunctioning. They will end up relying on electronic binoculars. They will look straight at us but they won't see us!"

Instantly they disappear. That is, their back sides disappear. It was almost comical looking at each other and seeing a front but no back. The Professor pulls his hood down over his face, stands, and looks out over the ridge.

"Isn't the sight beautiful, Peter? It's worth coming up here just to bask in the beauty. Look how far we've come. See how high we've climbed. Only my friend and his staff have seen this sight. The lodge is many miles south of us.

"If you look hard up there, you can just make out the falls at the upper end. Well, I was right. Did you see that flash just then? The enemy has men up there scanning the valley for us. We'd best start walking. It's still a good day's easy hike to get there."

"Easy! Nothing you say to do is ever easy, Professor," Peter complains.

They leave the safety of the shelter and begin to inch their way along the narrow ledge. The ridge on their right that had protected them disappears, much to Peter's disappointment. Once again they are both stretched out like spiders. How does the Professor keep on going like this? Suddenly, they hear the sound they have been dreading. A chopper is making its way up the valley. The enemy is making one last attempt to find them.

Following the Professor's lead, Peter stops. His poncho, anchored to his shoes, is stretched tight as he clings, spread-eagle, to the stone cliff. Peter almost loses his grip his hands are sweating so badly. All his old fears, the knot in his gut, his hair standing on end, have suddenly come back on him. The words race through his mind: *They'll see us! They'll see us!*

When the chopper gets about even with them it stops and hovers. Then it starts to come towards them. Peter holds his breath. A cold sweat pours out of him. His fingers are slippery and he has to move them a little to get a better grip on the wall. Just when it seems like it couldn't get any worse, they hear a second chopper! This one is coming in over the top of the cliff. They can't see it, but it sounds like it has stopped by the first chopper. The words shout in Peter's mind: *All is lost. All is lost.*

Suddenly a voice booms over a loud speaker, *"You in the black chopper. This is the police. It is illegal to hunt from a chopper, or to use a chopper to flush out the game. Get your chopper out of here now, or we will force you down."*

"Thank God for the police!" Peter exclaims in a whisper, taking a deep breath.

"Amen to that!" whispers the Professor.

The black chopper turns and leaves, and the police chopper follows it down the valley. They continue inching their way along the edge. At last they come to a place where the ridge rises up again on the right, and they can walk in safety.

"That scare deserves a lunch break; don't you think?" asks the Professor as he sits down. "Here, have a drink of my friend's energy cocktail. My friend knew we were at the critical part of our journey. He would have called the sheriff when he heard the chopper go over this morning. Perfect timing. They were curious about the shimmering of our ponchos. Even though they couldn't see us they were wondering what caused the shimmering."

As the afternoon sun starts to set, the wind comes up. The gusts make it hard to hang on as they "spider crawl" their way along the narrow ledge. In a few places the ridge rises up and they can relax and rest. But then it's back to the blowing and gusting. Finally, as the sun disappears over the high cliff, the Professor calls a stop. They have come to a place where the ledge widens to about fifteen feet. Several boulders lay along the edge on the valley side.

What appears to be a small grove of brush is growing between the boulders and the cliff face. It seems strange and out of place so high up on the rock cliff. But it is most definitely a welcome sight to Peter. The cliff slants inward a little more than usual. The brush has grown quite high and seems more like a small grove of trees.

Peter looks closer at the brush and discovers why it is growing there. There is a little trickle of water flowing out from the rock and watering the brush. It overflows the ledge like a dripping faucet, landing on the shale a few hundred feet below. The Professor sits down on a small boulder under the overhanging branches of a small brush tree. Peter joins him, glad to stop fighting the wind and enjoying the little shelter the brush offers.

The view from this vantage point is breathtaking. The top of the ridge is not far above them. Several hundred feet below the narrowing valley stretches out. The trees catch the last rays of the setting sun. The cliffs on the far side, catching the full force of the setting sun, seem to mirror the beautiful reds and blues and purples of the sunset.

"It's a beautiful view." The Professor's words break the silence. "My friend found this valley shortly after our Order broke up. It fit his needs perfectly. People come to the lodge to rest for a few days, enjoy hunting and hiking and swimming in the cool mountain water. His staff looks after all their needs, and he is free to pursue his research.

"We have to stay here and wait for the deepening dusk just before the moonlight breaks over the valley. You cannot see it because the door is closed, but right behind us a tunnel has been carved into the side of the hill.

"Prospectors once found a small vein of gold near here. It soon ran out. They tunneled a little further, hoping to find a new vein but all they found was the other side of the hill! The tunnel soon faded into local legend to be remembered only as the Fools Gold Tunnel. No one remembers where it is. Brush and trees have overgrown the openings.

"What the people didn't know was that my friend was behind the digging. The miners thought they were mining for gold. But what they were really doing was hollowing out the hill into a series of rooms. That way no one would be suspicious of the mounds of boulders and debris from the digging.

"We'll rest here a little longer, watching night come over the valley. When it's dark enough, the spy up by the waterfall will not be able to see us, or see the tunnel. It will only be open for a moment, and then closed before the moonlight hits it. Even if he sees something with his scanners, it will only be a fleeting thing, like a shadow, and then gone. Once inside, our escape will be complete, and we will have disappeared."

Those words, "our escape will be complete," do wonders for Peter's spirits. His heart grows light. He could almost sing! In seemingly no time at all, the last rays of the sun have been replaced by darkness, and the Professor says, "It's time."

He approaches a massive boulder lying against the side of the cliff. Next to the boulder is a hollowed out stone basin in which are five peculiarly shaped stones. Staring hard, Peter can just make out five indentations in the massive boulder. The indentations match the shape of the stones. The Professor places the stones into their matching holes. Slowly the boulder begins to roll to the left, revealing a large opening in the side of the hill, hidden from view by the shrub trees. He returns the peculiarly shaped stones to the stone basin.

Peter follows the Professor into the tunnel. The boulder rolls back into place, leaving the tunnel pitch black. The Professor removes a flashlight from his pack and shines it on the wall. Finding what appears to be a loose stone, he pulls it out. Behind it is a switch. He turns it on and the tunnel is flooded with dim light. Peter is amazed!

The tunnel looks like the inside of a marble palace. The sides are smooth as glass. The many varicolored streaks of minerals and crystals create a mosaic of pattern and color. The floor, as beautiful as the walls, has a square pattern etched into it that gives the appearance of a tiled floor.

"Long ago, my friend developed a technique using a laser beam to cut and polish the stone. When he feels the need to get away, he comes up here to relax and enjoy the beauty. When his joints start to get stiff, he comes up here, drinks the elixir of life, restoring his youth. He changes his name. No one recognizes him. He then goes into town and asks if the lodge is for sale. After some negotiation he will buy it. From himself, of course. Then he'll have an open house and invite the town's people to come for a free weekend, and he will start over again as a new owner. His staff are like Mrs. McD. He chose them carefully long ago and they are fiercely loyal."

A short way down the magnificent tunnel, they come to a beautifully carved wooden door. The Professor opens it, turns on a light, and they step into a large chamber that appears to be a living room. He turns off the light in the hall and closes the door. The room is filled with stuffed chairs, end tables with reading lamps, an extra-long sofa with an equally long coffee table grouped around the fire place. All around the room are shelves filled with books and vases and statues. A soft crackling sound from a fire burning in the fireplace makes one want to sit down and relax, which Peter does!

"We are safe at last. Before you sit down, will you slip into the bedroom on the left and bring us a couple pair of slippers? Ah, thank you Peter. That bed is going to feel good tonight. I'll check the computer to see if there's any messages."

Peter sits back and relaxes. It feels good to sit in a soft chair, his feet up, and nothing to fear. The Professor picks up a remote control and soon soft music fills the room. Peter is almost asleep when his stomach growls.

"Forgive my manners!" cries the Professor, jumping up. "I totally forgot dinner! My friend stocks a mean kitchen, and his cook is world class. Even one of his TV dinners is a gourmet meal. Let's see what we can find."

Peter follows the Professor into the room opening on the right.

It turns out to be a first class kitchen. Everything a cook could want all within easy reach. The cupboards are stocked full. A pantry off the kitchen is stocked full. The refrigerator is full of fresh food. And a mammoth upright freezer is stuffed full of everything one could imagine.

"To save time tonight, I'll heat up a couple of the cook's TV dinners. Why don't you make coffee?"

The coffee done, and the TV dinners microwaved, they carry the food into the living room to eat in front of the fire. They remove the foil from the remarkably full plates and discover these are no ordinary TV dinners. These are delicious chicken dinners with all the trimmings prepared by the cook at the lodge. One whiff and Peter realizes he is famished. The hike and mountain climbing have given him quite an appetite. It takes a little effort, but he manages to eat the whole thing! The Professor does the same, and now they both relax.

"We'll stay here two or three days. We've spent four days on the trail. The hike up to the falls and back takes five, maybe six days at the most. We've already been gone long enough to make it to the falls. They've scoured the valley and the cliffs. So if we don't show up in two more days Mr. Az will have to conclude we didn't come this way. My friend will let us know when it's okay to leave.

"Hopefully, between our disappearing and the tesseract activity, that will get Mr. Az off our trail for good. He'll have no choice but to send all his men to the chateau in Italy. Since it's new to him and he knows nothing about it, he will investigate it thoroughly. It won't be easy with the crowds. His men will have to blend in. He knows it could be a false lead, but he won't dare to pass up the possibility it might be real. He'll probably start to put pressure on TPF again. So let's sit back and enjoy our forced vacation." Then the Professor adds, with a twinkle in his eye, "As I remember, you daydreamed your way through your last physics class. So, tomorrow, we'll have class. Say . . . six-thirty in the morning?!"

Peter lets loose a groan that could have been heard half way down the valley if they'd been outside.

"Tomorrow we'll both sleep in," laughs the Professor.

Too tired to stay up longer, they both take long showers and crawl into bed.

Peter is awakened out of a deep sleep by the smell of bacon frying. "Why is someone frying bacon in the dorm?" he wonders as he struggles to open his eyes. Once opened he is startled fully awake! "This isn't my room! Where am I? How'd I get here? Oh, now I remember. I'm in the marble palace! I wonder what time it is?" He looks at his watch. "Almost noon!"

He hops out of bed and stretches. It felt so good to sleep in a bed again. The sunlight shining in through the window makes the whole room bright and cheerful. "I think I'll open the window and get a breath of fresh air," Peter mumbles as he walks over to the window. "What?" he almost shouts. "This isn't a window! It's a TV screen!"

The Professor hears him and walks in laughing. "Pretty convincing, isn't it? There's a concealed camera that looks out over the valley. You're seeing what the camera sees right now. We both slept late this morning. Almost too late for breakfast. But I refuse to start a day without breakfast! It should be ready to eat as soon as you get dressed."

The Professor goes back to the kitchen, and Peter heads for the marble shower. It had felt good to stand there and soak last night, but all he needs this morning is a quick wakeup shower. In no time he is out, dressed, and joining the Professor at the breakfast table.

"Eat first, and then I'll tell you some more about this house, or marble palace as you call it."

The Professor doesn't have to speak twice. A brief blessing and Peter tears into a huge stack of pancakes smothered in strawberries, maple syrup running down the sides, with eggs and bacon. When he can't eat another bite he pushes away from the table with regret. "There won't be any meals like this back at the college."

He helps the Professor rinse and stack the dishes in the dishwasher, turn it on, and adjourn to the living room.

"Wow!" Peter gasps, "What a view!" The whole side of the wall had become a gigantic window looking out over the valley on the other side of the rock mountain. Birds were flying down below. In the far distance the outline of a city could just be seen.

"The camera view you're seeing is what it would look like if we opened the 'front door' and looked out. When the miners were digging and blasting away, looking for gold, they drove right through to the outside. My friend leveled it off, and made a stone door to disguise the entrance from anyone looking in. To anyone outside, it looks like a small hollowed out area, about six feet by six feet, and three feet deep, with some boulders on it that form a railing. There is no way down to it and no way up to it."

Peter marvels at the technology that had been built into the marble palace. The camera views are so vivid it would be easy to forget you are in a confined space.

"We came in by the back door. You've just seen the front door. There is also a service door. The top of this cliff is flat. Helicopters can easily land. In case a wind comes up, there are tie downs to keep the chopper safe.

"A unique feature about this cliff is that there is a spur just above us that rises about forty or fifty feet straight up. My friend built a cabin that sits tight against the spur. It looks like an ordinary cabin on the outside. But inside he had used his laser to cut a large opening back into the spur, and then cut a shaft down to this level and installed an elevator. He brought all the furniture and appliances up by helicopter, stored them in the cabin, and then brought them down here.

"He let it slip that he was building a cabin on the table top, as they called it. Of course, everyone wanted to know why he built the cabin. They got their answer the day he brought in rock climbers and stone masons. Starting at the top they cut and chiseled a trail down to the foot, hundreds of feet below. It's a tough climb, with resting platforms cut into the rock about every seventy-five to a hundred feet. The view on the climb up is spectacular, to say nothing of the view from the table top itself.

"Only a few people can handle both the climb up and the climb down. Most only climb one way. That's where the cabin comes in. It is well stocked with food, has a bathroom, table, chairs and a couple of bunk beds. No one suspects the back wall opens onto an elevator. When climbers reach the top they make themselves at home in the cabin, and phone for the chopper when they're ready to go home.

"They pay a tidy sum, but everyone says the climb and view and food at the top are well worth it. It's a perfect cover for the many trips the chopper makes to keep this hidden palace clean and well stocked. The best place to hide something is out in the open. The best way to do things in secret is to always have something going on that gives a reason for what you are doing in secret."

Peter is awestruck by what he sees and hears as he listens to the Professor. It is some moments before he finally speaks. "Professor," his voice almost reverent, "the advancements in technology that this place represents are so amazing! How long will it be before modern science catches up with what your Order has accomplished?"

"Hopefully not much longer. Young scientists like you will soon be discovering more than even we know. The Prophet Daniel said knowledge would increase in the last days (Daniel 12:4), and by all the prophetic signs, these are the last days.

"But in the meantime, you're not going to be discovering anything if you keep daydreaming in my classes! It's time to start your physics lesson. This time, stay awake!" the Professor adds, smiling as he hands Peter pencil and paper and a clip board to write on.

Chapter 29

The Monks' Secret Weapon

"Sometimes birds can be a little annoying," Peter protests as he stretches, and then lies back down in bed. "Their songs are pretty enough, but I really didn't want to wake up quite so early. The sun is just coming up over the top of that far hill." He watches, fascinated, as the dark shadow of night retreats across the valley, making way for the bright sun's rays.

The fragrance of a fresh pot of coffee creeps into the bedroom and seduces him with its promise of "drink me and you will feel good." He hears dishes rattling in the kitchen. The Professor must be getting breakfast. He gives up, rises and sleepily stumbles for that irresistible pot of coffee. Entering the kitchen he is greeted by the Professor's smiling face and cheery "Good morning, Peter! Sleep well?"

"Your cheery voice is very irritating, Professor! Can't you at least wait until the coffee kicks in? Oh my head . . ."

"Was your physics lesson a little much for you?"

"A little much! Professor, you must have given me a hundred times more material than you gave the class! My poor head is still reeling from the knowledge glut."

"I did take advantage of having you as a captive student. We worked way into the night. You learned things that are far advanced over what your classmates are learning. You're a quick learner, Peter. How would you like to work with me in my real lab, not the mushroom cellar?"

Between the coffee and Professor's question, Peter is wide awake.

"Working with you, Professor, would be a dream come true! But I can't give up my job, and you can't let it be known you have a secret laboratory."

"I suppose you're right," the Professor admits, years of sadness showing in his voice. "I long for the day when the secrecy can end, and I can share my knowledge with my gifted students. But, on a more pleasant note, breakfast is ready!"

This time breakfast it is a heaping plate of waffles fixed any way you like them. A House of Pancakes breakfast would look pretty dull compared to the Professor's. All talk ceases while they eat.

"Today we'll just relax," the Professor announces as he puts the last dishes away, and Peter wipes off the table. "If the coast is clear, Louis will bring the chopper up tonight. Louis is my friend's pilot. He has a twin-engine plane at the airport. He'll fly us back home, which, in case you've forgotten, is in another country!"

"How will we get past customs? I don't have a passport."

"We have our ways," the Professor answers with that reassuring voice that means he's not going to tell you. "You can grab a book off the shelf, pick out a couple DVDs, nap, or just look at the inspiring view outside."

Peter grabs a book. Some stories are worth reading again and again. Right now, he feels like he's just been in one of the Narnia tales. He picks the first story and sits back in a soft easy chair with a cup of coffee by his side.

"Peter! Peter! It's lunch time." Peter had fallen asleep before he'd even opened the book! On the table are salads, gourmet lunchmeat, and a piping hot pie the Professor just took out of the oven.

"My friend's cook had everything ready for us, just waiting for us to pop the lids and dig in. I had a hard time deciding which pie to bake. I've heard it said that his apple pie is the best in the world. So I picked it. We'll soon find out if what I heard was right."

The one thing Peter doesn't want to hear when he's just eaten too much is someone saying, "We need to get some exercise and work this meal off!" But does the Professor listen to him suggest: "Let's take a nap"? No. So it's off to the exercise room.

"Tell you what, I've a better idea. We'll each get on a treadmill, adjust them the same, and see who can go the farthest in thirty minutes."

This is going to be a slam dunk! Peter tells himself, a little smugly. *No way the Professor can keep up with me. He's a lot older, and I'm at my prime.*

"You're on Professor. Care to make a little wager? If I win, I get an 'A' on the next quiz."

"And if I win, you cook supper and do the dishes."

Later, after a shower, Peter collapses exhausted in an easy chair. "I can't believe what happened, Professor. I was fully rested. No man your age should have more strength and endurance than me! I won the finals in track and field!"

The Professor obviously enjoys Peter's humiliation. "I won't hold you to cooking supper, Peter. I value my stomach too much! Anyway, while we're sitting here there is another story I want to tell you.

"I told you about Az visiting the monks in the Himalayas. I told you the monks became alarmed at what Az might do. They searched until they found us. They showed us how to resist having our memories erased and how to restore memories and how to resist the mind probe."

"I remember that, Professor. And I also remember you said I was unprepared to meet Az and you didn't have time to prepare me. What did you mean?"

"The answer to your question is in the rest of the story the monks told us. One day a missionary came to the monastery. How he found them, they did not know. A great love flowed out from him and embraced the monks. He seemed to regard them with reverence. He sat at their feet and asked them to teach him as much as they were willing to share. When they had finished they asked him, 'What is the source of the love that flows from you?'

"Politely and quietly, he told them the story of Jesus. He explained that God loved them so much that he sent his only son Jesus to die on the cross to pay the penalty for their sins. He told how Jesus had risen from the dead and ascended into heaven. The story moved them greatly and brought tears to their eyes. He did not ask them to abandon their lives as monks, but simply to ask Jesus to come and live in their hearts. The love and respect coming from this humble man won their hearts. They asked him for his Bible so that they could study and learn more.

"During this time, the missionary learned that locked up in a prison room were two mean-spirited thieves. They had been caught trying to break through a wall into what they thought was the treasure room. The monks had treated them kindly enough, but they responded to kindness with cursing. The monks were waiting until it was time to go to the village for supplies before they wiped the thieves' memories. The missionary asked if he might speak to the prisoners. They said yes.

"At first the thieves refused to listen. But the missionary kept coming back and loving on them. Finally, they let him tell them about Jesus. Their hearts were melted by the story of God's love for them. Both asked Jesus to come into their hearts.

"The transformation that came over them was like the difference between night and day. Their anger was gone. Love flowed out from them. They apologized to the monks for trying to break in and steal and begged the monks to let them do any work that needed to be done. 'Keep us bound,' they said. 'Just let us serve you.'

"The time came to return the prisoners to the village. The monks explained that it was their law that all who came to the monastery to steal must have their memories erased. The prisoners said they understood and gladly submitted to the treatment.

"As they stood there, love pouring out from them, the monks tried the fear treatment. It did not work. In fact, the fear started to come back on them. They found themselves fearing these men who exuded love. The monks were so stunned by this that they tried to send the two away loaded with gold and jewels, but the men refused it. They asked only that they be allowed to leave so that they could tell others about Jesus.

"That is how the monks discovered that the love flowing from a Christ-filled believer casts out fear. This truth is beautifully expressed by John: 'There is no fear in love – dread does not exist, but full-grown (complete, perfect) love turns fear out of doors and expels every trace of terror! For fear brings with it the thought of punishment, and so he who is afraid has not reached the full maturity of love – is not yet grown into love's complete perfection' (I John 4:18 AMP).

"Az does not know that one who loves with Christ's love cannot be cursed. The Christ-filled person who blesses and loves causes the fear, or curse, to come back on the person sending it. You'll find that in Proverbs 26:2 (The New Living Translation says it best). The monks who discovered this truth did not share this with Az. So he does not know the danger that awaits him if he tries to use the curse of fear on a Christian who has learned how to love."

The Professor is silent for a few moments, and then, jumping to his feet, and putting his hand on Peter's shoulder he says, "Well, Peter, I think I've finally told you everything. But let's not dwell on the dangers that may lie ahead of us. We are safe for now. Look at that gorgeous sunset!"

With supper over (and the dishes washed) they sit back in easy chairs to rest. Peter, gazing at the stars, tries to figure out which constellations he is seeing when a chopper pops up in front of the window, and flashes its light three times.

"That's our signal," shouts the Professor above the noise of the chopper.

Peter picks up his hiking boots and backpack and follows the Professor to the elevator in the back. A master switch turns out the lights and turns off the fireplace. The door closes and the elevator ascends to the cabin. Louis is waiting there with the clothes they'd left at the lodge. They quickly change clothes, toss everything else into the back packs and toss them into the chopper.

"It's been a long time, Professor. Our enemy has pulled off all his men. He's convinced you weren't here or else got away. Something happened to him in the valley a couple days ago. He can't explain it, but he's sure it wasn't you. At least that's the report that came back to us.

"He's hot on your trail, Professor. He's not going to leave you alone. He's pretty sure where you live and work. I fear a showdown is coming soon."

A short chopper flight to the air strip, and they are in a two-engine plane headed for home. Peter soon falls asleep, and the next thing he knows the Professor is waking him up.

"We've landed," he shouts above the engine noise. Not a word, though, about how they got out of the other country and back into this country without passports.

Mrs. McD is waiting. She brought the Professor's car and their winter jackets. They drop Peter off at his dorm room and head back to Mrs. McD's. She persuades the Professor that he ought not go back to his home in the dark. They'll drive out together in the morning. And Peter, Peter is so sleepy he flops down on his bed in his clothes, shoes and all.

point, made [illegible] seen [illegible] up [illegible] next things he knew th[illegible] beginning.

[illegible] us about [illegible] house. Nora, who thought about [illegible] of the [illegible] and back into his company [illegible] soon.

Mrs. [illegible] She brought [illegible] came that [illegible] Pete will [illegible] case back to [illegible] the [illegible] go back to his home [illegible] months. And [illegible] said all.

BOOK 3

Az You Were

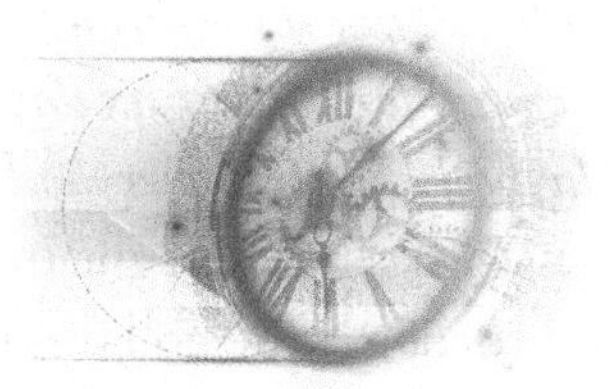

Chapter 30

Mrs. McD Tells a Tall Tale

It never pays to sleep in your clothes. If you twist and turn during the night they can get all tangled up around you, cut off the circulation and put your hand or leg to sleep. That is what Peter discovers when he wakes up. He tries to step out of bed only to find a numb stub where his foot should have been. It doesn't want to support him when he tries to stand up. He sits back down and tries to wiggle his foot to get the circulation going. Then it hits! It starts to tingle and feels like a thousand needles pricking. It brings tears to his eyes. It also makes him fully awake in a hurry.

As he sits on the edge of the bed, waiting for his foot to wake up, Peter thinks back over his unusual adventure of the last few days. *Let's see, how many days has it been? It was Wednesday morning when it all began. How many days were we gone? Let's see, it took us four days to climb and crawl to the marble castle. We spent two days in the castle, and came back last night. That's Wednesday, Thursday, Friday, Saturday, Sunday and Monday. That means today is Tuesday. My first class will be Twentieth-Century British Literature.*

Oh, No! I had a paper due today! How am I going to explain why I didn't get it done? How am I going to explain where I've been? What do I tell my instructors? What do I tell my boss? He's bound to be furious I didn't show up for work. I'll be lucky if I still have a job. And my friends? They won't leave me alone until I give them an explanation they'll believe. I can't tell them the truth. If I did they wouldn't believe me. It's not my nature to tell lies. They'll see through it right away. How am I going to explain where I've been for the last six days? I've got to come up with something in a hurry. Maybe I can stall everybody until I get a chance to talk with the Professor.

With that thought in mind Peter showers, dresses, dons his jacket and turns up the collar – there are snow flurries in the air. He steps out the door only to be greeted by the Professor, who is standing by his car waiting for him!

"Good morning, Peter! Hop in and we'll go have breakfast with Mrs. McD. One last good meal before you go back to the institutional stuff they call food. Don't worry about your classes. We'll fix you up with good excuses."

Peter is glad for the invite. It puts off the inevitable questions from everybody for a while. And it sounds like the Professor's got some ideas on what to say. He hops into the car, and they're on their way. This time the Professor drives normally, and soon pulls into Mrs. McD's driveway. They are out of the car and up the few steps to her merry kitchen in a flash, led on by a blast of the most delicious smells that seem to float them up the stairs. Mrs. McD, a big smile on her face, greets them with a cheery welcome.

"Come in, come in, Peter. You've had quite an adventure from what I hear. The Professor tells me you were even wounded, but carried on like an old trooper! Good for you. Well, enough small talk. I heard your stomach growling before you even got here! We'll chat after we've eaten."

Mrs. McD had fixed up the most delicious breakfast omelet Peter had ever had the pleasure of putting in his mouth!

"Mrs. McD, I didn't know an omelet could taste so good. You've got to be the best cook in the world. But these cinnamon rolls! I thought my mom made the best cinnamon rolls in the world. But yours beat my mom's hands down. Don't let her know I said that! May I please have another? Maybe two? I'll have to put in five hours in the gym to work off this breakfast!"

"You and me both," laughs the Professor, as he too reaches for another roll.

After they do their best to eat every last morsel of all the rolls, but fail, they sadly eye what is left. They push back their chairs and start to pick up their dishes. Mrs. McD stops them, "No, No. I'll take care of the dishes. You two go sit in the living room. I'll be in as soon as I'm finished."

Peter follows the Professor into the living room and plops down in an overstuffed chair facing him. When the Professor speaks it is with a contented look on his face.

"Well, Peter, you'll never get a breakfast like that in the dining hall. Are you glad you came?"

"Boy! am I glad! Mrs. McD's got to be a cook of the highest order!" he answers, an equally contented look on his face. Suddenly he remembers he needs help with his explanation of where he's been. "Professor, we were gone six days. I can't tell people about it. Besides, no one would believe me if I did. You said you'd fix me up with excuses. So what do I tell my professors? What do I tell my boss? He's gonna be furious I haven't shown up for work."

"I think Mrs. McD has all the answers for us. She may be a talented physicist in her own right, but she is also one shrewd detective, and very resourceful," he adds with a smile as Mrs. McD enters and takes a seat. "But before she gives us our alibi, she has a story I want her to tell you."

They look at her, and wait for her to speak. "Well, no doubt about it," she nods her head, "you two do need a lot of looking after. I've been looking after the Professor for well over one hundred years, Peter. It's been fun and never dull. Now you've come along and added more excitement to my job. I do hope you'll be a bit more careful than he is!"

"You're over a hundred years old?" Peter gasps. "I suppose I should be polite and say you don't look a day over fifty!"

Laughing heartily, Mrs. McD continues. "The Professor exaggerates a bit, Peter, but I love solving mysteries. That's why Dr. McD and I worked so well together. I worked as his lab assistant in my undergraduate years. It was easy for me to look at things differently than he. I'd see something he'd overlooked, or ask questions he'd not thought of. We grew very close, and fell in love. One day, however, he thought of a question I'd not thought of: he asked me to marry him!

"As I said, I enjoy solving mysteries. I was intrigued by the fact that behind every legend, every bit of folklore, there is always a story to explain how the legend started. One legend that caught my attention was the legend of the Nine Unknown Men. I got to thinking that it would make a great plot for a science fiction story to have the Nine Unknown Men still alive today, but with this difference; one of them would have turned evil with a diabolical plan to take over the world. The others were out to stop him. I had to decide what kind of evil plot he would devise. I told Dr. McD about my story idea, and he encouraged me to keep going.

"It would be logical for the Nine Unknown Men to leave a trail of evidence. I wondered what the evidence would be. What would it look like? I dug into all the versions of the legend I could find to see what they would suggest. It was quite a mishmash!

"One thread did seem consistent in all the stories. One of the Nine would step in and aid mankind in times of crisis, such as a disease epidemic. This seemed like the most promising trail to use for my story. If the story was true and they did step in to help as needed, there should be a trail of evidence that sticks out like a sore thumb if you knew what to look for. I had no choice. I just had to look for stories, folklore, myths that told of some unknown man or men appearing out of nowhere and helping in a time of crisis.

"It was fun. I was finding just the right historical spots to use in my story, when something unexpected happened. I was finding real life stories, instead of make believe ones! Dr. McD almost fell out of his seat when I told him what I'd found. I started to make some rough drafts on how all this could be woven together into my science fiction story. I made notes and documented the locations where the stories occurred and plotted them on the map.

"Then the stories suddenly stopped. I thought that strange. Then a wild idea hit me! What if all the stories I was collecting weren't just coincidences after all? This will make my story even better! What if one of the Nine really had turned traitor and wanted to take over the world? What if the others, to keep their knowledge from him, split up and hid? I knew right then that I now had all the elements I needed for a great science fiction novel.

"That would mean, of course, that the legend that they had discovered the elixir of life was true. Now, if the traitor used that elixir, wouldn't he be alive today? Would he be plotting and waiting to put his plan to work? What was he waiting for? What about the others? They had the elixir of life, too. Would they still be alive, keeping an eye on the traitor? This was getting better and better for my exciting thriller.

"Well, I'd set myself some tough questions to answer. I needed to find a new kind of trail of evidence to follow. But what kind of evidence was I looking for? The trail I'd been following was based on their stepping in and helping in a time of crisis. It was easy for them to step out of the woodwork, so to speak, give their help, and then step back into the woodwork.

"That storyline worked up until it stopped. I got to thinking about what was happening in the world at that time. Things were changing. Superstition was losing its impact. People were becoming more sophisticated, and educated. Inventions were emerging. That meant it wouldn't be possible any more just to pop in and out of the woodwork. Their strategy would have to change. But how? They had to keep their identities secret. So they would have to find ways to feed their knowledge to others in such a way the others would think it was their own. They would be the unknown assistant who helped, then disappeared. With that in mind I went back to study the history and legends of different cultures, beginning at the time when the stories of the Nine seemed to stop.

"Whenever I found a story that fit my criteria I marked the date and location on a map. Remember, I was just playing around with this. When I finished my research I looked at my map with all the locations and dates plotted. Suddenly I saw what I hadn't expected to see! All the locations grouped themselves into eight geographical regions!

"I looked and looked. All my detective instincts said there was far too much consistency for this to be coincidence. Could it be possible that the story of the Nine Unknown Men was really true after all?

Could my guess about a traitor and the Order splitting up be true? At this point all my detective instincts went on high alert!

"Just suppose it was true. Then what was the traitor waiting for? Maybe the answer to that was in the legends. The legends all said that their knowledge had been written in a book. That book disappeared. But in its pages, the legends said, were plans for building a time machine. 'So that's what he's waiting for!' I thought. He's waiting for the time machine. He doesn't have it or the plans for building it, else he'd have used it before now.

"That left me with one last question. What would the traitor do with the time machine? An article in a financial report suggested an answer to that question. It talked about the bankers of the world. The article made it clear that the people who really controlled the world were not the kings or dictators or politicians. It takes money to rule and control. The article concluded that he who controls the wealth, controls the world. Who controls the wealth? The world's bankers.

"When I read that, I knew I had everything I needed for my story. The traitor would use the time machine to go back in time and change things so that all of the world's wealth would fall into his hands. He wouldn't have to raise an army. No one would attack him. Everyone who wanted money would seek to gain his favor.

"He would decide who rose to power and who didn't. They would all have to do as he said, or he would pull the plug on their money. My book was practically writing itself! All I had to do now was figure out how the traitor would find the time machine. One day I got the answer to that, too! I read about a research and development company called Az Industries. In addition to manufacturing a variety of products, the company was pioneering the development of electronic surveillance devices based on the newly invented radio and telegraph. 'Aha!' I thought to myself, that is exactly what the traitor would be doing: finding ways to detect the presence of a time machine.

"The founder, Mr. Az, was said to be a recluse. It was a strange name. As I studied it I suddenly realized that Az is the first and last letters of the alphabet. Like Alpha and Omega, the First and the Last, the beginning and the end. And I thought, Az is a perfect name for the traitor to call himself in my story!

"One thing bothered me, though. The coincidences. There were too many of them. I couldn't get away from the question: is the story of the Nine Unknown Men true after all? That was an idea I thought I best keep to myself! Then one-day Dr. McD met the Professor and brought him home. We became good friends and had good discussions. Once in a while he'd say something that set the detective in me reeling. It happened again and again over the years. It got beyond the point of coincidence.

I found myself thinking, 'No, it can't be. Surely he's not one of the Nine!' I dismissed the idea. Yet, piece by piece the evidence built. The day Dr. McD died, the Professor came to see him. He asked to be alone with him. Dr. McD was a visionary. Nothing would have made him happier than to be on a spaceship visiting other planets. When I went in to see him after the Professor left, he said to me, 'Mrs. McD, I die a happy man! Take care of the Professor, will you? He's a bit older than he looks, and needs looking after.'

"That's when it all came together and I knew, just like a detective knows, when all the pieces finally fit. I knew for sure the Professor was one of the Nine. I knew my theory about a traitor was true! I was fairly certain it was Mr. Az. I was pretty sure he was looking for the time machine. I was pretty sure the Professor was its inventor.

"A few weeks after Dr. McD's death, the Professor asked me if I would consider becoming his housekeeper. I prayed about it and it seemed the right thing to do. But I couldn't tell him 'yes' until I'd unloaded all my suspicions on him. If it wasn't true, I figured he'd withdraw his offer, thinking I'd gone a bit daft.

"Well, I told him. He looked at me a little stunned, but he didn't deny a word of it. All he said was, 'Do you want to be my housekeeper?' When I said 'yes,' he took a small marble flask out of his pocket. He said it was a special mixture a friend of his had concocted to keep a person healthy. He didn't want me getting sick in the middle of helping him. I was pretty sure what it was, and by the next morning I knew. He had given me the elixir of life! I felt and looked twenty years younger! Like

Dr. McD asked, I've been looking after the Professor ever since. Now it seems I have to look after you, too!"

Her warm smile tells Peter this remarkable lady likes him very much and approves of him wholeheartedly. Her story also tells Peter that she has a very shrewd mind, like the Professor said. No one else would have ever gone to the effort to study, collect the clues, and then put the clues together like she did.

"Mrs. McD has been a marvelous help to me Peter. Her talents and skills go far beyond housekeeping and cooking. She is a genius. Now she's going to tell us what kind of story we'll be telling everyone."

As she sits back in her chair a look of obvious pleasure comes over Mrs. McD's face. *Being a conniving and astute detective while playing the part of a dumb housekeeper can be lots of fun*, she muses, thinking back over her adventures with Az's men, and the sneaky plan she put into action afterwards.

"When you two left in the Blue Orb I knew you wouldn't be coming back here. You'd have to land somewhere else, somewhere unexpected, and work your way back when it was safe. That's the only way you could keep out of Az's hands. We contacted TPF and he said he'd have the others start calling the tesseract machine when I gave the signal. I'd already notified the others when the Orb first landed to be on the lookout for you.

"Once you disappeared into the secret lab, I put into action a plan I'd been working on. First, I got rid of all evidence that you had been here. After Marybelle left I called the police chief and asked him to come by. He came just after the Men in Black got here. Once Hank got a look at the three men, he called for backup. The Men in Black heard the sirens and took off. Hank warned them they would be immediately arrested if they came back.

"After Hank and the boys left, I called our friend, Dr. Horrace Bottomly. You've never met him, Peter, but the Professor and I have been to his research lab. His field is Quantum Physics, specializing in teleportation of matter. I told him I needed a favor. I explained that you two had left on a top secret project and that we needed an alibi to explain your absence. He said it was the perfect time to call! He had just the excuse for you two rushing off without notice. The result, Peter, is this little article I cut from the paper a couple days ago." Peter takes the paper, reads the headline, and is astounded! The headline reads:

> STAR TREK TECHNOLOGY COMES TO LIFE!
> In a news release from a nuclear research laboratory at an undisclosed location, Dr. Horrace Bottomly, head of research, reports that a young physics student from our local college pushed the button that successfully dematerialized a small quantity of metal and sent it across space where it was successfully rematerialized in the first successful teleportation of matter. The student and his professor left the college unexpectedly, responding to an urgent call for help from Dr. Bottomly. Bottomly said they were up against a tight deadline and that substantial funding was resting on the success of this test."

"Quite a story isn't it. Peter?" asks the Professor. "Not as exciting as what we really did, but exciting enough. Mrs. McD has more to tell."

"Once I'd talked to Horrace, I called President Williams. He, of course, was excited to have a member of his faculty and one of his students involved in such a dramatic scientific breakthrough. He volunteered to make excuses for Peter with his teachers, and to get a fill-in for the Professor. I called your boss at the store, Peter, and he was glad you got such an opportunity. Just let him know when you can come back to work.

"That left just one more thing to take care of: how you got from here to there and back. Back, of course, was easy enough because a plane brought you back. I worked out a little scheme with our friend, Henry, who has a plane hangered about twenty miles from here. I asked Henry to find a couple people he could trust and make a fast trip to the coordinates I gave him. He would leave the two there, and return home. His log book would show he had taken two people to Bottomly's lab.

"The two people he took were given a gourmet meal, some gifts, a little cash, and put on a bus. Their trip was a diversion, they were told, to throw some industrial espionage spies off the track. So it was important not to say anything to anyone about the trip. Well," adds Mrs. McD, obviously proud of herself, "that's your cover story. The rest is up to you."

Peter is speechless. This is the most elaborate cover-up story he's ever heard! If this doesn't throw Az off the trail, nothing will. No wonder the Professor seemed unconcerned about any of Az's people being around.

"Are you ready for an alibi physics class?" asks the Professor. "We need a simple explanation for people. I think this will work: The only way you can dematerialize a cube of iron is to split it into individual atoms, send these across space, attached to a carrier, and then reassemble them at the destination. There is a problem. The atoms and molecules are in constant motion. How can you make a pattern or map of where each molecule goes if they are always moving? Without a map you can't reassemble them correctly. This problem is called the Heisenberg uncertainty principle. The first step towards solving that problem is to successfully send a specific number of molecules over a distance. That was what this test was about.

"Dr. Bottomly has been working on a device to compensate for the Heisenberg uncertainty principle. But to get funding for that research, he had to prove teleportation was possible. That's all you need to tell people. If people press you for more information, tell them you had to sign a paper agreeing that you would not divulge any information beyond this. That is not a lie, because you are going to sign that paper right now!"

Mrs. McD hands Peter a clip board and a pen. He signs, and passes it to the Professor. He signs it, and hands it back to Mrs. McD. She puts it in an envelope, seals it, and hands Peter some 8 x 10 photos.

"These are pictures of where you were. You are standing outside the sealed test area. You are looking through special glass that blocks radiation. The control panel is to the left, on this side of the glass. That's where you stood and pushed the red button. Every molecule made it across. Any information beyond this is information that you are not allowed to divulge even if you knew it. So you can truthfully say that you are not allowed to say anything."

"Mrs. McD, you are truly amazing. You've made fitting back into the college routine a piece of cake. You can be my defense attorney any day!"

"Well, Peter," laughs the Professor, "it's time we really did go back to college. In spite of all the excuses, you're going to have to make up the classes you missed!"

"You would have to say that," Peter responds with a groan.

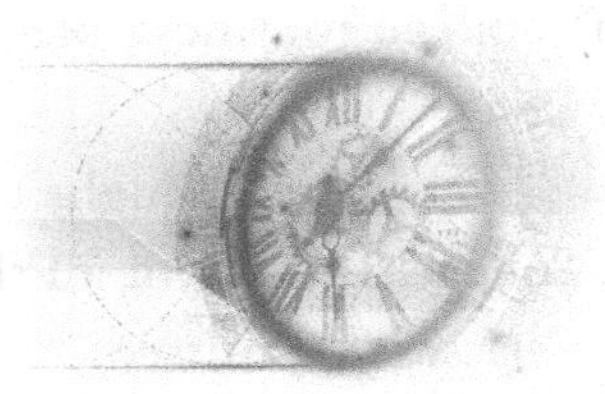

CHAPTER 31

A Babysitter for Peter

Two uneventful weeks pass. Well, almost uneventful. Peter is sure his professors have decided to gang up on him and give him long written assignments and papers to write in exchange for his "moment of fame!" He's gotten head cramps from all the notes he's taken, and he's spent hours and hours in the library trying to catch up. Mr. Johnson needed him a lot of extra hours in the store. He said it was because he knew how much Peter needed the money.

Early Sunday night, Peter rejoices as he puts the final period on the final paper, and is caught up. He's even happy when his alarm goes off the next morning. "At last I can relax and enjoy a regular day," he almost shouts. He'd been able to go to bed early for the first time since they'd returned. He feels rested. No flashbacks messing with his head. Just a good night's rest, a peaceful morning, an unhurried breakfast. No trouble staying awake during classes. Yep! Things are finally back to routine. Only the weather is unpleasant.

"What a morning!" Peter pulls his jacket tighter around him, shivering as he steps outside into a sticky mess of wet snow falling as winter fights with spring over whose turn it is. He sloshes his way to the library. On the way he stops by the college post office. No mail except a note from the President's office. He sticks it in his pocket to read later. In the library he hangs his wet coat on the rack, slips off his boots, and heads for a computer terminal. He'd looked forward to a course in Twentieth Century literature.

He just hadn't expected to do so much reading or write so many papers. This is Monday, and another paper is due Friday. At least this is about one of his favorite writers, C.S. Lewis, and his impact on Christian thought. The library's new computer program lets you narrow down your search to the specific subjects you are looking for, lists the books that meet your criteria, and describes the contents. It is a terrific time saver. He finds three books listed that look promising and heads for the stacks to get them. He finds a study carrel near a window, and takes out his notepad and pencil.

The note from the President falls to the floor. "Oops! I'd better read it," he whispers. The note reads: *Peter, there are a couple men who say they are from the government who will be here at 2:00 p.m. They want to meet with you in my office to talk about your trip. Please be prompt.*

The hair on Peter's neck stands up. His stomach twists into a knot. Ever since he first met the Professor this inner warning system started working. So far, it had never been wrong. The Professor said it has something to do with the Holy Spirit at work in us. When we take time to develop our relationship with the Holy Spirit and keep an ear tuned to his guidance, and follow it, we will receive it. He told about Agnes Sanford's daughter, who was on a train with a friend. She suddenly got that inner warning, grabbed her friend's hand and got off the train. The train wrecked before it got to its next stop.[1]

Peter grabs his stuff, and rushes out of the library. He runs towards the physics building, races up the stairs, runs down the hall, and bursts into the Professors office without knocking. Susan, one of his classmates, is standing in front of the desk, talking to the Professor.

"I hope I didn't do anything wrong," she is saying. "But when those Men in Black came into the Union three weeks ago looking for you and Peter, I didn't tell them what they wanted to know. Something inside me said, 'don't; evil.' I know it sounds weird, but I had to mislead to them. I told them you never came into the Union, and I had no idea where you were. I didn't do anything wrong, did I?"

---

[1] Sanford, Agnes, 1947, *The Healing Light*, St. Paul MN, Macalester Park Publishing Company.

"Quite the contrary, Susan," the Professor answers, smiling. "You did exactly the right thing. I'm so glad you were the one they asked. You gave us the extra time we needed to get away. Now, you had some questions about your homework?"

Peter pushes past Susan and thrusts the note in front of the Professor. He reads it. For a moment he is silent and thoughtful. Then he smiles and looks up at Susan.

"I'm sorry Susan, we'll have to reschedule our session. Peter has a problem that demands my immediate attention. Call me when you're free, and I'll clear my schedule."

Susan, slim, with long wavy auburn hair highlighting the delicate features of her beautiful face, is a very bright physics student. The smile she gives Peter as she leaves gives Peter the impression she'd be willing to go out with him any time! That thought comes to Peter as a total surprise. Girls were the last thing on his mind. He was too busy with classes and work, and too preoccupied with Az and the Blue Orb to give any thought to dating.

"Beautiful girl, isn't she?" asks the Professor, catching the look on both their faces. "I dare say she has the makings of another Mrs. McD!"

Is the Professor trying to play Cupid, Peter wonders? No, No. That's ridiculous. There is something sinister in the wind we've got to deal with, and it isn't dating! He sits down in a chair in front of the desk. The Professor looks at him thoughtfully for some time before he speaks.

"I had hoped Mrs. McD's ruse had safely gotten them off our trail until the Blue Orb shows up again. It hasn't shown up. Az is losing patience. The report has come back to me that now that he's had some time to think about it, he believes it was the 'Professor and his chosen one' who were in the valley. What he doesn't know for sure is who you and I are or where we are. That's what he's trying to find out. Are we the 'Professor and his chosen one,' or did we really go to Bottomly's? If he can break down your story, that will prove we're them. These so-called government agents will be his most trusted and trained men who alone know what he is looking for."

The Professor again looks thoughtfully at Peter. Suddenly he gets a mischievous and pleased look on his face. "Let's frustrate them, make them angry. They've gone to a lot of trouble to set up this meeting, thinking no one would miss a meeting with important government officials. So, let's start by making them angry. Call Dr. Williams' office and leave the message that you can't make the appointment today because you won't be on campus."

Peter calls Dr. William's office and leaves the message.

"Good. Now we've got to find some place for you to go, and a good reason for you to be gone. I know just the place. All I need is the reason!"

Once again, the thoughtful expression crosses the Professor's face. "Aha! I know who will make the perfect reason," he exclaims, grinning with an impish look on his face as he reaches for the telephone.

"I think Susan can help us. Let me see if I can find her." Peter, looking suspiciously at the Professor, wonders what he has in mind. Why would he want to involve someone else? After several calls he finally locates her.

"Susan, this is the Professor. Can you come back to my office right now? Good. We'll see you in ten minutes."

He looks up with a self-satisfied look, an obvious twinkle in his eyes like he is enjoying very much what he is doing. *This is not good*, Peter thinks. *He's up to something more than giving me an excuse, and obviously enjoying it*!

While waiting they go over Peter's story about helping Dr. Bottomly. He practices saying, "I can't tell you anymore. I signed a paper," while the Professor tries every way he can think of, and he's loaded with them, to trip him up. Peter stands his ground and doesn't flinch.

"You're good, Peter," the Professor finally admits. "They'll try to work around your answer, get you to slip up. Remember, the best defense is a good offense. Try to turn the questions back on them and trip them up every chance you get. The more you can make them look like dummies the better."

Just then there is a knock at the door, and a sweet sounding woman's voice asks, "May I come in?"

The Professor quickly hops up, rushes to the door, and pulls Susan in, saying "Susan! It was so good of you to come back. You've already met Peter. You two are my top physics students, and I've really enjoyed getting to teach both of you. How well do you know Peter?"

"I don't know him personally," Susan answers shyly. "We've been in several of the same classes. I work the counter at the Union sometimes, so I've waited on him. That's all."

"Then let me introduce you to each other. Susan, this is Peter. Peter, this beautiful brunette, who you've ignored all these years, and yet who has waited on you so faithfully in the Union, and who helped us get safely away, is Susan."

"Hi!" Peter shakes Susan's hand, a little nervously, especially after the Professor's flowery introduction, combined with the fact that he has no idea what the Professor's planning.

"Susan, I asked you to come back because I need to ask you to do a really big favor for me. I have an urgent need of a babysitter starting right now and for the rest of the day. Could you possibly do that for me?"

"I'll have to cut a couple classes, but I can make them up later. Yes, I'd be glad to babysit for you, Professor. Who is the baby?"

"Good! I'm glad you said yes, Susan. Who is the baby? Before I tell you, you need to know that you will find this a very strange request. This will be no ordinary babysitting job. It will take all your skills and patience, as this is no ordinary baby. In fact, this baby has been known to be quite unmanageable. He could drive you to your wits end," he adds with obvious enjoyment. "Can you handle it?"

Susan sees the mischievous gleam in the Professor's eyes. It makes her a little nervous, not knowing what the Professor is up to. But she does want to help him out if he needs her. So, with a little apprehension she answers, "I'm sure I can handle it."

"Now that that's settled, and you've been warned, let me introduce you to the baby. His name is Peter! I want you to babysit Peter this afternoon and tonight, away from the campus."

"Babysit!" Peter gasps. "I don't need a babysitter!"

"Now, Peter," the Professor shakes his finger as though scolding a child. "You know Mrs. McD said you needed looking after! That's all I'm doing. Just seeing that you get looked after!"

The mischievous gleam in the Professor's eyes does not put Peter at ease. Peter sputters to no avail. Susan doesn't know whether to laugh or shake her head in disbelief.

"I know this is a strange request, Susan. But I really do need your help. I want to get Peter away from the campus this afternoon. There are some people looking for him who claim to be from the government. We both know they aren't. They want some information Peter has, and we don't want them to get it. They called Dr. Williams to make the appointment, just to be sure Peter would be there. We want to aggravate these men, make them angry. To do this I want to get Peter off campus. I thought that a young man spending the day with a pretty girl would be an excuse anyone would believe. It will make them mad to think Peter has stood them up for a girl. How about it, Susan, will you do this for me? Will you babysit Peter?"

"When you said it was a strange request Professor, that was an understatement! If anyone else were to ask me to do this, I'd say 'absolutely not!' But I trust you. Somehow I sense in my spirit that it's the right thing to do, which surprises me to say the least! What is it exactly you want me to do? What do you mean by 'babysit'?"

Peter's face gets very red. "This is downright embarrassing" he mutters, half under his breath. "Here I am, a grown man, well almost, and you're talking about me like I'm a baby!"

Ignoring Peter, the Professor continues with his plan. "This is what I thought we would do, Susan. One can't blame a fellow for wanting to spend a day with a pretty girl. That's a pretty good excuse for not going to a meeting you just learned about an hour ago. But Peter doesn't have a girlfriend and there is no time for him to go find one. So I'm doing the next best thing. I'm getting him a babysitter.

"I know it won't be easy. So, I'm going to call Mrs. McD to help you. I'll ask her to come by and take you two to her home for the rest of the day. You'll love her. She's also a great physicist in her own right, and she is one shrewd sleuth, as Peter can tell you. She's an expert at asking critical questions. She'll help you babysit him and keep him under control," he adds, winking at Peter.

With that settled, he calls Mrs. McD. "I've got something I need you to do," is all he says. Hanging up the phone he turns to Susan, "She said she'd drop everything and meet us in the faculty parking lot. We'd best get out there in a hurry. I'll join you for supper, and then we'll plan the evening." So saying, he slips on his coat and galoshes and ushers Peter and Susan out.

The wet snow is still falling, but not so hard. There are signs of it clearing. Maybe spring won this fight after all. They slosh their way to the parking lot. Just as they get there, Mrs. McD drives up in her vintage car.

"Well! What's this? A girl? And a very pretty one, too. I like her looks. You've got good taste, Peter."

Again Peter's face goes red. But before he can say anything, the Professor speaks up. "That's not quite the way it is, Mrs. McD. This is Susan, one of my top students. I've asked her to babysit Peter for me this afternoon! I told her you'd take them to your house and you'd help her."

"Come now, Professor. That's not the whole story. You've cooked something up. What's going on?"

"Peter just got a note from Dr. Williams that two government agents were coming to interview him this afternoon. Both of us sensed immediately that these were not government agents. We suspect you know who is back on our trail, trying to crack our alibi. We thought it would be fun to aggravate them a little, maybe get them to slip up and reveal who they really are. It seemed to me that the most logical reason for a young man not to be on campus would be because he was with a girl. Since Peter hasn't cooperated by getting a girlfriend, I decided to fix him up with a babysitter! Who better than my pretty young physics student?"

"You do have good taste, Professor. But it's a miracle you got her to agree! Well, I told you Peter was going to need looking after. That's no small task. I'll be glad to help you babysit Peter, Susan. I think we can find some toys he can play with. When he's taking his nap we can get better acquainted. I sure hope Peter's potty trained!" she adds, winking at Peter.

Peter's only consolation in this conversation is that he notices that Susan's face is also red, whether embarrassed for herself or for him, or just from laughing. He wouldn't blame her for backing out now. He sure would if he could. The only thing Peter knows for sure is that the way Mrs. McD picked up on this, this could turn into one long afternoon of being the focus of a lot of jokes.

"Come on you two," Mrs. McD hurries them into the car. "Time's a-wasting. We'd better get going before those so-called agents arrive and see you. Don't worry about lunch, Susan. I'll fix us a good lunch. Oh, and we'll fix a nice warm bottle of milk for baby Peter!"

"Please! Mrs. McD!" Peter pleads. He holds the door for Susan to sit beside Mrs. McD, and he slips into the back seat. He feels like he needs to say something to Susan. "Susan, I apologize for Mrs. McD and the Professor. I don't know what's come over them. They're not usually like this."

"That's okay, Peter. I like them both very much. If my doing this can help you and the Professor, I'm really glad to do it. I saw those strange men snooping around campus this last year. They made my skin creep. Then, when those Men in Black came looking for you three weeks ago something in me shouted 'danger.' They asked me a lot of questions about you and the Professor and I gave them all kinds of wrong information. All the while they were talking I kept thinking, 'there's something evil going on, and it's directed towards the Professor and Peter.' I was so glad when I saw you and the Professor escape out the back door. I've been praying for the both of you a lot."

Susan's words leave Peter speechless. The words are not lost on Mrs. McD, either, who is now smiling from ear to ear.

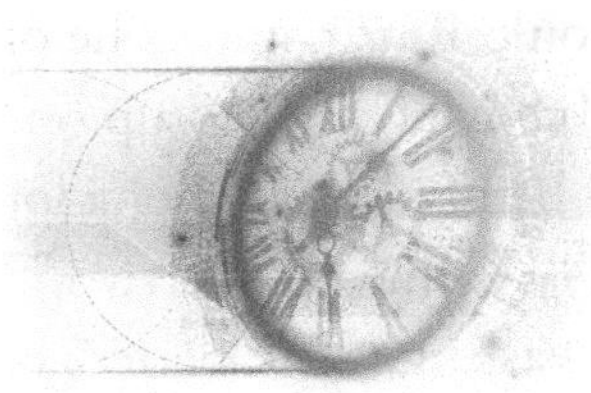

CHAPTER 32

Looking After Baby

A few blocks away from the campus, in a semi-secluded area, Mrs. McD tells Peter, "Scoot down in your seat so no one can see you. Good. Stay down until I've parked the car and closed the garage door. I've had a feeling someone's been watching my house for the last three weeks. Just in case they are, I don't want them to see you, Peter. Okay? They won't think a thing of seeing Susan. I'll let you know when it's safe to get up."

Mrs. McD continues the drive to her home, finally turning into her driveway. The garage doors open, and she drives in. The doors close and she gives the all clear. Peter sits up, opens his door and steps out. Susan is already out of the car, following Mrs. McD as she leads the way through the door into the house and up a few steps to her welcoming kitchen. They are immediately flooded with the wonderful odors of fresh baked bread and rolls and cinnamon buns and chocolate chip cookies.

"Oh," gasps Susan, "this is just like my mom's kitchen. So colorful and full of light and all kinds of good smells. It's almost like going home!"

These words please Mrs. McD, who immediately forgets Peter and concentrates all her attention on Susan. "Tell me more about your mother. Is she a physicist?"

"No, mom is a pastor's wife. Dad says mom always wanted to be a missionary. He says she married him so that she could have her own private mission field! Mom agrees. She says dad is quite a handful! Mrs.

McD, do you have any aspirin? I stayed up late and got up early to finish a paper that was due today. I'm starting to get a headache. Usually a short nap takes care of it, but I'm not going to get a nap today, not with this babysitting job."

"I don't have any aspirin, Susan, but I've got something far better. I've got a Relative who loves to heal headaches, and refresh our bodies. He's my Elder Brother. His name is Jesus! Just sit in that chair, relax, and let his healing power flow into you when I put my hands on your head."

The instant Mrs. McD places her hands on Susan's head she feels power flow out of her hands and into Susan.

"Wow! You absorbed that like a sponge."

"My headache's gone too. I knew it would be. I did like my dad said to do: 'Keep your "expectorator" turned on and plugged into Jesus.' Mom says it's like the woman with the issue of blood who expected and knew that as soon as she touched Jesus' garment she would be healed. Dad calls it the BER of faith: believe, expect, and receive. I should have remembered that in the first place before I asked you for aspirin."

"Amen to that!" Mrs. McD is thrilled to hear Susan talk about prayer and faith with such conviction. "I can see that you and I are going to have lots of fun sharing things."

Sharing together is what they do. They talk about Jesus, talk about their favorite dishes and some sneaky ways to fix things so they taste terrific. They become so completely engrossed in talking that they forget all about Peter. Peter waits patiently while they go at women talk a mile a minute. Finally, he cries out, "Hey! I'm the baby and I need my coffee and cookie!"

Laughing, Mrs. McD mockingly slaps herself gently on the cheek and blurts out, "Oh my goodness, we forgot the baby! Susan will you get some cups out of the cupboard while I get some cookies? There's a tray under the sink. We'll take them into the living room and drink our coffee by the fire. There's a sippy cup for baby Peter."

The warm fire, the hot coffee (drunk from a sippy cup), and the supremely delectable chocolate chip cookies get the best of Peter, and he dozes off. Suddenly he feels his shoulder being shaken, and he hears Susan's cheery voice, "Did baby have a nice nap? Lunch is ready!"

Looking up sleepily, yawning, Peter, acting on a sudden impulse, puts his hand on Susan's and says, "You know, if this wasn't Mrs. McD's home, and if you weren't so pretty, I think I'd resent being called a baby, but it sounds nice coming from you."

Susan quickly pulls her hand away, turns and goes back into the kitchen. Peter, out of the corner of his eye, sees her blush. But that's okay. He's blushing too, now that he is fully awake and realizes what he just said! "Boy, did I act like a fool," he mutters.

Peter is wide awake after his little nap. He wants to talk to Mrs. McD privately to see if she knows anything new about Az and his goons. He doesn't get a chance. She and Susan are too busy talking about recipes and Susan's mom and how much Mrs. McD has in common with Susan's mom, and a whole lot of other stuff. Peter gives up trying to ask Mrs. McD anything.

However, he is informed by Mrs. McD that Susan helped prepare lunch. He quickly decides that he is obviously outnumbered and outgunned as far as these two are concerned. He contents himself with listening as he eats. Susan and Mrs. McD talk like they've known each other for years. When lunch is over he discovers that there is one advantage to having Susan there. He is excused from washing dishes, told to go to the living room while the two women wash up the dishes and clean up the kitchen.

When the dishes are done, the two women also retire to the living room. It feels good to sit and relax around the fire while the snow outside is still falling in big wet clumps. No one says anything. And then a little smart-alecky urge hits Peter and he blurts out, "What are we going to do now? Baby wants to play." Too late he realizes that may have been a mistake!

"Oh, goodness me!" exclaims Mrs. McD. "What poor babysitters we're being, Susan. We've forgotten all about the baby."

She rushes to a side closet and brings out a basket of baby toys. She and Susan make Peter sit on the floor, while they roll a ball back and forth with him.

"Isn't he the nicest baby, Susan? He rolls the ball ever so nice."

Peter realizes he is in over his head and he doesn't know how to get out of it. He stops rolling the ball, and they immediately give him some puzzles for toddlers to put together. As soon as he puts those together they hand him pictures to color. Finally, they try to get him to play with some pull toys. Peter can't take any more!

"Okay, okay, enough already!" Peter protests, while they laugh and laugh and ask "Is baby tired of playing with toys?"

"Yes, I'm tired of playing with toys. I'm tired of being a baby. And I'm sorry I made that stupid comment that baby wants to play! Please let me grow up!"

Peter helps Susan pick up the toys and put them away. He puts another log on the fire while Mrs. McD and Susan rustle up an afternoon snack of coffee and of course, Mrs. McD's famous chocolate chip cookies. Finally, everyone is back in their easy chairs, enjoying their afternoon cup of coffee. Susan breaks the silence.

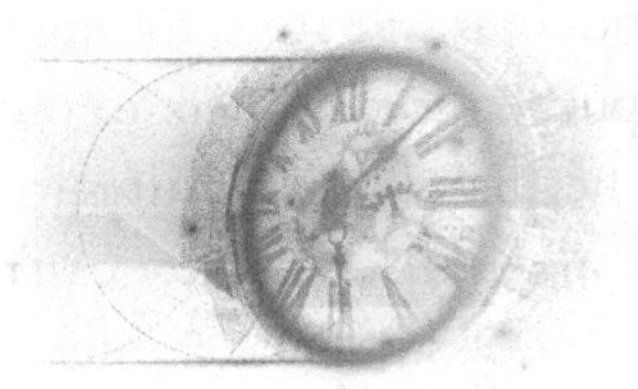

CHAPTER 33

The Second Mrs. McD

"Mrs. McD, the Professor said you are a shrewd detective. As we've talked I realized you are interested in many of the same things I'm interested in. That makes me think you might also be interested in a legend the Professor told us about. It grabbed my attention and I've not been able to get it out of my mind. Whenever I have any free time, I sit at my computer and play around with it. I enjoy solving mysteries, but this one has left me with a lot of questions and no answers. Maybe I'm just being foolish. Peter will probably think me stupid for keeping at it, but do you know anything about the legend of the Nine Unknown Men?"

The room becomes suddenly silent. *Not another Mrs. McD!* Peter thinks to himself. Only the crackling of the fire can be heard. He waits, wondering what Mrs. McD will say. He studies her face. It is so obvious she wants to tell everything to this girl who seems so much like herself. But she isn't sure how much is safe to tell, or if Susan would believe it if she did tell her. She cannot reveal the Professor's secrets. She definitely can't let it be known that the Professor is one of the Nine. Susan looks back and forth between Peter's face and Mrs. McD's face. Intuitively she realizes her question has touched on something that goes a lot deeper than she'd imagined.

Finally, Mrs. McD asks, "Why do you ask, Susan?"

"My father taught me that behind every myth and legend there is a truth, regardless of how obscure or distorted it may have become. People dress up in tales what they do not understand. The legend of the Nine Unknown Men is so interesting, and has so many versions that I wanted to know the truth behind the legend. I thought maybe that if you had heard of it, you might have some ideas to help me. Something had to have happened to give rise to the legend. Can you help me Mrs. McD?"

"I don't know if I can help you, Susan. Tell me what you've learned so far."

"I've spent a lot of time on the internet looking up everything I could find. There are many forms of the story. Most seemed to agree that the Nine Unknown Men had a two-fold mission. The first was to preserve their knowledge and keep it hidden from people who would misuse it. The second was to step in, in times of great need, and help. For example, to show how to make a much needed medicine.

"Then the thought came to me that I was going about this all wrong. Since the internet wasn't going to give me the answer I was looking for, I should treat this as a mystery to solve. That meant the first thing I needed to do was take some aspect of the legend that would most likely leave a trail of evidence, if the story was true. It was easy to pick that. It was the part of the legend that said that when there was a crisis, a stranger would suddenly appear from out of nowhere. It might be to show them how to make the medicine to cure a disease. It might be to provide some technical or scientific information that was needed. Then he would disappear."

Mrs. McD's eyes glow. "I like the way you think. That's the secret to good detective work. Don't be distracted by other things. Concentrate on one thing at a time until you nail your suspect. Have you come up with anything? Have you found a trail of evidence?"

"That's just it," Susan answers. "I haven't had time to work on it very much. But it did seem to me that there were stories of unforeseen help showing up whenever help was needed. Then something happened that didn't make sense. The stories suddenly stopped. Tall tales don't end that way. They hang on. They aren't like superstitions that stop and are then made fun of as civilization develops and science replaces superstition. These stopped abruptly. What really bothers me most is that just before the stories stopped, I had reached the place where it looked like there might be corroborative evidence to support the stories. Now I want to know more than ever if there is any possibility the legend could be true?"

"Susan, I commend you for how well you've done your research. It's frustrating when a mystery takes a sudden turn like that. Then you have to raise new questions to explore. As a detective your next step should be to form a working hypothesis to explain that sudden stop, and then see if you can find anything to support it. In other words, form a hypothesis that gives a logical reason why, if the legend is true, that the appearances in time of need suddenly stopped. Based on your hypothesis describe the kinds of new evidence you would expect to find. That will tell you what to look for. Then all you will have to do is to look and see if you can find evidence to support your new hypothesis."

"I did ask that question," Susan continues. "I reread the original stories to see if there were any clues that might explain it. Several accounts said they had discovered an elixir that prolonged life. That would explain why the stories covered so many centuries, but not why they stopped suddenly. There had to be another reason. I thought of several possibilities but only one of them made sense."

"What was that?"

"It seems kind of silly. I haven't had time to figure out a way to check it. But it would help explain some of the other references in some of the stories. What if one on the Nine turned traitor and wanted to rule the world instead of helping it? That would explain why the others went into hiding and hid the book of knowledge to keep it from him. It was rumored that instructions for building a time machine were in that book. If that were true it would make sense that the traitor wants the time machine. He wants to go back in history and cause changes that will result in giving him complete control of the world. And if that is true, the Nine must still be alive today to stop him. What's really weird is that I find myself wanting that to be true!"

Again there is silence. Susan looks back and forth between Peter and Mrs. McD. Peter has a stunned look on his face. Susan can't tell if it means she is on to something, or that Peter just can't believe she'd be that silly. But Mrs. McD. Her expression has changed too. At first it was one of real interest in what she was hearing. But the more Susan said the more Mrs. McD's expression changed from interest to that of amazement at what she was hearing, and finally to that of one who is holding things back she wanted desperately to share.

Finally, Peter speaks, "She's you all over again, isn't she Mrs. McD?"

"She is indeed. She's asking the same questions I asked. It won't take her long to come to the same conclusions."

"Are you going to tell Susan the rest of the story?"

"The rest?" Mrs. McD pauses thoughtfully, "Oh I think we'd best let the Professor decide that. It's not my place or your place to say more."

Susan sits, looking first at Mrs. McD, and then at Peter. She realizes now that there is more to the story that they know, and that she's come close to knowing.

Peter, looking at her with admiration, gets a very strong impression that it will be impossible to hide anything from this girl, who is turning out to be a most remarkable girl. A girl in whom he finds his interest is rising!

What is it they aren't telling her, Susan wonders. There is more to the story then either are willing to tell. It has something to do with the Professor. From long practice of seeking the guidance of the Holy Spirit she automatically prays, asking the Holy Spirit to tell her what she is missing. Suddenly an expression of joy sweeps over her face.

"Thank you, Holy Spirit," she speaks softly. With eyes aglow, and a look of great admiration on her face she speaks in a soft, self-assured voice. "The story is true. There is a traitor. He is after Peter and the Professor. The Professor is one of the Nine Unknown Men. The traitor is after the Professor's time machine."

Utter silence envelopes the room, except for the crackling of the fire. The three of them sit quietly, realizing that something holy has just happened, and that a holy presence fills the room. The silence is broken only when the Professor walks into the kitchen, greeting everyone with his cheery, "Hello, how's the babysitting?"

He is greeted only by silence. Everyone turns towards him and he sees the expressions on their faces. Peter's and Mrs. McD's expression is one of the awe. On Susan's face he sees the glow of one who has just received a word of knowledge. Admiration and wonder fills her face. Jumping up she runs to him, throws her arms around him and hugs him with all her might. Finally, the Professor places his hands on her shoulders, pushes her back so that he can look into her glistening eyes.

"You know, don't you?" he asks in a gentle voice.

Too overcome with emotion and love for this man to speak, she nods. He looks at Mrs. McD, speaking softly, for this turn of events does not anger him. He had suspected that this girl, who seemed so much like a young Mrs. McD, would put the pieces together. Just not this quickly.

"What happened?"

"She started asking about the Nine Unknown Men. Seems she had been studying the stories like I once did. She had come to the place where the stories stopped. And she had already theorized there was a traitor. Peter asked if I was going to tell her more of the story and I said that would be up to you. Then all of a sudden her face changed to a look of wonder as words of knowledge flowed into her mind. We were left speechless as she told us the rest of the story. There was absolute knowing and confidence in her voice. She even had it right that Az was after you and Peter and the time machine!"

"Well, Susan, it looks like I picked a most excellent babysitter for Peter! Az is the name the traitor calls himself. It's not his real name. The so-called government agents are some of Az's men. Peter will meet with them tomorrow morning at eleven. No, don't be concerned. He's quite able to beat them at their own game. It'll be touchy, but I believe Peter can do it.

"Now, speaking of babysitting, did Peter behave himself?"

"Well, he did get a little testy when we ignored him," Susan laughs. "But just like a baby, put something in his mouth and he shuts right up!"

"Enough!" Peter protests. "You said something about doing something tonight, Professor. Is it permissible for a baby to take his babysitter to a movie?"

"You'll have to ask the babysitter."

"Susan, if I can get the Professor to drop us off, would you do me the honor of going to a movie with me tonight?"

"I'd love to Peter. But only if you promise to behave and not throw a fit!"

As everyone laughs, Peter groans. Will he ever live this down?

Mrs. McD and Susan slip into the kitchen to cook supper. The Professor joins Peter in front of the fire.

"The men came and they weren't very happy. I think they almost caused a scene! Patience was never a virtue with Az, and evidently not with his men either. Dr. Williams called and asked me to make sure you are there tomorrow. It would be fun to stand them up again, but that might invite trouble we don't want.

"Well, it looks like God is giving us more help in our battle with Az. I've sensed in my spirit for some time that Susan would be helping us. God recruited her without our help. I'm glad it happened like this. When we let God work His will and His timing, it's done right. It's when we get impatient and get ahead of God that we make a mess of things. Patience is one of the hardest lessons Christians have to learn."

"Supper's ready," Mrs. McD calls from the kitchen.

"Wow, that was quick! I hope we're not getting raw steak, Mrs. McD."

"Professor, you complain about my cooking and you'll get raw steak," Mrs. McD snaps back.

"Now, now, Mrs. McD. I was only kidding. Goodness, you try to liven things up a bit and she bites your head off!"

Susan and Peter have a hard time eating, they keep laughing so much, as the Professor and Mrs. McD tease each other, and them. Thankfully they only mention "baby Peter" once or twice.

With supper over and the dishes done, the Professor takes Peter and Susan back into town and lets them off at the movie theatre. They catch the early show. They have just enough time when the show ends to get Susan back to her dorm before curfew. Her parting words to Peter are, "I really enjoyed babysitting you, Peter. Maybe we can do it again sometime." Unfortunately, she says it loud enough, and on purpose, so that some friends hear her.

Peter's face turns beet red, and Susan laughs, "Bye."

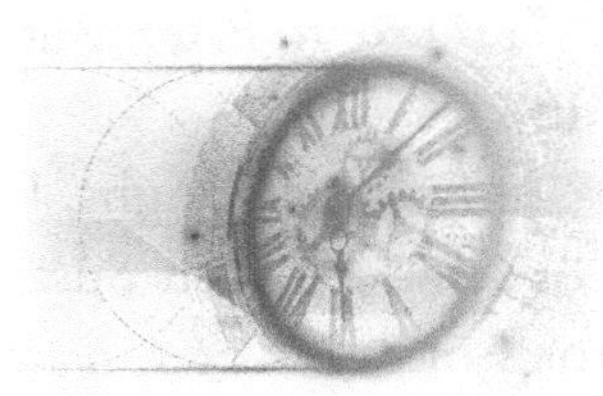

CHAPTER 34

Mocking the Enemy

Peter's dorm is across campus from Susan's. The temperature has dropped and the clumps of wet snow that had been falling have turned into frozen clumps of snow that crunch as he walks. Suddenly he remembers that he has a paper due in two days, and he left all the books he was using in the library, which is now closed.

"Boy, I'm going to be hard pressed to get that paper written on time," he says to himself. "I'd better get a good rest tonight because I'll probably have to put in an all-nighter tomorrow."

Back in his room, Peter gets ready for bed, all the while thinking about the strange day he's had, and the meeting he's going to have with Az's goons. "Sometimes, when you need to sleep it's hard to sleep," he complains. "Maybe a cup of hot chocolate will help."

He heats the water in his small microwave, adds the instant cocoa mix, and drinks it slowly. His mind drifts back to the strange moment when Susan suddenly knew who the Professor really was. The hot cocoa begins to do its job and Peter, overcome by tiredness, quickly falls asleep.

"If you're going to lead a double life, shouldn't you get double sleep?" Peter asks himself when the alarm goes off. "It's only five a.m.! Mr. Johnson expects me to be there by six. I wonder if it's possible to sleep while restocking shelves?" Having finished with his usual grumbling he takes a quick shower, dresses, and heads for the store.

This whole thing with Az is starting to give me the jitters, he thinks.

I know he won't make a move until after the interview today, but I keep feeling like someone is watching me. Boy I'll be glad when I get to the store.

Peter's feelings are shared by Susan who also wakes up early knowing Peter will leave for work about five-thirty. She quickly prays for Peter's protection. It was a prayer patterned after the Passover in Egypt when the Hebrew people put blood on the door posts of their homes. She prayed, "In the name of Jesus I cover Peter with the blood of the Lamb to be a shield and a protection."

The morning passes without incident. As soon as his work is done Peter heads back to the campus and the dining hall. The morning has turned bright and clear.

Peter thinks back over yesterday's strange events. *My date with Susan last night was a lot of fun. I'm really impressed with her. But it's too dangerous to ask her out again. She knows too much, and I don't want to give Az any reason to go after her. So I'm going to have to content myself with hanging around with Jim and Ed and George, and frankly, none of them look as pretty as Susan! Well, I just have time enough for breakfast, and then off to class, and then that meeting.*

Peter hurries through breakfast - a far cry from one of Mrs. McD's - and heads for his nine a.m. class, eating a last piece of toast as he hurries along, hoping there's no pop quiz on a chapter he hasn't had a chance to read. Fortunately, there is no quiz, and he does not get called on to answer questions. A relieved Peter steps outside the building.

"Well, it's time to face the so-called government agents. Everything inside me says danger, these are Az's men. I'm sure glad Susan said she'd be praying for me." The old bell tower clock is striking eleven. "Good, I'll arrive about ten minutes late! That's the first step in throwing them off balance and making them mad."

Peter enters the Administration Building, and ascends the steps to Dr. Williams' office. His secretary is busy typing some letters.

"Hi, Mrs. B., is Dr. Williams in? I think he's expecting me."

"Hello, Peter. You're late! The government agents are getting very impatient. I'll tell Dr. Williams you're here."

Mrs. B. knocks on the President's door. "Peter's here, Dr. Williams."

Mrs. B. holds the door and Peter enters. Dr. Williams is seated behind his massive desk. Seated on chairs to the left are two men in dark suits. Everything about them speaks danger. When people are walking in darkness, those who are walking in God's light can sense it.

"Peter, this is agent Hobbs and agent Smith. I'll leave you alone to talk."

"No, Dr. Williams, don't leave. I don't trust these men. I don't think they're who they're pretending to be." Peter's words, spoken with authority, startle Dr. Williams, and clearly upset Agents Hobbs and Smith. Students don't talk like that.

"It's quite all right, Dr. Williams," Agent Hobbs speaks up. "We're only here to ask a few routine questions, that's all. There's nothing to be concerned about. It's okay for you to go."

Peter immediately responds by declaring, "If Dr. Williams goes, I go."

Agents Hobbs and Smith are taken aback by this unexpected response. Dr. Williams isn't sure how to respond. He hadn't expected Peter to act like this for no apparent reason. He really doesn't have time to stay, what with an important trustee meeting in just a few minutes.

"Really, Peter, I don't think you have anything to be concerned about," Dr. Williams tries to reassure Peter. "I don't think these men mean any harm."

"That may be so, sir. But if you go, I go."

Hobbs and Smith try to hide their emotions, but Peter can see he's getting under their skin. This is not going the way they had planned. Seeing how stubborn Peter is, they are forced to change their strategy. Hobbs and Smith confer with each other. They don't dare return empty handed to Az with the excuse that they were outsmarted by a young kid. They decide to play it Peter's way.

"There's really no reason for you to stay, Dr. Williams. But if the only way Peter will talk to us is with you present, we agree to that."

"See, Peter. It's okay."

"With all due respect, Dr. Williams, I still do not trust these men. If you go, I go."

"Well, all right, Peter, if you insist," Dr. Williams says with a sigh and sits back down in his chair. Peter casually pulls up a chair to the corner of Dr. Williams' desk. He places it so that the corner of the desk is between him and the Agents. This is a little psychological maneuver that is like raising a barrier. It is not lost on Hobbs and Smith, who are having trouble hiding their obvious irritation. Peter sits back and waits.

Finally, Smith speaks. "We do not believe your story about helping Dr. Bottomly with his experiment. We know what he is working on. As an undergraduate student you couldn't possibly know anything about his advanced work. The idea that your Professor would know anything about his research is equally ridiculous."

"Well, gentlemen," Peter speaks up immediately. "It's obvious you know nothing about scientific research. Research like Dr. Bottomly is doing costs an immense about of money. Money doesn't grow on trees. I've seen a shoe tree, but no one has seen a money tree. You have to submit reams of documentation to justify what you want to do in order to get any money. And the people who give you the grants want results. They expect regular research updates, and they set time limits when they expect to see results."

Peter notes with satisfaction that his comment about the shoe tree and money tree are not appreciated. Not only do the agents not appreciate it, they are frustrated because nobody gets away with treating them that disrespectfully, and they can't do anything about it. Peter's tone of voice sounds like he is treating them like simpletons.

"Dr. Bottomly," Peter continues, "was at a critical point. He had submitted his request for additional funding to cover the next phase of his research. But first, he had to prove that this phase was successful. Everything was riding on the success of this test. He had to produce results or they'd pull the plug on all his years of research. Dr. Bottomly was positive he had it right. But, with everything riding on its success, he called on his old friend, the Professor. The Professor has helped him many times by pointing out things in his calculations and research that Dr. Bottomly had missed. That's why he called and why we left in a hurry. I got to go along because I've been doing some independent research on Dr. Bottomly's papers."

As Peter watches the two men, he's almost enjoying taunting them.

He knows they aren't going to like what he says next! "I can't tell you anymore. I signed a paper."

"All right," Agent Hobbs speaks up, "you talk a good story. But how are you on actual facts? You say you've been studying Dr. Bottomly's writings. Okay, so have we. Now tell us what he says is the process involved in teleportation."

Peter answers, almost flippantly, "I can't tell you anymore. I signed a paper."

"So that's going to be your excuse for ignorance! Let's just see how smart you really are. Let me tell you how it works. I will purposely get parts of it wrong. Then you tell me what's right and what's wrong."

"I can handle that," Peter answers matter-of-factly.

"We know from the theory of quantum entanglement that you can instantly transfer the characteristics of a piece of matter from one spot to another. However, the matter itself is not transported. The actual matter is destroyed at the sending point in obtaining the information that is sent to the receiving point. The receiving point takes the information and reproduces the matter."

"I have no idea what you're trying to get at," Peter answers. "All you've told me is what everybody knows. If you gentlemen are expecting me to add to what you've just said, like I told you before, I can't tell you anymore. I signed a paper."

"We're not asking you to tell us more. We're asking you to tell us if what we said was right or wrong. Your answer will tell us whether or not you've been lying."

"So far you haven't given me anything to lie about. I'm certainly not going to volunteer information to you that you don't know. Like I said, I can't tell you anymore. I signed a paper."

"All right. Let me put it this way," says Hobbs, who is starting to get red under the collar as he tries his luck with Peter. "Teleportation is accomplished by splitting the matter being sent into its atoms, attaching the atoms to the information stream which carries them to the destination where they are reassembled. Dr. Bottomly has discovered how to do that."

"You've got a nice theory," Peter answers. "But you haven't taken into account Heisenberg's uncertainty principle which means your theory can't work. But as far as what does work, I can't tell you. I signed a paper."

Hobbs' and Smith's level of irritation is definitely rising. The veins on their necks are starting to stand out!

"You give us no choice but to show you a picture. Do you know what this is?" He hands Peter a picture of Dr. Bottomly's lab, an exact duplicate of the one Mrs. McD showed him. Peter reacts instantly.

"Where did you get this? This is top secret information. Dr. Williams, call the police. These men are imposters. They're industrial espionage spies. They're trying to learn Dr. Bottomly's secrets by tripping me up. I'm keeping this picture for evidence." Peter folds the picture and puts it in his pocket.

The two men, hostile and angry at being bested at their game, quickly rise, saying, "That won't be necessary. We think your story of going to Dr. Bottomly's lab was a cover-up for something else you and the Professor were doing. We intend to get to the bottom of it. We're leaving, but you haven't heard the last of us."

They exit. Dr. Williams looks stunned. "Peter, you were right! Their credentials looked very official. I apologize for not calling to find out if they really were who they said they were. I'm glad you spotted them. I'll have the campus police keep a look out for them. Be careful. You got them upset and they won't forget it."

Peter breathes a sigh of relief as he leaves Dr. William's office. *A good offense is the best defense,* he thinks to himself. *The only thing they learned was that I knew what Bottomly's lab looked like. And I had an air tight reason for the quick trip to help him. I wonder how they got a picture of the lab. I must mention this to the Professor.*

Peter glances at his watch and sees that it is close to lunch time. He hurries down the hall and exits out onto the high portico. Looking around, he sees no one. He starts down the steps and just as he reaches the bottom of the last step and turns towards the dining hall, his arms are suddenly gripped so tight he can't escape. It's the two pseudo agents. They had waited outside for him, hidden from view.

"Make fools of us, will you," growls the man called Smith. "We'll teach you some respect."

Hoping he can get them to loosen their hold so that he can get away, Peter immediately responds, "I didn't make fools of you. You did that all by yourselves!"

This inflames their anger, makes them reckless as Peter had hoped. But they squeeze his arms tighter instead of momentarily losing their grip.

"We'll see who's the fool now. You're coming with us. Don't try to get away. Don't make a sound. We can break your arms like match sticks and we'll do it if you don't cooperate. Now move."

They shove Peter ahead of them, keeping close to hide their tight grip on his arms. Peter sends up a quick prayer, "Holy Spirit, don't fail me now." They head towards the visitor's parking lot. When they parked they were forced to park in a tight place. Fortunately for Peter, unfortunately for them, more cars had pulled in to park. Now they will have to maneuver their car a bit before they can speed out of the parking lot. The lot is full with many people coming and going. This forces them to take their time and be careful not to arouse suspicion. They squeeze Peter's arms extra tight, almost breaking them, to let him know not to make a sound.

They reach their car. Hobbs shoves Peter into the back seat. Peter quickly moves to the other side and opens the door. Smith climbs in after him, grabbing Peter's jacket before he can get out of the other door. Hobbs gets behind the wheel. Once in their car, they turn loose on Peter viciously, spewing out their anger. They tell Peter they're going to crack his alibi if it's the last thing they do. Smith starts the interrogation.

"Admit it. You never went to Dr. Bottomly's lab. You don't even know where it is. You were with the Professor in his time machine. You and the Professor landed at that other guy's mountain resort and escaped into the hills. That's why you were gone so long, trying to make it look like you'd been with Bottomly."

"Wow! What kind of drugs are you guys on? What I want to know is why do you even care? I'm just a college kid. I get invited to watch something momentous happen and you guys pounce on me like I'm some dangerous criminal. Of course I don't know where Dr. Bottomly's lab is located. The pilot was given the coordinates to fly to, not the name of an airport, so I figured it must be a private airport out in the middle of nowhere. You can get the coordinates from the pilot's log book if you want them that bad. It's no secret. And a time machine? You've got to be kidding. Oh sure, I know a lot of people who've built time machines - in science fiction stories, not in real life. You don't really think time travel is possible, do you?"

Peter can almost see the steam rising from their necks and cautions himself, *These guys are really steamed now. I'd better not antagonize them anymore. They look like they're ready to start beating up on me!*

The engine roars to life and Hobbs starts to back up. But his way is blocked by a police cruiser pulling in behind him. Peter wonders if he can get the chief's attention.

Just as the police cruiser comes to a stop, the police chief jumps out, gun in hand. He rushes to the driver's window and points the gun at Hobbs. "Okay you two, step out with your hands up. Don't try anything or my men will fire. You okay Peter?"

This last frustration, on top of Peter's belligerency, must have been too much for Hobbs and Smith. They start to let out the most vitriolic stream of cursing and threats ever heard. Of course, this does not endear them to the police, who jerk the doors open, drag Hobbs and Smith out, and clamp hand cuffs on them.

"I'm taking you in for resisting arrest and attempted kidnapping. You okay, Peter? You do want to press charges?"

"Absolutely!" Peter answers. "I don't appreciate being called a liar, threatened and kidnapped. As far as I'm concerned, you can throw the book at them."

Just then the Professor runs up, out of breath. He gasps, "Peter! Thank goodness you're safe. Thanks Chief. I appreciate your quick response more than you'll ever know."

"Thanks for alerting me, Professor. Ever since these guys showed up at Mrs. McD's we've been on the lookout for them. I should have slapped them in jail then. Attempted kidnapping, along with aggravated assault, is a serious offense, to say nothing of breaking and entering Mrs.

McD's. If they stay around long enough for a trial, we'll send them up for a long stretch in prison."

"Confidentially, Chief," the Professor speaks in a low voice so that Az's men cannot hear him. "I doubt if you'll get a chance to bring them to trial. Their boss will have his lawyer here before tonight. You need to talk to the judge and explain what's happened. He needs to set their bail as high as he can. Their boss' lawyer will try to get them out tonight. If he does, they will never come back to stand trial. He doesn't want anyone to know his name or have his name brought up in any trial. Just be sure the judge sets bail as high as he can, knowing they won't be back. Make their boss pay dearly for this. By the way, I'm sure Mrs. McD has some of her fresh baked bread she'd love to trade for a report on this arrest!"

"Thanks for the offer, Professor, but you know it's illegal to bride a police officer! I will stop and see her, though. As you say, she will be happy to hear that we've taken these two thugs in. They won't be bothering her or anyone else for a long time. I'll send a tow truck and impound their car."

With that, the police chief drives off, leaving Peter and the Professor alone.

Peter turns to the Professor. "Thanks for the rescue. Those guys were strong. My arms are still hurting. I don't think they were supposed to kidnap me. They were overconfident of their ability to trip me up and get me to admit the trip to see Dr. Bottomly was a fake. I think the reason they tried to kidnap me was I'd made them so mad they wanted to beat me up. I outflanked them every step of the way. I even told Dr. Williams to call the police because these guys weren't government agents, but industrial spies. Here's something that worries me, though. Maybe you ought to tell Dr. Bottomly about it. They had this."

Peter takes the picture out of his pocket and gives it to the Professor. "I'd like to stay and talk for a few minutes, but I've got to go. Its lunch time and I promised the guys I'd eat with them. Professor, I don't suppose you'd consider eating with the students today? The food won't be anywhere near as good as Mrs. McD's, but we'd enjoy your company.

We're going to talk about your last physics assignment, and I thought maybe if you were there . . .?"

"Nice try, Peter. But my job is to give the assignments, not do them! This thing with the police will silence Az for a few days. He's got to get his men out of jail. He'll have to take them out of state to keep them from going on trial. Az won't take a chance on their keeping his name out of it. The temptation to tell all can be pretty strong if it means getting out of going to jail. He'll have to pay a pretty hefty bond since there's no possibility that they will come back and face a trial. That's good news for us. It will give us a little breathing space. Now, off to lunch or you'll miss your friends."

Peter says goodbye to the Professor and heads for the dining hall. Meanwhile, back in the shadows, unseen by anyone, stands a young woman who watched the attempted abduction. When the thugs grabbed Peter she called the Professor. She was so thankful when the police chief drove up and blocked the thugs' car, that she dropped to her knees and prayed, "Thank you Father, thank you, thank you." She, too, leaves to go to lunch with some of her friends.

As Peter walks towards the dining hall he suddenly becomes so hungry he could eat a horse! Bursting into the dining hall he says hi to Linda, showing her his ID and heads for the serving line. He fills up his tray, a lot more than usual. The gang is saving a place for him. They call him over to their table.

"Wow," says George, "you got a tapeworm?"

"No. This morning has been something else, and it has given me an enormous appetite. After my eight o'clock, I went to a meeting in the President's office. I was supposed to meet with some guys who claimed to be government agents come to ask about my trip to Dr. Bottomly's. Turns out they were industrial spies. I gave them so many wrong answers and tripped them up so bad that Dr. Williams realized they were spies and started to call the police.

"I thought they'd gone, but when I got down to the bottom step of the administration building, they grabbed me and kidnapped me. They had me in their car ready to take off when the police chief drove up and blocked them in. Seems they'd been watching them. Long meetings and getting kidnapped can make a guy extra hungry."

Amused at the look on his friends faces Peter chuckles, thinking, *Sometimes it's fun to tell the truth just to see how people react to it, especially when the truth seems so far-fetched.*

The guys don't let Peter down. They don't believe a word of it.

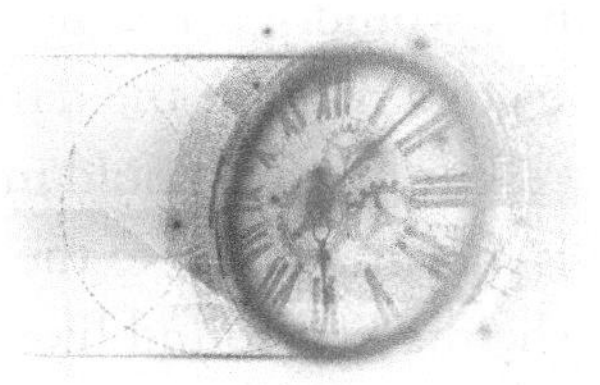

CHAPTER 35

Days of Peace

How long were you in the President's office?" they ask, making all sorts of fun at Peter's Expense. "Fifteen minutes? Half an hour? That's better than three hours in the gym from the looks of your plate! And you were kidnapped for five minutes? Guys, let's package this up as a miracle weight reduction program. All the girls will be lining up to buy it! We'd even cut Dr. Williams in on the profits!"

"Guys, remember, we're here to discuss a physics assignment, not my morning escapades! Besides, it was a battle of wits - not half-wits like you guys!"

Pushing their trays aside, they take out their books and begin. All they've got to do is memorize some quantum mechanics formulas, explain them, and work a couple problems using them. Slowly but surely everyone begins to get a handle on it.

"Well guys," Peter speaks up, calling the session to a close, "the kitchen crew is giving us the evil eye. We'd better call it quits for now. Besides, I've got to go to work."

As they pick up their trays and take them to the counter, Ed asks, "Did you notice the girl who checked our IDs? Her name is Linda. Seems like a pretty nice girl. She's a friend of Susan, that girl in our class. I asked Susan if Linda was going out with anyone, and if she thought Linda would be willing to go out with me. She checked, and thought

Linda would. I asked her when I came in today. She said yes, and now I've got a date for the dance Saturday! You guys going?"

"Funny you should mention Susan," George speaks up. "I asked her this morning to go to the dance. She turned me down. The weird thing is she made it sound like she was very honored that I'd asked her. Said she'd love to but she isn't dating right now. She's working on a project off campus that's taking all her spare time. That's the first time I've ever had a girl make me feel good when she says no! She even offered to help me get a date with someone else. She'll let me know later today if another girl I was wondering about would be willing to go out with me."

Peter is surprised to find himself pleased that Susan said no. *She's just an acquaintance who also happens to know the Professor's secret, nothing else. So why am I pleased,* he asks himself, *and why do I have this suspicion that what she's working on involves me? Well, no time to figure it out. I've got to get to work. Mr. Johnson is shorthanded today and it's one of the busiest days of the week. I'll be running back and forth between restocking shelves and running a cash register.*

When Peter enters the store, Mr. Johnson's eyes light up! "Peter, boy am I glad to see you. Our sale this week is a big hit. This place has been jumping like crazy!"

The afternoon is the busiest Peter had ever seen. But by six o'clock the rush is over, and Mr. Johnson is able to let him off on time. That's good because Peter is expecting to pull an all-nighter if he has any hope of getting his paper ready to turn in tomorrow morning.

He makes it to the dining room just as they are about to close the serving line. Linda smiles, saying, "You're pushing your luck coming this late. I hope you like a cold supper, Peter."

Peter answers teasingly, "But you'll warm it up for me won't you?" She gives him a dirty look.

Supper over, which was hot in spite of what Linda said, Peter heads for the library. It's the first chance he's had to get back after getting Dr. William's note. He hoped the books he'd picked out were still available. They were, and the desk clerk lets him check them out overnight. Books in hand, he goes back to his room. He checks for his jar of instant coffee.

"Good," he says aloud to himself. "I'll probably need a lot of this before the night's over."

With everything ready for his long night he sits down at his desk. He first opens his Bible and reads the scriptures for the day. He likes reading at night best. He is seldom interrupted by phone calls, or by his growling stomach wanting to be fed. His Bible reading finished, Peter turns to John 14:26, "But the Helper, the Holy Spirit, whom the Father will send in my name, he will teach you all things and bring to your remembrance all that I have said to you." (ESV) He then prays, "Father, I come to You in Jesus' name to ask for Your help. I know John 14:26 isn't talking about my research paper. But it does say that the Holy Spirit will bring things to my remembrance. And in John 16:23 Jesus promises, 'In that day you will ask nothing of me. Truly, truly, I say to you, whatever you ask of the Father in my name, he will give it to you (ESV).'

"Father, my study plans got interrupted by the trouble Az caused. That day at Mrs. McD's with Susan was fun. Thank You for arranging that, and for letting me be there when Susan received that word of knowledge. But Father, now I'm in a bind. That's why I'm asking you in Jesus' Name to ask the Holy Spirit to quicken my thinking and understanding as I go through this material. And then give me insight and guidance as I write my paper. Thank you, Father. I ask this in Jesus' Name."

The prayer ended, Peter begins to read and take notes, with his ear tuned to "hear" the Holy Spirit's guidance. Peter is amazed by the insights and understanding that pour into his mind. The paper seems to organize itself and write itself as he reads. The understanding and insights come so fast he forgets all about drinking coffee. The paper is done by three a.m.! As he pulls the last page from his printer he exclaims, "Wow! Thank you, Holy Spirit."

His work done, Peter crawls into bed and immediately falls into a deep sleep. When his annoying alarm clock goes off, he is surprised to find he feels as rested as if he'd had a full night's sleep. In fact, he feels perfectly at peace, as though everything is right with the world. He's not felt that peaceful in a month. That's when he realizes he has not sensed any uneasiness from waiting for Az to do something.

This sense of peace continues for the next several days. When he does think about it, he knows Az will be up to something. He is thankful for these few days of "out of sight, out of mind." It's fun to relax and just be a normal student. Even the Professor seems totally relaxed and unconcerned about anything except for his "diabolical pleasure (as his students call it) in giving pop quizzes."

After about a week of this peacefulness, an uneasiness begins to creep into Peter's spirit. He can't quite put a finger on it. It just feels like something isn't right. When the feelings don't go away but grow stronger, Peter decides he needs to talk with the Professor about it. He wants to know if his imagination is playing tricks on him, or if the Professor has sensed something not quite right, too.

Finally, two weeks to the day of his encounter with Hobbs and Smith, Peter makes an appointment to talk with the Professor. Peter arrives for his appointment a little early, and sits in one of the chairs outside the Professor's office. As he waits he reflects back over events of the last two weeks. Things have been almost too quiet.

The judge took the police chief's advice and set the bond at half a million each, cash, and refused to lower it. "This bond is the only hope we have that you will be back to stand trial," he told the men. "If your boss wants to throw away a million dollars that's his business. But I warn you, if you don't come back on the date I've appointed, I will send out a warrant for your arrest and return to my jurisdiction."

There's been no sign of Az or his men since then. No word has come from any of the Eight. Even so, something isn't right. Peter feels it in his bones. "It like I'm waiting for the other shoe to drop. I wonder if the Professor has this same uneasiness. Or am I getting paranoid, making it all up in my head? I'll soon find out."

Just then the door opens. A young woman, whose delightful voice he'd recognize anywhere, is speaking. "Thanks, Professor. You've been a great help. I'll keep a sharp eye out and let you know if I see or hear anything unusual." The voice is Susan's!

Peter rises quickly to greet her. "Hi Susan! I've missed seeing you around. You sure get prettier every day."

Boy! he thinks. *That sounded so corny.*

"Thank you, Peter," she smiles. Then, taking his hand she adds, "I'm so glad those awful men who tried to kidnap you got caught. I was worried when I saw them grab you. The Professor was afraid something would happen and asked me to keep an eye on you. I'm glad I did. Mrs. McD was right. You do need looking after," she laughs. "Bye."

"Come in, Peter, come in," the Professor calls.

"Professor, Susan tells me you had her watching over me the day those goons tried to kidnap me!"

"Susan is a lot like Mrs. McD. She was worried about what would happen to you if you got the best of Az's goons. She came by to see if there was anything she could do to help. I believe she was responding to a prompting of the Holy Spirit because I did need her help. I knew that if you got the best of Az's goons, they'd want revenge when you came out. I'd already alerted the police that those two were back in town and might try to abduct you. I had Susan watch the front door of the Administration Building. She saw them come out and then hide. She called me and told me what they'd done. That's when I called the Chief and asked him to come immediately. There was no way they could have gotten you out of the parking lot.

"Susan came to see me just now because something's bothering her. She feels a disturbance in her spirit. Now, what did you want to talk about?"

"Professor, I have this feeling like I know in my gut that Az is up to something really bad. I can't shake the feeling. It's getting worse. Am I being paranoid?"

"No, you are not paranoid. Mrs. McD and I have felt the same uneasiness. Susan felt it too. That's confirmation that we are being warned. We always need to look for confirmation when we are being led by the Spirit. Satan delights in trying to mislead us. In 2 Corinthians 11:14 Paul warns us that Satan can disguise himself as an angel of light. And Jesus tells us in Matthew 10:16 'Behold, I am sending you out as sheep in the midst of wolves, so be wise as serpents and innocent as doves (ESV).'

"The next step after our guidance is confirmed is to ask for guidance as to what to do next. How is the rest of your day? Are you busy right now? Do you have to work? Can you get away for the rest of the day?"

"That's a four-part question! I'm free. I'm not busy. I don't work today. I can get away."

"Good. I think we need to sneak off to Mrs. McD's for some serious praying. The sooner the better. We can talk there and pray and see if we get any words of knowledge that will help. Bring your books, and we'll go get my car right now. Oh, I'd best call her and tell her we're coming!"

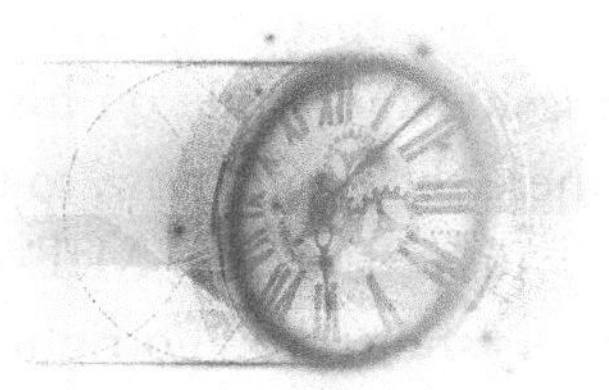

CHAPTER 36

Taking Stock

After "warning" Mrs. McD, the Professor grabs his jacket, locks his office, and leads the way to the faculty parking lot. They put their stuff in the back seat, and Peter sits in the front beside him. The Professor could drive the most expensive car made, but he prefers to drive an old car that's given reliable service over the years.

Peter settles back for the short trip to Mrs. McD's, glad to be doing something. It was a relief to learn that all four of them had been having the same uneasiness and that he wasn't being paranoid. The Professor turns into Mrs. McD's driveway, presses the remote to open the garage door, and drives in. The door closes behind them. Mrs. McD's car is not there.

"Don't worry about Mrs. McD, She'll be here soon. She's running a little errand we both thought wise. Let's go in and see if there's a pot of coffee brewing."

The smell of freshly brewed coffee fills the air when they open the door into the house. Mixed with it is the smell of some fresh baked cookies. Her kitchen always smells good.

"One of the reasons I asked Mrs. McD to be my housekeeper was her cooking," the Professor confesses. "Of course, it was for her other skills that I really hired her. But still, getting a good cook too was frosting on the cake!"

"Professor, there are four cups and four plates on the table. Is Mrs. McD expecting company?"

"As a matter of fact she is," answers the Professor, with a bit of a mischievous smile on his face that Peter's not too sure about. "That's where she's gone now, to pick up our company."

Just then Mrs. McD's car comes rolling into the garage. Two car doors shut. "You go right in, dear. The Professor and Peter are already here. The coffee should be ready.

Peter hears familiar footsteps. Then, standing in the doorway is Susan. Her face breaks into a joyous smile as she sees him.

"Hi, Peter. I'm going to be your babysitter tonight!"

"Oh, no! Not again! Professor!"

Mrs. McD, Susan, and the Professor burst out laughing. "Well done, Susan! You got him! No, Peter. Susan is not here to babysit you... this time!" he adds.

"Let's all sit down first," suggests Mrs. McD. "Then we'll explain what this is all about."

"We're all here because we're all worried about the same thing. We've sensed evil in the wind. Mrs. McD agrees with me that we need to prepare ourselves."

"That's right. Peter," Mrs. McD adds. "You're wondering why I asked Susan to join us? What you don't know is that Susan and I have been spending a lot of time together. We've sort of become like mother and daughter."

"You should be warned, Peter," the Professor interrupts, "part of the time they've spent together they've been talking about us. My ears have been burning something fiercely every time they've gotten together. I suspect you and I don't have any secrets left that they haven't figured out."

"Now Professor, you know full well Susan has been helping me in my research. Talking about you and Peter? - *Pshaw!* We've had more important things to do than to waste our time on unimportant trivia."

"Trivia? Mrs. McD, I'm cut to the quick. I, THE Professor, am only trivia?"

Once again Susan and Peter find themselves unable to contain their laughter as they listen to Mrs. McD and the Professor tease each other.

"You'll have to forgive Mrs. McD, Peter. Sometimes she can be most difficult," the Professor "explains."

"Professor," Susan asks, "Mrs. McD said that the research we just finished she will be giving away. She said you give your research away, too. Why?"

"We do not want to draw any attention to ourselves. Others get to take credit for it and that leaves us free from any publicity. Our wealth we keep secretly hidden away, drawing on it for our labs and for our charity work, which we also do secretly."

"Az, on the other hand, lives extravagantly," Mrs. McD adds in a tone of voice showing her disapproval. "He insists on taking full credit for all his technology, even though others may have invented it. His gives to charity only when it will advance his projects."

"But enough of that talk," the Professor breaks in. "If we really want to get started right, we must put first things first. We need to get ourselves in a proper frame of mind, and I know of nothing better than coffee and cookies."

"Now, now Professor. Aren't we getting a little pudgy around the middle? Seems to me you've been spending far too much time lately 'getting into a proper frame of mind' and out of a proper frame of body! These two are young, still growing, and need lots of energy. Whereas you need to burn off some energy!"

"Mrs. McD, you cut me to the quick again! First you call me trivial, and now you are suggesting I'm getting pudgy around the middle? Why it was only a couple weeks ago Peter and I were mountain climbing. Getting pudgy indeed!"

Peter and Susan continue to laugh at this good natured banter. It is so obvious how much they admire and respect each other.

"Well, I suppose Peter and Susan might feel a little awkward if we didn't join them for a cookie or two," Mrs. McD answers like a mother speaking to a child. "And of course we don't want them to feel awkward. So, just to be polite, mind you, I'll pass the cookies to you after I pour the coffee."

"No, Mrs. McD, let me," cries Susan, jumping up and grabbing the coffee pot. She carefully fills Mrs. McD's cup first, then the Professor's, then Peter's, and lastly, her own. "I'm sorry, Peter, this isn't cappuccino. I know how much you like it."

Wow! mused Peter. *There's something about this girl that gets under my skin.*

The Professor and Mrs. McD continue to engage in small talk, and Peter and Susan sit as quietly as they can while holding their laughter in check, listening. Mrs. McD talks about her prayer group.

"Gossip group!" chimes the Professor, at which Mrs. McD takes his cookie from him and says, "Sometimes I think a good spanking would do you a world of good! Now, if you promise to behave I'll give you back your cookie."

In a pretended meek reply, he answers, "I promise."

Shaking her head, she adds, "Some men never grow up. See what I have to put up with?"

The coffee and cookies are soon gone. Peter and the Professor excuse themselves, or rather they are summarily dismissed by the women and sent to the living room. Susan helps clear the table and wash the dishes. They giggle like two young girls, making Peter and the Professor wonder what they could possibly be talking about. Probably about them. The dishes soon done, they join Peter and the Professor around the fire.

"Well," the Professor begins, "let's see what we know.

"Well, one thing we know for sure," Peter begins, "is that Az was not happy with the fact that I frustrated his men so badly. It was bad enough that I got the best of them, but it must have really upset him to have his men arrested."

"Peter's right," Mrs. McD joins in. "Az trains his men well. No ordinary person could have gotten them so angry or remained un-intimidated by them. Neither should there have been anyone around to stop them when they foolishly tried to kidnap Peter. What will Az conclude from this? Is there any chance he'll think you had something to do with humiliating his men and getting them arrested, Professor?"

"That is possible, but not probable," the Professor explains thoughtfully. "Hobbs and Smith revealed they were working for Az when they said 'time machine' to Peter. But Peter just laughed at them and accused them of being on drugs."

"I've been thinking, Professor," Susan speaks up after some moments. "I don't think Az learned anything from the failed kidnapping. The fact that the police were waiting for them, and knew they were after Peter, actually leaves him with only one logical explanation for Peter's behavior. If his men had been industrial spies, you and Peter would have been on your guard to protect Dr. Bottomly's secrets. That explains Peter's actions."

"Susan's right," Mrs. McD agrees. "All Az got was a logical reason for why Peter acted as he did. My hunch is that he will try another tactic to get his proof. He needs to know as quickly as possible if you two are the ones he is looking for. Sending Hobbs and Smith tells me he thinks the best way to get his proof is through Peter. He doesn't dare harm Peter; that would tip his hand. So he is cooking up some other scheme to get the information from Peter without you or Peter knowing it."

"Professor?" Susan asks. "Peter spoke about Az's mind probe when you were on the mountain. I've read about experiments based on the electro-magnetic impulses of our brains. They claim that they will be able to read any person's mind by merely aiming the device at the person. Has Az been working on that?"

"Susan, you may have just answered our question! There are rumors he has been working on that. So far he's not been successful. He's grown very impatient and he might try to use it before it's ready. The only way he can learn what he wants to know and not tip his hand is to probe your mind, Peter, without you knowing it. His impatience for proof and the fear that we will use the time machine to block his plans may be getting the best of him. He may be getting reckless."

"Maybe that explains why I have this feeling that Az is planning something really evil. And it feels just like the mind probe felt," Peter interjects.

"I think you and Susan have nailed it, Peter! A mind probe of the whole campus. That would be the most logical thing for him to attempt now."

"What will he do if that doesn't work? The pressure of time running out for him may cause him to try to do something careless and drastic," adds Mrs. McD, concern evident in her voice. "If he does, he might decide just to grab both of you. I dare not think what he would do to you."

"But won't that also put you and Susan in danger?" Peter asks. "If he knows about you two won't he try to get at us through you?"

"That's a good point Peter," the Professor answers. "I share your concern. However, look at the facts. Mrs. McD took herself off the endangered list the first time we dealt with Mr. Az's Men in Black. They've got her labeled as a feisty housekeeper who knows nothing. When they came bursting in here looking for us, they found the same feisty Mrs. McD who scoffed at the idea of a time machine, and who also happened to be friends with the local police, who keep an eye on her. No, Mrs. McD is safe."

"But what about Susan? Do they know about her? Is she safe?" Peter asks, anxiety for her safety rising in him.

"I don't think so, Peter. I had no intention of getting Susan involved. She's brilliant, very pretty, and has an analytical mind like Mrs. McD's. When I asked her to help us by being your babysitter I only meant it to be a onetime thing. She had no reason to know more than that it was a favor to help us expose Hobbs and Smith. They didn't see her that morning when she was spying for me. Since Susan was already worried something bad might happen, she was a natural choice for a look out. So she is not in danger from that."

"But Susan is in danger," Mrs. McD corrects. "When she first started praying for you two, that put her in danger. Satan knows her name now. Just as we've been praying for your protection, Peter, the Professor and I have been praying for her protection, too. Satan will have difficulty getting through Az's inflated ego to tell him about Susan. But it could happen, maybe."

"I'm sorry I goofed up your plans, Professor." Susan's voice is soft and full of trust. "Peter, thank you for worrying about me. It makes me feel safe."

"You didn't goof up my plans, Susan. The Holy Spirit goofed them up. When the Spirit poured that knowledge into you it took it out of my hands. I should have realized the Spirit was up to something in the beginning when you told us that you had sensed evil and had prayed for us when the strange men came on campus. Even then the Spirit was preparing you. You were responding to His guiding."

"Need I remind you Professor that that is why we are all here now?" Mrs. McD interrupts. "Enough talking. We need guidance from the Spirit as to what to do next. We have been warned that evil is coming. We've a pretty good idea of the form it will take. We need to prepare. Things are finally coming to a head with Mr. Az. It is time to pray.

"Many people go about prayer all wrong. They come with a list, and then try to convince God as to why he should give them the things on their list. That's not prayer. Only beggars go up to strangers and ask for things. We are not beggars, and God is not a stranger. We have taken the time to get to know God. We study His Word. We talk to Him as we work and play. We praise and adore Him as the Creator and one deserving of all our praise and adoration. He is the Lord our God, and we are the sheep of His pasture.

"We are coming to our Father Who we know and love, with Whom we've shared our most intimate thoughts and dreams, and Whose dreams we have shared as we've studied His Word and talked over with Him what we have read. As a result of this fellowship with God we have learned to trust Him, to rely on Him, and to know that His will for us is the very best, and we desire to please Him in all we do and say."

"Well said, Mrs. McD. When we do ask Him for His help and guidance we shut up and wait on Him to speak, to give us His guidance. We search the Word to see if He will quicken a verse or story to us. We write down what comes. To be sure that we're not listening to the wrong voice, ours or Satan's lying voice, we ask for confirmation, words of scripture. Most importantly, we obey. First comes fellowship. Then comes guidance.

"Mrs. McD has a pad of paper, a pencil, and a Bible for each of us. We need to be clear and in agreement on what we are asking. Write this down: 'What are we being warned about, and what do we need to do?' Are we all in agreement with this question? Do you think there is a different question we should ask first? No? Then let's enter into prayer. Write down whatever thoughts come to you, or scriptures, songs, anything. Guidance can come in many ways. We need to be alert and not discount anything."

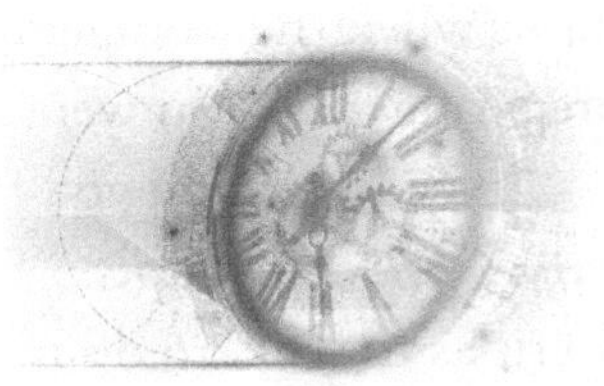

CHAPTER 37

Battle Strategy

God might tell each of us the same thing," Mrs. McD adds. "Or each of us may get a different part of the answer. Maybe a verse of scripture, or a memory, or even a word or a song. Each may seem meaningless by itself. But when put together they coalesce into a whole. Professor, say 'amen' when it seems right. Now let's pray. Father, we come to You in the mighty Name of Jesus seeking Your guidance and instructions in this matter we've been discussing. Reveal Your will and guidance. Remove anything from our thoughts that is not of You. Our desire is to obey and glorify You. Satan, according to 2 Corinthians 10:4 and 5 we cast down every stronghold you have erected in our minds, and every high thing in our minds that exalts itself against the knowledge of God. We release our minds to be reconciled to God. We release our minds to obedience to Christ."

Peter closes his eyes and listens. Try as hard as he can, he can't get his mind to focus on anything but his escape from the mind probe in the valley, when the Word of God stopped Az.

After several minutes the Professor says "Amen" and asks everyone to share. It is silent for a while.

Finally, Mrs. McD speaks. "I remembered something from my childhood. One wintry day we went to the library to hear the story lady. She told the story of Peter and the Wolf. On the way home it started to snow again. The wind whipped the snow into a fury, and then I heard a dog howl. I thought it was a wolf, and I remember running as hard as I could to get home before the wolf got me."

Encouraged, Peter tells about the mind probe.

"It's strange," Susan speaks next. "What I got doesn't make any sense alongside your stories. I kept hearing Psalm 91, verses 9 to 11 over and over in my mind. 'Because thou hast made the LORD, *which is* my refuge, *even* the most High, thy habitation; there shall no evil befall thee, neither shall any plague come nigh thy dwelling. For he shall give his angels charge over thee, to keep thee in all thy ways.'"

Everyone looks at the Professor. His eyes are closed. Finally he opens them and speaks. "I saw in my mind the story of the Passover. I saw them take the hyssop, dip it into the blood of the Passover lamb, apply it to the door posts of their homes. The death angel passed over them.

"I asked the Lord how all of this fit together, then I saw it. Peter's guidance showed us that Az is planning to assault this college campus with his mind probe. Mrs. McD's guidance warned us that no one would be safe from the lion seeking whom he can devour. Susan saw the promise of protection. I saw what God wants us to do. He wants us to lay down a Bloodline around the campus. Now we need to pray again. We must ask if this is the correct interpretation. If not, what is? And is there more?"

This time after their prayer, Peter's mind is at rest. He seems to hear, or see, or feel the impression, "Yes." So do the others.

"Who's up for a hike?" the Professor asks. "We want to get it done before Az strikes."

"Professor, what is a Bloodline?" Peter and Susan ask.

"Laying down a Bloodline is a form of spiritual warfare, a modern day application of the story I just told from Exodus chapter 11," the Professor explains.

"There is tremendous power in Jesus' Blood. When He gave His life for us He shed His blood. His blood cleanses us of all sin (I John 1:9). His blood redeems (Colossians 1:14). His blood atones for our sins (Romans 5:11). His blood enables us to overcome (Revelation 12:11). His blood has power because it is His life that is in His blood (Leviticus 17:11). His blood gives us a recreated human spirit (2 Corinthians 5:17).

Wherever His blood is applied His power is applied. And it does much more.

"Because of the fact that His life is in His blood, wherever His blood is applied, His power is applied. When we lay down a bloodline, or cover someone with the blood of Jesus, His life is present. We can lay down a bloodline around ourselves, our families, our homes, our property, our places of business, and decree that nothing shall cross that bloodline to harm us. This is not a magic incantation. It is simply affirming a fact. However, as always, there is the man side and the God side. You must do the man side first. You must apply the blood in faith, believing. Then God will do the God side."

"I never realized how much power and authority is in Jesus' blood," exclaims Susan.

"It's pretty exciting when you see it at work," Mrs. McD exclaims. "Do you remember the story Lee Mathews told, Professor? Lee Matthews lived in Minneapolis, Minnesota. He had become interested in the occult when he discovered he could use it to help him sell insurance and investments. Then he got born again and became a witness of Jesus. That led to the story he shared."

"I'll take over now," the Professor interrupts. "This needs a man to tell it right!"

The look Mrs. McD gives the Professor could have singed his hair! Then she laughs. "This is one of the Professor's favorite stories. He gets so tickled with the power of the bloodline."

"Lee was speaking in a college. A lady was walking by the open doors and heard him say something about Satan being a yellow bellied rascal and nobody needed to be afraid of him. She stopped and turned. She couldn't believe her ears. She came in and listened. At the end of the fifth session she got born again, and baptized in the Holy Spirit. It turned out that she was a witch and active in a coven.

"Lee went back to that same college a couple months later. The former witch was there with several others she had invited to come. The lady was frightened. The man who was the leader over the whole area for Satanism said he was going to come in the middle of the meeting, and beat Lee up to show that Lee didn't have any power.

"The lady was scared. Lee told her she didn't have to worry. He had prayed over the room. They had commanded that no evil spirits could enter while Lee was speaking. They'd pleaded the blood of Jesus. Nothing could happen.

"Well, the man came. He stood back at the door. Three times he walked like he was going to come in, but he never came in. When the lady left, the man was very, very angry. He'd lost face after bragging about what he was going to do. He said, 'I'm going over to your house tonight. I'm going to burn it down. If you call the fire department or if you call the police, I'm going to kill you.'

"This wasn't an idle threat. He had killed others. She was very frightened. She came to Lee and said, 'You're going to have to come and pray over my house.' Lee said, 'No! The same blood that I speak about will work for you. I'm not going to be here next week. You learn to do it now.'

"The lady walked around her house praying, 'In the Name of Jesus I lay down a bloodline around my house.' She commanded that no demon could cross that bloodline to enter, and any that left could never come inside again. She did it very enthusiastically. Like James says, the fervent prayer of a righteous person avails much. The man showed up right at eleven-thrity with about six people. One was carrying a can. They walked around outside the bloodline for about twenty minutes and left."[1]

"So you see, Peter and Susan," Mrs. McD breaks in, "it's the power of the blood. When you speak it out with faith there isn't a demon in the world that can cross it. Az has allowed himself to be controlled by Satan and his demons. He can never cross the bloodline once we lay it down. We will also pray a covering of blood over the whole campus. Just remember, it has to be spoken out with faith. It isn't something we try, it's something we do."

---

[1] Matthews, Lee (Not his real name), was a popular conference speaker and spoke several times in the author's church. At the request of his family his name has been changed for this story.

"Boy, that's a lot to digest. I've never heard of a bloodline before. Why don't we hear more about it?" Peter asks.

"We don't hear because most people have forgotten that we are at war. The warnings and instructions of Paul and James go mostly unheeded because Christians have been lulled into a false sense of security. Because Christians have stopped fighting, immorality and lawlessness have begun to take over. Because we know the truth, we must keep calling people to arms. A bloodline is a strong, power filled way to pray.

"I can hardly wait to do it," Susan cries out joyfully. "What a wonderful thing to do for our college and all the students!"

"Amen!" adds Peter.

"Then let's go! Grab your coats. You may get a bit chilly before we finish laying down the bloodline," warns the Professor, hopping up and grabbing his own coat.

Everyone heads for the Professor's car. Soon they pull into the faculty parking lot and begin their prayer walk.

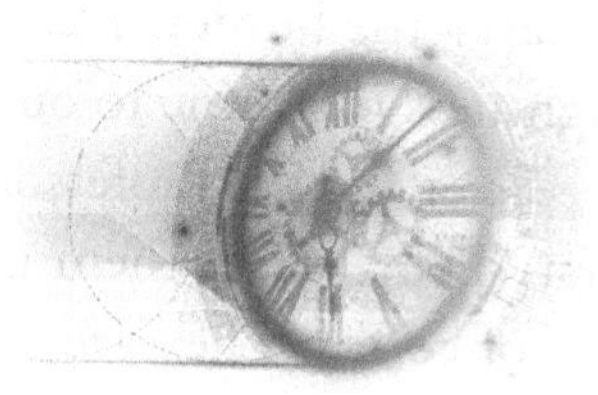

CHAPTER 38

Invasion of Darkness

When the prayer walk ends and they've piled back into the car, Mrs. McD announces, "Now there's no sense in you young folks missing supper. You come back home and I'll fix up a good meal for you. I suppose we can even find something for the Professor. Unless you'd rather scrounge around in your mushroom patch, seeing as I didn't leave you any supper."

"There's no sense in these kids suffering alone, Mrs. McD. I'll do my best to eat whatever you fix. It's the least I can do!"

"The least? The kids will be lucky if you leave anything for them!"

Peter asks jokingly, "Can't we just get along together?"

And Susan adds, "When we get home we're putting you two in separate rooms! Peter and I will fix dinner."

"No! No!" cries the Professor. "Anything but that! Don't let Peter cook! I'll behave."

"He started it!" Mrs. McD gets in the last word.

Now all four of them are laughing.

"Laughing is good," Mrs. McD observes as they pull into her garage. "Once the Professor has obeyed all God tells him, and he feels peace in his spirit, he becomes light-hearted, joyful and silly, like a little child whose daddy has just stepped between him and a bunch of bullies. One of his favorite sayings is, "Do the man side first, and then God will do the God side.' Or, 'Obey and get out of the way!' He doesn't have to carry the burden when God is carrying it. Our work is now done. Lightness has come to our spirits."

Peter and the Professor gallantly allow the women to enter the house first. They follow them up the stairs but don't get a chance to grab a cup of coffee. They are immediately ushered into the living room and told to sit and wait.

"What about coffee?" the Professor pleads.

"May I remind you, sir, that patience is a virtue?" Mrs. McD fires back.

"Virtue? I don't need virtue. I need coffee," he pleads again. Before he can say anything else Susan brings them each a cup of coffee.

"No cookie," she replies to the question on the Professor's face. "It's too close to supper. While you're waiting, you can go wash your hands."

"Women!" the Professor grumbles.

Meanwhile Mrs. McD and Susan rustle up supper. She keeps a supply of partially prepared meals on hand so that she can quickly put a meal together when needed. When everything is ready Susan invites the men to come and take their seats. "Now, no fighting at the table," she says.

Mrs. McD keeps the table talk lighthearted. "Everything is in God's hands. We turned it all over to Him. Won't do us any good to rehash everything, and it could get us off trusting into worrying. Time to get our minds on something else. How are your classes going? I hear your physics professor is something of a nut case! What crazy thing has he got you doing now?"

The Professor opens his mouth as though asking "me?"

Peter answers. "He hasn't teleported into class lately. But his last lecture was a little off the wall! He called it 'The Quantum Physics of Mushrooms'."

Susan rises to the Professor's defense. "You'll have to admit it was a fascinating lecture, wasn't it, Peter? He disassembled the mushroom back to its atoms, and then inside its atoms. It is amazing how everything comes together to make something like a delicious mushroom."

Their conversation centers around the marvels of God's creation. And speaking of creations, Mrs. McD makes a point of telling Peter which parts of their meal were Susan's creations. Peter finds himself eying the Professor and Mrs. McD suspiciously, thinking, *are they trying to fix us up? I admit Susan is smart and pretty, and right up there with Mrs. McD as a cook, too! But this isn't the time. It's too dangerous until this thing with Az is settled.*

When no one can eat another bite, the Professor pushes his chair back, rises and announces, "You two ladies have outdone yourselves. Thank you for a most delicious meal. I'm sorry to eat and run, leaving you with all the dishes, but I'd better get Peter back to his dorm. We don't want the two of them arriving together. I'll volunteer to go first."

"Now isn't that just like a man?" Mrs. McD turns to Susan. "They'll use any excuse they can come up with to get out of doing the dishes! Of course he's right. We don't want the two of you seen together. But even so . . ." she looks accusingly at the Professor.

Peter and the Professor sheepishly excuse themselves. The Professor is quiet on the drive back. Finally, he speaks, "Peter, we've surrounded the campus with a bloodline. But the store where you work is unprotected. Az knows where it is. When he hits that Bloodline and can't mind probe the campus, his anger will explode. He doesn't know about the power of the bloodline. He is already angry about the valley. He is also angry because you outsmarted his smartest men. He may lose control. He may try to grab you when you're off campus. Be watchful."

After the Professor drops him off in front of the dorm, that warning echoes in Peter's ears. Elated as he was with the spiritual warfare they had accomplished, now he's not so sure. They hadn't walked a bloodline around the store. He will be working all day. How will he protect himself? Back in his room, he undresses and hops into bed. Sleep does not come. He tosses and turns.

Unable to sleep he prays. "Father, there is something missing. There's got to be more to spiritual warfare than just resisting or holding on. James 4:7 says 'resist the devil and he will flee from you.' If all we do is hold up a protective shield won't the devil keep at it to wear us down? Why would he flee? The only reason for the devil to flee is something's scared the bejeebers out of him! But what? Second Corinthians 10:4 says 'the weapons of our warfare are not carnal, but mighty through

God to the pulling down of strong holds.' What is this weapon, and how do I use it?"

As Peter waits on the Lord in prayer, other verses come to mind. Philippians 2:10-11 says "at the name of Jesus every knee [must bow], of things in heaven, and things in earth, and things under the earth; And that every tongue [must bow] confess that Jesus Christ is Lord, to the glory of God the Father" (AMP).

"Yes! That's it! The name of Jesus is a weapon! Matthew 28:18 says Jesus has given me the power of attorney to use His Name. I can bind evil by the authority of His Name like He said in Matthew 18:18. I don't need to worry about Mr. Az. When he tries to mess with my mind, I'll bombard him with the name of Jesus!

"But that's not enough. I don't want to just see Mr. Az bowing in fear. He was a great man, like the Professor. My heart goes out to him. What happened to him? What bitterness drives him? When Peter and John saw the lame man at the gate of the Temple, their hearts went out to him, and they commanded him to be healed (Acts 3:6). Can I command Mr. Az to be healed in his heart in the name of Jesus?

"No. Not even God did that. All I can do is love on him as God loves on us. I need to make myself a clear channel through which God's love can flow. Then, when he messes with my mind, and only finds the name of Jesus and God's love, then maybe he will repent and return to the Lord. Thank you Father for giving me the answer. Now, according First John 1:9, forgive me of all my sin, and cleanse me of all unrighteousness. Put your love for Mr. Az in my heart."

Peter looks at the clock. "Good heavens! It is almost morning. Where did the night go? There's only a couple hours left to sleep! Better set all three alarm clocks."

Almost as soon as Peter's head hit the pillow, the first alarm goes off. He's surprised at how wide awake and refreshed he feels. There is a lightness and joy in his heart, buoyed by the hope that Az will respond to God's love. He showers and dresses quickly. His new shirt with the store monogram fits nicely. Grabbing a light jacket, he heads for the dining hall.

As he walks along he looks out over the city. There seems to be a darkness that comes up to the campus and stops where they walked the bloodline. "Well!" he muses. "We were right. Mr. Az came during the night. I wonder how he will respond, butting up against God's love? It looks like I'll soon find out. But breakfast first."

The dining room is pretty much deserted. The gang's sleeping in. Being first has its advantages. Everything is fresh. The toast is actually crisp, and the rolls have not been picked over! Peter is famished. The night of prayer used a lot of energy. A double helping of eggs and toast and two of the gooiest rolls, along with two cups of coffee leave little room on his tray. He picks a table with a good view of who is coming in just in case one of the gang shows up. No one comes. Peter takes a last swallow of coffee to wash down the last bit of a roll. It's time to head for work. He puts his tray on the dirty dish conveyor and leaves the dining hall.

He heads for the store. He pulls his collar up. It may be turning spring but the wind still has a little nip in it. He enjoys walking to the store. It's good exercise and the air is fresh, not like the library. There's no sign of anyone on the streets except for a few delivery trucks. He arrives at the store just as Mr. Johnson unlocks the door.

"Hi, Mr. Johnson. Beautiful day."

"Hi, Peter, right on time as usual. First, we have to set up the displays for this week's specials. Ready for some hard work?"

"Yes sir. I can use some hard work. I'm starting to get a little flabby from all those delicious college meals!"

"You're going to need more than hard work if you're starting to think those college meals are delicious," Mr. Johnson laughs. "You're going to need a taste bud transplant! I've eaten there. I know! This week we're having a big sale on our store brand canned vegetables. They unloaded a big truck load of them in the back storeroom yesterday. I was thinking we could stack cases of the vegetables in a pyramid at the end of each isle. Cut the tops and front off the boxes, and then build a can pyramid around the outside of the whole thing. That should give us plenty of stock on the floor."

"I'll get right on it."

Peter estimates how many cases of each vegetable he'll need for each pyramid. He loads the hand truck as full as he can get it, and brings the cases out. He's a pretty fast worker and the pyramids take shape in no time. A different vegetable at the end of each isle, starting at the front of the store. It hardly takes any time to do the first side. He goes back to the front and starts to do the other end of the isles. He thinks about Mr. Az as he stacks, picturing him standing there. He speaks the name of Jesus over him, and tells him how much God loves him.

With the can pyramids built, Peter starts to check the shelves and restock them. It's still pretty early in the morning and there have only been a few customers. Restocking is a never ending job and there has to be enough stock on the shelves to cover the morning rush.

Meanwhile, the Professor and Susan have been making plans of their own. It started when Susan woke up early with the words 'Peter needs you" running through her mind. She began immediately praying for him. The Professor woke up with the same uneasiness, and the words 'call Susan' running through his mind. While he hesitates to get her involved any deeper he can't ignore the guidance.

"Who could be calling this early?" Susan wonders out loud as she answers the phone. "Good morning. This is Susan. How can I help you?" she asks.

"An emergency has come up and I desperately need a babysitter right now! It can't wait. You'll have to drop everything else this morning. I'll pay double your usual rate. Can you come?"

Susan instantly recognizes the Professor's voice. "Is this the same baby I've babysat before? Or is it a new one?" she asks. "If it's the same one, I'll have to have more than double my rates!"

"You do drive a hard bargain, Susan, but I'm so desperate I'll pay your higher rate. Yes, it's Peter. He needs watching again. But this time I want you to go where he is."

"I'm glad you called, Professor. When I woke up the words "Peter needs you" were running through my head. I started praying for him right away."

"That's very interesting, Susan. When I woke up the words "call Susan" were running through my head. That confirms our guidance. Now for your babysitting task. Az still doesn't know about you, so he'll ignore your presence. Find a place where you can watch the store in secret. Look for any unusual cars with darkened windows, like a limousine. That will be Az. I want you to guard Peter.

"When Az finds his mind probe is blocked at the edge of the campus, he'll be steamed. He knows where Peter works, so he will go there and try to use his mind probe on Peter again. Az is going to meet a formidable opponent when he comes up against Peter. When that happens Az is likely to send his men into the store to grab Peter. If you see strange men trying to sneak up on Peter, grab Peter's arm and run."

"Is that all?" Susan asks. "Just grab his arm and run? Run to where?"

"That's where you're going to have to trust the Spirit to guide you. Whatever pops into your head to do, do. That will give Peter a chance to recover, and then you can work together to get back to the campus. Once you're back here you will be safe. If my hunch is right, this will get Az and his men into so much trouble with the local police that they won't dare to show up here again for some time."

"I'll do it Professor. I really want to help Peter, and this is something I can do. I'll take my cell phone and keep you informed."

"Thanks, Susan. Remember that greater is He that is in you than he that is in the world. And you are covered by the blood of the Lamb."

Susan dresses in old blue jeans, a worn, faded sweat shirt that used to be red, and an old spring jacket that had seen better days. She pushes her hair straight back in a ponytail, fastens it, and sticks the hair up under an old ball cap. She looks more like a street urchin than a college girl. Putting her cell phone in her pocket and grabbing a granola bar for breakfast, she steps outside and begins walking slowly towards Peter's store.

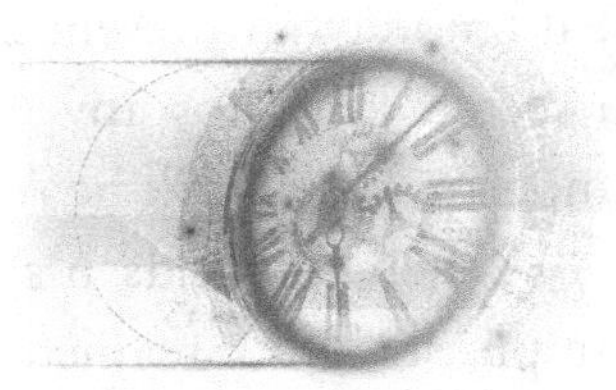

CHAPTER 39

Cans, Oil and Flour

At first the streets are empty except for an occasional car or truck. It's too early for most shoppers to start their rounds. Az wouldn't likely be driving around in a limousine just yet because he would want to be as inconspicuous as possible. This gives her ample time to find a well-situated seat in the doorway of the pawn shop next to the grocery store. She leans back and watches.

By eight-thirty the traffic starts to pick up a little. It's still too early for more than a handful of people. Just then she senses a pressure in her head, as though someone was trying to get into her mind. It quickly passes but it was all she needed in order to know Az had come. As she watches, a black limousine with dark windows pulls up and parks in front of the store.

Inside the store Peter feels Az trying to get into his mind. He smiles and directs his thoughts towards Az, saying, *Welcome Mr. Az, Jesus is here. He loves you. The Word says that at the Name of Jesus every knee shall bow, and every tongue confess that Jesus Christ is Lord. Let Jesus be your Lord once again, Mr. Az. He loves you so much. Jesus, please bless Mr. Az. Thank you.*

Suddenly Peter is aware of a great change in the mind probe. For a moment he senses that Mr. Az is feeling great pain in his head, like a searing hot iron. Just as quickly the mind probe stops and he senses a horrible rage taking its place. Peter feels a great sadness, knowing that Az has refused God's love.

Peter keeps on stacking cans, waiting to sense what Az will do next. Will he leave? Will he try again? Several minutes pass. Meanwhile, Susan has quietly entered the store through the back. She stands where she can watch Az's car. Two men in black get out and head for the store. Susan acts quickly. Running up behind Peter, she grabs his arm and shouts, "Az! Knock over the cans! Run!" A quick glance and Peter sees it all. Two men, dressed in black, are coming at him, one from each side.

In rapid motion Susan pushes over a can pyramid on the right. The man in black trips and falls. Peter pushes over a pyramid on the left and the second man in black trips and falls.

"Quick!" cries Susan. "We can't run out the front. Az is there. We've got to find a place to hide." She pushes Peter towards the back storeroom door just as the men in black get up and race after them. The door slams shut, hitting the men in the face and stopping them for a second. Inside the storeroom Peter spots a pile of empty boxes.

"Quick," he shouts, "help me push them in front of the door."

"The lights!" cries Susan. "Turn off the lights."

The men in black back up and then hit the door with their shoulders, crashing through just as the lights go out. Momentarily blinded, they trip over the empty boxes, cursing as they do. In the darkness Peter sees daylight around the edges of the back door. Susan rushes towards the door, pushes it open.

"Don't go out!" Peter warns, grabbing her hand, and pulling her behind a stack of boxes. They crouch down and watch. The men in black, seeing the back door open, rush through it. Peter jumps up and quickly closes it and bolts it.

"Peter, we've got to get back to the campus. It's the only safe place."

"We can't go out the back way now. We'll have to go out the front door. If we're lucky we'll get a good head start before those two realize we tricked them. It'll be a long run back to the campus, Susan. Are you up to it?"

"Peter, Az is parked right out in front," she cries urgently. "We can't go that way either. We're trapped!"

"Not quite," Peter answers. "When Az tried to probe my mind I told him how much God loved him. It seemed to cause a tremendous amount of pain in his head. I think he is still in too much pain to follow us. It'll be safe to run past him. We'll have a good head start on his men. Oh, and if he sees you he may try to probe your mind. Just keep thinking Jesus, Jesus, Jesus. His mind is so weak right now that that will stop him."

Peter opens the door into the store just far enough to see what is happening. Mr. Johnson is looking at the mess, when suddenly two more men in black rush past him, knocking him off his feet.

"Oh, oh," Peter whispers, "two more Men in Black. It's time for Plan B."

"What's Plan B?"

"I haven't thought of it yet!"

"Then follow me!" whispers Susan, again grabbing his arm and standing close by the doors. The two men slam into the doors. In that brief instant, before their eyes adjust to the dark, Susan pulls Peter past them and runs into the store. "Call the police!" Susan shouts to Mr. Johnson, as Az's men turn too late and try to grab them as they run past.

Peter grabs some cans of vegetables and throws them at the men. They jump, trip and fall, letting out a stream of curses. One grabs for Susan and Peter hits him square in the face with a can of corn. Susan grabs a bottle of cooking oil. She dumps it on the floor behind her in the path of the man in black. He slips and slides into a rack of flour. A bag bursts covering him and everything else with flour.

Just then the other man grabs for Peter. Susan hits him with a frying pan.

"Ow, that's got to leave a bump!" Peter shouts.

The flour-covered man grabs Susan. Without thinking Peter dives hard into the man's back, causing him to let loose of Susan, lose his balance again, and slam into the shelves. Peter loses his balance, too, and the two men pounce on him before he can get away. Susan continues to belt them with the frying pan. They shield themselves with one hand while they hold Peter tight with the other, one on each side. Mr. Johnson joins in the struggle trying to force the men to let go of Peter as they try to push their way to the front doors.

Just then two police cruisers pull up, sirens blaring. The police rush into the store. The two men, holding a firm grip on Peter's arms, turn and rush towards the store room door.

"Quick," Susan shouts. "They've got Peter. They're escaping out the back door." The Chief orders two of his men to go outside and run around the back.

The Men in Black, covered with white flour, slam into the back door only to find it is bolted. They are in such a hurry to get out they fumble with the bolt. By the time they get it unbolted and rush out the police are there, guns drawn. The Men in Black draw their own guns. Using Peter as a shield, they rush towards the police, shouting at them, "Get back or we'll shoot."

The police, unwilling to take a chance on hitting Peter, hold their fire. The Men in Black think their only danger is in front of them. They don't look behind. But the police see Mr. Johnson come out the door, seething with anger. These men made a mess of his store, and then kidnapped Peter. He takes a quick look around and grabs the two by four used to bar the door, and rushes out. The police, seeing him come, keep stalling the flour covered Men in Black, warning them to put their guns down. Meanwhile, Mr. Johnson, swinging the two by four, comes up behind them, and clobbers the man holding Peter. In the confusion Peter pulls away, and the police arrest the two men.

Peter goes back into the storeroom and joins Susan. She had followed Mr. Johnson and watched from the doorway.

"Thank God, you're safe," she exclaims with relief.

For the moment both Peter and Susan are safe. But only for a moment, and only as long as they stay inside the store and only as long as the police stay. The first two Men in Black are out there, waiting for them to come out. The chief and two of his men are occupied with supervising the two men they've captured. The other two officers are out searching for the other two men in black.

When they arrived with their cruisers, the police tried to block Mr. Az's limousine. But while they are busy with Az's men, Az's driver maneuvers his way out of the blockade. Now free, he speeds away, but not far. Meanwhile Mr. Johnson, still seething in anger, is standing over

Az's two men, with his two by four ready to whack again! He and the police force the men to clean up the mess and rebuild the can pyramids.

"I can't do nothin'," one of them bellows. "That kid hurt my back when he slammed into me."

"A lot more than your back will hurt if you don't start cleaning up this mess," Mr. Johnson bellows back. "Unload all those shelves where you made a mess and start cleaning it up. Here's a mop. Wash the shelves down. Once you get them clean, wipe them dry. Then scrub your mess off the floor. Don't you leave a single speck of dirt or I'll use your face to clean it up."

"Boy!" Peter observes, "I'm sure glad I don't have to clean up that mess. It'd take me the rest of the day."

With clean-up settled, Mr. Johnson focuses his attention on Peter and Susan.

"You two are a mess," he says, observing their disheveled and floured looks. "You can wash your hands and faces in the bathroom, but I don't have any clothes you can change in to."

"That's okay, Mr. Johnson," Peter replies. "We can go back to our rooms to clean up. I'll grab a bite to eat at the dining hall and then come back to work."

Mr. Johnson looks first at Peter, and at the men who are grudgingly cleaning up the mess.

"Peter, I don't think you'll need to come back. When these goons finish cleaning up this mess, I'm going to set them to work cleaning up the whole store and restocking the shelves. These goons are going to earn your money for you today. After they're through here, the Chief is going to take them to jail and throw the book at them."

"That's right," the Chief adds. "And if they don't have enough money on them to pay for the damage they caused, we'll tack it onto their bail. Only this time their bail will be one million dollars each, cash. I told them to never set foot in this town again. They chose to disobey my orders. So, they'll pay for it, but good."

"As long as you don't need me, Mr. Johnson, Susan and I will leave. We both need to get cleaned up before we can eat."

"You go right ahead Peter. You deserve the rest of the day off. But why don't you wait and let the police take you back? The other two goons are still out there looking for you. So far they've eluded the two officers who are looking for them."

"A police escort would be nice, Mr. Johnson, but we can't wait that long or the dining hall will be closed. The police can't leave right now. They have their hands full looking after these two goons and searching for the other two," Peter explains. "If the other two hoodlums are trying to avoid the police, as well as watch for us, there's a good chance we can make it back to the campus before they catch up with us."

Mr. Johnson is doubtful, but before he can answer, the police call him over with a question about the cleanup.

Susan shares Mr. Johnson's doubt. "It's not going to be easy getting back to the safety of the bloodline, Peter. It's not just the two goons who are looking for us. Az is out there too. I feel it in my spirit. Do you have a plan?"

"I've been thinking of something that might work," Peter responds thoughtfully. "Let's review what we're up against. There's Az. Like you said, he is still out there somewhere, waiting for us to leave the store. He still has two men out there, hiding and watching for us. Each will be watching two sides of the store. If we just rush out and make a mad dash for the college they'll be on our heels so fast we might not make it to the bloodline. We need to do something that will give us a good head start."

"I agree. If we can get a block ahead of them we can easily out runthem. Any ideas?"

"Well, this idea has been bouncing in my head. I'm tired of being chased. It's time we started doing the chasing, don't you think?"

"I'm with you on that score Peter. But how can we do that, seeing as how we are the ones being hunted?"

"I was thinking we could start by working on Az. When I responded to Az's mind probe this morning by witnessing to him, he recognized me. From my two experiences with his mind probe I think I've learned a secret. In order to use his mind probe technology, he has to open his own mind, too. He's not worried about that because he believes that his mind is so superior he can force his will on anyone. He can't believe anyone can resist him. He has no fear of anyone attacking him back.

"That's his weakness. The Name of Jesus gets through all his defenses and causes him severe pain. It did back in the valley, and it did just now. Now he's consumed with anger mixed with his pain. I felt his anger explode. It was like a gigantic ego declaring, 'No one dares oppose me and live!' He is becoming more and more reckless. He broke away from the police, but he's still here. He is determined to find us. Yes, us. He knows about you now. He'll tell his thugs where we are. If we can use that against him by making him think we're where we're not, it will give us a good head start. He'll try to probe your mind first. So it's your turn to give him a headache and feed him false information!"

"Peter! We are to love our enemies, not torment them."

"That's exactly what we're doing, loving him. It's just that our love causes him pain. What's the one thing we desire most to happen to Az? Isn't it to let Jesus back into his heart? His headache comes from resisting Jesus. When he tries to probe your mind, he needs to hear the name of Jesus. He needs to hear that Jesus loves him. It will either soften his heart, or cause him pain and inflame his anger even more."

"How do I do it?"

"Let your compassion flow to him as it would flow to anyone who needs to know Jesus. As you do, keep repeating over and over, 'Mr. Az, in the name of Jesus, please let Jesus into your heart. He loves you very much.' At the same time, keep thinking 'Bus Station.' If both of us project that same thought he just might send his goons there and give us more time. That's my plan."

"It sounds good in theory. Don't we have to wait until he uses the probe before we can speak to his mind? What if he doesn't? If he does use the mind probe, what if he doesn't fall for 'Bus Station?' What if he can tell it's wrong information? Do you have another plan?"

"Yes. But it's not as nice as my first plan. It'll be harder because it will take a lot of hiding and waiting as well as running. If we give the goons the slip, Az will search for us with his mind probe, and tell the goons where we are. First we'll have to slip out a side window. The storeroom sits back a little further than the building next door. Once we're out the window if we can slip around the back of the building next door without being seen, we can sneak down the alley and get away. But if we are seen we'll have to look for places to hide and try to block Az's mind probe from giving us away."

"Peter, I've an idea to make your plan work perfectly! The building next door. It has a barber shop and pawn shop in front, but the back is rented out as a warehouse. If we can sneak out of Mr. Johnson's office window into the alley we'll be right across from the fire escape. We can climb the fire escape and maybe they won't see us. If they do see us, we'll be almost at the top before they can start climbing."

"But what good will it do us to be on top of the building, Susan? If they see us and climb up after us won't we be trapped?"

"No! That's the great thing about it. We can get into the warehouse through the fire door on top. It's left unlocked. We'll bar the door once we're inside. While they're trying to get in, we can go down the stairs and out the front. That will give us even more time to get back to the campus before they can catch us. Even if Mr. Az sees us, his men will have to get down from the building before they can follow us."

"Good thinking, Susan."

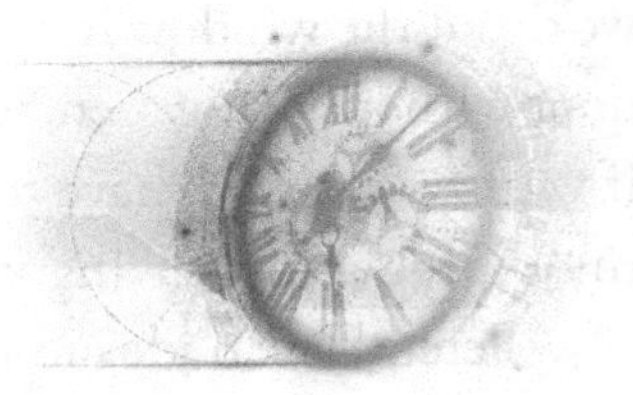

CHAPTER 40

Playing Dress-Up

Mr. Johnson, would you mind if we climb out of your office window in case those goons are waiting for us outside? We think it will be safer than going out the door."

"Yes. I'll help you. Peter. I'll stay by the window and if they're out there I'll help you back in before they can catch you. We'll keep these two goons so busy they won't know what you're doing and can't pass the word to their boss. Who would think a little article in the newspaper would cause you so much trouble! I never dreamed industrial espionage could lead to something like this!"

Mr. Johnson opens the window and gives Peter a boost up. He looks around, sees no sign of anyone. He slips out the window, letting himself down silently to the ground. He waits, looking for any sign, even a shadow moving. Seeing none he whispers, "It's all clear, Susan."

Mr. Johnson gives Susan a boost, and Peter helps her land, making no sound, still looking for any movement or shadow. Quietly they head for the fire escape. Like most old fire escapes this one is a bit rusty. As they start to climb the ladder creaks and moans. This alerts Az's goons and they come running.

Peter and Susan are only halfway to the top when the goons reach the bottom and start up. With a burst of speed Peter and Susan race to the top as fast as they can. Once over the top they dash to the fire door. It too has become rusty and at first resists being opened. Peter grabs a nearby two-by-four that was used to prop the door open and brings it down hard on the latch handle, forcing it to turn and unlatch. Dropping the two-by-four, Peter wrenches the door open.

"Quick!" shouts Susan, pulling Peter in after her. "Pull the door shut, and hold it while I drop the bar in place."

The goons pull hard, trying to wrest the door from Peter's grasp. Susan slips the bar in place just in the nick of time.

"Those bolts are almost rusted through," Peter shouts. "It won't hold them very long." Just then Peter spots a freight elevator in the back.

"Susan, hit the call button and call up the freight elevator. Then help me jam everything we can into the stair well. It will take the goons a while to clear the stair well. We'll jam the elevator so they can't call it back up."

Susan hits the call button and joins Peter. They shove everything they can into the stairwell, and then rush to the freight elevator. Just then the fire door opens.

"Quick," Peter grabs Susan's hand. "Get on the freight elevator."

Peter hits the down switch. The elevator comes to a stop at the bottom. Peter jams the door open to keep the elevator from moving.

"Now we've got the head start we wanted," Susan whispers as she slowly pushes the warehouse door open. The alley is clear. Turning to Susan, Peter gives her a high five.

"We did it! We should be a good two blocks away by the time they get back down the fire escape. Run!"

Meanwhile, the goons realize the elevator has been blocked, along with the stairwell. Az probes their minds and learns that Peter and Susan have given them the slip. He has his driver drive down the street, looking for them, while his goons climb back down the fire escape.

Peter and Susan start running for all they're worth. Peter thought he was a pretty fast runner, but Susan puts him to shame. It takes everything he's got to keep up with her! He'll never live it down if the guys find out he was beat by a girl!

They almost make it to the end of the second block when a black limousine comes careening around the corner, blocking their way. The driver starts to get out. Without thinking Peter heads for the driver's door. Giving it everything he's got, Peter slams hard into the driver's door, crushing the driver against the car. The driver screams in pain.

"Follow me," Susan cries, running past and dashes into a ladies clothing store. Inside, Susan steers Peter behind some racks of dresses. They crouch down and look out between the dresses, breathing hard.

"I said Az was still here," Peter whispers.

"I felt him probe my mind," Susan whispers back. "I did like you said. It felt like he screamed, and stopped. I don't think he will try again. But it was just long enough for him to guess where we are. Now what?"

"I think I hurt his driver pretty bad when I slammed the door against him. He won't be coming in. Az will probably wait for his two goons to come and send them in after us. I don't think he will dare try a mind probe again. Too painful. You know, if we could disguise ourselves, I bet we could walk out the front door right now and he'd never guess."

"Peter, that's a great idea!" Susan's face lights up as she immediately heads to the sales counter.

The store, Peter notes, is an exclusive lady's store. The white stalls around the outside are filled with the latest colorful fashions, some on hangars and some spread out to show off their styling. Racks of beautiful dresses, slacks, and blouses fill the floor. A fashionably dressed and attractive older lady stands behind the U-shaped counter at the front.

"Hello, Susan! What a pleasant surprise. And I mean surprise! You two look a mess! Why did you come bursting in so fast and then hide among the racks? Are you playing some kind of game?"

"No, Mrs. Morgan. I'm afraid it's not a game. We need your help. There's a couple men, bad men, following us. It's a long story, but they are after Peter."

"Oh, yes. I know all about you, Peter. You're one of the politest and helpful clerks Mr. Johnson has ever employed. And to think, you got to take part in that science experiment, too. How can I help you two, Susan?"

"We're trying to get back to the campus before those men catch us. If you could dress us up in some of these clothes so that no one can recognize us, I bet we could walk out the front door right under their noses. Will you help? We'll come back later and pay."

"I'll be glad to help, Susan. It's the least I can do for the best sales lady I've ever hired!"

"You work here?" Peter asks, surprised.

"You hold still, Peter," Mrs. Morgan orders. "Susan has a gift for helping people pick out the clothes they will look the best in and be happy with. Some of my customers like her so well, they won't buy unless she's here. Now hold your arms up."

"Ow!" Peter gasps at the sudden pain. "Must have hurt my shoulder when I hit the car door."

Mrs. Morgan finishes taking measurements and then selects some long dresses from the racks. "Long enough to cover your shoes," she states. And tops them off with big bonnet hats to hide their faces.

"Quickly, you two. Take these clothes into the dressing room and get yourselves dolled up. Here's a couple shopping bags to put your own clothes in. Here's a wig for Peter. Can't say as you'd make a very attractive woman, but do your best!"

They go into one of the dressing rooms, and close and latch the door. Susan helps Peter strip down to the waist, taking care not to make him move his shoulder too much. She rolls up his pant legs. She carefully examines his shoulder and concludes it is only a bruise, nothing broken. Noticing the scar she asks, "What caused the scar?"

"It's from a bullet wound I got when the Professor and I escaped from Mr. Az. It was nothing."

Somewhat awed by this news, Susan is quiet for a moment as she helps Peter slip on the women's clothes, taking special care not to hurt his shoulder. She tucks his hair under the wig. A little powder over his whiskers and a little lipstick add the finishing touches. Lastly she puts the big bonnet on his head. Peter looks in the mirror.

"There, you have just come up in the world, Peter! You are now a woman! Look at yourself in the mirror and see how much better you look."

What Peter sees is not his idea of a pretty woman. "Well, definitely not my choice for a date." Then he looks at Susan and says, "But

I've seen worse!" Susan responds to his teasing insult by giving him a friendly slap on the face. "Ouch! What's that for?" he asks pretending hurt.

Just then they hear voices. The goons! They've come into the store. Mrs. Morgan's voice snaps out an order. "Not in there! I have customers in there getting dressed and you may not peek, you perverts!"

"Wow!" Peter whispers. "She can be real bossy when she wants to."

Susan, meanwhile, puts on her clothes. She had been looking pretty scruffy when they came into the store. The full length dress she chose to wear is very pretty. Using the dress as a tent she slips off her sweat shirt and jeans. She lets her hair down, and it flows gently over her shoulders. Peter stands open mouthed at the transformation.

"You're absolutely beautiful!" he whispers.

Susan looks at him and laughs. "Close your mouth and stop drooling! Put your clothes in your bag and let's go." She does the same. Then she gives Peter one last going-over. "Try to keep the dress covering your shoes. They're a dead giveaway. And if you possibly can, try to walk gracefully like a lady, and not that awkward clumsy look of a boy." Peter pretends a hurt look.

Susan leads the way to the checkout counter. "Thank you so much Mrs. Morgan for all your help. The clothes are just beautiful. We'll take them."

"Sign right here," smiles Mrs. Morgan. "And remember, bring them back if you're not completely satisfied."

Susan signs first, using a fictitious name and Peter signs after her using another fictitious name. They pick up their bags and walk slowly out of the store, walking right in front of the goons, pausing to look at the racks of clothes, feeling the cloth, pulling the garments out sideways to get a better look. Outside they pause to look at the window displays.

They slowly walk to the end of the block and turn left. Once out of sight of Az's limousine, Susan picks up her dress, and shouts, "Run!" Halfway down the block she crosses the street and runs into an alley. The alley runs all the way to the end of the block. Only two blocks to go and they'll be safely on campus.

"Quick," Susan cries, urgency in her voice. "Change back into your clothes."

Peter slips off the bandana and wig and dress, rolls his pant legs down, and painfully slips on his shirt. Susan slips her jeans on underneath the dress, pulls her sweatshirt over the top and stuffs the dress up under the sweatshirt.

"Az tried to probe my mind again," she says breathlessly.

"I saw a chance to give us more time. I told him we were dressed as two women, and then hit him with the Name of Jesus again. He recoiled in pain. He saw us come out of the store. He saw us turn left. His men will be looking for two women. If we run hard, I think we can make it to the campus."

Peeking out of the alley, they see no one. They step out cautiously, turn right and go back to the main street. Az's limousine is gone. They turn left towards the campus and run for all they're worth. This time Susan is lagging. Peter takes her hand to help. One block down, one to go.

Peter looks behind. The two goons are hot on their tail. Out of the corner of his eye he catches sight of the limousine. Only half a block to go. The limousine stops and Az waits. The goons are gaining. Just a few more yards. With a last burst of energy Peter speeds ahead, pulling Susan with him. With the goons just a couple steps behind them, they cross the bloodline.

They hear what sounds like two *thumps.* They stop and turn around. The goons are laying flat on the ground, stunned, as though they'd run into a brick wall.

"I bet they ran into our Guardian Angels," Peter says.

Az's limousine starts up and comes towards them. The engine stops dead at the edge of the bloodline. Neither Az or his men can cross the Bloodline to reach Peter and Susan.

Again Peter says, "Angels. We are safe."

With a great sigh of relief Peter and Susan turn and head for the Professor's office.

"Susan, I am so thankful you were there this morning. That was an amazing stroke of luck!"

"It wasn't luck, Peter. I was babysitting again. You sure do need a lot of looking after!" she adds, laughing.

"Hmm, I see there's a story here. Want to tell me about it?"

"I woke early with the words running through my mind, 'Peter needs you.' So I began to pray for you. While I was praying the Professor called. He said he needed me to do something very important. He said Az was here. Then he said, 'I need you to babysit Peter again!'"

"Oh no, not the babysitting thing again."

"Like Mrs. McD said, you sure do need looking after! The Professor said that this time I was to do it in secret. He said Az doesn't know about me, and won't suspect anything. Besides, he said, Az will be so preoccupied with you that he will ignore my presence. It's you he wants.

"The Professor has a lot of confidence in you, Peter. He said Az will meet a formidable opponent when he tries to use his mind probe on you. He was confident that you'd be just fine. But he was worried about Az. He thought Az was getting reckless. The patience that has carried him for so many years has run thin now that he knows there is a time machine. He's afraid Az might become extremely angry and throw caution to the wind. Do foolish things. Then he told me, 'Your task is to guard Peter. Look for any unusual cars with darkened windows, like a limousine. That will be Az. In anger at being bested at his own game he will send in his goons to grab Peter. If you see strange men trying to sneak up on Peter, grab his arm and run.' That's it, Peter. I couldn't resist his babysitting offer. The pay is too good! Triple this time! And look, today we even got to play dress-up!"

Peter stops. He looks at Susan, and asks, "Is that all I am to you: a babysitting job?"

Without batting an eye, she answers, "Of course!"

Peter groans.

Safely back on campus they arrive at the Professor's office. They share briefly with the Professor what happened. He laughs heartily over the goons having to clean up their own mess. He laughs even harder when Susan tells him how they got to play dress up. "We'll have to tell Mrs. McD all about it. I bet she'd love to sew some dresses for Peter!"

"*Professor!*"

CHAPTER 41

The Calm Before the Storm

They leave the Professor and go their separate ways to their dorms to clean up. The gang sees Peter come into the dorm, looking a mess and carrying a shopping bag from a ladies clothing boutique. Peter doesn't even try to explain.

"Not only would you guys not understand, you wouldn't believe it if I told you. But it was a rather unusual day at the grocery store."

Mr. Az, meanwhile, is not having a good morning. He is puzzled and a little worried. Why did his men fall flat on their faces when they were so close to grabbing Peter? They claimed they ran into a wall. Why did his car die when he tried to drive onto the campus? How could two smart-aleck kids escape from his highly trained men in black? His surveillance technicians were unable to detect anything that would explain what had happened. He will put his best scientists to work trying to solve this mystery.

There is one bright spot in this otherwise miserable morning. He has learned what he came to find out. The Professor is the one of the Nine he is looking for: the builder of the time machine. Peter is his protégé. Only the Professor could have developed the mental ability to resist the mind probe. Only the Professor could have taught Peter how to resist. Now he knows they were both in that mountain valley. He recognized Peter's mind. His search is finally over.

But, there's the local police. He could blast them all with his mind probe. But he is so close to grabbing his prize, his time machine, he doesn't want to do anything to jeopardize that. Well, he'll play along with their stupid game, but they will all pay for it later. Once he has his time machine he'll make that boy, Peter, and that girl, pay double for their insolence. His head still throbs from those smart-alecks! He'll get his revenge on this town later.

For now he can finally focus on bringing his forces to town and getting them ready to sweep down on the Professor when the time machine is activated. He will bring his men into the area without alerting that meddlesome police chief. Wherever the time machine lands they will be ready to pounce. His new surveillance team will be set up ready to go in just a few days. Not only will they catch the first signal from the time machine, they will be able to locate it within three feet. Finally, the last piece of his master plan is ready. In the meantime, he will send out false information saying he has gone off to other countries looking for the time machine. That will put the Professor off guard.

Mr. Az's men do not share his feelings of success. This has not been a good day for them. They spent most of the day cleaning and restocking shelves. They'd been "forced" to dust the light fixtures, clean the tops of display cabinets, wash and scrub the toilets, wash the windows. They had been threatened with going without meals, cleaning the jail, washing the police cars and being jailed without bail if they didn't do a good job. When they're finally done, the chief throws them into jail, subjects them to a humiliating full body search, and forces them to wear prison garb. Az's lawyer tries everything he can to get the bail reduced, but to no avail. The judge "throws the book at them" and sets their bail at one million dollars each, cash, plus expenses. Az pays it grudgingly.

Nothing is heard from Az again, except Az's own rumors. But word of his activities, which he tries to keep secret, leak out. Little signs are picked up by the other members of the Order and told to the Professor. He knows when Az's men begin to infiltrate the area. He knows when the new surveillance is installed. Periodically, just to anger Az, he lowers the secrecy curtain when Peter is there.

Everyone relaxes, knowing things will remain quiet until the Orb shows up. All four of them, Mrs. McD, the Professor, Peter and Susan, are glad for this little respite from dealing with Az. There aren't many weeks left of the spring semester. There are term papers to be written, tests to be taken, lab work to complete, and special study projects to complete.

Susan, in addition to her regular studies, continues to help Mrs. McD in her research. This enables her to write a couple extra credit papers. Occasionally Mrs. McD and Susan invite Peter and the Professor to dinner. They talk about many things, laugh and joke and play games. Mrs. McD always makes a point of telling Peter which things Susan has cooked. And, of course, the subject of babysitting always manages to come up!

Peter is completely engrossed in his studies, in writing papers, taking tests, working at the store, and practicing with the baseball team. He spends several long days in the Professors lab working on extra credit papers under the Professor's guidance, enjoying coffee breaks and eating Mrs. McD's famous chocolate chip cookies.

After several weeks of this busy pace it all comes to an end with the last day of classes, and with the last reports and papers turned in.

The Professor and Mrs. McD announce that it would be quite appropriate to celebrate the end of classes with a picnic. A restful break before studying for finals the following week. All the classes end on Friday. The last papers are turned in by the five p.m. deadline. Even Mr. Johnson had told Peter to take Saturday off.

Just because he can, Peter does not set his alarm clocks. He wakes up a little later, not much, but this time it's on his own! He barely makes it to breakfast before the serving line closes. "Cutting it a little short, aren't you, Peter?" Linda asks as she is about to lock the door. "I hear you've done so bad in Physics the Professor has to spend the whole day today tutoring you. Susan said the Professor wasn't sure he could help, but he was going to try! She said she is going along so the Professor will have something pretty to look at when he can't take looking at you anymore."

"You really know how to hurt a guy, don't you, Linda! I was going to tell you how pretty you look today. But after those remarks I'm not going to tell you! Now you'll never know. To think, I could have made your day!"

"That's the trouble with you guys, Peter. You think all it takes to make our day is to be noticed by one of you. That's so nauseating."

Peter decides there is no way he is going to win this debate. "Okay, Linda. You win. This time. I misjudged you. I shouldn't have tried coming in here with my full brain tied behind my back! I should have kept half of it out to use with you."

"I don't know which is worse - a no wit, or a half-wit!"

"Okay! Okay! You win. Care to join me for breakfast?"

After a leisurely breakfast Peter hurries back to his room, grabs his stuff, and heads for his car. "Finally," he almost shouts as he tosses his backpack and jacket onto the back seat, "a Saturday with nothing to do! Finals may start Monday, but today, no school, no books, no work. Just relax. I've been looking forward to this day for weeks. A day at the Professor's home always means a day of fun."

Oh, they all know Az is around, prepared to pounce. But, like the Professor said, Az won't do anything until the Blue Orb shows up. Until then it's party time! Peter stops before getting into the car, just to look around and breathe in the fragrant smells of spring. He takes a deep breath. The lilacs, blue and purple and pink and white, showing off their beauty against a deep blue sky, fill the air with their delicate fragrance. It's one of those days when you want to drive slowly with your windows open to take it all in. But that will have to wait until another day. He'll be late if he doesn't hurry.

What a day this is going to be, Peter smiles in anticipation as he starts his car and pulls out of the parking lot. Mrs. McD will be driving up with the food. She's cooked one of her fabulous meals with Susan's help.

Speaking of Susan, Peter muses, *I've hardly seen Susan since that business with Az and his goons! Not that I haven't thought about her. We had quite an adventure together. I really would like to get to know her better. But that will have to wait until this business with Az is over. She's already been exposed to too much danger.*

The Professor will be teaching before the day is over! It's in his blood.

Anything you didn't get in the classroom he'll bring up sooner or later. You'll know it before you go home. Even if it is something you don't need to know, he'll start teaching it! But it's his stories; that's what makes it all worth the effort. He can tell stories that keep you on the edge of your seat for hours! There are so many things he's done and places he's been, and never been able to share them until now when Susan and I came along.

As Peter turns into the Professor's driveway he sees the Professor working in his flower garden. He loves flowers, and Mrs. McD uses them to make beautiful bouquets. You can bet the house will be full of the delicate fragrance of lilacs with bouquets of them in every room. Peter parks his car and hops out.

"Hi, Professor. What a beautiful day. Can I help you?"

"Thanks for the offer, Peter, but I'm just about done. There's a fresh pot of coffee on the porch. Pour us each a cup and I'll join you in a minute."

Two porch chairs have been pulled together in front of the picture window on the left. A small stand sits in between them. On the stand is a tray with a coffee pot, two cups, and what has to be some of Mrs. McD's cookies under a napkin.

Peter pours the coffee and waits. The Professor hops up the steps like a teenager. He hands Peter a cup, takes the other cup and sits down beside Peter. The plate of cookies does not go unnoticed! With a grin he whips off the napkin and both reach for a cookie.

"Business later. Cookies first!" the Professor smiles with a look of contentment as he takes another cookie. The cookies are quickly finished, and coffee pot drained dry. Together they sit and bask in the warmth of the sun's rays that stream in under the edge of the porch roof. Peter turns and watches the Professor. He's known him long enough that he knows that this is just the sort of thing that gets him telling one of his amazing stories.

"Peter." This isn't the Professor's storytelling voice! This is his serious voice. Something must be up.

"This day will turn out to be most unusual and unexpected. The Blue Orb showed up for a moment last night. This may be our third and final trip. No word has come to me on that yet. You know Az is waiting. He will have detected the Blue Orb's landing. We're going to have visitors before the day is over. I've no idea how it will all turn out. I've warned Mrs. McD. She insists on bringing Susan. Says she knows it's the right thing to do.

"Don't worry, Peter. I don't believe Mrs. McD and Susan are in any danger. Az is only interested in us. He won't bother them. He knows only you and I travel in the time machine. He didn't pounce last night because you weren't here. But now you are here. His surveillance will have told him that you've come. He'll come straight here. It's just a question of whether or not he will wait until the Orb comes again and then pounce, or pounce first and wait for it to appear.

"I must remind you again of all you've learned about love and fear. Az will try to defeat you with fear. Love is a matter of the will, not of feelings. By an act of your will, you choose to love and to give Christ's love. In the presence of Christ's love there can be no fear. That's why the Apostle John wrote that 'love turns fear out of doors and expels every trace of terror!' (I John 4:18 AMP). No matter what happens, you must keep loving Az with Christ's love. Do not let fear or hate enter your mind for one second."

"I've been working on love," Peter answers. "I used to get really upset with some of our customers at the store. But ever since I began to intentionally love them, I've seen a lot of change. Some customers have opened up and I've been able to pray with them. Some are carrying around some really heavy burdens. That's why I was able to intentionally love Az when he came after me."

Just then an old rattlely car turns into the driveway and pulls up beside Peter's car.

"Well, here's the ladies now! Let's give them a hand."

Jumping up, the Professor heads for Mrs. McD's car. Peter follows close on his heels.

"Mrs. McD," he shouts gaily. "You really should trade that car in for a new one. The way the rust and parts are falling off, it's turning into a stone age car and cluttering up my lawn! It's really a shame that you make Susan pedal too!"

"Oh, I don't mind," Susan speaks up. "The exercise does me good!"

"Now listen, both of you," Mrs. McD answers in her best scolding voice. "I'd buy a new car if you weren't so stingy and paid me a decent wage! And as for you, Susan, if it's exercise you want I can fix that!"

"Now, now, Mrs. McD, let's not get all huffy! I did offer to buy you a new bicycle with a basket and everything, anytime you wanted it."

"A bicycle is not a car."

"Come, come, let's not split hairs. After all, this is a beautiful day for a picnic. It's going to be a great day with pleasant company, namely me. What have we got here?" he asks, lifting up the cover of her big basket. Just as quickly Mrs. McD shoves the lid down, and scolds, "Now, Professor, none of that! You wait for dinner like the rest of us. And stop acting so uppity. Honestly, as old as you are, you still act like a spoiled brat!"

Susan, laughing at their antics, notices Peter start to peek. She quickly steps in front of him, saying, "And that goes for you, too, Peter!"

"What good's a picnic if you can't sneak a peek and a taste?" asks the Professor.

Mrs. McD turns and in mock sternness orders Peter and Susan to take the baskets into the kitchen. "And Susan," she adds, "slap Peter's hand if he tries to reach in the basket again!"

Peter and Susan carry the baskets into the house. When they're out of earshot Mrs. McD turns to the Professor. "I talked to the police chief just after you called, Professor. I told him we had reason to believe those men would be coming out here today. He said if I signal he'll be right out."

"Very good, Mrs. McD. That's all we can do. It's up to the Blue Orb now. So let's relax and enjoy ourselves as long as we can. Maybe we'll get to eat before the excitement starts. Peter and I already finished off one pot of coffee. If you'll fix another, we'll pull up a couple more chairs. We can sit out here, enjoying the view. I do love spring."

"And maybe you can tell us a story or two? We all love your stories," Susan pipes in as she and Peter rejoin them on the porch.

"Well, I suppose I might be persuaded to tell one or two. Oh, oh! I think we're about to have some unexpected company."

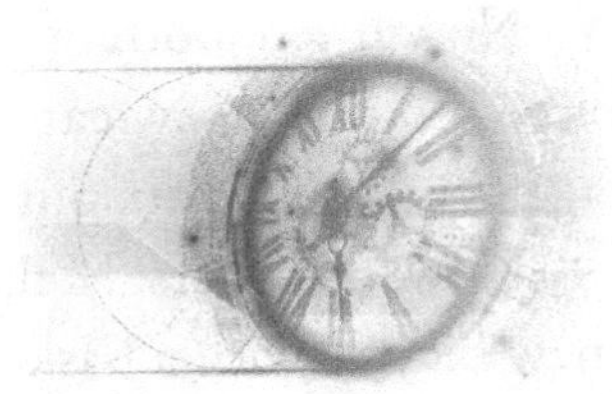

CHAPTER 42

The Thing About Andrew

Peter looks up, following the Professor's gaze, and sees three black cars turning off the road into the driveway. The third car appears to be a limousine. Eight Men in Black emerge from the first two cars. The hair on the back of Peter's neck bristles. There's no need for "warning" to run through his mind. He had already met four of these men before.

The eight men approach the porch. One of the men, who Peter does not recognize, but who seems to be the leader, climbs the steps and stands directly in front of the Professor in a manner designed to intimidate.

"Are you the Professor?"

The Professor, who cannot be intimidated, looks at the man, and says nothing. But his expression says, "What business is that of yours?"

The Intimidator, is taken aback by the Professor's silence. He asks again in an authoritative voice that expects an immediate answer: "Are you the Professor?"

Again the Professor does not answer, but responds with a look of total disinterest, bored by the man's presence. It has its effect. The man turns red in the face. He moves towards the Professor menacingly, as though he is ready to strike. Everyone's attention is focused on them. This gives Mrs. McD the chance to pull out her cell phone and dial the police chief's number. The chief answers just in time to hear the stranger demand a third time, almost shouting, "Are you the Professor?"

The Professor, in a calm voice, asks, "Who wants to know and why?"

Whether he meant to say it or not, the stranger blurts out, "Mr. Az wants to know."

That was all the police chief needed to hear. "Time to go, boys!" he hollers to his men. They rush to their cars and head out for the Professor's, sirens wailing.

"You can tell Mr. Az that I am the Professor. Everyone around here knows that."

"Who are these people?"

"You already know," the Professor answers. "Why do you bother to ask?"

The man does not answer. He barks orders to four of them to search the grounds and the woods behind the house. They split up and begin searching all around the outside of the house. They walk on the flowers, poke into bushes, and forage into the woods. If making a mess of everything was their intent, they were doing an excellent job of it.

The boss man motions to the other three, and the four of them, shoving Mrs. McD and Susan aside, rush into the house. The Professor motions to Susan and Mrs. McD to sit down. From inside the house comes the sound of furniture being thrown about, pounding on walls, doors being opened and slammed shut. Dishes breaking. This is more than Mrs. McD can take. No sooner does she sit down than she bounces to her feet again, rushes in, and starts to give the men one whale of a tongue lashing. She is fearless. Susan starts to follow, but the Professor motions her to stay seated.

Peter can imagine the utter chaos they are creating and the anger that must be rising in Mrs. McD.

"Get out of our way, old woman," one of them shouts. Then comes the sound of what must have been a whale of a wallop with an iron skillet, and cries of pain. "You two, grab her before she kills us."

Peter and Susan and the Professor remain seated. Peter studies the Professor's face. Written all over his face is love. It is easy to see that the Professor is looking upon these men with love. Peter does his best to follow his example. Even Susan is following the Professor's example. Angry men, and evil men, feed off the anger and fear they generate in others. But if no fear or anger is coming back at them it confuses them and weakens them.

Finally, the eight men return, four of them fighting off Mrs. McD as they come out of the house. Whatever they were looking for they did not find, either inside or out.

The boss man speaks into what looks like a cell phone. "We've searched everywhere. Can't find a clue . . . Nothing... No secret panels . . . We checked for hidden switches and all that . . . There is a mushroom cellar . . . Yes, sir. We checked it thoroughly. Our instruments couldn't detect a thing . . . We looked for doors, levers, the whole works, and found nothing . . . What do you want us to do?"

He nods, and motions the men to go back to their cars. Then the limousine pulls forward and parks in front of the Professor. A chauffer gets out of the limousine and opens one of the rear doors. A man steps out. Instantly Peter realizes he's come face to face with Mr. Az. He is like the Professor and yet not like the Professor. Peter had sensed a hidden power in the Professor, but this man seems to wear his power like a coat. He approaches the porch, climbs the few steps, and stops directly in front of the Professor.

"Hello Professor," he speaks with an unfriendly smile. "It has been many years since we last spoke with each other. In case you have forgotten, let me introduce myself. I am Mr. Az."

"Hello, Andrew, for that is your real name."

"Not anymore, Professor. Unlike you I have grown far beyond that name. My knowledge and wisdom have grown by leaps and bounds. I have become Mr. Az, the Beginning and the End. I am Mr. Az, the savior of this world. At long last I shall fulfill the plan I laid out before you long ago, the plan that would end war forever. But, come, let us go inside where we can talk in private. Oh, and bring your upstart student. But not you."

These last words, angry and scathing, he directs at Susan, who starts to get up. "You must be that pesky idiot brat who thinks she's so smart. You may have fooled my men. But you didn't fool me for one second. I'd teach you a thing or two right now, but it's not worth wasting my time.

"Now move," he snaps out, pushing the Professor and Peter. "Or shall my men carry you?"

The Professor winks at Susan, and mouths the words, "You got to him! He doesn't dare mind probe!"

The three enter the house. The living room is a shambles. Peter helps the Professor turn the chairs upright and the three sit down.

"I am here, Professor, because you've finally built your time machine. Oh, don't deny it. I know you have. It's here. You activated it for a moment last night. I know the energy footprint. My surveillance teams have tracked down every use you've ever made of your time machine. We know every place where you landed and every place from which you took off. Your little maneuver last winter was brilliant. Something I would have done. But, you didn't fool me for one second. I knew you were just playing around with all the tesseracting, trying to make me think you were jumping all over the map. But I saw through it right away. I knew where you were all the time."

"Andrew, Andrew. I'm sorry to disappoint you, but you are quite in error if you think I have built a time machine. When I built that model that we all saw vanish, I thought it might be useful one day. But since then I've come to realize how dangerous it would be if it fell into the wrong hands, your hands. I abandoned it long ago. I don't know what you think I've built, but it isn't a time machine."

"Professor, I am not here to banter words. I know you have it and I'm here to get it. I need it." His voice rises to almost a maniacal pitch. "I will not be denied. I have waited centuries for this moment. Peter is your protégé, isn't he? It would be too bad if something bad happened to him. You might survive torture, but I doubt if he would."

"Andrew, Andrew, what has come over you? You were never like this. What happened?"

"You happened, Professor," he spews the words out with great anger, and then is silent. "We were so close to stopping all the misery in the world. It would have been so simple for us to step in and begin ruling benevolently."

Once again he lapses into silence. Police sirens can be heard in the distance, coming up the valley. Andrew seems oblivious to them. Then suddenly, he rises to his feet.

"I've no time or patience for any more talk. Take me to your laboratory."

"Andrew, you're quite welcome to see my laboratory. But it won't be what you are expecting. Come."

Susan and Mrs. McD, hearing the sirens, sneak quietly in the front door, and hide where they can hear. Peter sees them out of the corner of his eye. The Professor rises and leads the way out of the living room towards the kitchen. Andrew grabs Peter's arm in a vise like grip and shoves him in front. They follow the Professor into the kitchen and out the back door to the anteroom. The Professor opens the door on the right that leads into the dark cavern where he grows mushrooms.

"Welcome to my laboratory, Andrew. It's not secret. The whole town knows about it. I cultivate mushrooms here and experiment with electronic and magnetic bombardment to see if I can make them grow bigger and improve their flavor. The town has a mushroom festival every year and they almost always clean me out. Over there you see my lab set up with the radiation generator and my electron microscope."

While the Professor talks, Andrew becomes more and more agitated at this seeming delay. Suddenly he whips a revolver out of his pocket and holds the muzzle up to Peter's head!

"Show me your lab Professor, or I'll kill Peter." He cocks the gun. This sudden change of events puts Peter's resolve to love to a test he hadn't anticipated. Much to his surprise, he is not scared. While he doesn't know what God's plan is, he knows that God is in this. When all is said and done God will be glorified. That's good enough for Peter. It comes to Peter, *It's Andrew who should be scared. He has no idea that this is God's time machine, not the Professor's. He has no idea what will happen to him if he steps inside it. But then, I've no idea what will happen to him either! But, one thing is for sure. God is going to have him in a place from which he cannot escape or run away!*

The Professor hesitates. He'd planned to drag his feet to antagonize Andrew. He knew once Andrew stepped into the Blue Orb he would get the shock of his life. But he never thought Andrew would draw a gun and threaten Peter. He starts to speak. "Andrew, Andrew, there's no need for that."

"I'm not bluffing, Professor," Andrew threatens. "Show me the lab or I will blow Peter's head off." He fires a shot past Peter's head, into the mushroom cavern.

Susan, who has been watching from the doorway, screams, "Peter!"

"Quiet, impudent brat," Andrew spews back at her and slams the door behind him.

"You win, Andrew. Follow me." The Professor is reluctant to give in, but he's too worried about what Andrew might to do Peter to keep stalling. He walks over to the wall where he rubs his hand slowly back and forth. He stops and the shape of a hand glows. He places his hand on the glowing hand. He speaks, "This is the Professor. Please open."

There is a pause, and then a computer voice speaks: "Hand print recognized. Voice recognized."

Slowly the outline of a door appears in the wall. There is the sound of stone moving on stone until the wall opens and they step into a tunnel. With Andrew behind Peter, the revolver still pointed at his head, they walk along quietly until they are stopped by a dead end.

As before, the Professor places his hand against the wall. There is a slight glow where his hand touches. A small door becomes visible and opens to reveal a retina scanner. A voice speaks, "Hand print accepted. What is your Name?"

"I am the Professor."

A pause. "Retina scan accepted. Voice recognized."

The little door closes and a massive door takes shape in the stone and opens. They step inside. Once again Peter is in the Professor's amazing secret laboratory. Even though he has worked in it several times alongside the Professor, it still amazes him anew.

"This is more like it," Andrew's sharp voice snaps out, with a very slight tinge of admiration. "This is a proper looking laboratory. It looks like you've done very well for yourself, but nowhere near as well as I have done. Now, where is the time machine, Professor?"

The muzzle of the revolver continues to press hard into the back of Peter's head. Even so, Peter notices a slight tremor in Andrew's hand he'd not noticed before. Andrew cannot hide his excitement over finally getting his "prize."

"The time machine will materialize when it is ready," the Professor answers. "That's one of its built in features. If it stayed around, it would arouse suspicion. Your readings should have told you it isn't fully here yet. So we might as well make ourselves comfortable and wait. Come and join me while we wait. I'm sure you've lots of questions you'd like to ask. I know I have a lot."

The Professor nonchalantly goes over to his desk and sits in an easy chair. Andrew, ever suspicious of a trap, refuses to budge or take the revolver from Peter's head.

"You're not going to catch me in one of your traps, Professor. I know you. You're just as sneaky as you were back then, when you turned everyone against me. Just remember, my first reaction if you try anything will be to squeeze the trigger and that will be the end of Peter. You don't want his death on your conscience, too… if you have a conscience."

"Andrew, Andrew, don't be so suspicious. Only people who fear, set traps and look for enemies under every stone. I have no desire to trap you. If you had just asked I would have told you all about the time machine. But tell me, how do you plan to use it?"

"I will go back in time to certain strategic points and make little minute changes. All of the wealth in all the world will fall into my hands. Then I will begin to rule this troubled world with the benevolence and justice it deserves. Men will be free to develop and grow in their innate goodness, unencumbered by power mongers and cruel rulers. I shall be the power behind the throne. I will keep rulers, kings, governments, scientists, industrialists, in line because they will all have to come to me for money, and do what I say or lose it."

"Don't you understand?" asks the Professor, breaking in on Andrew. "Every man has free will. You cannot force him to be good. He has to choose to be good by choosing to become redeemed. As long as human nature remains unredeemed, your plan will not work. Every unredeemed man belongs to Satan. Satan will not allow you to step in and steal his slaves. There is no way we could have stepped in and wrested unredeemed man from Satan's control, because Satan is the god of this world."

"Come, come, Professor. Don't tell me you still believe that old wives' tale? I, at least, have a better opinion of man than you do. Man is neither good nor evil. He is like a piece of clay. We had the opportunity to mold him into greatness. But you turned the rest of our Order against me. Because of you, mankind has had to endure hundreds of years of war and suffering. The blood of countless thousands of innocent people is on your hands, Professor. And for that you do not deserve to live."

While Andrew is talking, the Blue Orb begins to materialize. All conversation stops as they watch it fading in and out until fully materialized. All this time, Andrew keeps his revolver pressed against Peter's head. Pushing on the muzzle, Andrew prods Peter to walk around the Orb while he carefully examines it. As anxious as he is to reach out and touch it, he doesn't for fear it might be trapped. As they watch, an opening appears in the side.

"I was expecting something very crude, Professor. This is a surprise. I must admit that I am amazed that you, of all people, could possibly come up with such a marvelous piece of engineering. It wouldn't surprise me if it was your student who had to design it for you! Too bad you won't be around to see all the good it will do. But, as I said, you deserve to die. I do not believe in violence, but I have counted the days until I could take your time machine and end your miserable life."

Peter feels the nozzle of the gun being removed from his head. He turns, just in time, to see it flash as Andrew fires it at the Professor. The Professor slumps over in the chair. A horrible sickening feeling comes over Peter. Then something rises up within him and suddenly he rams hard into Andrew. Andrew's gun flies from his hand as the force of Peter's blow propels him towards the Orb. He raises his arms to shield his face as he slams into its side. But instead of slamming into the side of the Orb, the Orb turns and Andrew plummets through the doorway and into the Orb.

Quickly Peter jumps in after him. The opening closes. Once again Peter is surrounded by a musical humming. He expects Andrew to jump up and give him an angry tongue lashing. But nothing happens.

Peter looks down at Andrew and sees the last thing he expected to see. Andrew is doubled up, on his knees, hands over his head, and shaking with intense fear. As Peter looks, he sees a pathetic old man cowering on the floor of the Orb. All anger drains away. In spite of the ugly thing Andrew has just done, a great pity for him wells up within Peter, and a great longing that Andrew would yield to the Father's Love.

CHAPTER 43

Rebellion in Two Places

A gentle beeping sound draws Peter's attention to the control counsel. The ruby red lever is flashing, beckoning him to touch it. He does, and the Blue Orb suddenly leaves the Professor's lab. Once again, the Orb is immersed in a wild dance of brilliant colors in constantly changing patterns. As before, it feels like everything around is rushing past while the Orb sits still.

Just as suddenly it all stops. Peter knows they are in the in-between place. At the same time a verse of Scripture floats up into his mind: "take no thought how or what ye shall speak: for it shall be given you in that same hour what ye shall speak" (Matthew 10:19). Peter understands that God is going to speak to Andrew through him.

Everywhere Peter looks through the crystal clear walls of the Orb he sees the familiar millions of glistening stars and planets. For a moment he basks in the beautiful sounds and melodies coming from the stars and planets themselves as they blend into a vast symphony. How can Andrew fail to be impressed at this wondrous display of beauty and sound? He glances down at Andrew. A look of severe pain covers Andrew's face, his eyes are squeezed tightly shut. He has covered his ears as though shutting out noises he cannot stand. Peter is puzzled by Andrew's actions.

"Turn off that cacophony of noise," he cries out in pain. "How dare you assault my ears with such a hideous clamor of sounds? How dare you try to blind me with that hideous light? Turn it off or I'll make you so sorry you'll wish you'd never been born."

"Andrew, this is the beautiful, wonderful music of the stars, not noise. The glorious display of lights are the glistening of the stars and planets. They are a feast for the eyes. Just listen to the music. It thrills the soul."

Andrew, who seems unable to move, answers Peter with a burst of blasphemy, so opposite to the beautiful music, that Peter is taken aback. Suddenly he feels the urge to command Andrew to sit up on the bench.

"Andrew, Jesus commands you to sit beside me on the bench."

Andrew struggles mightily to resist the command. But he is unable. Slowly he rises and sits beside Peter. The look on his face reveals that, added to his fear, is a white-hot anger and an expression that says that nobody tells him what to do and gets away with it, not even Jesus.

"Andrew," Peter hears himself say. "Your mother named you Andrew after my disciple. She dedicated you to be the man who leads others to me. At first you did. Then you changed and became bitter instead of turning to me. You have lessons to learn that you've refused to learn in all your long years. I have tried to break through your stubbornness, but you refuse to listen. Now I am giving you one last chance. Surrender your anger. Repent of your rebellion. Watch and listen and learn or it will be too late for you."

Surprised to hear himself speak like that, Peter listens but no other words come. Andrew remains silent, seething in an anger he is powerless to express. Peter wonders if those words, spoken from God's heart, are having any impact at all. After a few minutes of silence he decides to start talking and see what happens, trusting that God will put the right words in his mouth.

"Andrew, I'm going to call you by your real name as Jesus did. In the Blue Orb only truth can be spoken. The Professor did not build this time machine. This is God's. He sent it to the Professor to take three trips back to the beginning of time. This is the third trip, and this trip is just for you because God loves you so much. In here you are in the presence of holiness. That is why you fear.

"But, Andrew, there is nothing to fear. God planned this moment for you because He loves you so much. In all the years you've renounced and hated Him, He has never renounced or stopped loving you. He is giving you one last chance to know the truth and be guided by the truth. When you see what happened in the Garden of Eden when man fell, you will learn why man is Satan's slave. Man, himself, made Satan the god of this world.

"Man is not an innocent lump of clay waiting to be molded, as you say. He is born a slave of sin with a sin nature controlled by lust and greed and evil. Only when man's sin nature is transformed into God's nature will the evils of this world cease. It is only by God's mercy and love that man can be born again and receive a recreated human spirit. You learned this at your mother's knee. But in your pride and arrogance you renounced it. You vowed you could not and would not love a God who allowed the evils of war and suffering that tore your parents from you. Humanism became your religion, when in fact humanism was your enemy, not God."

As Peter listens to these words flowing from his own lips, compassion for Andrew rises up within him. He reaches out to put his hand on Andrew's shoulder.

"Don't touch me!" Andrew shouts. "When we get out of this thing I'll show you who's to be pitied. You've obviously developed some kind of force field that makes me helpless. Well, I won't be helpless when this thing lands. When I get out you'll regret ever using it on me."

The ruby lever begins to flash again. It is time to continue the journey. Peter reaches out and touches the lever. The familiar *whooshing* sound fills the Orb. When it comes to rest, the Orb is once again back at the Garden. Words of explanation fill Peter's mind. Instinctively he knows that these words are for Andrew, and he is now Andrew's guide.

"Andrew, this is the Garden of Eden. Look and see." Unable to resist Peter's command, Andrew looks. He sees and he does not like what he sees. "You're using some kind of holographic projection," Andrew fumes. "That's not real. I know what you're doing. You think you can stop me with this elaborate hoax."

"Peace. Be still, Andrew. Look and I will explain what God is showing you. Look to the elegant mansion in front of you. That is where

Adam and Eve live. Eve had not been created when God created the animals, and Adam spoke their names. She was not there when God told Adam about the Tree of the Knowledge of Good and Evil. But she was there when God said 'This Garden is for your delight: a place to enjoy and be supremely happy in. It is yours. I have crowned you with glory and honor. You are its King and Queen. Rule wisely over the fish of the sea, the birds of the air, and over every living creature that moves upon the earth. The care of all living things is your responsibility. Utilize the earth to its fullest, developing all its vast resources. Be fruitful, multiply, and replenish the earth.'

"Look closely at this man and this woman, Andrew. They are dressed in the glory of God so that we see them only as glory-dressed beings, even as God is hidden in glory. That is why they appear to us as man-shaped lights. Look at them. There are no words to describe the majesty of these two beings. Power and stateliness radiate out from them. The intelligence and wisdom of their Creator is built into them. Their intelligence is beyond measure."

Andrew, unable to resist, looks at the scene before him. In a low voice, using all the control he can muster, he speaks, "I don't know what you are trying to do with this charade, but it won't work on me."

"Andrew," Peter continues, "listen carefully. God did not give this Garden to Adam and Eve. He leased it to them with instructions as to what they were to do. While this was going on an evil, seductive, deceiving archangel named Lucifer, who you know as Satan, has been watching from the shadows. He has been at war with God. While defeated once, he has not given up planning and scheming.

"His thoughts dwell on that Lease. The earth had once been his to rule. In his mind he believes God stole it from him. Now he knows how he can get it back. He believes he knows the details of the Lease. He thinks that if he can get possession of the Lease he will become the ruler of this earth, and man will be his slave (Romans 6:16), just as you believe that if you can get hold of a time machine, earth and man will become your slaves.

"Once Satan has that Lease, he plans to use this earth as the staging area for his next attack on God's throne. The question in his mind is how can he get the lease? How can he trick the Man into sinning against God? See how he lurks in the shadows: a darkness in the midst of shadows? He begins to scheme a plan.

"He cannot reveal himself in the Garden. God is holy. Adam and Eve are holy. The Garden is holy. If Satan tries to approach Adam and Eve they will see him for the evil that he is (Isaiah 14:16). No, he must find a dupe, a vainglorious creature he can con into doing his bidding. He knows Adam and Eve will not knowingly sin. They will have to be lured into sin without knowing they are sinning. He will focus his attack on the woman. 'Yes, that's it,' Satan says smugly. 'She obviously suffers from the same weakness God suffers from. That Love drivel.

"'That's the reason I attacked God's throne. He's weak. Love is weakness. You can't run a universe on love and joy and laughter. My attack on God's throne would have worked if the rest of the angels had seen how weak God and His love thing really are. Well, I'm not through yet. I will win, and those who opposed me will pay. Meanwhile, I will work on the woman.'

"So Satan begins his scheming. First, he will let enough time pass for the woman to feel the full weight of the responsibility of rulership and care of the animals and the earth. Then, he thinks, 'I'll find a vain creature to help me, and I'll start planting ideas about needing wisdom to rule wisely. That'll get her.'

"Satan bides his time. Of all the animals the serpent appears to be the vainest. See the serpent, there, Andrew, strutting around, acting superior? See Satan whispering to him from the shadows? The serpent is gorgeously arrayed in colors that sparkle in the sun like living jewels. It is the most colorful and intelligent and crafty of all the animals (Genesis 3:1), and walks uprightly (Genesis 3:14).

"The Serpent was created before Eve. When Eve was created, he knew that she was created equal to Adam, having been taken from his side. Like all the other animals, he was in awe of her. To be able to spend time talking with her was a joy to him. And it was a joy to Eve, for the Serpent seemed to have greater wisdom than all the other animals. But the Serpent was also vain. He knew he was wiser than the other animals. So, Satan began to work on the Serpent's vanity. He suggested to the Serpent that there was a reason why he was so wise. He was the one God had created to be Adam's helpmeet in governing the animals, not Eve. Eve was a usurper.

"The more Satan reinforced these ideas in the Serpent's mind the more the Serpent began to lose respect for the woman. At last, the stage was set for Satan to carry out the next part of his plan. So it was that Satan coached the Serpent in just what questions to ask the woman. Being very crafty and thinking himself very wise, the Serpent looks forward to asking the Woman Satan's questions."

"Balderdash! Nonsense!" snaps Andrew. "The last thing I need is some upstart, stupid brat feeding me a bunch of nonsense."

Nonsense? Peter can tell by the look on Andrew's face that he knows it is not nonsense. It is truth he has been running from. Truth he wants to accept, but can't. Peter continues in the hope that he will finally let the truth in.

"We are about to see the events unfold on that fateful day, Andrew. Look, there is the Serpent and Eve. Eve is sitting on the white marble wall that sets off the beautiful garden within a garden, in which grows the Tree of Life and the Tree of the Knowledge of Good and Evil. The Serpent stands at her side, speaking to her. Listen…"

"Mistress, I was here before you were created. I saw the trees in the Garden. I'm worried because you've been eating the fruit of the trees in the Garden. Didn't God tell you not to eat of the fruit of the trees in the Garden?"

"Oh, no," Eve reassures the serpent. "We can eat from all the trees except the tree in the middle of the Garden. God said don't eat of that tree, or even touch it, or you will die."

"I think you got that wrong, Mistress. Remember, I was there. You won't die. What will happen if you eat it is you'll be smart like God. You'll know everything from good all the way up to evil. God would never put anything bad in the Garden."

Eve begins to reason with herself. *Having the care of all the animals as well as the earth itself was a heavy responsibility. In addition, they were to utilize the earth's vast resources and develop them to their fullest possibilities. They hadn't even scratched the surface of possibilities. She loved these creatures and wanted to do well by them. The fruit did look very luscious. And the wisdom and knowledge she would gain, she convinced herself, was just what she needed. Surely God would want that. God would never deny them the knowledge and wisdom they needed. Now that some time had passed and she had gotten the feel of what ruling this earth entailed, she was ready for more knowledge and more wisdom.*

As Peter listened to Eve's thoughts he suddenly realized that he had been guilty of doing the same thing; of failing to acknowledge God in all His ways and letting God direct his paths, as Psalm 3:6 instructed. *That was what had happened to Andrew. He fell into the trap of trusting his own wisdom rather than God's.*

"Remember Andrew, Eve was brilliant beyond anything we can imagine. Her intelligence exceeded yours as the heavens are higher than the earth. She is not vain. She has only love for God, Who she loves with all her heart. She had no desire to disobey God. Satan is right that her weakness is her love. As smart as she is, the responsibility of ruling wisely, lovingly, weighs heavily upon her.

"Eve begins to reason with herself: If eating the forbidden fruit would give them the wisdom they needed to rule the earth wisely, to care for the animals and the earth carefully and lovingly, and to develop the earth with all its vast resources to its utmost, then eating the forbidden fruit is a wise thing to do. Perhaps God actually wants them to eat it, now that they see how much they need it.

"Remember, Andrew, love is central. God is love. The earth and garden He prepared for the Man and Woman are altogether lovely, a gift of love. Love is the atmosphere of earth. The Man and Woman dearly love God and the earth, and the animals and birds and fish. The plants and trees grow and blossom and bear fruit to bless the Man and Woman.

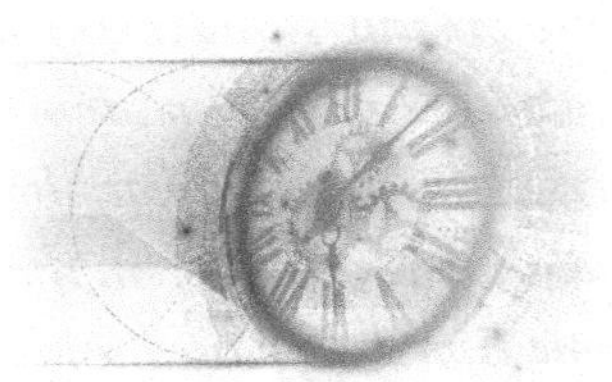

CHAPTER 44

Be Afraid, Very Afraid

The temptation to which Eve yields is not to disobey God. It is to substitute her wisdom for God's wisdom. It is to rationalize and think that God intended that she eat of the tree to gain help in obeying God and fulfilling the task that God had assigned her. It is her great desire to rule wisely those she loves so much that is her downfall.

"Her motivation is love. She feels the need of wisdom. She does not have the promise of Scripture that we have that says, 'If any of you lack wisdom, let him ask of God, that giveth to all men liberally, and upbraideth not; and it shall be given him' (James 1:5).

"Andrew, the deception that trapped Eve has trapped you. It is the greatest temptation every Christian faces. It is the deceptive trap of human wisdom (James 3:15-17; Romans 1:18-25). It is to substitute our wisdom, our ideas, and our plans in place of God's. We forget that 'The fear of the Lord is the beginning of wisdom' (Proverbs 9:10).

"Look, Andrew, look at the scene that is unfolding before us. Eve is convinced that eating the fruit of the tree is wise. She is reaching up. She plucks the fruit. She eats. She turns to Adam who is with her, and gives him the fruit to eat.

"Look at them and see what is happening. The glow of light that surrounded them is dimming. The form of a naked man and a naked woman begins to emerge from what had once been a covering of light. Suddenly they realize that if God sees them like this He will know that their covering of holiness is gone. For the first time in their lives, they know fear.

"They turn and run into the woods, hiding behind bushes. Grabbing the biggest leaves they can find they work feverishly weaving the leaves together, trying to make garments to cover their nakedness. They cannot look at each other. See how Eve hangs her head and cannot look at Adam, asking, 'How could you have let me do this? You knew it was wrong.'

"Adam, who was not deceived by the serpent, is looking at Eve with a look of disgust, as if to say, 'How could you have done this to us?'

"Man is not an innocent lump of clay waiting to be molded, as you say, Andrew."

"Whatever it was that Adam and Eve had hoped would happen, it didn't. See how feverishly they are working, trying to get the leaves to stay together to cover them. Look at that dark figure, Andrew, strolling up and down and saying 'Yes, Yes, I did it. God thinks He is so smart. But I showed him!' Watch him now as he strolls up to them. That is Satan. Gleefully he grabs the lease from Adam and waves the lease under their noses."

Just then a voice, melodious and malicious and cunning and commanding, breaks through into the Orb with a fierceness and power that shakes the Orb. "Mine! All mine. You pathetic images of a pathetic God. The earth now belongs to me. That is the rule of Law. You betrayed God like I knew you would. You betrayed all living creatures. You have sold me your birthright. You are mine, you pathetic God-images. You are my slaves (Romans 6:16; 8:20-22; John 14:30). What's more, you're going to help me assail the throne of God, and win!"

Peter turns, and looks at Andrew sitting on the seat beside him, cowering, the veins on his face and neck sticking out as though they would burst.

"Andrew," Peter asks, "surely you cannot be unmoved by what you just saw happen? What you have hoped to do by using a time machine won't work. Only God can undo the mess."

"Oh, I'm moved alright!" There is bitterness in his voice. "If that's what really happened, how could a loving God have allowed it? A loving God would not allow His creation to be entrapped by evil."

"Andrew, Andrew, you still do not understand. Listen to the rest of the story. Even now it is beginning to unfold before us."

Peter is amazed to hear all these words that have been coming out of his mouth! They could only have come from God. Andrew's need seems to be pulling it out of him. Maybe that's how being led by the Spirit works. Where there is a great need, and your heart is open to the Spirit and the person in need, He gives you the words to say. (John 14:26; 15:26; Acts 6:10; I Corinthians 2:4, 12:8)

"There is more to the story, Andrew. Have you forgotten all that you were taught? Satan thinks he has outsmarted God, but you and I know something he doesn't know and that he is about to find out. Watch. He is about to rejoice in his cleverness. He believes that what he holds in his hands is a title deed. He does not know it is only a lease. He believes there is nothing God can do, no way God can help the man. The man belongs to him, Satan. He has shut God out of the earth. Now he can use the earth as his staging area in his fight against God.

"Andrew, have you forgotten what it is that Satan does not know? He does not know about the fine print in this lease. Both he and Adam and Eve are about to find out. Yes, it's true, Adam and Eve have lost their home, their kingdom, their freedom. That one act of disobedience made Satan the ruler of this world (John 14:30). What Satan said to Jesus was true. All the kingdoms of this world were turned over to him, and he had the authority to give them to whomever he wanted to give them (Luke 4:6).

"Watch, Andrew, and relearn what you once knew about the love of God. It has turned to evening. Do you see the bright light moving in the Garden? God, who dwells in unapproachable light (1 Timothy 6:16), is walking in the Garden, looking for Adam and Eve. You can see the glee on Satan's face. He thinks he has God just where he wants him. God's rule of law says that he who sins must die. But, Satan believes God cannot kill the sinners because now, by law, they belong to Satan. God is trapped by his own laws."

"Adam. Adam." The words well up from the Garden and resound in the Blue Orb; the words of God calling.

Andrew begins to shake uncontrollably.

"Adam, where are you?"

"Here," a fear filled voice cries from the bushes.

"Why are you hiding in the bushes?"

"I, I heard You walking in the Garden, and I was afraid?"

"Afraid? Why should you be afraid, Adam? And how did you learn fear?"

"There's more."

"More, Adam? What do you mean more?"

"I'm also naked and I didn't want you to see me naked."

"Who told you that you were naked?"

"I ate the fruit of the Tree of the Knowledge of Good and Evil. But it's not my fault. Honest it isn't. It's that woman You gave me; that woman who was supposed to be with me and be my helper, she gave it to me!"

"Eve, is this true?"

"Yes sir. The serpent deceived me and I ate the fruit. Adam didn't stop me. He was with me and he didn't stop me."

"Satan!" God's voice rings out so fierce it shakes the Orb. Andrew slides off the seat onto the floor, cringing in fear, and Peter once again commands, "Andrew, Jesus says to get back up on the seat and listen."

"Satan!" God calls again. Satan, confident of his victory, strolls majestically into the Garden, his garden that God had stolen from him. "Satan," God speaks in a commanding voice, "Read the lease!"

There is a moment of silence. Suddenly a cry of angry horror rings out across the stars.

"Do you know what that cry means, Andrew? I will tell you. Satan has just discovered that he has sealed his own doom. He has just discovered that God has a secret plan written in the rule of law (Ephesians 1:4). That plan is that God chose us in Christ before the beginning of time. Before He created us He loved us! And Satan has just learned that in the fullness of time God Himself will bear the punishment for every person's sins, from Adam's even to yours, Andrew."

"You tricked me!" Satan's words hurl across the heavens, shaking the Orb. "But remember, by Your own rule of law, I am the Prince of this world. Adam has sold out to me and I own him."

"He is your slave for the present, Satan, but remember all souls are mine; as the soul of the father, so also the soul of the son is mine (Ezekiel. 18:4). It is true that it is written in the rule of law that the soul that sinneth, it shall die. But Satan, there is another law written long before you were created. I choose now to set that other law into motion.

"Serpent, come here." God's command rings out across the Garden. Slowly, from his hiding place, the serpent emerges. He walks uprightly, his splendid coat of beauty sparkling even in the twilight. Shaking like a leaf he slowly approaches the light that is God.

"Serpent, you have brought a curse upon yourself. All that you had and knew of bliss and comfort and joy in this Garden you have lost. I do not take it from you. You have taken it from yourself. It is written in the rule of law.

"Because you have done this, you are cursed above all cattle, and above all wild animals; upon your belly you shall go, and dust you shall eat all the days of your life."

"Andrew, watch," Peter commands. Even as God speaks the arms and legs of the serpent begin to shrink back into his body. His beautiful covering changes into dull scales. He sinks down to the ground, his body elongating to the shape of a snake. Just before the look of intelligence leaves the serpent's face, God speaks again. His words, like mighty claps of thunder, resound into the heavens. You know that these words are directed to Satan, as well as to the serpent.

"I will put enmity between you and the woman, and between your seed and her Seed; He shall bruise your head, and you shall bruise His heel."

The snake slithers off into the trees. Turning to Adam and Eve God speaks again, but this time there is a great sadness in his voice. "Adam and Eve come, sit beside me here. There is much I must tell you."

Peter can tell by how gingerly they move that Adam and Eve are very much afraid.

"Fear not, my son. Satan meant this for evil. But I mean it for good.

My will and purpose will be accomplished. In the fullness of time, many long generations from now it shall be done and you shall inherit the kingdom I have prepared for you from the foundation of the world (Matthew 25:34).

"There are three things you must remember and you must tell them to your children and they to their children. The first is that I love you. Your sin has not changed My love, but it has broken My heart and broken our fellowship. You had the freedom to choose good or evil. If you had chosen the good I would have given you the fruit Myself and you would have been blessed by it. Instead you chose to steal the fruit. When you did, you sold your birthright and your soul to Satan, but not your spirit. Satan's fate will be decided on the Day of Judgment.

"Under the Rule of Law the wages of sin is death (Romans 6:23). I warned you about that before. By your deeds you have chosen death. But I love you too much to let you die eternally. In the fullness of time I will take your death upon Myself, and thus fulfill the Rule of Law.

"The second thing to remember is why I could not stop you from eating the forbidden fruit. I created you in My image, after My likeness. I gave you the freedom to be yourself, to make your own decisions and choices just as *I AM WHO I AM and WHAT I AM, and I WILL BE WHAT I WILL BE* (Exodus 3:14). If I tried to stop you, I would have broken the rule of law and all of Creation would have disintegrated. I would not be God and you would not be man (Colossians 1:16-17).

"The third thing to remember is the YES DOOR. Satan has taken your place as the Prince of this world. He will fill the world with wars and suffering (John 16:33; Matthew 24:6). He will constantly tempt you to sin, for when you sin you act as his slave doing his will (Romans 6:16-18). He thought he had shut Me out. But remember, the earth is Mine and My purpose will be established and I will accomplish all My good pleasure (Isaiah 46:9, 10). I have reserved for Myself an open door, a direct line of communication and power. Your 'YES' gives Me the authority to bless you and meet your needs."

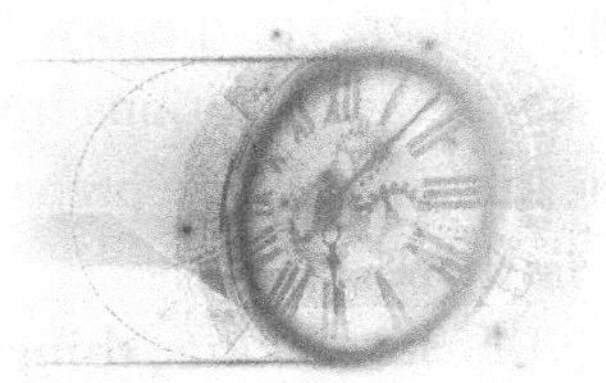

CHAPTER 45

What Happened to Andrew

Just then Peter hears the ruby lever beeping. He gently touches it and they are instantly back in the in-between place. Andrew's face is white. The muscles of his face twitch as one who has so many things to say they are blocking each other. Peter doesn't think it will do any good, but he senses God telling him to try one more time to reach Andrew's heart.

"Andrew, God has let you see these scenes in the Garden because He loves you so much. In His eyes you still are the magnificent person He created you to be. It is His will to forgive all your sins and heal all your diseases. As far as the east is from the west, so far has God removed your transgressions from you" (Psalm 103:3, 12).

"God wants to bless you with every spiritual blessing (Ephesians 1:3). All He needs is your permission. We are the ones who release God's power to meet our own needs and the needs of the people for whom we intercede. Of us it is said, one can put a thousand to flight, and two, ten thousand (Deuteronomy 32:30)."

"Shut up!" Andrew shouts at Peter. "I am not going to fall for your claptrap, or be preached to by a pathetic excuse for a student. You and the Professor have rigged up an elaborate charade but I know the truth. You're not going to take me in by all these lies. Get this over with NOW."

With that Andrew folds his arms and glowers at Peter. The ruby lever begins to beep, and Peter pushes it again. Once again Peter hears the familiar *whoosh.* The sides of the Orb turn an opaque blue and he can no longer see outside. The familiar slight jar tells him that the Orb has landed. An opening appears in the side of the Orb.

Andrew pushes him aside and jumps out. Peter follows. Andrew turns and faces Peter with all the venom and hatred and viciousness his mind can muster. Peter looks at him, loving him and pitying him, his heart breaking as he knows God's heart is breaking.

"Andrew, please repent and come back to God."

Peter's words inflame Andrew even more. He looks at Peter with fire in his eyes. Then, with all the power he can muster, he utters the curse of fear that erases memories and destroys minds. For a moment he stares at Peter, a look of stark terror comes over his face. A horrible shriek escapes his lips. He falls to the floor. Just then the Professor comes to Peter's side.

The Professor!

"I thought you were dead!"

"No, I'm not dead! At least not yet. When the Blue Orb showed up last night I slipped on a bullet proof vest! Knowing how much Andrew hated me, I thought he might try something like that. He's had a lot of years to use my face in target practice! I figured he wouldn't aim for my head, because he would want me to live long enough to witness his success.

"What convinced me was how hard he tried to capture you. I suspected it was to pilot the time machine. It set him back when you resisted him twice. But his massive ego convinced him you'd not do it again.

"Poor Andrew. In the beginning he was a very dear friend. Now he has become the victim of his own cunning. The very curse by which he meant to destroy you has come back upon him. If only he had known: Like a fluttering sparrow or a darting swallow, an undeserved curse does not come to rest (Proverbs 26:2 NIV). Now he has destroyed his own mind. He will live the rest of his life in fear with no knowledge of who or what he was. In death he will go where he did not want to go.

"What do we do with Andrew? We can't bring his mind back. He destroyed it with his curse. Perhaps the kindest thing is to let his driver take care of him. You take his arm on that side, and I'll take his arm on this side. All set? Andrew, start walking. That's it. Keep going. We'd better go back through the mushroom cellar. We don't want the fireplace opening up."

Andrew does not speak. He appears disoriented. Peter and the Professor half carry him. They walk along silently. Up ahead the tunnel turns to the left as it leads up to the fireplace. The Professor stops. He moves his hand back and forth on the wall until the handprint begins to glow. With his hand on the handprint he speaks.

"Please open." They hear large slabs of stone moving, rearranging themselves. Slowly an opening appears in front of them and they are standing in the midst of mushroom beds.

"This way," the Professor directs as he moves towards a door on the end. The door opens and they find themselves once again in the anteroom off the kitchen. Peter is glad to see the kitchen door again with its old fashioned square window. He opens it and they are greeted with a hubbub of noise.

"Now you, be careful of those dishes," Mrs. McD orders. "You've already broken enough. You," she orders another man, "get the broom and sweep up all the pieces. I want this kitchen spic and span." Two policemen, with guns drawn, are standing guard.

"Hello, Mrs. McD," the Professor speaks loudly to get her attention. "Looks like you've got quite a crew working here. We won't get in your way. We just want to take Andrew outside so his driver can take care of him."

"You go right ahead, Professor. Susan's bossing the clean-up in the living room, and I've got these scoundrels under control!"

Andrew's men, seeing their helpless boss, a blank look in his face, are shocked. Afraid of what will happen to them now, they turn back to quickly obey Mrs. McD. Together the Professor and Peter half-carry Andrew down the hall towards the front door. As they come to the living room, they hear a familiar voice. Susan, sounding like a drill sergeant, is overseeing the putting up of the books and furniture back in place.

"Keep going, Andrew," commands the Professor when Andrew starts to stop. Susan hears his voice and looks up. Tears are streaming down her cheeks. Worry and anger are written all over her face. She sees Peter. The worry and anger vanish. Her face lights up with a beautiful smile.

"Oh, Peter I was so worried," she exclaims, rushing towards him. She reaches up and presses her lips hard against his. Then, just as quickly she pulls away. He looks at her beautiful face flushed with embarrassment and a look of shock. Embarrassed at her impulsive action? And shocked at what she felt?

"Peter, I'm sorry. I . . ."

Peter looks into her eyes, equally shocked at what he felt, and says, "Wow! Can we do that again?"

"Yes!"

Again she presses her lips hard against his. Peter can't explain it, but suddenly he wants to put his arms around her and hold her tight. He lets go of Andrew and starts to put his arms around Susan when the Professor speaks.

"Peter, our work isn't done yet. We have to take care of Andrew."

"Oh, I'm sorry Professor," he answers, reluctantly letting go of Susan, and once again helping support Andrew.

Meanwhile, the rest of Andrew's men look at him, shocked to see the helpless figure that once held many in fear of his anger. Like the other men in black, they too suddenly become anxious about what will happen to them. The Professor and Peter take Andrew down the steps and to his limousine. There they hand him to his driver.

"Take good care of Andrew," the Professor tells the driver. "Yes, his real name is Andrew. He has suffered a tremendous blow to his mind. I'm afraid he will never fully recover. Be gentle with him. He was once a very brilliant man, and he did many good and noble deeds to help mankind. He deserves to be treated well.

"Tell his second in command what has happened. He will have to take over the running of the company. I'm sure he will be able to arrange for someone to care for Andrew. Perhaps over time, with loving care, he may begin to remember a little about who he is. Maybe you can help him do that. Goodbye."

With that the Professor closes the door and sends the limousine on its way.

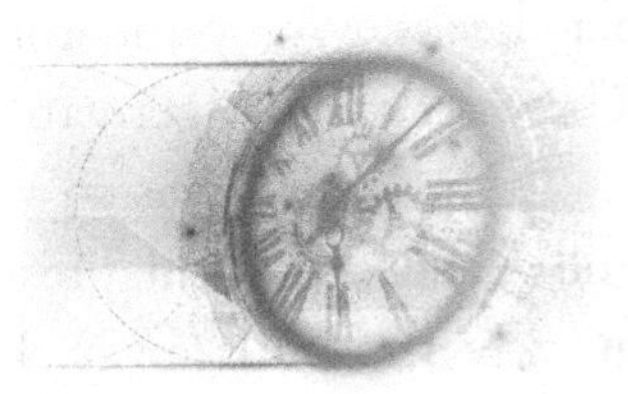

CHAPTER 46

Forced Seating

You okay, Professor?" The Chief of Police asks after spotting the Professor and Peter exit the house. "We came as soon as Mrs. McD called. Looks like these fellows gave your house quite a going over. We'll take 'em down and book 'em after Mrs. McD is through with 'em."

"Oh, hello Chief. We were so wrapped up in getting that gentleman back to his car I didn't see you. Thanks so much for coming. Don't press charges. I suspect when Mrs. McD and Susan get through with them they will have had all the punishment that's needed, and maybe more!"

"I'll agree with you there," the chief laughs. "Boy, did she tear into them something fierce! Wouldn't surprise me if she made them do some extra odd jobs while she's at it. Like a mother tiger when her cubs are threatened she was. I think we'll stay around until she's done with them. I don't want to see any of them sneaking off."

Peter and the Professor realize that probably the best place for them right now is out of Susan and Mrs. McD's way! Between those two the men in black don't have a chance! Looking at Peter and smiling the smile of a job well done, the Professor speaks.

"Well, Peter, with the problem of Andrew solved, the Nine Unknown Men can come out of hiding. You've met four of us now. There are four others. I dare say there may be some exciting adventures ahead if you're interested. I'd like to see TPF perfect the tesseract now that we know it works over long distances. And it is safe now to build my time machine. Would you like to join the fun?"

"Would I ever! When do we start?"

"Whoa!" the Professor laughs. "First things first. We still have to get this mess cleaned up and then eat our picnic lunch. The Chief is going to want some explanation about what's been going on."

Peter moves one of the extra chairs over and they invite the police chief to join them on the porch.

"Well, Chief," says the Professor, chuckling to himself, "I suppose you want to know what this was all about? You know how rumors spread? Someone started a rumor that I had acquired an ancient manuscript that told how to build a time machine.

"Can you think of anything more ridiculous than that somebody hundreds of years ago designed a working time machine? Why it was only about a hundred years ago that we got out of the horse and buggy and into cars! There are some strange fanatics who will believe almost anything. This guy was one of them, a very rich one of them. You've already met some of his goons, as Peter calls them. This morning, while Peter and I and the ladies were sitting here on the porch, he came in person.

"He came and sat out here in his limousine. This time he brought eight of his men. They trampled my flower beds, poked their noses into every nook and cranny and then ransacked the house. When they couldn't find anything he came in himself. He said he wanted the manuscript. Of course, I didn't have one to give him. He also insisted I had built a time machine, and he wanted that, too. Said he had proof. He claimed I have a secret lab here and insisted I take him to it. So we took him to our 'secret' mushroom patch. That wasn't what he wanted. He did a lot of ranting and raving. He actually pulled a gun and threatened to kill Peter if I didn't show him my secret laboratory."

"We heard Susan let out a scream, and holler 'Peter'. She was so scared something bad would happen to you, Peter. Mrs. McD told us about the gun. She said not to worry. The Professor's never lost a student yet, although he's flunked a few! I figure she said that to calm Susan down."

"I think our visitor must have had a stroke, blown a gasket, so to speak. Suddenly he collapsed right on the floor. He went totally dumb. Didn't know who he was, or where he was. We carried him to his car and told his driver to take care of him. I'm glad Mrs. McD's got her work crew going. I wasn't looking forward to cleaning up the mess they made."

"Professor, you've always been a good story teller. We've gotten many a good laugh out of your tall tales. But this real life adventure beats them all! People sure are strange."

This is amazing, Peter thinks to himself. *The Professor has told them the truth in such a way that they see it as a real life tall tale. A very rich man hung up on some strange fanatic belief. But that is really not so strange*, Peter muses. He'd met people who have the weirdest ideas about God, the Bible, and Jesus. They are so convinced their ideas are correct that they refuse to learn the truth.

With the story of what happened told to the police chief's satisfaction, he and the Professor start talking about sports and politics and other things adults talk about. Peter tries, but he cannot keep his mind on the conversation. He keeps thinking back to Susan's kiss. Did Susan feel what he felt? He's sure she did.

Finally, the Men in Black come out, followed by Susan and Mrs. McD. "Now, one more thing," orders Mrs. McD, "You men take out all the money you've got in your pockets. Give it to the chief. Chief, you count it. They've got to pay for everything they broke."

The men, who are accustomed to living a very lavish life style, and who are expecting to be taken to jail, do as they are told. Among the eight of them they come up with $4,327.52.

"Now Chief, you take that money and keep it. I'll send you the bills for the broken dishes. You put the rest in your benevolence fund."

The chief looks at the eight Men in Black. "I should arrest all of you on several charges. But I'm not going to because of what happened to your boss. Rest assured, if one of you shows your face around here ever again, I'll arrest you instantly and book you. Is that clear?"

"Yes sir."

"Now go. I'll be right behind you so don't try anything."

Peter, the Professor, Mrs. McD and Susan follow the chief to his car.

"Goodbye Professor, Mrs. McD, Susan and Peter. We'll see you in town. Maybe even help Mrs. McD eat some of her bread?" he adds, a wistful look on his face and an equally wistful look on the faces of his men.

"I'll give you a call when I'm baking again. Goodness knows you've all sure earned it."

The chief and his men and the Men in Black drive off, leaving the four alone. As they step back up on the porch, Mrs. McD rearranges the chairs. She groups the Professor's chair, her chair, and a third chair, which is almost big enough for two, so that everyone can see each other, and also look out over the beautiful meadows. She turns the other chair over.

Looking at Peter, she states, "Looks like you and Susan will have to share that big chair." Peter looks at Susan, and both their faces turn red.

"Go on, go on," orders Mrs. McD, "sit."

It's a tight squeeze. Peter likes it. He likes sitting that close to Susan. He's sure she likes sitting close too. He senses the same slight tremor he felt when she kissed him and he started to hold her tight.

"Well, Mrs. McD, this has been some morning. I hope the dinner you fixed is worth all we've been through to get it! They didn't eat any of it, I hope?"

"Everything's fine, Professor. I just thought Susan and I'd rest a few minutes. It was a lot of work bossing all those men around."

"Work? Why I thought you rather enjoyed it. Four men jumping at the snap of your fingers. You sitting there filing your nails, giving yourself a manicure, being waited on. What more could a woman want?"

"There are times when I wonder why I ever said I'd work for you."

Once again Peter and Susan laugh as these two friends tease each other. Peter hadn't meant to take Susan's hand in his, but it just happened. It didn't go unnoticed by the Professor and Mrs. McD. They both look at Peter and Susan, almost laughing, their eyes full of merriment. Mrs. McD speaks.

"We wondered how long it would take before you two finally

realized you were in love. Oh, we saw it the first day when Susan came to babysit you, Peter. It was written all over your faces, though you couldn't see it. But we could see how the Holy Spirit had drawn you two together."

"Yes," the Professor agrees. "When Susan told us she saw the strangers on campus and felt an urgency to pray for us, I knew the Holy Spirit had been at work, preparing her, preparing her heart. I would never have involved Susan in any of this business with Andrew. But we didn't have a choice. The Holy Spirit put her on the team without asking us. I, for one, am glad. Susan saved your life twice, Peter."

Peter squeezes Susan's hand and whispers, "Thanks."

"Speaking of Andrew, Mrs. McD, the Andrew problem that kept us going all these many years is finally solved. I've long thought that when it was solved there would no longer be any need for the Nine Unknown Men. Technology has progressed so far, and mankind has matured so much we just aren't needed. True, we've all got some projects we want to finish. Now that it's safe we'll be getting together and helping each other.

"I was thinking that with Andrew out of the way and our projects finished, it was time to stop taking the elixir of life and let nature take its course. But lately I'm not so sure. Mrs. McD, neither of us had any children or grandchildren. When I saw the love that was going to blossom between Peter and Susan I began to wonder. Suppose they do get married? Suppose they do have children? Do you think they might let a couple old fuddy-duddies like us be grandparents to their children?"

"Oh yes," cries Susan. "It would be thrilling to have you be grandparents to our children, wouldn't it Peter?… That is… if we do get married and have children?"

Peter, looking stunned, answers, "I haven't even had a chance to say 'I love you,' and already I'm married with kids!"

"On that note," Mrs. McD bursts out laughing, "I think it's about time to fix our picnic dinner. Marriage and children may be a long time off, but dinner is now. Come Susan, we'll get the food ready while the Professor and Peter fix the picnic table."

Printed in the United States
By Bookmasters